all the best
Hugh.

TO KILL KAT

by HUGH RUSSEL

Index

Cover design and illustrations: Hugh Russel

Cover photo of Kat Pawelsierakowski|

Silhouette of man with gun Pixattitude

Back cover photo: Denni Russel Photography

Sculpture image of Emperor Leopold I: Robb@de.wikipedi

Image of Charles VI: © National Portrait Gallery, London

Photos Hotel Ibrahim: The Closure Library Copyright

Printing: 2021

Library and Archives Canada

Paperback ISBN: 978-1-7773671-9-0

eBook ISBN: 978-1-7777946-1-3

For information about this and other books by Hugh Russel

Contact Negative Space Publishing:

negative.space.publishing@gmail.com

For Cheryl, Denni and Nicole

Acknowledgment

This story has been brewing in my head for decades in many different forms but once I had the first book in the bank the rest followed relatively quickly. During that time my family and close friends have been put through the ringer answering my pleas to read my drafts. I can't count the number filed away on my computer or in boxes and file folder written in pencil.

I would have thought that I had taxed them beyond their limits, but to my surprise they have never complained. Well OK, they've complained, but they still read them and for that and for many other reasons, I love them dearly and appreciate their forbearance.

First among them would of course be Cheryl, who has stayed with me through thick and thin for more than fifty years now. She has read and reread ever draft of every letter, rant, short story and novel I have written since the beginning. She says that because of my interesting and rather novel approach to spelling and punctuation, she wouldn't have it any other way. Then there are the two Tony's, Hillman and Reynolds who have been true friends for nearly as long. Their comments and support have been an enormous help to me.

And many thanks to my enthusiastic team of readers Frances MacFarlane, Susan Brown, Barb Bailie, Nancy Pease and Evelyn Fotheringham.

I want to mention Nancy Frater, owner of Booklore in Orangeville. She has been a wonderful source of information about the world of publishing.

I'd also like to praise my publisher and the wonderful team of editors there who have done such an amazing job getting this book out. Also I am deliriously happy to heap thanks on my hard working and truly talented agent, who's amazing friendship has meant the world to me. If either one happens along, in the near future, I am sure all of the forgoing and more will be greatly deserved by her/him/them or they and that would delight me no end, fingers crossed.

Prologue

From travel writer, Reginald Pritchard - Harding's book, My Travels Through Umbria, Pritchard - Harding offers a short history and tour of the area surrounding Lago di Peredicci. The countryside is typical of Umbria, filled with exquisite rolling farmland and treelined country roads. Since the late 1800s, Peredicci, a small village perched on the shore of Lago di Peredicci, has been attracting tourists to savor the spectacular views through all four seasons. Its crystal-clear water is deep and teaming with fish, and on the far side are three idyllic pine and cypress covered islands.

In 1659, during the reign of the Holy Roman Emperor Leopold I, (on the right) 1658 – 1705, a monastery was commissioned in Umbria. It was built on a peak of a small mountain in the Appennini Mountain Range, overlooking the tiny village of Peredicci. The retreat was called the Abbey di San Martino. Historians of the time noted that the abbey was typical of the genre, but the orchard, vineyard, and gardens were exceptional. Their network of paths connecting the gardens was extraordinary. As well, it was rumored that there was a secret passage through the mountain though no one has ever found it. Over the generations the monks produced a fine olive oil, sweet figs and a full-bodied red wine.

As charming as it is now, there was a chapter of Peredicci's history that was far from placid.

During the War of the Polish Succession (1733–35), Leopold's son Charles VI, (on the right) the last male member of the Bourbon line, was involved in a conflict with both France and Spain. On Friday,

April 13th, 1739 the French attacked the Abbey, the monks, being peaceful and pious men, gave up without resistance. Even so, the soldiers beheaded the abbot and took the monks away in chains.

Explosives were placed inside the buildings and as the monks and villagers watched, the Abbey was reduced to rubble and the orchards and vineyard burned.

Leaving only the foundation completely intact, the soldiers took the twenty hapless monks, along with the men and boys of the village, and locked them in large steel cages fixed to barges by the shore. They were then towed out into the middle of the lake and while the women of the village watched the soldiers scuttled the barges. It took nearly an hour for the last one to finally slip beneath the surface.

The rape and murder of some of the women followed and the village was torched before the French left.

Later, people who had escaped into the area surrounding the lake returned and began to rebuild the village with stones brought down from the Abbey.

PART 1

Chapter 1

By The Sea Of Azov

Berdyanskaya Spit, March 12, 2004

Ten minutes ago, she was cold and tired; time to head in and sit by the fire with a mug of tea before bed.

But that was ten minutes ago.

She had been standing on the rise above the house, watching the Sea of Azov from the Berdyanskaya Spit when a tiny flash of red light drew her eye. She saw it for just a second, sitting on the foil between the calm black sea and star-studded sky.

Ten minutes ago, it hadn't been there.

She stared out trying to figure out why a flashing red light would set off an alarm bell in her head. What danger could it possibly represent to her? "Oh, for Christ's sake Katrina, get a grip." She was about to chalk it down to nerves, but something made her pause. "What if ..." she paused again. "No, I've just been alone too long and it's beginning to get to me. I mean, come on, it's just a light for heaven's sake, and even if it was a signal, they're certainly not communicating with me." It flashed again and again in a vaguely familiar pattern. She couldn't take her eyes off it. But then, who are they communicating with? How likely is it that it has anything to do with me? She was about to turn back to the dacha but stopped. "Unless it does."

The repetitions were coming faster now. It blinked, quick, slow, on and off. Peeling back the fur lined hood of her long, white parka, she concentrated on the light again and began to see the full pattern. Wait a second ..., oh Jesus, that's Morse code.

• •• —• ——• •• — ——•. After a pause, • •• —• ——•
•• — ——•.

(E, I, N, Z, U, G)

"It's German, einzug. Holy shit! Einzug…, Move in!"

Then she realized that she was standing out in the open, with the full moon lighting her up like a stage light?

My shadow must be thirty feet long. Seized by a sudden and uncharacteristic bout of panic, she ducked down. I might as well be shouting, Hey guys, I'm over here!

"Jesus Kat, come on!" she said, standing up. "They can't see you from our there." Her eyes were drawn to a flash in the east, up the road to Berdyans'k. Was it in answer to the ship's signal?

It sure looked like it. The vehicle's headlights flashed twice then it began to move towards her. She was the only resident on the spit in the winter, so if it were here to visit someone then… "Oh crap, they're definitely coming here." But they can't be coming for me. Everybody thinks I'm dead. She took a breath to calm herself down.

It took a moment for the penny to drop. Vlad! she thought. They must be coming for Vlad. Damn.

They were about to breach the walls of her sanctuary and that really pissed her off. In addition to that, they were doing it to get to her friend, to someone she loved. It didn't matter that he wasn't there, the intent was crime enough and inevitably, the penalty was death.

She sprinted for the dacha to gear up for war. Leaping onto the porch, she slammed into the door with her shoulder as she pressed the latch. Bursting into the room, she slid into the metal locker Vlad had given her. He had it engraved with the words Spem Pacis Quam Bellum, Hope for Peace, But Plan for War. There is always war, she thought. She unlocked the cabinet and grabbed her go-bag. Taking out her SIG P226 she slid the 15-round magazine out into her palm, checked its load then reinserted it in the grip and chambered a round. After screwing on the silencer, she stuffed it in the deep pocket on the right side of her parka.

She had switched over to fight mode automatically, her safety was no longer her concern. All she could think of was keeping Vlad safe.

That was the mission. No matter who was coming for him, this would be their last stop.

Reaching for the rifle, an H & K G28 E3, a gift from Vlad she remembered that first lonely Christmas in Berdyans'k and how surprised she was when the messenger arrived, with a package addressed to Miss Katrina Mogilevski. The card said, Happy Christmas to my beloved daughter, from her adoring father.

She checked that the safety was on and checked its load. Snapping the mag back, she screwed on its suppressor and put two full clips for each gun into her left pocket. It was time to go.

She locked the cabinet and left, closing the cottage door behind her. Long ago, she had done a recon of the property and selected her defensive position. It was behind the house in the trees, two hundred meters up the small hill. She ran there now and neatly disappeared behind a natural berm of snow-covered rock.

A tall, black truck-like vehicle was silhouetted in the light of the moon and it was moving quickly towards the cottage. She had perhaps two minutes before she had company.

There was time to think as she waited for them. Petrus had tried to murder Vlad in San Diego, but with Kat there to protect him, the attempt failed miserably and in gratitude, Vlad unofficially adopted her. The arrival of ship and the vehicle must have meant that they were still trying to find him. Happily, it also meant that he was safe somewhere. Whoever was after him must have known that Vlad was responsible for what she did to Petrus and is looking for revenge. This attempt would fail too. She had no doubt at all. With the edge of her hand, she packed down a small divot in the snow in front of her to rest the barrel of the rifle. It never occurred to her that these people might be friendly. Friends don't visit in the middle of the night. "The only way to stop the enemy is to kill them before they kill you," she murmured, then relaxed while she waited for the vehicle to arrive.

There Are No Do-Overs

On the lane of Kat's dacha

As the vehicle approached her house, the driver doused the lights and shut off the engine letting it coast off the road onto her lane and roll to a stop.

Four men dressed in black battle dress emerged and leaving the doors ajar so as not to make a noise. They crouched over and ran quietly to the house. It was a well-practiced strike team, kitted out with Kevlar vests, night vision goggles and close combat automatic weapons.

Those NVGs would be next to useless under a full moon, everything would be too bright. But if they insisted on using them, maybe it would give her another advantage. The vests weren't going to stop the rounds her rifle would deliver. The equivalent of a .308 slug, these things would make some serious holes, and no matter where they hit, it was likely to be a kill shot.

The timing of the attack meant the leader expected the target to be asleep inside, so as far as he was concerned, the advantage was all theirs. If Vlad had been in bed, he would have been right, and Vlad would not have stood a chance. How unfortunate for them.

Who says insomnia isn't good for you? she thought grimly.

Moving up to the door, the point-man reached for the latch and tested it, then he fitted a small snake camera under the door to have a look inside. "Klar," he whispered to his team.

It was a textbook entry; the Seals and Special Forces would have done it just like that. The door swung open, they lowered their NVGs, crept in and a moment later they opened fire with everything they had. Bullets tore through the walls as if they were made of paper. Even the cement tiled roof couldn't stand up to the barrage.

Their mission wasn't just to kill the target, they were there to obliterate him. The bullets blazed a path of destruction well beyond the building. As Kat's rental Volvo was ripped apart the gas tank erupted, and the flames consumed everything in it that would burn. Even a few of the trees that surrounded Kat were hit, and one small pine close to her was felled as if someone had taken a chainsaw to it.

As suddenly as it began, it was over.

In the deathly silence that followed she thought they must have discovered that their efforts had been fruitless. One man shouted, "Scheiße!"

Another concluded, "OK, er hat draußen zu sein!"

She heard them stomp down the stairs and hurry across the living room floor to the door. Leaning against the berm, Kat tucked the butt of her rifle against her shoulder and concentrated on what was left of the front door. She dialed in the scope, rested her finger above the trigger and waited.

"Here they come." The hit squad walked out onto the porch and trundled down the stairs which placed them directly in her kill zone. She waited until they were all outside and then realized that perhaps she'd waited too long. The leader spotted the tracks in the snow that led up the small hill to her hide. He looked up as if he could see her.

"Aw shit."

Pointing to her general area he signaled for them to move in.

Aiming for his NVGs Kat dropped him before he took a step. Her second shot hit the man beside him, sending him into the deep snow.

Despite her suppressor, the sound carried across the snow and drew fire from the other men as they charged her position. Staying low, she aimed for their heads and quickly fired off two more rounds. The soft thuds could be heard clearly as the projectiles hit their marks. Then there was that awful silence again. There was no way they were going to get up, but she checked them anyway.

Death on a battlefield is ugly and to have been the cause of it left only regret. Like their leader, the last two had taken a bullet through the optics and the result was nasty, but surprisingly, the man next to the leader was still alive.

"Oh Jesus." She dropped the rifle and took out her pistol. His NVG was undamaged, but the helmet had hole in it. It taken the force of the round. He must have turned his head at the moment of impact. After tossing his weapon away, she straddled his hips, removed the goggles and undid his chinstrap. When she tossed away the helmet, she saw that the wound wasn't serious. There was a lot of blood on his face, but her shot had just plowed a furrow across the skull over his ear.

She pressed the barrel of her SIG into the soft tissue under his chin and speaking in German said, "You are very lucky to be alive." His eyes blinked as he tried to focus through the blood. She wasn't going to help him. She waited until his eyes locked on hers then asked, "Who are you?"

"But," he began, looking stunned, "you are a woman."

"That's ten points for you, Einstein. Tell me who you were sent to kill."

"I'm not telling you anything," he said.

"Oh, I think you will." She touched his wound with the barrel of her gun. As if there was another person inside her watching what she was doing, she realized that a part of her wanted to hurt him. She had no idea where her cruel streak came from.

She tried to control it, but the emotion was too strong, it just seemed to take over.

He winced and then his eyes widened in recognition. "No …, it can't be."

"What … another revelation?"

"They said you died after you killed Petrus!"

"Did they? Well, thank goodness for that. You came after Mogilevski." He averted his eyes. "A simple yes would do. Was the target Vladimir Mogilevski?"

"Yes, alright. We were told he would be here."

"There, you see, I told you that you'd talk. OK, now tell me, who wants him dead?"

"He killed Petrus."

"No, he didn't but that's not what I asked, is it? I want to know who you are working for."

"It doesn't matter what you do to me, my people will find you both soon and they will kill you."

"People have been promising me that for years but, as can you see, I'm still here." She had an urge to smack him but resisted, took a deep breath and quietly coaxed him, "Let's go over it again. Who sent you?"

He glared at her, tight lipped and she felt some sympathy for him.

"Aw. OK, listen to me guy, I think your willingness to sacrifice yourself for the bastard is admirable. But trust me, whoever it is, he doesn't deserve your loyalty. Now come on, be smart for a change and tell me who he is."

Thinking that she was distracted, he began moving his right hand down to his belt. The hand rubbed against her inner thigh. "Woops!" She jammed her gun against his jaw and said, "Do you honestly think I couldn't feel that?"

"Alright, alright!" He stopped, but only because he had located what he was after. Closing his fingertips around the handle of his knife he drew the weapon from its sheath.

The sympathy was short lived and pressing her gun into the soft flesh under his jaw she pushed his head back into the red stained snow. "Stop squirming and tell me who sent you."

As if that was his cue, he swung his arm up aiming for her throat, but the movement was instantly telegraphed through her body and Kat's reflexes took over, she blocked the attack with her left arm while simultaneously squeezing the trigger. It was a twitch, not a deliberate desire to kill him, but even so, the result was terminal. With a pop, brain, blood and bone erupted from the top of his head like a volcano, drenching the snow.

"You dumb-ass, how stupid was that?! Shit!" She sat back feeling awful. She had done what she had to do, but for two years she had been at peace, or at least resigned to her lonely existence. This sudden burst of violence was a shock to the system and the need to cause pain was deeply unsettling. What had she become?

POLICING HER BRASS

1:25 am

After surveying the tiny battlefield, Kat was amazed that she was still breathing. "How many lives do I have left now?" She stood up and only then realized that his knife was dangling from her sleeve. There was so much blood around her that she was unaware that some of it was hers. She put the gun in her pocket and removed the knife letting it drop beside the body, then walked into the house.

They'd destroyed much of the interior, but she hoped there was something she could salvage from the wreckage. The armoire next to her weapons locker was kindling, but there was only surface damage on the locker. She opened it and removed the go-bag and checked that she hadn't forgotten anything. There was her purse, a change of clothes, flat shoes for running, a thin blanket, ammunition for the SIG, water and chocolate. It was all she needed for now. She put the gun in the bag then carefully examined the contents of her shoulder bag. The wallet had a small amount of Ukrainian money, her Spanish passport, driver's license, and credit card. She removed the cell phone and after checking that it still had a charge, Kat returned everything to the soft sided suitcase.

There was blood dripping onto the floor from her arm. It could have been the cold or the adrenalin that numbed her senses, but until that moment she hadn't realized that she'd been cut. Removing the bloodstained coat, she examined the tear. *Aw shit, I really liked that coat.*

She carried the medical kit from the locker into the bathroom and was surprised to see that the sink was in one piece. It was freezing cold, but she had to assess the damage. So, even though she was shivering the sweater came off and she ripped the shirt sleeve open to her shoulder. The knife point had made a shallow gouge across her forearm. "That's not too bad," she said and washed off the blood then used Steri-Strips from the kit she closed the wound then covered it with a gauze bandage. She looked in the mirror, "Groan." her face was covered in blood. With a heavy sigh, she put the rest of the dressings in the go-bag for later and washed her face.

The wood stove had been destroyed and there were so many holes in the walls that hundreds of little jets of wind off the sea came through unimpeded. Her shivering getting worse, and her joints were stiff and painful. She had to get upstairs and find something warm to put on before she froze to death. she.

Thankfully, there were some things that had survived, her good coat, was intact and she shoved her arms into the sleeves and buttoned it up before she went any further. She found warm socks, a warm jersey shirt, and a sweater, some underwear and a pair of jeans that were serviceable, though they had some new holes that could optimistically be considered fashionable. Tossing her blood-soaked snow pants to the floor she put on what she had found and went back downstairs. There's going to be a big shopping trip in my future, she thought, that is, if I actually have a future. Satisfied that she had salvaged all she could, she left the house.

The only positive thing she could draw from the attack was that whoever sent the gunmen was after her friend, Vladimir Mogilevski and didn't know she was alive. Since the assassins were dead that bit of information would remain a secret for a while. She had to do some cleanup to destroy any evidence that she was in residence, but her secret had a shelf life. It was inevitable that they would figure out who had done this and come after her. How long that would take was anyone's guess. If she was careful she might be able to disappear again.

Her rental car was a burning wreck, but it didn't matter because waiting for her a mere hundred meters down the lane was a shiny new Mercedes G 350 SUV.

She ran to the truck, opened the driver's door, tossed in her go-bag, then followed it in and pulled the door closed. Miraculously, the keys were in the ignition, so setting her Sig down on the dashboard, she, started the engine, turned up the heater to high and took a moment to steady her breathing. She had some time to let the adrenalin faded with the shivering and began to calm down. The gas tank was nearly full. "They must have just filled it up in town."

She left it running, hoping that it would warm up soon. It did thankfully and she was able to start thinking about her next move. She narrowed her list down to two things to begin with. First thing, finding clues as to who sent the men and coming up with a way of obliterating the evidence.

The clues were few and not very helpful. The musky odor of four sweaty men, and their fast-food leftovers mingled with gun oil, told her that they had come a long way. The small B in the blue field on registration plates said the vehicle came from Berlin. They could have flown into Kiev and picked up a vehicle for there, so why had they driven all this way?

Moving on, Kat found the ownership papers and insurance card in the glove box. The Mercedes belonged to a company called Zapf

Industries of Delaware, USA, but the insurance slip had a Berlin address. "Oh wonderful, Zapf is a ghost company."

When she was comfortable warm, she got out and opened the back of the SUV and found that it was filled with weapons stowed away in boxes. "Who-o-o-o-a. Talk about overkill, they could start a war with this. ~ There were flash-bang grenades, German DM51 fragmentation grenades, ammo clips and four soft bricks marked PE-4, the British version of C4. A smaller box had everything to make the stuff go boom.

"The men on the ship must be waiting for an explosion, ~ she thought, and for the first time since the killers arrived Kat felt a smile coming on. "I have to clean up my mess, so why not give them what they want?"

She drove closer to the dacha and carried everything inside, then went out to collect the bodies and their weapons and dragged them inside. Her lovely rifle was useless to her now, so she tossed it in too.

It took a moment to set up the PE-4 where it would do the most damage and when she was done, she hopped into the Mercedes and drove a little way up the road. All it took was a little finger pressure on the detonator and there was a huge boom. The shock-wave rocked the truck violently and a shower of light debris dusted the truck. She wiped her prints off the detonator and tossed it out the window on her way to Berdyans'k.

If the people on the ship were watching for an explosion, then they got their money's worth.

On The Horizon

2:47 am

The captain of the Russian salvage vessel Красной Звезды (Red Star) was watching from the flying bridge and saw the show, and then became concerned when he heard nothing from the tactical squad. He went back into the wheelhouse and radioed the squad leader. After several unsuccessful attempts to make contact he knew that mission had gone south and sent a team in a zodiac to investigate. They drove their craft up onto the slush covered beach and with guns at the ready closed in on the burning wreckage of the dacha.

At about the same time, Kat found a safehouse in Berdyans'k.

The dacha was still burning but the sailors saw the four bodies, burned beyond recognition and their weapons had melted into a mound of twisted metal. All the sailors could do was remove anything that remained that might identify the charred bodies and take pictures.

The 2nd officer radioed the ship. "There is no sign of Mogilevski, and the team's vehicle is gone."

"So, they failed," he said.

"Yes captain. Captain, I don't think he could have done this by himself."

"Is there any sign of how many people were guarding him?"

"No, but I found footprints around the area. It looks like there was a woman here."

"That means nothing to me. Very well. We will leave the investigation up to the Swiss. Have you cleaned the sight?"

"We have, yes sir."

"Good. Return to the ship."

As soon as the sailors rejoined the Red Star, they hauled up the Zodiac and headed back to port at Odessa on the Black Sea.

The captain had served under the old boss Delph Petros and he knew what failure meant. He waited until the ship was secured and his crew had disembarked before he sent in his final report to Switzerland, then he disappeared without a trace. When the report was delivered to the intelligence office in Zürich the head of the agency was not happy. The captain's decision to disappear had been prudent.

CHAPTER 2

Berdyans'k

7:10 am

The sun seemed to arrive just moments after Kat closed her eyes. Exhausted, she slept soundly for two hours in the small hotel room. When she awoke, she took her gun into the bathroom, showered and toweled off before she inspected her wound. The Steri-Strips had done their job beautifully, the wound had held the cut together and it was clean. She applied a new bandage, dressed and left the room.

The young woman behind the desk in the lobby appeared to be surprised to see her. But she smiled brightly and said, "Oh, good morning, can I help you?"

"Good morning, I'm checking out now."

"Excuse me, madam?"

"Um ..., I stayed here last night. I'm checking out now."

"Checking out?"

"The large man checked me in. I'm Mrs. Franco," she said, delivering the name as if asking a question.

"Oh, sorry I was not aware that we had any guests. Please, let me see." She looked through the small stack of paper in the drawer. "Ah," she began cautiously, "did you happen to pay in cash?"

"Yes," said Kat, expecting trouble.

"I understand now. That was my husband's uncle Torben. Sometimes he destroys the registration and pockets the money. I will have a talk with him later. I hope you slept well."

"I did, thank you. Would you be able to call me a cab?"

"Certainly. Did he charge you the rate listed on the wall?"

"Yes, he did."

"Then I owe you some money. Those are the summer rates."

"Don't worry about that, I don't mind."

"Thank you. What room were you in?"

"210."

"Thank you. The taxi company is very close." She typed something into her computer then called the taxi company. "It will be here in two minutes. It was quite a night, yes?"

"Was it?" Kat asked, masking her alarm.

"The moon was so bright. My husband and I sat up late staring at it."

"Oh yes, the moon was huge. I suppose I was too tired to appreciate it."

The woman tapped the keys on her terminal, hit enter and the printer spat out the receipt. "Here you are. And thank you for staying with us."

"Thank you," Kat said, and went out to wait for the cab.

At the train station, she bought a ticket to Kiev then went to a kiosk for a breakfast coffee and roll. Stopping at the news stand, she picked up the morning paper and a book for the trip. There was nothing in the paper about her, that is Anita Franco, or the fire.

The train eventually arrived and waited in the station for exactly twelve minutes before it headed back up the track.

It took the rest of the day to get to the Kyiv - Passazhyrsky train station and she hurried out with the crowd to get a taxi to Boryspil International Airport. Once in the terminal she looked at the newspapers of the day and was relieved that there was still no report of a fire on the Berdyanskaya Spit. She went into a stall in the women's washroom, wiped her gun down, disassembled it and ditched its various parts in waste baskets around the terminal.

It was getting late, but she had to book a flight out of the country. Moving up to Ukrainian International Airlines desk Kat smiled.

The woman smiled back at her. "Good evening, madam. How may I help you?"

"What is the first flight out of the country?"

"I am sorry but we have no more flights out today. Where did you want to go?"

"You know, this may sound strange, but I don't really care. Why don't you surprise me?"

"Uh, very well," the woman said, scanning the computer schedule. "We have a flight going to Istanbul tomorrow afternoon at 1:20. Would you like me to book you on that flight?"

"Why not? I have never been to Turkey."

"May I see your passport, please?"

"Yes, of course," Kat said, handing it over.

"Thank you," she paused, "Señora Franco." She checked the name against the no-fly list and Kat had a momentary chill as she realized what the woman was doing. Of course, since she was dead, she wasn't listed. "And do you have any seating preference?"

Relieved she said, "First class if you have it."

"Of course. The flight comes to ₴8,684 hryvnia and how will you be paying?"

"I have cash, if that's alright."

"That will be fine. Do you have any luggage to check?"

"Just this bag," she said.

"That you may take on board with you."

"Wonderful." Kat took out her wallet and put the notes on the counter.

"Thank you, madam." After counting the money, the agent produced the ticket and her boarding pass and handed them over the counter. She checked her computer again and said, "Again, your flight leaves tomorrow at 1:20 from gate D 12. Enjoy your trip, Señora Franco."

"Thank you." Kat started to walk away then turned and asked, "Is there a hotel nearby?"

"The Boryspil Hotel is just a short walk from Terminal D. Take the elevator down to the street level; go out the front door then turn left."

Callers From Switzerland

12:20 pm

Two agents were assigned to the Vladimir Mogilevski case. When they looked through the photos of the carnage at his dacha, they noticed that the car was a rental from a company in Kiev. Taking the first flight from Zürich to Kiev in the morning, they arrived just as Kat boarded the train in Berdyans'k.

Showing the photo of the license plate to the manager of the rental agency, the lead investigator asked him, "Can you tell us who rented this car?"

At first, the manager refused, but when they offered him a hefty bribe he quickly found the information. "Ah, here it is. A white, 2002, Volvo long term lease, rented by a young woman, Anita Franco."

"Did you say Anita Franco? No, that can't be."

"That's what it says on the form."

"It is not correct. Look again."

"I don't need to I served the customer myself. She was a very shapely young woman."

"Russian?" the second investigator asked.

"No, her passport was Spanish, but she spoke Russian."

"Did you photocopy her driver's license?"

"Of course, it is company policy."

"You will make a copy for me. It is very important that we locate this woman. Did she give an address in Kiev?"

"No, in Berdyans'k, that's down on the coast."

"Yes, we know where that is."

Turning away from the counter the senior agent called Zurich to report what they had discovered.

"What did they say?" asked the junior agent.

"Find the woman."

"Do you think she will still be in Berdyans'k?"

"No, but it is where will have to start our search."

"We were told that the hit team was eliminated by Mogilevski's security force."

"Obviously, the report from the Red Star was wrong."

"What do we do now?" asked his partner.

"We drive to Berdyans'k."

Returning to the rental agency, they picked up a car and began their journey down to the coast.

Hours later, after a treacherous drive, they arrived in the seaside city on the shores of the Sea of Azov. Armed only with a grainy picture and a vague idea that someone in the area might remember her, they began by going to the only place that was open at that hour and struck gold. They found the Mercedes in a hotel parking lot.

When they showed Kat's photo to the young woman at the hotel desk, she confirmed that she had spent the night and left that morning.

"Do you know where she went?" the first man asked.

"She took a cab, that's all I know. Why are you looking for her?"

"What was the cab company?" he asked.

"She told them, and they left without answering her question.

"It is the off season," the cab company's dispatcher told them. "We had only two cabs working this morning."

The driver remembered her of course, "... a beautiful woman and very nice too, she gave me a big tip."

"Where did you take her?"

"I dropped her off at the train station."

"Do you know where she was going?"

"There is only one train in the winter, and it goes to Kiev."

"So, if she bought a ticket," began the second man, "then she must be in Kiev."

"Or any town in between," corrected the senior investigator. He looked at his watch. It was a quarter past nine. He said, "We can be back in Kiev in nine and a half hours."

"Are you gentlemen thinking of driving there tonight?" asked the cabbie.

"Yes, what of it?"

"I hear there is a storm up that way. The road will be covered with snow and ice. It will be impossible in the dark."

Frustrated, the agent considered his options for a moment. "When is the next train?"

"Wednesday."

"Wednesday?! What kind of a place is this?"

"It is a summer destination. No one comes here in the winter."

"Well to hell with that."

"We'll drive in the morning?" asked his partner.

"What choice do we have?" They drove back to the hotel, booked two rooms and went to bed.

Chapter 3

You Can Run

1:30 pm Saturday

When she ventured out the following morning, Kat checked the newspapers and still there was no mention of the dacha fire, and no sign that anybody had taken any special notice of her. She had lunch at the hotel and then walked back to the airport. Her flight left right on schedule without incident.

As soon as she was up in the air, she tried to reach Vladimir. The call went directly to voice mail, so she left a message in Russian. "Vlad darling it's me, your little Kitty. It has been too long Darling, and I ache for you. You have my number so call me soon. There is so much I have to tell you."

He didn't call.

The plane landed at Ataturk Airport and she lined up in the crowded arrivals room to go through immigration. After handing her passport to the customs officer she waited while he looked her over and studied the document. He didn't speak Spanish and assumed that she didn't speak Turkish, so he asked, "Do you speak English?"

"Yes."

"What is the purpose of your visit?

"I'm just taking a little vacation."

"And how long will you be staying?"

"A week perhaps," she said.

"And where will you be staying?"

"This is sort of a last-minute trip and I haven't booked a hotel." He looked at the small bag she was carrying and studied her eyes closely.

"You are traveling light, madam. Will you be doing any shopping?"

She smiled. "Oh, you know how we women are. How could I resist doing a little shopping while I'm here?"

"Alright, though you may find it difficult to get a nice room. Enjoy your stay in Istanbul." He stamped her passport and handed it back to her. "Next."

But Can You Hide?

4:45 pm

Kat found a kiosk to change her Ukrainian money into Turkish lira, put the money in her shoulder bag and went outside to find a taxi. The snow had stopped recently but had already turned to brown slush on the roadway. She was glad that the driver spoke English "Would you take me into the old city?"

"Most assuredly," he said, and nosed his way into the traffic nightmare that is Turkey. During the drive, he complained about the condition of the roads. It wasn't until they reached the city limits that he asked, "Where in the old city do you wish to go?"

"I need a bank, a Lloyd's if there is one, and then I want to do some shopping."

"There is a Lloyd's bank very close." He took a turn and in no time stopped at the bank.

"Can you wait for me?"

"Of course, madam."

A few minutes later she emerged with enough money to last her a month in the city. "Thanks for waiting. Now, can you take me to a women's clothing store?"

"It is nearing closing time, madam. Which one, there are so many."

Grasping at what little she knew about Istanbul she said, "Is there a street near the Blue Mosque that has dress shops?"

"Oh yes," he said. "I know just the place for you. I have a friend who owns a cafe near Turkocaği Street. There are many dress shops there."

"That would be fine."

He drove her into town and through the narrow byways of the Sultanahmet district and dropped her off on a street that had several attractive women's clothing stores.

She poked around quickly before finding Gürbüza, a little shop with a nice selection. The shop keeper welcomed her in Turkish, but when Kat smiled apologetically, she easily transitioned into English. "My name is Kayra, how may I help you today?"

"Hello Kayra, it is wonderful that you speak English. I need some things that are comfortable to travel in."

"I have a good selection of dresses and ensembles. Have a look around and if you find something you like let me know."

"I know you are closing soon I won't keep you."

"Don't worry my dear, I am in no hurry. Take your time."

"Thank you." Kat went through the racks and picked out everything that caught her eye. When she had an arm full, she said, "I'll try these on."

"Certainly, the change room is right back here." She showed her to a large dressing room behind a curtain. After trying on a number of outfits, Kat picked out the ones she wanted and took them out to the counter.

"You have made some wonderful choices. I will wrap them up for you."

"Kayra, I wonder if you might be able to help with another matter."

"Certainly, if I can."

"I need a place to stay. Would you be able to recommend a nice hotel ..., something nearby?"

"You don't like the hotel you are in now?" She looked alarmed. "Has something happened to you?" Kayra asked, only because she assumed that every tourist who came to Istanbul had booked their hotel before they came.

"No, no, it's just that this was a last-minute trip and I have just come from the airport. There are so many hotels that I didn't know how to choose one."

Kayra had admired Kat's large diamond engagement and wedding rings. "And you are traveling alone without your husband, I think."

Kat also looked at the rings and thought of Harm. "Yes, my husband is gone now. Cancer," Kat said.

"I must apologize, forgive me for being so nosy."

"There really is no need."

Kayra opened a drawer in the sales desk and produced a business card from the Ibrahim Pasha Hotel. "You must try this one," she said, as she placed the card in Kat's hand. "It's not too far from here and I believe it is one of the most beautiful of the small hotels in the city. My cousin Jefi is the owner. Shall I call him and tell him that you are coming?"

"Why not, thank you," she said, and her smile seemed to make Kayra very happy.

"You are going to love your stay in Istanbul, I assure you."

"I'm sure that if everyone is as kind as you then I will."

"Why, thank you," she said, giving her a warm smile, "I am happy to be of assistance."

Kayra took great care packing the purchases in tissue paper and then placing them in sturdy boxes with string handles. "May I suggest that I send these to the hotel for you?"

"Thank you, that would be perfect." Kat said, handing her the money for her purchases.

"Wonderful, then it is settled," she said, "I will call Jefi and tell him you are on your way."

Hotel Ibrahim Pasha

6:50 pm

As Kat opened the shop door and stepped out onto the street she was reintroduced to the noise and smell of exhaust on the narrow road.

She thought about taking a cab, but quickly gave up on that idea. The street was an inland Sargasso Sea filled with becalmed drivers.

Kayra had said that the hotel was relatively close. Buttoned to the chin in her warm coat, she studied the tiny map on the back of the card and decided to walk.

By the time she reached Terzihane Sk., she was very cold and thinking about sitting in front of a nice fire with a cup of tea.

It was a quiet little street, not much more than an alleyway really, and in the middle of the block stood the Hotel Ibrahim Pasha. As promised, it was a charming little boutique hotel. There was a fire burning in the grate and a comfortable love-seat that beckoned. Like a moth to the flame, she stood close with outstretched hands.

A tiny movement under the front desk caught her eye. His chin never left the back of his paw, but an old golden lab managed to look up at her through the droopy openings that passed for his eyes. "Hello pup," she said, and his tail twitched slightly. "Are you looking after the place? Yeah?" Just a suggestion of a wag seemed to be enough as far as he was concerned. As she was wondering where the owner was, the dog let out a half-hearted woof, put his head down, closed his eyes again and began to snore softly.

She sat in front of the fire and warmed herself, feeling at ease in the quiet comfortable simplicity of the hotel.

"You must pardon my lazy friend," said a voice from the landing. "His name is Godot." She turned to see a pleasant looking man in his fifties enter the lobby with a cup in his hand. "In his own way," he continued with a little laugh, "he and I welcome you to the Ibrahim Pasha. I am Jefi Ozan. And you must be Señora Franco?"

She nodded, stood up and smiled, "Yes, hello."

"Ah hah, very excellent." He put the cup on his desk. "Of course, it was my blessed cousin Kayra who called to tell me you were coming. She described you perfectly."

"It's a pleasure to meet you Mr. Ozan." She looked down at the sleeping dog. "Tell me, was there any particular reason why you named him Godot?"

"Oh, it is a tired old joke but it's because in a way, I am forever waiting for him to do something. Since he was a small puppy, he has been like this."

"He's lovely."

"I'm happy you think so. Call me Jefi, please. So ..." he said, with obvious pride, "... what do you think of it?"

"I think it is quite wonderful."

"Good. Now please sign the register for me." She did. "Very good, thank you, may I see your credit card please?"

"I'm sorry but I never use the thing. Would it be a problem for you if I paid in cash?"

"Of course not, the card is just a formality, you understand. I will not put the charge through and will accept your payment in cash when you check out."

"Oh," she said, wondering if the risk was worth it. Obviously, anywhere she went the request would be the same. "Alright." She removed it from her wallet and handed it to him. "Here you are."

"Perfect."

"I'd love a cup of tea, if that's possible?"

"Of course, here have this one, I just brewed it and have not yet touched it."

"Thank you." She tasted the drink. "M-m-m-m, that's just what I need, thanks." It was hot and sweet and warmed her all the way down. "I hadn't realized there were so many hotels in Istanbul. I passed dozens on my way here."

"We Turks are a very hospitable people. Your card," he said, handing it back to her, "and may I say that it is a pleasure to have you as our guest, Señora Franco."

"Thank you." She took it and placed it back in the wallet.

"Let me show you up to your room."

"Are you all alone here?"

"We are not very busy this time of year, so housekeeping comes only when needed." He took her go-bag. "I have selected one of our deluxe rooms for you where I am sure you will be most comfortable. Come, I will show you up." She placed the empty cup on his desk and followed him to a small landing at the foot of a wide marble spiral staircase. "Through here to your right is our breakfast room. There you may make tea for yourself any time you wish."

"It's very homey."

"Thank you. And as you can see, we have an elevator. My apologies, it is a little slow. Though, not so slow as Godot thank goodness."

"That doesn't matter."

"Good. You will be on the third floor."

The lift stopped and the door opened onto a narrow hallway. "Ah, at last we have arrived. Your room is just in here." He opened the door to a spacious suite.

There was a small balcony with a table and two chairs looking out onto the alley. "See," he pointed. "Look there, you can see the Blue Mosque to the south."

"It's amazing." There was a queen-size bed and a long leather couch by the balcony door. A small table on the other side of the door held a heavy wooden bowl with dates, figs and a pomegranate, a bottle of water, two glasses and a vase of fresh flowers. "I hope I have made the right choice for you."

"This is perfect, and the flowers are lovely."

"I am so pleased. When your packages arrive, I will bring them to you at once."

"You are very kind." It was more than she had expected and was sorry that she would only be staying one night. Perhaps now that she was safely away from Ukraine, she could afford to spend a little more time in Istanbul.

"How long will you be staying with us?"

"I was just wondering that myself. I'm not sure, perhaps three or four days, if that is alright?"

"Certainly, that's fine. Stay as long as you like."

When the door closed, it felt like the danger had been locked out forever. She pulled her cell phone from her bag and speed dialed Vlad's number again. Again, it went to voice mail and she left another message.

"Vlad it's your Kitty Kat again. I'm beginning to feel unloved," she said. "Call me." She disconnected and put the phone by the bed. Where the hell was he? She began to worry that they had already found him.

She had a shower hoping it would help her relax. At first, the warmth soaked in and felt wonderful, but she closed her eyes and the river monsters from St. Petersburg returned. She had been clubbed on the head and thrown into a cold, black river where she imagined hideous sharks and eels were about to take her. The memories of that attack overwhelmed her, and she fell back against the shower wall.

Quickly she opened her eyes and shut off the water. She stepped out into the light. Reaching for a towel she was going to head into the bedroom to dress when she noticed the hotel's terry robes hanging on the back of the door. It was a pleasant reminder of the first time that she and Harm made love, a happy time, and it helped to calm her.

Taking the man's robe, she wrapped herself in its plush softness and pulled the cord snuggly around her waist.

There was a knock at the door. "Yes?"

"It is Jefi, Señora Franco. I have your packages."

She opened the door.

Seeing her in her robe he said, "Forgive me, I should have called up first."

"It's alright, come in."

"Shall I place these on your bed?"

"That would be fine. Thanks."

"You are most welcome," he said, and left.

She immediately began opening boxes selecting warm things to wear, then dressed quickly. Looking in the full-length mirror on the inside of the bathroom door she checked for tags she might have missed. "OK ..., now that looks really good," she said.

Feeling better, she sat down on the couch wondering how safe she really was. Would they try to find her? Could they come after her here? She shook her head. "They weren't after me."

She called down to the front desk and a young man answered. "How may I help you, Señora Franco?"

"Oh uh, hello, is Jefi there?"

"He has gone for the night. I am Rafi, his son. How may I help you?"

"Oh, it's alright, thank you. I just had a question for him," she said, and hung up the phone.

Jefi had said it wasn't going to be put through and even if he did put the room on the card she might stay on for a few days. It would it take them that long to trace the transaction. They'd have to discover the fire first then trace the car and that would take time. She had to calm down.

She decided that just to be safe she would stay one more night and then head for Spain. But, if they did come, what kind of a defense could she put up without a gun?

She looked around the room.

"Well, I could always hit someone with that fruit bowl." The ridiculousness of that idea almost made her laugh.

She grabbed her purse and coat and left her room.

Downstairs she met Rafi and told him that she was going out for a walk. She wanted to look at the Blue Mosque and get a better idea of where she was.

"I wish for you a pleasant evening, Señora Franco."

"Thank you. Oh, perhaps you could suggest a restaurant nearby."

"Indeed, I can." He gave her instructions, and she went out and began to walk. Her destination was the area near the Sirkeci train station where he said there were many good and inexpensive restaurants.

Turning right, she went down the short block past a parking lot to the great pedestrian mall. It was lined with trees and right in front of her was the Walled Obelisk he had mentioned.

The mall was nearly empty, and the streetlamps bathed everything in soft yellow light. She felt exposed, but she pressed on in the shadows under the trees.

She found a suitable restaurant and after dinner she took a cab back to the hotel. The young man was seated at the reception desk doing homework. "Ah, Señora Franco, Usted está aquí. Hola," he said, as he stood up.

"Oh, hola Rafi, Tu Español es muy bueno," she said, looking at the books.

"I try," he said, reverting to English then bowed awkwardly and produced a key from the pigeonhole.

"Thank you. You must be in college."

"Yes, the Marmara University Rektörlüğü. I am studying to be a biologist."

"A biologist? I'm impressed. The university is just around the corner, isn't it?"

"Yes, it is very close."

"Good for you, that's wonderful. Goodnight Rafi."

"Buenas noches, Señora. I will lock up for the night now."

"Lock up? It's only just after 10:00 isn't it? What about the other guests?"

"But Señora Franco, you are our only guest." He went to the door and locked it then turned back to her and bowed again. "My father will be here in the morning to prepare your breakfast. Duerme bien."

"Gracias." Kat went to the elevator while the young man went back to his books. She watched a bit of Turkish television without understanding a thing, which was fine, it was just the distraction she needed. Eventually she shut it off and turned in for the night.

Chapter 4

Given License

Sunday, March 14

After speaking to several people at the Kiev airport the two men from Zürich found the agent who sold her the ticket. "Let me see the picture again. Oh yes, I remember her. I looked after her on Friday. I thought it was strange, because she asked for the next flight leaving Kiev. It didn't matter to her where she went so, I suggested Istanbul. She paid for her ticket in cash."

"I'll take two tickets on the next flight to Istanbul."

"Two tickets for Istanbul, Turkey, Monday March 15."

"Wait, the flight leaves tomorrow?" the agent asked.

"Yes sir, Monday afternoon at 1:20."

"Then never mind that. Give us two seats on the next flight to Zürich." While the men waited for their flight, intelligence analysts at the Kroner Agency in Zürich used the information to assemble a new dossier on Anita Franco, which was passed up to the head of the agency.

Much of it was distilled from the burst of media attention she received beginning with her wedding in Ibiza to Paulino Franco, up to the report of her disappearance from her hotel in Berlin. There was little official documentation beyond her birth certificate and school records up to the second year of Bacillerato (high school). Her parents died the year she turned fourteen and after that she became a non-person, no driver's license, no police records and no employment records.

Checking into Paulino Franco, the analysts found little to prove that he existed at all. That led them to believe that Anita Franco probably created the character then 'killed him off' to explain how she came by her sudden wealth. Their conclusion was that she was an assassin, a part of an elaborate plan created by Vladimir Mogilevski to assassinate Petrus.

The full report was sent to the client. The command that came back was simple, 'Find her and bring her in'.

Word was put out all over Europe and Asia that she was a top priority and had to be found and the client wanted her taken alive. A bounty of one hundred thousand Euros was offered to the one who captured her and brought her to Zürich. Apparently, there was some confusion about that detail amongst some of the lower ranks. The understanding they had was dead or alive.

A Distracted Moment

Having gone through the various possibilities, Kat was sure that staying one more day wouldn't be a problem. The sunrise was glorious, the day was the first warm day they'd had in some time and, like everyone else, she was out enjoying herself. She spent it exploring the old city on foot. She had a delicious dinner in a traditional local restaurant and headed back to the hotel with a new suitcase to replace the go-bag.

When she pushed through the door of the Ibrahim Pasha, Rafi was at the desk again engrossed in his studies. Not wanting to disturb him, she reached for the key herself. He smiled and said, "Good night, Señora Franco," then got up to lock the door.

As soon as she got in the room, she kicked off her shoes and began packing her new suitcase with all the things she bought. It had been fun, but two days was pushing her luck. She had to move on in the morning.

CHAPTER 5

NIGHT CALLERS

Monday, March 15, 1:52 am

The harsh sound of a motorcycle turning onto her street woke her. But when it screeched to a stop right below her window, she became fully alert and her pulse quickened. It was 1:50 am. Since she was the only one staying there, that meant there was only one reason to come calling at that hour. When the engine shut off, she jumped out of bed.

"Well, so much for 'hope for the best'," she said. They were coming for her. She knew it. She could feel it in her bones.

She shoved the pillows under the covers. There was no time for underwear as she jumped into her pants and yanked a cashmere sweater over her head. On her way by the side table, she grabbed the fruit bowl, dumped its contents on the floor and headed for the bathroom. That was when the terminal countdown began.

10.

9.

There was the unmistakable blast of a shotgun then a scream and shouting down in the lobby.

8.

As she moved across the room, there was another scream and a gunshot, a smaller weapon this time. She was sure that Rafi had been killed. "Oh Jesus, why shoot him?!"

7.

More shouting from below, and her heart was pounding so hard, it threatened to break ribs.

6.

Someone was running up the stairs.

5.

Kat ducked back into the bathroom, lifted the bowl over her head and waited.

4.

The gunman kicked the door in and fired five times into the bed.

3.

Kat stepped out of the dark.

2.

He saw the movement out of the corner of his eye.

1.

She smashed him in the face with the bowl.

0.

It broke in half and the sharp edge cut his forehead open and blood erupted from his nose and mouth. He rocked back hitting his head on the door jamb. Amazingly, he was still standing. A blow like that should have killed him but it didn't.

The blood blinded him. He swung the gun wildly and wasted three more rounds. She blocked his arm, grabbed him by the wrist and pulled him to her. At the same time, she spun around and slammed her elbow into his face. He shot back and slammed into the door jamb with a horrible thunk.

While twisting the gun from his hand it went off, shattering the balcony's glass door. She drove her knee into his groin which put him down on his knees. Now, with control of the gun, she kicked the door closed and smacked the side of his head with the butt of the gun. He fell on his shoulder but, again, he was only dazed.

She asked herself how many bullets were left. "He'd fired 9 shots here, this is a ... a Turkish Luger TP9 SF which holds ..., Shit! It holds ..., 18 rounds. Did he fire the shot downstairs? OK I've got maybe 8 left."

Kat grabbed him by the hair and pulled him up on his knees. She put the gun to his head and said, "Who sent you?"

He didn't respond. She heard a second man running up the stairs shouting. She let go of the gunman's hair and he flopped to the floor again. Kat moved stepping away from the door just in time, as the second man arrived on the landing.

The shotgun blast tore a hole in the door a foot in diameter just where she had stood a half second before. He kicked open what remained of the door while pumping another shell into the chamber.

Kat turned back and squeezed off three rounds into his chest. He dropped like a stone and the shotgun tipped into the room.

That's 5 left.

The first man regained some mobility and reached for the shotgun. Kat shot him in the back of the head. She had 4 rounds left, but she wouldn't need them now.

In the short silence that followed, she slid the magazine out of the gun and checked the load. There were 3 rounds in the clip and 1 in the chamber. She pushed the clip back in and raced down the stairs calling Rafi's name.

He didn't answer.

Taking the steps two at a time she called again, "Rafi!"

"I'm here," he said weakly.

"Oh, thank God, I thought they'd killed you," she said, as she arrived on the main floor.

"He shot me."

She found him covered in blood lying at the foot of the landing, with one leg dangling from the overturned chair. "I am so sorry, Rafi." She looked around making sure they were alone. Pushing on the safety, she tossed the gun onto a nearby couch and put her hand on his arm. "Where did he get you?"

He moved his hand away from his chest to show her. "It hurts."

"I know. Try to lie still and let me have a look." She gently lowered his leg and pushed the chair out of the way. After unbuttoning his shirt, she peeled it back and looked at the wound. The bullet had gone right through. The hole in his shirt told her that there was probably material inside him. If they didn't get it out the wound would fester.

There was a good chance that he wouldn't live long enough to worry about it. Rafi was bleeding out. She felt completely helpless.

"It doesn't look like it hit anything vital," she said, but that was just wishful thinking rather than fact. "You are going to be OK, Rafi." All she could do was apply pressure, but knew it wasn't enough. "Why aren't the police here yet?" She looked at the wall clock, 1:52:45. The assault had taken less than three minutes. Response time would be ..., what ..., five or ten minutes? Would he survive that long?

"I couldn't reach the phone," said Rafi.

"I'll do it. What do I dial?"

"112."

"This is going to hurt, but you're going to be OK." She pushed down on the wound with one hand and he groaned and twisted. "Try to hold still." She dialed with the other. Naturally, the operator answered in Turkish but Kat spoke in English, "I have a medical emergency."

"Acil durumun doğası nedir?"

"I'm sorry, but I don't understand. I'm at The Hotel Ibrahim Pasha, I need help!"

"I speak English. What is your emergency?"

"There has been a shooting!!"

"I understand, I'm sending an ambulance and the police to the Hotel Ibrahim."

"Thank you." she wasn't thrilled about the police coming, but there was nothing she could do about that.

"Is the victim conscious?

"Yes, please hurry."

Rafi groaned "The ambulance will be there in five minutes," the dispatcher said. "Please stay on the line."

She put the phone down, so she could use both hands to put pressure on the wound. "This was my fault. I gave your father my credit card. I knew I shouldn't have done that, but he said he wouldn't put it through. But even if he did, I don't know how ..."

"I put it through. I had ..."

He put the charge through when he came in, so that her bill would be ready when she checked out. He thought he was just being efficient.

"I am sorry."

"There is nothing we can do about it now. Please hold on, Rafi, the ambulance will be here soon."

"Who are these people?"

"I wish I knew, but I don't."

The Second Wave

A policeman on a motorcycle arrived first and stood his bike beside the one the gunmen came on. Kat noticed that they looked identical, but she didn't care about the police right now, she wanted to see the ambulance. The cop stepped through the broken glass with his gun drawn and approached Kat cautiously.

"I need help," she said desperately.

He said, "Ayağa kalk ve ellerini kaldır." (Stand up and put your hands up)

She couldn't understand him, but it sounded like an order. "I don't speak Turkish."

His response was to push his gun against the back of her neck and repeat it. She figured out what he meant, but she couldn't let go of Rafi. She shook her head.

The cop pushed her with the gun and yelled. Rafi was sweating and shivering. Suddenly, his eyes rolled back, his body went limp, and he lay as still as death. "Rafi! Rafi, wake up!"

The cop kept yelling at her and prodded her with the gun again until she just lost it.

She spun as she stood, stripping the gun from his hand. Now she had his gun pointing in his face. He looked and smelled like he had just soiled himself. She ejected the shell from the breach and dropped the magazine on the floor, then tossed the gun on the couch with the other one. "Enough!" she shouted, in Russian and put her hands up. He stood stock still, obviously terrified and confused.

The ambulance arrived next and two paramedics rushed in. They cautiously walked by her to take over with Rafi.

Right behind them another policeman rushed in and pressed his gun against her head. He looked terrified too, so she kept her hands up. The first officer retrieved his gun and left the building.

Another motorcycle cop arrived and ran in pointing his weapon. Now both men were shouting at her. "Do you speak English?" she asked. It had no effect. "Lei parla Italiano? No? Sprechen Sie Deutsch?" Still nothing. "Well then, let's try Russian."

The man she disarmed returned and slapped her across the face with the back of his hand, then picked up the discarded clip. When he got it back together, he chambered a round and pressed the barrel against her chest.

"Hayır!" shouted the other two.

"I guess that was a no then," she said, with a bloodied lip. The third man stepped behind her, pulled her arms down one at a time and cuffed her hands.

The medic covered Rafi with a sheet and stood up shaking his head.

"What? No! He's not dead! No," Kat shouted, turning in horror. She was slapped again and pushed back onto the couch beside the Luger.

The policeman realized his error and dragged her onto the floor. Her sweater and jeans were soaked with Rafi's blood. She could feel it drying on her face and caked in her hair just like before when the four men came calling at the dacha. Blood was all she could smell, and she shivered in the cold night air.

Several minutes later two plain clothed detectives arrived. She watched as one of the uniforms went out and greeted the senior detective with a salute as he rose from the car. The detective was a short, dark skinned man, heavy-set with a long, hooked nose which he held high, as if the air were cleaner up there. He looked like a comedic caricature of a detective, a nasty version of Inspector Clouseau. His trench coat hung from his shoulders like a cape and the uniforms all seemed to be afraid of him. Things were already horrible, but Kat knew from the way he looked at her that it would get worse.

His dark inquisitive eyes quickly took in the scene as he stroked the small strip of a mustache outlining his upper lip. He surprised her with his first question spoken in Spanish. "What is your name?"

"How did you know I was Spanish?"

"Just answer the question, please."

"Anita Franco."

He looked at his younger partner as if to say, I told you so. The partner was taller but lacked the authority that the senior man seemed to exude. Perhaps it was his lack of chin, the pockmarked skin and hooded eyes that made him appear both creepy and ineffectual.

The senior man pointed upstairs and gave the partner an order. The skinny man nodded, chose a few men from the expanding pool of police and headed upstairs.

Kat was still on the floor. On his own now, the detective leaned down to examine her, as if she were an attraction at the zoo. He sneered. "I understand you also speak English," he said, switching languages again. "Fortunately, my colleagues do not. I choose English because I wish this to be a private conversation. I am Detective Burakgazi." He straitened up and the corners of his mouth pulled back into an ugly smile. "So ..., you are the infamous Señora Franco. It is an honor."

"How do you know me?"

"My people have been looking for you for days."

"Your people?"

"Oh? Ha-ha-ha. You thought we wouldn't find you? So, you are not as clever as they say. The credit card brought us right to you."

"What are you going to do?"

"I have instructions that you are to be taken to Zürich. You may get up now." He studied her from head to toe, stroking his mustache with the back of his finger as she stood. He said, "But with the right incentive I might be persuaded to forget that."

"And how persuasive would you like me to be?" she asked, knowing exactly where his mind was headed.

"I am sure you will think of something," he said. He paused when his partner returned saying he had done as he was asked. The officers came down with the bodies and removed them from the hotel. The medics took Rafi's body out to the ambulance and departed.

Taking out his gun, a Luger, just like the one she took from the man upstairs; he ordered all the uniformed officers to leave immediately. He fed a round into the chamber, switched off the safety and pressed it against her blood-stained chest. "The reward for your capture is 100,000 Euros."

"I could double that if you let me go," she said quickly.

"I'm sure you could," he said, tracing her breasts with the barrel of his gun, "but you would have to do much more than double it to persuade me to betray my employer."

"Tell me what you want."

"How much is your life worth to you? My instructions were to deliver you alive, but I might just say that it was impossible. They would accept that, knowing your potential." Burakgazi turned to speak to his partner. "Durum kontrol altında, simdi git!" (The situation is under control, now go.)

"What's happening?" she asked, but he ignored her.

His partner said, "Ancak yardıma ihtiyacınız olacak." (But you will need help.)

"Bu bir emirdir, simdi git," he replied. (That's an order, go now) The younger man began to argue. Burakgazi cut him off with a slash of his hand and jerked his head towards the door. "I have told him to leave us, but the fool insists that he remain for my interrogation." The younger man looked at her and made a disgusting licking gesture with his tongue between his fingers before he left. "But I ordered him to get out." Burakgazi's face split into a twisted smile and he said, "It is just you and me now, Señora Franco." His eyes locked on hers as he traced circles around her nipple with the barrel of his gun.

"What do you want to do, shoot me or ... more of that?"

"Shall we go to your room?"

He pushed her toward the elevator and followed with the gun at her back. As he leaned around her to push the elevator button, his hot breath touched her neck, and he pressed his body against hers. She shivered and that seemed to amuse him. "Oh, you are going to feel a lot more of me before we are done."

Eventually they reached her room and he surprised her by removing the cuffs. "This will go so much better for you if you cooperate."

"How unoriginal, detective."

He slapped her face. "I am going to enjoy hurting you." He took her by the arm and put the gun to her shoulder.

"No, no wait! Wait a second ..., I'm sorry OK? I get a little lippy when I'm stressed. And besides, if you start putting holes in me it's going to make pleasing you difficult."

He moved back and said, "So you will cooperate?"

She nodded. "Anything you want."

"O-o-o-o-w ..., very well then."

"I gather you are with Zapf Industries," she said, studying his reaction. He didn't know what she was talking about. "I mean that's who you work for, right."

"I have never heard this name Zapf before. Where did you hear it?"

"Oh, it just turned up in conversation with a man in Ukraine."

"You have been misinformed. The organization I belong to is Rote Faust."

"Rote Faust? How interesting, and what does Rote Faust do besides try to murder people in their sleep?"

"The Americans will know all about it soon enough."

"Why, what is going to happen?"

"Enough of this, you are wasting my time. I tell you what I am prepared to do. For a significant act of contrition and a million Euros, I will let you go."

"A million? Is that all?"

"It is enough for a modest man such as myself."

She pulled at her sweater suggestively. "Look at me, detective, I'm covered with blood and it is sticking to my skin." She began to lift the sweater just enough to get his undivided attention. "Let me have a shower. After that we can discuss that act of contrition you wanted." He smiled but didn't move. "Of course. Stay and watch. I don't mind."

"Alright," she said, as she backed away from him into the bathroom.

He followed, saying, "You were very lucky to get out of Ukraine alive."

"Oh, I don't know. I handled myself pretty well, I think."

She began to slowly remove her sweater, stopping just short of revealing a breast. His eyes widened. She didn't think he would be drawn in so easily, but thought it was worth a try. "How would you like to put you hand there?" He lowered the gun and reached for her.

In one swift motion, she blocked his hand with her right arm and drove her left fist into his neck crushing his throat. The gun tumbled to the floor. His tongue stuck out and his hands went to his throat. His eyes filled with tears and terror. As he struggled for breath, she delivered a powerful blow with the heel of her hand slamming his nose into his brain. It made a nasty crunching sound as he died. His lifeless body instantly turned to gelatin and dropped to the floor. She stepped over him, then taking him by the arms dragged him out into the hall.

She picked up his gun and tossed it onto her bed, then stripped down leaving the bloodstained garments on the floor. She showered, then picked out the last things she packed before she went to bed, dressed quickly and pulled on her coat. After closing the suitcase, she left the gun on the bed and took the stairs down to the lobby.

Carefully, she scanned the street for movement. When she was sure that it was deserted, she walked down to the mall. Crossing over to the street by the university she turned south on Safi Hamami Sk.

Following the route she had taken the previous day, she came to the crossroad near the Sarnic Hotel. There was a taxi parked out front and the driver was asleep behind the wheel. He was startled when Kat rapped on his window, but he rolled it down. "Evet hanımım?"

"Do you speak Russian?" she asked in Russian.

"A little," he said with a yawn.

"Good." She opened the back door, tossed her case on the seat and got in. "Take me to the airport." She handed him a wad of bills over the back of the seat. "Hurry please, or I'll miss my flight." It was far too much but he grinned as he stuffed the money into his pocket, and they sped off.

Chapter 6

New York, New York

Monday March 15

At the start of morning trading, a broker in New York, acting on behalf of an anonymous buyer, bought 20 tons of gold at the spot price of $426.5 an ounce paying $223,201,695.10.

This purchase was larger than the holdings of several small countries, so there was a great deal of interest in the identity of the buyer. It was hypothesized that the buyer was a government, which, for its own reasons, chose to remain anonymous.

No one considered the preposterous idea that an anonymous megalomaniac planned to destabilize the world order, cutting off American influence in Europe and, given time, eventually naming himself Emperor of Europe. But that was indeed his plan. The trade was reported in the Wall Street Journal on page 13, below the fold. A few commentators wrote articles suggesting the possible motivation for the purchase, such as preparations for war, but no one had been able to identify the purchaser. The world was in such turmoil that it was soon old news and forgotten by Wednesday.

To Familiar Ground

10:20 am

The first flight out of Istanbul was to Madrid leaving at 6:25 am and once she was buckled into her seat, she didn't open her eyes until they landed at Madrid - Barajas Airport. Feeling the pressure ease somewhat, she thought she might stop for a sweet roll and espresso before hopping on the metro.

That thought sustained her in the line-up at customs. But as soon as she was cleared and walked out the door she was spotted by a hefty, middle aged man covered with tattoos. He began snapping pictures. He called out to her in a voice that filled the terminal. "Hola ..., Señora Franco!" Everybody within earshot turned to look. "Hey! Mira Anita!"

"Oh Christ, that's all I need." She quickened her pace, but he continued after her. She called over her shoulder, "Listen, leave me alone, please."

"What brings you back to Madrid? Hey, Anita Franco, look here," he shouted, as if she were deaf. All the while he was snapping pictures. A few curious travelers began taking pictures too. She tried to hide her face and started running, but he chased her and some of the travelers joined in.

After a few strides in the crowded hall of Terminal 4, she realized that she wasn't going to get rid of him by getting into a foot race. She stopped and turned on him saying as sweetly as she could, "Listen Señor, can we just not do this right now?" He just grinned and kept on snapping pictures. "OK, Shit for Brains, if you don't stop, I'm going to break your fucking camera!" There was a collective gasp from those around her, but he just laughed and continued snapping away. She snatched the camera and yanked it out of his hands.

"Hey! Madre de Dios," he said, and tried to get it back, but she slammed him in the chest with the palm of her hand. The force of the blow came as a total surprise. He was a big guy, but there was expert technique behind that blow, and it stopped him cold. She raised the camera above her head and was about to slam it down on the floor.

He put up his hands and shouted, "No-no-no! Please don't. I'll stop!"

"You'd better." She flipped open the little door on the side of the camera and removed the two SD cards then handed the camera back to him.

"But they had ..."

"I won't warn you again!" He was going to protest but she cut him off. "Do you understand?"

"Si," he said, rubbing his chest.

She dropped the cards in her shoulder bag and walked away. He stood speechless watching her go. Before she was out of sight his impromptu entourage gathered round him chattering excitedly about what she had just done. "I had no idea she was so strong," he said, still rubbing his chest.

"I think she may have broken my rib."

Kat walked on to the Metro line 8 and took the train to Nuevos Ministerios without any further interference. Unfortunately, another problem popped up while she was dealing with the paparazzo and she had missed it. A man in the crowd heard the photographer shout out her name. He had other business at the airport, but he realized that he had stumbled onto something much more profitable. He watched with great interest how she dealt with the nuisance. Now aware that he had to keep his distance, he followed her to the train.

Once in the city center the memory of her last stay here took over and she asked the cab driver to take her to the Only You Boutique Hotel. The man followed in another cab and drove by as hers stopped at the hotel. She should have known that this was a mistake, but she was tired and angry. The woman at the desk remembered her the moment she walked through the door. "Hola, Señora Franco, bienvenida de vuelta al Madrid."

"Ah ... hola buenos," she read the young woman's name tag. "Helena, hola. I'm surprised to be remembered after all this time."

"I recall exactly the night when you returned with Antonio Alvarez. My God, he is so dreamy, don't you think? I have seen all his movies. Who could forget that night? It is a pleasure to see you again."

Kat realized what she had to do before she compounded her error. "You know, Helena, I am sorry, but I can't stay here." She ran out of the hotel and caught the attention of her driver before he left.

She tapped on his roof. "Si, señora, did you forget something?"

She jumped in dragging in her bag behind her. "Please just drive. Anywhere, I don't care."

"Si, señora."

The man from the airport had his cab driver circle the block before dropping him off. Unfortunately for him, by the time he found a spot to wait for her she had already moved on. He waited there the rest of the day before he gave up and returned to the airport.

Kat had to smarten up in a hurry, or she wasn't going to survive this. She knew it was going to cost her dearly, but it was time to take cover and call in the cavalry. "Señor, I've changed my mind. Could you take me to a Lloyd's bank and some place to buy a phone?"

"Si, no problem."

A Call For Help

12:48 pm

After a brief stop at the bank, the driver delivered her to the entrance of the Plaza Callao on Calle Gran Via. "This is as close as I can take you, señora. You must cross the street at the light. The Phone House is just on that corner."

She looked across at the huge, maze-like pedestrian mall, lined with shops and restaurants and jammed with people. The driver was pointing towards the corner of Calle Preciados.

"OK, I see it," she said, as she read the meter. Handing him thirty Euros as she got out, she said, "Keep it and thank you."

Satisfied that she was alone, she entered the Phone House. After showing her passport and paying €20 cash, she left with a prepaid phone and a SIM card. She walked through the maze of cross streets and alleys looking for a quiet place where she could make a call.

She was also getting very hungry and spotted Cañas y Tapas, a tapas bar down the street from El Corte Inglés. It wasn't busy at all and the proprietress was standing in the doorway, watching unhappily as the crowd passed her by. Kat approached her. "Hola. ¿Hay una mesa tranquila en la parte posterior?" (Hello. Do you have a quiet place in the back?)

The woman's face lit up. "Si, te lo mostraré. Ven por aquí." (Yes, I'll show you. Come this way.) The room was dominated by the three huge copper beer barrels suspended from the ceiling above the bar. Kat had never seen anything like it. She had an awful vision of whatever was holding them up giving way and the people below being crushed and/or drowned in the ensuing flood of beer. The hostess seemed unconcerned and took her to a table in a narrow room at the back.

"What can I get for you"

One of the copper barrels was labeled San Miguel. "A small San Miguel and a little fried fish."

"Bien," the woman said, and disappeared.

Kat pulled out her new phone, inserted the SIM card and tapped in a number she hadn't used for quite a while. "Maryland heating and air conditioning," said the operator.

"My furnace isn't working, I'd like to speak to the manager please."

"Serial number please."

"MI 55-31-86"

After a short pause, Devlyn picked, "So, Katrina," he said, "would I be correct in assuming that you are in trouble again?"

"Oh, for God's sake." Hearing his smug tone made calling him even more difficult. "Yes. I'm in Madrid, Paul, and people are after me."

"No fucking surprise there! What people?"

"That's just it, I don't really know. One group seemed to be working for some company that probably doesn't exist and the other group is calling themselves Rote Faust." She told him everything that had happened over the last five days.

When she finished, he said, "I suppose the cop is dead as well."

"That's not helpful, Paul. I didn't have a choice."

"Yeah, right. OK, so you're in Madrid now. That's good, I can work with that, but before I do anything are you prepared to accept my conditions?"

"You never said what your conditions were."

"We'll get to that, but our problem right now is that you're a cop killer. Interpol will be after you."

"This is a goddamn nightmare."

"Yeah, I hear you. So, who knew you were in Ukraine?"

"Apart from Vlad, no one. And I trust him completely," she said.

"Then how did they find you?"

"I'm guessing that they were after Vlad."

"I'm sure they regret that."

"They didn't have time."

"Ouch. OK, where are you staying?"

"I haven't found a safehouse yet," she said. "There is something else, Paul. When I arrived this morning, I was met by a paparazzo at the airport. The guy recognized me the moment I cleared customs. That's crazy, right?"

"Did he get your picture?"

"Yeah, but I got his camera away from him and took out the SD cards. The problem is there were other people taking pictures. He was pretty pissed at me, so I wouldn't be surprised if he gets hold of some of those pictures."

"Shit. So, we have to assume that the bad guys will know that you're in Madrid."

"Yeah, I'm open for suggestions."

"Alright, do you have any cash?"

"Yeah."

"OK, good. Change your appearance as much as you can and find an-out-of-the-way place, a young people's hostel maybe, or a B&B where you can lay low for a while. Call me when you're safe and I'll arrange to bring you in."

"How long is a while, Paul?"

"I don't know but fixing this is 'priority one'."

That was a surprise. She wondered what was going on. "Thanks Paul."

"Don't thank me yet. We still have to talk about the conditions."

"OK, what are they?"

"I'll tell you when I see you."

"You know Paul, I have a feeling that killing Petrus was like lopping off the head of the Hydra."

"Katrina, you were warned."

The Hostel Falfes

K at had to get busy losing herself in the big city. With just under €10,000 she had more than enough to find food and shelter for a while. After she ate lunch, she went to a cab stand to hire a driver for the day.

She asked him to help her find an out of the way place where she could hide from her abusive husband.

They drove all over Madrid looking a safehouse. Finally, at a quarter to seven, she selected a hostel in Tetuán, near the Santiago Bernabeu Stadium.

The driver warned her that it was a rough district, but she said it was perfect. She assured him that her husband would never look for her there.

She wheeled her baggage over the threshold and as she stopped to look around the sparse modern lobby, the manager looked up from his reading material and said, "Hola, señorina, ¿Qué puedo hacer por ti?"

"Hola, I want a single room with a bath or shower if you have one."

He got up from his chair, put his magazine down and stared at her with interest, then leaned over the counter to see what she had brought with her. "English?"

"Close enough."

"That is a big suitcase. You are planning to stay for a long time?"

"That depends."

He noticed the rocks on her finger and looked at her suspiciously, "This is not a place where I would expect to see a woman like you. Are you are hiding from someone, your husband perhaps?"

"Does it matter?"

"No, not to me," he said.

"Have you a room for me or not?"

"I have a single with a private bath at 23 Euros."

"That sounds fine."

"I'll need to see some identification."

"Would this do?" she said, counting out a hundred Euros. "If I only stay a couple of days, then you can pocket the rest. How does that sound?"

"That would be acceptable. You just have to sign the register." She did, using the first name that came to mind. He read it upside down with raised eyebrows, "You are Frieda Kahlo?"

"Yes."

"Frieda Kahlo," he repeated, with amused skepticism. "The dead Mexican painter?"

Oh fuck, well isn't that just peachy, she thought. The guy had to be an art lover. "Do I look dead to you?"

"On the contrary, señora," he said, staring at her with a smirk on his face.

"I happen to share a name with a famous person and it only causes me problems. You have no idea how much I hated my mother for doing that..., among other things. And no, I don't paint."

"I didn't think so," he said, and the smirk broadened into a wicked smile. "It is obvious that your talents lie elsewhere."

"All I want from you, señor ..., is a room. Can we just stick to that?"

The smile withered but the attitude remained. "I only meant that ..."

"It's OK, I know exactly what you meant. May I have my key now?"

He reached down to his terminal to enter some information into his computer, slid a plastic card through a scanner then dropped it on the counter saying, "You are in room 221," then pointed, "up the stairs over there."

"And will you carry my bag for me?" she asked sarcastically.

He laughed and went back to his magazine.

As soon as she was in her room, she called Devlyn.

"Where are you now?"

She looked around her at the room's décor and said, "I'm in a very cheap and oppressively red room at the Hostal Falfes, registered as Frieda Kahlo."

"Frieda Kahlo ..., the painter? You've got to be kidding me."

"Shut up! I'm tired and it was the only name I could think of. This little gem of a place is in the 'not so very trendy Tetuán district', so I doubt that anyone will be looking for me here. I think I'm safe for a while. But please don't make me stay here any longer than necessary. The color alone is going to drive me insane."

"Since when did you start caring about the décor?"

"Again, not helpful."

He laughed. "Alright, sit tight and I'll figure out how to get you out of there." He disconnected and she sat for a while staring at the fire engine red walls. It had been a trying day and she was done in. As far as she was concerned it was still siesta time, so she kicked off her shoes, stretched out on the bed and instantly fell asleep.

An Uneasy Prelude

9:40 pm

The evening had cooled off quite a bit and the cold seeped through the block walls. The room didn't have a heater, so she woke up chilled to the bone. A sweater would be welcome, so she opened her suitcase and pulled out a warm pullover.

She was hungry again and went out in search of sustenance. After about ten minutes she found a pleasant family restaurant. She asked for a table in the back corner away from the door. It was warmer back there and the lighting was softer. "This will be fine, thank you."

"Can I bring you something to drink?"

"A glass of red wine." She looked at the wine list on the chalk board. "El Condado de Oriza Crianza, please."

"Right away, señora."

As the room began to fill, she watched from the corner, growing lonelier and increasingly more depressed with each extended family's arrival. They were all talking happily and laughing. The kids were running around, pausing briefly on a grandfather's knee to eat something and then off again.

Feeling like a visitor from another planet, she sipped the wine while she considered the menu. Finally deciding on breaded veal, fried potatoes and another glass of wine, she sat back and watched them as if they were actors in a play.

They looked so happy. She wondered what it would have been like to have a normal childhood. Hers was nothing like this. She never had a family dinner of any kind. No grandparents, no siblings, no play dates with other kids, no birthday parties. "No wonder I'm a crazy person."

Perhaps it was a combination of the wine and watching the children that caused her to drift inward, remembering everything, regretting everything. The childhood that was stolen from her, the abuse heaped on her by her uncle and the perverted old man who paid him by the month to use her as his personal sex toy.

Everything that happened to her since Uncle Ernesto died was a direct result of what those two men had done to her. She was sorry for the blood she spilled for her country, but she had no regrets about the deaths of Ernesto and that pervert Sebastiano.

She raised her hand and the owner smiled and came over. "Si, señora?"

"Otra copa de vino por favor."

"Ciertamente"

The woman smiled and went to fetch the bottle and refilled her glass. "Gracias," Kat said.

"De nada."

She slowly turned the glass around with her fingertips watching the wine slosh around the bowl and found herself wondering if love would ever come her way again. The woman soon returned with her order. Kat nodded her thanks and sipped some wine.

The food was simple and good. Even so, her she didn't have much of an appetite. After picking at it for three quarters of an hour, she had had enough of the place. Enough food, enough wine and more than of enough family time. Maybe it was just as well that she missed that whole business of babies, toddlers and school kids. With no place in particular to go, she paid her check and went out into the cold night air.

Walking down the street, window shopping through the glass of darkened shops something caught her eye. Taped to the window was a picture of a woman not unlike herself, but with stylishly short, black hair. Touching her ponytail, Kat looked at her reflection then looked up at the name painted on the window, Masajemania Salon. She remembered what Devlyn had said about changing her appearance and decided to return on Tuesday morning.

As she walked back to her room all her thoughts about her past conflicting with her need for a family began to congeal into a mess she had to sort out.

CHAPTER 7

CONTACT

Tuesday, March 16, 11:14 am

Kat stayed in her room until 7:30 am then, with a scarf to cover her head, she went out to find a café solo and a sweet bun for breakfast. It was a crisp morning. During the night, frost had settled on the rooftops and awnings. The brilliant sun beaming down on a cloudless sky would soon clear that away. She was glad to have both the dark glasses and a warm coat. Warmed by a fine cup of coffee, Kat went back to the salon and pointed to the picture in the window. "I'd like it to have a cut like that."

"Perfecto," the hairdresser said. "We'll start with a wash and then I cut. I promise you will love it." After the first snip Kat preferred not to watch.

Instead, she concentrated on the gossipy articles in a recent European edition of Architectural Digest. The featured property was an incredible glass house just outside Zürich. She read the article with mild interest and admired the photos, then moved on, forgetting about the house the moment she put the magazine down. During that hour of cutting and styling, she read four and a half magazines. An article in a movie magazine about the actor Antonio Alvarez had her smiling as she remembered that last night in Madrid with him almost two years ago. He was a good lover but not as good as Harm. Could anybody be as good as Harm? She wondered fleetingly if loving him made all the difference or had he become greater in death than he'd been in life?

The hairdresser patted her on the shoulders and said, "There you are, señora, we are done."

Kat put the magazine down to look at the result. The woman had done a fantastic job and Kat thought it looked better than the picture. Even so, it was a bit of a shock to see the new her. In her whole life, she had never had more than an inch taken off. "Wow."

"This is a good look for you, no?"

Kat wasn't sure. "You think so?"

"Oh yes! You look like a different person." Kat turned her head from side to side, and sensing that she needed reassurance, the woman said, "Don't worry, señora, you will get used to it very quickly and your husband will love it."

"I hope so. It does look good. You know what? I love it. Thank you."

"De nada."

I do look like a different woman. And somehow, I feel different.

Shopping was beginning to be a distraction from the constant pain she lived with, but she had no place to put the things. Making do with window shopping, she headed back to the hostel and every window she passed, reinforced what a change cutting her hair had made. "If the paparazzi spotted me now, they wouldn't have a ..." Her phone rang. Only one person had the number. She took it from her purse and said, "Hola, Paul."

THE CAVALRY

1:20 pm

Just the fact that his voice was familiar made her feel safer. "Hey Katrina. You sound like you're out on the street."

"Yes, I've just been to the hairdresser."

"Can you talk?"

"It's too loud out here." She looked around and saw a café two doors away. "Give me a second, I'm going inside."

"Sure, do whatever you have to do." Kat stepped off the street into the Café Mies, a nice place with soft lighting and practically empty.

The owner glance up. "Ah-h-h ..., Hola señora. ¡Bienvenido!"

She was amazed at how quickly some men seemed to notice the wedding ring.

"Hola, café solo, por favor." She pointed to the back of the room, "Can I sit over there?"

"Perfecto, señora," he said, and started on the coffee.

She sat down then returning to English, "Sorry about that. So, how much trouble am I in?"

"Don't worry about that now."

"OK-a-a-a-a-ay," she said, stretching the word out and up. "Should I ask why?"

"It's no longer an issue. You said you went to the hairdresser?"

"Yeah. Oh, hold on a second. Are you telling me that I just got my hair cut off for nothing?"

"Hey, it probably looks great, don't sweat the small stuff."

"It may be small stuff to you, but it sure was a hell of a fucking biggie for me." She took a breath and calmed down. "What's happening at your end?"

"My end is that I am currently parked in front of your hostel."

"Are you kidding me?" she said, "When did you get here?"

"About five minutes ago, just long enough to find out that you aren't here. Give me your location and I'll come to you."

She gave him the directions and ended the call.

Seven minutes later, Devlyn came through the door wearing the aviator shades and that old leather jacket he had on when they first met. Other than needing a shave, he hadn't changed at all. Kat felt unexpectedly happy at seeing him. She stood up smiling. "Hola."

"Hola, Katrina," he said, and took off his sunglasses. "Girl, you took magnificent."

She had been expecting an 'I told you so' lecture but no, it looked like he was genuinely happy to see her. "Thanks stranger." Still undecided as to how to proceed, she gave him a casual European embrace and platonic kisses on each cheek. He apparently wanted something more substantial but she put a little space between them.

"Do you want something?"

"Si," he said, without letting her get too far away.

"I meant to drink, Paul."

"Oh." Looking over his shoulder at the man at the bar said, "Café Americano." Redirecting his attention towards her again he grinned. "You really do look fantastic."

"Really? The hairdresser told me I looked like a different person."

"She wasn't kidding. If you hadn't stood up, I wouldn't have recognized you." He drew her close and kissed her neck.

"I have changed, I'm not the same Katrina you knew."

"Come on, get serious."

"I am serious. Listen, after two years of living with that name you gave me, two years of being in exile, alone, speaking nothing but Russian and Ukrainian, of course I've changed. With two notable exceptions, everyone I knew thinks I'm dead."

"OK." His grip loosened. "What do you want me to do?"

This was the moment she had hastily prepared for. She sat down and the barman placed his cup on the table. "Gracias."

"¿Otro café para ti?"

"No gracias," she said. He smiled and returned to the bar. "To start with, we need to talk about a solution to my situation," she said. "You said you could bring me in. Is that going to be a problem?"

"Not at all, provided you accept the conditions."

"Let's go on the assumption that I do. Paul," she said pointing to the other chair, "you're making me nervous, could you please sit down?"

He sat. "Better?"

"Much."

He tasted the coffee as his expression turned serious and lowering his voice, he said, "Katrina, the whole world has started to come unglued. You may have heard that the Middle East problems are spilling over into Europe."

"The Russian media doesn't pay much attention to what's going on there."

"Not surprising I suppose. People are getting incredibly nervous because we're seeing something new developing. European nationals in every country are forming in groups and having secret meetings. There's talk of some sort of terrorist activity starting up here that is totally unrelated to the Middle-East factions.

"I've been given command of 6-6-MI. During this crisis, I've moved office to The Hague temporarily and am working out of an office at the Europe headquarters. Europol has had some intel …"

"Europol?" she said, interrupting him and he knew what her objection would be.

"Ease up. They're under new management."

"I hope he's better than the last guy."

"I think he is. Katrina, the crazies are coming out of the woodwork. Our sources say it's just a matter of time before they do something big."

"This is going to be really bad, isn't it?"

"Yeah, really bad. They haven't sent out a manifesto yet but we're hearing some disturbing things coming from unexpected places. And there's some nut-job stirring up more trouble, saying that if he were the President of the EU, the terrorist problem would go away."

"Is there even such a thing as a President of the EU?"

"Actually, there is but I don't think the position has the power to do what he thinks it does."

"Who is this guy?"

"He is a multibillionaire named Arnulf Jäger."

"So, the Euro-King in waiting is a billionaire nut-job. Typical." Devlyn shrugged. "OK. Who are these terrorists aligned with?" He shrugged again. "Does Jäger have anything to do with them?" Kat asked.

"We can't rule anything out at this point and it's weird that Jäger is campaigning for the job at all."

"Why?"

"No one is running an election." He sipped his coffee.

"Yeah, that is weird alright. Does it fit with anything else you've heard?"

"No, not specifically. So, if it's the same group and they've infiltrated the police in Turkey, then we're up to our necks in some major shit." His phone rang and after saying "Devlyn," he just sat there and listened. "Jesus Christ. OK." He ended the connection and looked at her.

"What?"

"Rote Faust just sent a manifesto to a paper in Munich. They said Americans must leave Europe immediately. The purge has begun."

"The detective didn't say anything about a purge."

"Yeah, well maybe he just forgot to mention it. There's another mystery that happened at home. I don't know if it's connected, but someone bought a shit load of gold the other day when the price was relatively low. It made some waves, but Wall Street said, 'What are you going to do? Shit happens'. Washington was a little more concerned. They think Iran is behind it. If something bad happens, and the price goes through the roof, the implications of that will be more than a little disturbing."

Kat was concerned that they were missing something. "What about the Russians? They could be involved as well."

"Boy, you've really got a thing about the Russians, don't you? No, I don't think so. The name is German."

"Sure, but we've dealt with Germans criminals working with the Russians before. They're always looking for a way to destabilize the West. Funding a terrorist organization is standard operating procedure for them." While Devlyn considered that Kat said, "We should be looking for a connection there."

"Agreed. Why did they go after you?"

"They weren't after me. They wanted Vlad for killing Petrus. Everyone thought I died with Petrus."

"Fuck lady, you scare me sometimes. You know that?"

"I scare myself a lot."

He didn't touch that. "Apart from the name, did you get any other intel in Istanbul?"

"The detective said I had a price on my head, and he wanted to take me to Zürich. God-knows-why."

"Alright, it seems clear now that the timing of the manifesto and what happened to you isn't coincidental. Whatever they've been planning is going to start soon."

"Is this where the conditions come in to play?"

"I knew you were sharp. Yeah. As soon as you called, I reported to G-2 and told him you were alive and, I won't lie to you, he was not overjoyed. He hit the roof."

"He was never a fan."

"True, but then I said that you could be useful, and I told him I wanted to bring you on my team. He wasn't thrilled about that either. I said your experience would be invaluable."

"Is this official?"

"Oh, it's official alright. I'm bringing you in, but you are going to have to work with me. We need anything you can tell us about these people, every bit of intel you've managed to collect since this started. If I know anything about you, Katrina, it's that you're always on the job. G-2 cut the orders himself. If you accept, you'll be reinstated with a clean slate and a promotion, plus back pay and benefits."

"Reinstated? You mean I have to go back to MCI?"

"If you want to get out of this mess then that's the deal."

She thought about it for a moment and then said, "Alright, I accept."

"Good. I thought you would, so I brought some things for you." He checked over his shoulder, then took out an envelope from his inside jacket pocket and pushed it across the table. It contained a few familiar objects; her badge, her Military Counterintelligence ID and her passport. "As of now, Katrina Fernando has officially risen from the dead. You can let go of Anita Franco forever."

She twisted her rings around her finger, a habit she'd gotten into when she was thinking. As much as she loved the idea of being Kat again, she wasn't sure she wanted to give up Anita. "You know what? I think I'm going to hang on to the Franco passport. You never know when I may need her again."

"What about the rings?"

"Harm gave them to me. I was married, remember?"

"Yeah, I remember. OK, keep 'em."

"Thanks," she said, although she didn't know what she was thanking him for. "OK, what happens now?"

"You're to accompany me to the Netherlands, Lieutenant Colonel."

"Excuse me?"

"Yup, you're a Lieutenant Colonel now, congratulations."

Not quite believing it she joked, "So we're finally the same rank."

"Dream on, Katrina, I'm a full Bird Colonel now, so I'm still your boss. Our assignment is to collaborate with Europol, Interpol and all the other European agencies." Her eyes immediately teared up. "What's the matter? Hey, I thought you'd be happy about this."

"I am, it's just that I'm ... a little overwhelmed by all of this. When do we leave for The Hague?"

"The meeting is at 08:30 tomorrow. We have a flight at 20:15."

"What? Jesus what time is it now?"

He looked at his watch. "14:10. You haven't gained any weight over the past year, have you?"

"Why?"

"Because I brought you a new uniform. My car's outside, we should get going." He dropped twenty Euros on the table, and they left.

By Her Rules

As they drove back to the hostel, Kat couldn't help feeling that she was letting herself be used all over again by the same people who had already taken so much from her.

She had agreed because it was the price she had to pay to get a little security. But now security wasn't enough for her. She didn't need the clemency, the promotion, or the money. What she needed was everything that had been taken away, her husband, the family, a normal life. Casually she looked over at Devlyn sizing him up for a little pay back. He smiled at her, she smiled back. If he was comfortable using her whenever it suited him then it was time for her to use him when it suited her.

He probably knows I don't really like him, but I know he doesn't care. He wants me, that's plain enough, and it would not take any effort at all to get him to do what I want. She looked out her window as the neighborhood passed by.

She looked at him again.

He knew that was more to come. "Something on your mind?"

"There isn't ever a time when there isn't something on my mind."

"Well?"

"It's nothing important. It'll keep for another time," she said smiling. He shrugged, unconcerned. His thoughts were more important anyway. She could see that as clearly as if he'd said as much out loud. "Is that my uniform back there?"

"Yeah."

"I'll have to try it on."

"There's no time for alterations, Kat, so it better fit."

"I haven't put on any weight, so it should." She touched her belly then slowly moved her hand to her thigh, consciously lingering on a highly suggestive area to draw his attention. He looked, and she pretended she didn't notice. "It will be cold waiting in the car for me, you should come up to my room while I change.

There was no emotion involved in the act she performed. The object was simply to have him do his part and then she would be done with him. Although she did manage to make him feel that he was the best she'd ever had.

Afterwards he lay beside her panting and glistening with sweat. That was a skill she developed to stave off the beatings Ernest would give her when he had complaints about her performance. Devlyn's prowess was an illusion. "Wow, that was awesome," he said, and she smiled as she got out of bed. "I did not see that coming."

"That's not the impression I got at the café," she said.

"It was on my mind, sure, but I never thought I'd actually ... you have no idea how long I've wanted you."

"Oh, Paul, you're an open book."

"It was that obvious, was it?" She didn't reply. "So, was it good for you?"

"It was what I expected."

"What can I say, you bring out the beast in me."

"I'm going to have a quick shower."

"Ah, Katrina?"

She turned. "Yes?"

"Everybody has been underestimating you, me included. I look at you now and you look incredible, but ..."

"But?"

"I'll be honest with you. I expected a lot when I selected you. I had a plan to make you into a honey trap."

"I eventually saw what you were doing, Paul."

"Of course you did. That's what I'm saying, but I had no idea that you had such unbelievable strength and power. I won't underestimate you ever again."

"Uh huh."

"I'm glad to have you back," he said. "I think we'll be great partners."

She paused. "Partners?"

"Yeah, we're partners now."

Perfect, the very thing to shut him down forever. "Then we can't ever do this again."

"What? But I ..."

"Partners can't be lovers, Paul. That would only lead to problems and that's the last thing either of us needs, right?"

He let that disappointing bit of news sink in then said, "Yeah ... agreed."

Chapter 8

A Soccer Tour

Near Lyon, France, 11:23 am

The Golden Foxes, a women's soccer team from Indiana's Sifton College, was in France to compete in the first match of their six country European tour. None of the twenty-two young women had been beyond the borders of the continental US before and most had never been outside the State of Indiana. They were being chaperoned by their head coach, Haley Griffith, her assistant, Joanne Rhodes and the team manager, Rosanna Hemp. The team doctor, Bethany Rogers, a specialist in sports medicine, was along for the ride.

So far it had been a terrific ride too. During their first three days in Paris the excitement level was sky high. They'd seen everything and done everything they could imagine in the City of Lights and now it was down to business. After a late night in the capital, they headed out to their first game in Lyon at 6:00 am. Suffering from a collective hangover, they were tired, somewhat subdued and thankful to be able to just sit and watch as the countryside flashed by their windows.

The game schedule would take them to the Netherlands next for a game in Rotterdam, then on to Munich, Germany; Vienna, Austria; Copenhagen, Denmark; and finally, they would cross over to Stockholm, Sweden, for the last match. The first match was going to be held in the Plaine des Jeux de Gerland, a 2,200-capacity stadium home of the of Division 1 Féminine champions, the Olympique Lyonnais Féminine. A hundred American fans and family had flown over from Craigleith, Indiana to watch the tournament and were waiting in Lyon to cheer on their girls to victory.

After being on the bus for five hours the young women were getting a little restless. Coach Griffith was sensitive to the collective mood of her team and thought it best to do something proactively. Sitting in the seat right behind the driver she leaned forward and asked, "How much further to Lyon?"

"It's about an hour and a half, madam."

"Then I suggest we have one more stop now to stretch our legs."

"Very well," the driver said, "I know of a patisserie in Trévoux where we could stop. It's just a few minutes from here."

"That sounds perfect." She stood up and faced the back of the bus. "Alright, ladies, listen up. We are going to stop for a pee break just down the road." The team cheered. "OK, quieten down, quieten down. You can have twenty minutes to do your business. Get some fresh air and get back on the bus ... and that means twenty minutes ... or less this time, ladies."

They groaned. "I'm not kidding guys, twenty and that's it."

The bus went around a traffic circle on the far side of La Grange aux Délices and pulled off the Route de Lyon onto a mall parking lot. The driver parked behind a gas station. The pressure of the flood of girls against the door seemed to open it and everyone rushed off. They chattered excitedly as they walked back to the sidewalk then crossed the busy road as one large mass. Traffic was forced to stop in both direction and the angry drivers honked pointlessly as the team, oblivious to the danger, shouted and laughed on their way to mob the little shop on the far side.

It was a small patisserie with only a few tables and only one toilet, so it took a while for the overwhelmed baker's assistant to accommodate the group. They went inside in shifts and came out refreshed with coffee and their entire production of eclairs.

During the quiet that followed, a minivan carrying six men slipped in beside the bus. They had been tailing the team from Paris waiting for a moment just like this. The leader got out and went over to the bus and knocked on the door.

Being a curious man by nature, the driver opened the door and found that he was staring down the barrel of a pistol equipped with a silencer. "Oh, mon Dieu! Don't shoot me, please."

"Get down from there," the gunman ordered. Trembling, the driver immediately raised his hands and complied. "Over to the van." As he was pushed over to the van, the side door opened, and the other men emerged wearing trench coats and hats. They took up positions near the bus and watched the women from a distance.

After fifteen minutes, the team began to amble back to the mall parking lot and filed onto the bus. The four chaperones came along behind, making sure that everyone was back on board safely. Just as Dr. Rogers was about to climb in, Coach Griffiths said, "Now where the hell did the driver get to? Hey! Has anybody seen him?" She looked up at the faces peering down at her from the windows.

The team captain opened her window and said, "He's not in here, Coach."

"Thanks, Cathy. Well did anybody see him in the bakery?" All she got were shrugs, so she turned around to scan the lot. "This is just great." Her attention was drawn to the van as the side door opened. It was dark inside, but she could see the familiar shape of her driver. "Frank, what the hell are you doing in there?"

In answer to her question the driver tipped over and fell out onto the pavement. She screamed. Her eyes were fixed on the gaping hole in the back of his head. Suddenly everyone was screaming. The gunman got out and stood over the body.

Haley turned and shouted, "Get on the bus! Get on the bus!" As she pushed Bethany, Joanne and Rosanna to the door she yelled, "Rosanna, start it up." An instant later a bullet pierced her back between the shoulder blades, erupted from her chest then continued through Bethany's thigh. Haley dropped to the ground and the doctor fell back on top of her grimacing in pain. As she started to get, up a second bullet hit her just above the right ear and exited from the left. She sprawled beside Haley.

Joanne turned on the top step and the next round hit the twenty-two-year-old volunteer in the chest. She fell forward out of the bus onto Bethany, leaving the team manager exposed. She turned to look, and the last bullet went through her head hitting her above the eye. Her head slammed against the side window where the bullet had shattered glass. She slumped over the wheel pressing down on the horn.

One of the men rushed up and pushed her aside. The rest of the men surrounded the bus, now filled with a cacophony of screams and crying. The gunmen had covered their faces with surgical masks, four held submachine guns, the fifth had a video camera recording everything.

The leader quietly stepped onto the bus removing the silencer from his gun. He fired a shot through the roof and shouted, "Assez!" The screaming stopped suddenly and the man with the camera appeared standing on the steps behind him recording their reactions. He said something in French and the women, all in their late teens, had no idea what he just said, but from his actions and his tone, they understood the meaning.

The camera man said in English, "If you try to run, you'll be shot.

"Commencez maintenant," said the leader.

The women hurried off the bus. The gunmen on the ground forced them to line up beside the bus, then he said, "Maintenant, chacun d'entre vous répétera votre nom à la caméra."

"We don't know what you are saying!" Cathy said.

"Merde!"

The cameraman said, "OK. Each of you will repeat your name to the camera. Got it?" He moved in close and focused the lens on each of the terrified women. Their voices trembled as they stared wide eyed into the camera and gave their names.

When the close-ups had been recorded, the cameraman moved back for a group shot then turned the lens on the leader who read the statement he had rehearsed many times. "Let this be your warning! This is just the beginning for you Americans. From now on, for you ... there is only death."

CHAPTER 9

A NEW WAR

The Hague

Devlyn's new attitude toward Kat was refreshing. She wasn't sure whether it was because of the sex, or if he really did develop a new appreciation for her abilities. Whatever it was, she was beginning to change her opinion of him. He had become more deferential and his bully commander attitude was gone. She wondered how long it would last.

Now that she was wearing a uniform again, she felt a change in herself as well. The new silver oak leaves on her collar gleamed in the harsh Iberian sun and the number of service ribbons on her chest had grown. She suspected the last one was to signify what Devlyn euphemistically called the Battle of Werneuchen, but she had no idea and didn't ask.

She had the uncomfortable feeling that wearing the uniform was a mistake. It wasn't that she didn't feel good being back in the unit, the feeling came from the reaction of people seeing the uniform.

US uniforms were not a common sight in Madrid, and she was well aware that the Spaniards were not overly fond of Americans to begin with. People were staring strangely and keeping their distance. It seemed obvious that they knew something that she didn't. "Paul, will you excuse me for a moment, I have to go into the ladies' room."

"Are you alright?"

"I don't know. I have an awful feeling that something's wrong."

"Wrong? What do you mean wrong? Are you getting sick?"

"No, it's more of an intuition. Excuse me, I won't be long, I just need to splash some water on my face."

She stood in the vestibule for a few minutes watching the expressions of the women going in and out. Now she was sure that something terrible had happened and somehow it related to her or them. She straightened her cap, pulled her shoulders back and walked to the exit.

When she emerged, Devlyn was standing just outside with his back against the wall and arms folded. He pushed away and adjusted his lid. "Are you all set now?"

"You know, I don't really have an answer for that." A voice came over the speaker announcing the flight to the Netherlands. "I suppose it's as good as it's going to get." They passed a news stand on the way to the gate and Kat saw the headline.

"Holy shit."

"What is it?"

"Paul, look at this." She picked up the paper and pointed to the front-page banner.

US BUS ATTACKED IN FRANCE

"Yeah, I heard, I was going to tell you about it on the plane."

They both stared at the headline and Kat said, "I think your right, Rote Faust has finished their planning phase now."

"That's what we're are going to The Hague to discuss. Come on, let's get to the plane." When they arrived at the gate Kat's attention was drawn to a crowd in front of a television and she just caught the tail end of a report. The terrorist attack in France was the big story.

"Look they're boarding us now. We'll get a detailed report when we meet tomorrow in The Hague."

The Enemy Has a Name

9:15 pm

Deplaning Paul said, "I took a cab when I went out to the airport this morning, but someone from the office will be here to pick us up."

Kat pushed ahead saying, "I want to find out what happened in France. There must be a television around here somewhere."

"We haven't got time, Katrina. We'll be briefed at the meeting." They couldn't help noticing the large, heavily armed police presence as they walked through the terminal. "We'll find out soon enough. Oh, that looks like our guy over by the carousel."

When the Europol agent spotted Kat, he couldn't help smiling. "Hello, Kat, I am surprised to see you again, I thought you were dead."

"A good surprise, I hope." She threw her arms around him like an old friend. "Hello, Henrick," she said.

"A wonderful surprise, I am overjoyed.

He noticed her new rank and said, "Congratulations on your promotion, it was much deserved I am sure. And welcome back Colonel Devlyn."

"Agent De Jonckheer," said Devlyn, with a touch of a growl in his voice. Kat was sensing a bit of jealousy. "And … how do you know Agent De Jonckheer, Lieutenant Colonel?"

"Henrick drove me into town the last time I was here." She turned back to Henrick. "Have you got your sister's car this time?"

"No," he managed to control his smile, "She was using it today, so the agency kindly let me have a more comfortable company car."

"What's this about his sister's car?" asked Devlyn.

Henrick explained, "I had to use my sister's car when I picked up Colonel Fernando the last time. It was a very small car and I had trouble fitting inside it." Then he added, "I would have enjoyed seeing more of Colonel Fernando then, but unfortunately that was not to be."

"I saw something on the news in Madrid about an attack on a US bus in France. Do you know anything about it?" Kat asked.

"All of Europe has been put on alert. It was terrible, a women's soccer team from America was attacked. The French have released very few details so far."

The car sped out onto the highway and they traveled for the next twenty-five minutes in silence. Traffic was light going into The Hague and a little busier in town as they made their way to the hotel.

Reservations had been made for her at the Novotel den Haag City Centre and Henrick dropped them off saying that he would pick them up in the morning at 7:30 am.

Devlyn said good night at her door. "I have an apartment not far from here. I'll come back in the morning and ride over to Europol with you and Henrick. I think under the circumstances we should dress in civvies from now on."

"I agree. Good night, Paul." Kat watched him until he reached the elevator before she went into her room. Closing it behind her she sensed a darkness that had nothing to do with the night. She couldn't help wondering if either of them was going to survive this.

The next morning Henrick ferried them to the Europol building on Eisenhowerlaan. Kat was impressed by how different it was from the old Catholic boys' school the agency used to call home. The new building was a somber, gray brick and glass edifice with four towers that straddled a long two-story structure. Her first impression was that it looked like a 3-D business graph. Interesting architecture, but not stunning.

It stood behind tall panels of bullet proof glass on a street lined with cylindrical, stainless steel barriers. As they drove up to the entrance, four of the barriers sank into the ground at the curb and four more just inside on the left. Then four more vanished into the ground as the gate swung open allowing them to pass.

They were met by another agent at the security gate in the underground parking. "Ah, here you are Special Agent Devlyn and Ms. Fernando," said Agent Allard Wolters.

"It is Special Agent Fernando," said Devlyn. "And she is a Lieutenant Colonel now."

"Oh, I was not made aware of your promotion, Colonel. Congratulations."

"Thank you. It was a bit of a surprise to me as well."

"You are just in time; people are gathering in the conference room now. Thank you, Agent De Jonckheer, I will take them up."

As he escorted them through security Wolters said, "I heard that you had died, Colonel Fernando. I am glad to see that the reports were inaccurate."

"Well thanks again, Agent Wolters. As it happens, so am I."

CONFERENCE ROOM BRIEFING

Wednesday March 17, 10:20 am

Europol's new director was a dour Dane by the name of Mikkel Bech and the burden of office seemed to be exceedingly heavy. He looked gravely worried as they entered the conference room, giving Kat the awful feeling that things had just gotten worse.

He quickly confirmed her suspicions by saying, "I realize that this meeting was called on short notice, but the crisis is developing so quickly that we are hard pressed to catch up with events. Please come in and take a seat."

Before Devlyn was able to sit at the table, Kat could see that he had already established his place in the security network of Europe. Most of delegates greeted him like an old friend and shook his hand. When everyone was seated, Director Bech opened the meeting.

"Thank you all for coming gentlemen and you, Col. Fernando. The President of the United States is scheduled to speak to the American people from Washington in a few minutes. We shall be listening in, but before that happens, we have some time to discuss what has happened across Europe since yesterday.

"I don't have to tell you that we have been working to identify and prevent threats from the likes of Hamas and al-Qaeda for years. Our resources have been stretched to their limit dealing with those problems. And now we are faced with something new.

"The author of these horrific atrocities has identified itself as Rote Faust, the Red Fist. They are perhaps more radical than al-Qaeda though their radicalism is not born of religious zealotry. They have no religion, no nationalism, only a cause, and that is to rid Europe of everything American.

"An incident happened late yesterday afternoon in France, near Lyon. Because of it, our international threat level has been elevated to the highest it has ever been. We have intercepted a video file from Rote Faust intended for the American people. I will play it for you now, but I must warn you that this is extremely difficult to watch."

The screen on the end wall came to life as the lights dimmed.

The leader of the terrorist cell filled the frame, his face covered by a surgical mask and he spoke English slowly with a thick French accent. "Let this be your warning! This is just the beginning for you Americans. From now on, for you ... there is only death."

The video cut to the body of the driver falling out of the van and then proceeded to show in horrific detail the murders of the team's four chaperones. "From this moment, no American will be safe in Europe." The camera moved to take close shots of the bus driver and the three women on the ground. Then the woman slumped over the steering wheel as the camera moved onto the bus. Inside, it moved from her to the leader's back and then panned across the terrified faces of the women's soccer team in their seats. The leader fired a shot into the roof then gave his instructions to the young women. They watched as the girls filed off the bus and were lined up against it. "This," he said, "is how we will deal with every one of you that we find here." In the close-ups that followed each girl gave her name, then it cut back to the speaker who turned to the men holding submachine guns. Until that moment, it was obvious that the young women had no idea what was coming.

He raised his arm.

The gunmen turned their weapon towards the young women. When his arm dropped, their screams were abruptly cut off by gun fire and the twenty-two young college students were dead. The camera zoomed in for another close-up as the leader shot each woman in the head. He had to stop and reload before he finished his task. He turned to the camera again, "We are Rote Faust. Americans ..., hear this; wherever you are, you will end up like these women. We will slaughter you like pigs. If you stay here none of you will be safe ever again. Leave Europe now, or you will be pulled out into the street and butchered. This is the end of your occupation! The cleansing has begun!"

The screen went black.

There was stunned silence in the room until the lights went on again and then everybody began speaking at once. "Ladies and gentlemen, please. May I have your attention," said the director, and the pandemonium faded into silence. "Alright, until yesterday we had no idea that Rote Faust existed. Now, unfortunately, we know only too well.

"It is clear what they want and what they intend to do to get it but we don't know why. The number of attacks has escalated sharply since this atrocity.

"We have just received a report of an attack on a Paris restaurant where gunmen killed five people and wounded eight. All were American tourists. The gunmen managed to escape. We have a report that several gunmen were killed last evening while trying to breach the American Embassy in Lisbon. Three Marines were wounded. There was a bombing of a hotel in Brussels, frequented by Americans, this morning. As of our last report thirty-seven are dead and a hundred and fifteen are injured. The death toll is expected to rise.

"What is troubling, is that not one of our intelligence services had detected any activity or even the existence of the Rote Faust leading up to these attacks. We are dealing with several well-organized cells who are communicating with one another through a system that we cannot detect let alone penetrate. My hope and expectation, is that this deficiency will end soon.

"That is your job. Find out who these people are. Find out how they communicate. Find out where they intend to strike next. You must do it quickly, before they strike again. Americans in Europe and Europeans everywhere are depending on you.

"We have information that these attacks were preceded by two seemingly unrelated attacks, one in Ukraine and the other in Turkey. Their target was a house on the coast of the Sea of Azov. A member of this Antiterrorist Task Force, an American Army Counterintelligence officer, happened to be in residence there and foiled the attack. Until that despicable atrocity we just witnessed, it was assumed that there was only one intended target. A Russian named Vladimir Mogilevski. Colonel Fernando has been brought up from assignment in Madrid to brief us on what she has so learned thus far."

She had no idea that she would be asked to speak, and she had no idea that she had been on 'assignment' in Madrid. She was so upset by the video that she was trembling. "Special Agent Fernando, if you please."

Reluctantly Kat stood up. "I…, I hardly know what to say after that." She placed her fists on the table to support herself. "My information is, uh … quite limited I am sorry to say."

She looked around the table at the all male group, wondering how they were going to react to what she had to tell them.

"I was only able to find bits and pieces from my two encounters with members of the organization, one in Berdyans'k and the other in Istanbul. I got two names. Zapf Industries and Rote Faust.

"The first attack came during the night 8 days ago, at the dacha where I lived. Four men came by road and stormed the house. They were expecting to find the Russian citizen the director mentioned, asleep inside. I was outside when they attacked.

"I engaged them, killing three outright and wounding the fourth. I questioned him, but the information he gave was limited.

"Later, when I checked over their vehicle, I found that it was registered to Zapf Industrial of Delaware, USA, with an address in Berlin. Perhaps someone from the German delegation can track down Zapf for us.

"Since then I have been pursued by agents, whom I had assumed belonged to Zapf, but in Istanbul I learned that they were members of Rote Faust." Director Bech raised his hand. "Yes Sir?"

"Pardon the interruption, Special Agent Fernando, if Mr. Mogilevski wasn't there at the dacha, where is he?"

"I don't know, sir. In the sixteen months I lived in the house I had no contact with him. I have since tried to make contact, I have left messages, but have had no response."

"How unfortunate, it would be interesting to hear what he has to say about this."

"I agree."

"If you would, Special Agent, please continue with your report. We have the official report from the Istanbul police. Perhaps you can give us a brief description of what actually happened."

"Certainly, I arrived in Istanbul two days after the Berdyans'k attack. During my second night, a two-man team raided the hotel killing the night clerk. I was able to neutralize them. There was a language barrier between me and the police officers who responded, so I was not able to explain what happened. When a senior detective arrived to take charge, he held me at gun point until the bodies had been removed." She paused for a sip of water.

"Then he sent everyone away. Once we were alone, he tried to extort money from me. He told me that there was a bounty of a hundred thousand Euros on my head, for my role in the death of Delph Petrus."

"And were you responsible?"

"Counterintelligence was not involved. The detective informed me that he was a member of Rote Faust and that he was supposed to turn me in to their leader in Zürich. He did not give me the name of the man to whom I was to be presented. But for a million Euros and sex, he would set me free. He said that if I didn't agree to pay him, he would kill me."

A member of the panel from Italy stopped her to ask a question. "As I recall Delph Petrus was killed by a Russian assassin. Are you admitting now that the Americans had him killed?"

"No. May I continue?"

"But you did ..."

"I have already answered that question. Now, may I continue?" Director Bech nodded. "Thank you. I convinced the detective that I would do anything if he would release me."

The Italian interrupted again, "By anything, you mean that you would have ..."

"Sir, this is not a courtroom it is a debriefing for the purpose of bringing you up to date on the activities of Rote Faust prior to yesterday's attack. I asked ..."

"Colonel ..."

"I asked him," she said, refusing to yield to the Italian again, "if Rote Faust was in the business of attacking people in their sleep and he said that the Americans will know all about that soon enough."

"And then you killed him. Why did you not try to interrogate him further?" asked the Italian.

"Excuse me? Look," Kat said, showing her frustration, "I was in Turkey, I was alone, I had already been attacked twice by these people and the man was going to kill me. I would have thought even you could see that I was in no position to be taking prisoners."

Director Bech was irritated by the interruptions and glaring at the Italian said, "Of course, we all appreciate severity of situation. Please continue Colonel Fernando."

"Thank you. We have since learned that the gunmen who attacked the hotel and murdered the hotel employee were both members of the police force. If Rote Faust has infiltrated law enforcement institutions in Turkey, then wouldn't it be prudent to assume that they have people in positions of authority throughout Europe. Perhaps even in this room," she said, looking squarely at the Italian.

He blanched and sputtered, "That is a groundless accusation, Colonel. I …"

"That could be the reason we have not been able to identify them or crack their communication network."

"I am inclined to agree with you, Colonel Fernando," said the director, also making eye contact with the member from Italy. "We must redouble our efforts to root out this cancer wherever it is. Thank you, Colonel Fernando."

She nodded and sat down.

"I see that it is nearly time for the President's address," said Director Bech, and signaled for the operator to turn on the television and dim the lights. Everyone turned their chairs toward the screen again as the images appeared.

The lead-in to the Presidential address was in progress with a network anchor in New York hosting an expert panel providing commentary on the massacre of the soccer team.

He touched his ear, then ended the discussion saying, "I have just been told that the President is about to speak. We now take you live to the White House."

Washington   D. C.

2:08 pm

The press secretary spoke from the podium, "Ladies and Gentlemen, the President of the United States."

It was an election year and President Darcy Lake, a Democrat from Michigan, had been hoping to be brought back for a second term. As far as he was concerned, the soccer team tragedy, and the other attacks in Europe had just ended his run for office.

Like a few of the men before him, he had come into office confident in his ability to manage the country's affairs. At the beginning of his Presidency he was a handsome young man with a thick mane of dark hair, strong opinions, and big ambitions. That no longer described the man who walked up to the podium in the White House press gallery.

As he stared into the camera, America and the rest of the world saw a middle-aged man who was profoundly distressed and exhausted He leaned forward on the podium, his arms outstretched and his hands gripping the edges for support. Looking away from the camera for a moment, he focused on the people gathered in the room to record and report on what he was about to say. He shook his head sadly, seemingly unaware that he was going live to the country. With his guard down, it was perhaps the first time Americans were seeing the real Darcy Lake.

Then, straightening his back, he once again made contact with his audience through the lens. The people must have been able to feel the effects of the relentless stress of the office. There was a noticeable tremor in the hand that held the prepared remarks, he cleared his throat then began to speak.

"My fellow American at home and abroad," he paused, and let it stretch on so long that his staff was afraid that he couldn't continue.

"Mr. President," someone prompted him from off camera.

He let go of the paper and put both hands flat on the desk and said, "Tragic events in Europe have forced us to once again change the way we must view the world around us. This has become a terrible ... and dangerous time for all of us."

He paused and looked down at his hands as he summoned the strength to continue. "Without mercy or the slightest trace of humanity, innocent, young American lives have been taken." He paused again as he stared straight into the camera. There was no question about how deeply troubled he was. "I have no doubt ..., that by now most of you have seen ..., or have been told about the video released over the Internet by the terrorist organization Rote Faust, the Red Fist.

"Twenty-two college women, the flowering youth of our nation, together with their coaches, the team manager, the team doctor and their French bus driver, were gunned down a short time ago. This beastly and brutal assault was carried out by a group of cowards."

His voice was beginning to fail, so he paused once more to collect himself. A sip of water, a cough and a shake of his head. He looked up and continued, "In Paris, five more Americans were murdered in a restaurant shooting. In Brussels, eighteen people died in a hotel bombing and it is believed that twelve of the dead were Americans. In another bombing in Madrid, seventeen more were killed, six were Americans.

"In Lisbon, Portugal, terrorists attacked the American Embassy, seriously wounding three Marines, one of the Marines has since died." He looked down at the paper and lifted it to read. "We are receiving new reports of attacks every few minutes, from nearly every part of the continent. The terrorist organization responsible for this outrage is large, mobile and well equipped. As far as we know, these butchers are predominantly European and, as such, are inconspicuous in the general population, they are essentially invisible.

"Having said that, I want to stress at this time, the vast majority of Europeans are not our enemies, they are victims just as we are. These terrorists lurk among them like a cancer. Make no mistake, they will be found, and they will be brought to a swift and terrible justice.

"Clearly, Europe is no longer a safe place for our citizens to travel. I am initiating a travel advisory for all Americans. During the foreseeable future, Americans should avoid traveling anywhere in Europe until this threat has been eliminated.

"For those of you who are currently in Europe, both tourists and nonessential American personnel, I urge you to take shelter, be vigilant, and cautious, and I strongly suggest that you make immediate plans to return home. Airlines are being asked to reschedule flights to deal with the evacuation. We are reinforcing security at all American embassies and consulate offices, and European authorities are doubling their security at every airport.

"Your government is doing its best to protect its citizens on the continent. Our diplomatic and consulate personnel are working to capacity to help with evacuation. If you choose to do so you may, with valid identification, seek shelter at your nearest American military base anywhere in Europe. Contact your local consulate to locate the base closest to you and notify the base that you are on your way. We anticipate that they will be swamped, so expect delays. You will need to use extreme caution and be patient during this crisis."

While the President was speaking, just south of Paris in Fontainebleau, Valeri and Gill Matheson, newlyweds from New Rochelle, New York, had just finished breakfast and had checked out of the Hôtel Le Country Club on the Seine. They had a spectacular week and were heading home when they were taken from their cab by four masked men. The gunmen forced them out onto the lawn, knelt them down and shot them.

"I have been in touch with the Prime Ministers of Canada and Great Britain and they have assured me that their embassies and offices will be available to assist you as well.

"After consultation with the Joint Chiefs and our NATO Allies, I am declaring this a state of emergency."

Seconds later, outside the Residence Grand - Duchesse Josephine-Charlotte, a retirement home in Luxembourg, the Barton family of Montgomery, Alabama, was gunned down in a drive by shooting. All five members of the family were killed in the incident.

"No effort is being spared in our determination to track down these killers and wipe them off the face of the earth. Every law enforcement agency we have with a mandate to operate outside the United States, is being mobilized to work with European agencies against this threat.

"God bless and keep you safe …,"

Luke Gardner, an American economist, was shot dead in an elevator in the Deloitte building on the General - Wille - Strasse, Zürich.

"… and God bless the United States of America."

Following his address, the media returned to their broadcast news.

The screen went black in the Europol conference room and, for a few seconds, the room remained dark and silent. When the lights came on again the attention turned back to the head of the table.

The videos of the execution style shooting of economist Luke Gardner and the Paris restaurant shooting were released at the end of the speech in time for their wrap-up broadcast.

"Alright," said the director, holding his cell phone so that he could read a text message, "I have just been advised that during the President's impassioned address, Rote Faust has been streaming live images of these killings to the Internet and they are going viral. Every government in European is trying to cut them off but, I am told, that will take time.

Time has been on the side of the terrorists and we can't afford to allow that to continue. I'm calling upon you people to make the best use of the time we have to shut them down."

CHAPTER 10

THE GOLD TRADER

Wall Street, New York, 5:18 pm

Following the President's address, the price of gold shot up to $1,230.45 an ounce. Before the close of the market in New York, Billy Rourke, the trader acting for the anonymous investor, sold the twenty tons he purchased on Monday and his commission would be enormous. Reporters asked him who he was trading for, but he honored his commitment not to divulge the name of his client.

The sale moved all the way up to the Wall Street Journal's page three this time. Their financial investigative reporter Saul Bartel interviewed Rourke and tried, unsuccessfully, to get him to divulge the identity of the investor. Bartel asked if there was any truth to the rumor that he was acting for the government of Iran. Rourke flatly denied that, and the interview was over. The story did not make it through to the next news cycle.

At 5:20 pm, as Billy Rourke was on his way home, he was struck and killed by a taxi while crossing Wall Street. A witness said that the trader had tried to cross against the light. It was listed as an accidental death; no charges were laid, and the investigation ended there.

It was later discovered that a homeless man Buddy Williams, also witnessed the incident. He claimed that Rourke was pushed into the street by a guy in a three-piece suit. His description of the killer perfectly matched the man who witnessed the trader cross against the light. Buddy was African American, a Vietnam Vet with a history of mental illness, PTSD and drug abuse, so his statement was ignored.

The next morning his body was found in a cardboard box in an alley. Cause of death was listed as accidental drug overdose. No investigation was made. A day later, 53-year-old Habib Dhil, the cab driver who ran down Mr. Rourke, suffered a heart attack and died. His family said he was in perfect health.

PAN EUROPEAN MOVEMENT

Thursday, 8:00 pm

After viewing the American President's address, Conrad Bliss a popular political television talk show host in Berlin interviewed Arnulf Jäger, a regular commentator on the European political scene and a vocal proponent of the Pan European Movement.

"For those of us unfamiliar with this movement could you briefly tell us what its aims are?"

"Certainly," said Jäger. "It is independent of all political parties, but has a set of principles by which it appraises politicians, parties and institutions. The International Pan European Union has four main basic principles: Liberalism, Christianity, Social Responsibility and Pro - Europeanism. We wish to bring unity and prosperity to everyone in Europe."

"Isn't that what the EU is doing?"

"No, I don't believe that it is. The Pan European Union was a popular idea proposed back in 1923 and has become even more relevant today. Europe is suffering a crisis of leadership. The EU is run by nationalistic politicians with too many differing ideas on how to solve our problems. Their ancient and irrelevant rivalries are holding us back.

"The reality is that the EU is nothing more than separate and unequal states forced together in a chaotic and wasteful circumstance. None is equipped to deal with the social unrest, none has the authority to act unilaterally for the good of all. Without that power, there is no solution."

"But Mr. Jäger, what you are suggesting is not the original Pan European ideal."

"Yes exactly."

"But it was intended to unify the European economies for the purpose of trade and social issues. What you are proposing sounds more like a European dictatorship."

Without denying the statement Jäger said, "What is needed now is a truly unified Europe. We cannot allow old thinking to obscure what Europeans truly want. One new unified government that would not be distracted from its proper destiny. It would deal with the social and political turmoil that is at the heart of what is going on right now. This turmoil is what interferes with reason and good judgment."

"And how do you see your idea of a single government bringing an end to our current crisis?"

"These attacks," Jäger said, "are a direct result of the inability of the governments of Europe's leading nations, Germany and France ... and of course Great Britain as well, to deal with the essential issue, which is ..., the dominance of American interests in the Europe economy."

"It sounds like you are supporting the aims of Rote Faust."

"Not at all. I do not condone the violence that is sweeping the continent now. I condemn it and I mourn the loss of so many innocent lives. What I am saying is that we must find a political solution to the underlying problems that created Rote Faust in the first place. Obviously, people across the continent are fed up. Europe's security community sees this as an organized terrorist group, but I assure you that they are mistaken."

"Are you saying that you don't see them as terrorists?"

"No, of course I do. But we are dealing with a group of like-minded idealists."

"Idealists?" Bliss asked incredulously.

"Yes absolutely, though sadly misguided. I believe they are only a radical expression of the sentiment held by the entire population of Europe, a sentiment that has existed since the end of the Second World War."

"Aren't you misrepresenting this situation and the level of anti-American sentiments? Europeans are not at war with America."

"Yes, perhaps I am, that is true for now. But I think you are missing the point. Are we prepared to wait until we are at war? I think that would be a terrible mistake.

Perhaps Rote Faust is simply a movement, a manifestation of the same ideals that Lech Wałęsa espoused during Poland's Solidarity movement of 1980, but much larger of course. It is seeking to create a union of the workers of Europe. Their perception of America's presence in Europe amounts to an economic occupation by a foreign power. This is unfortunate. No, it is tragic. But we cannot ignore the sentiment of the people. If I am elected, my goal as the Pan European leader, charged with the welfare of all its people, I would be able to bring peace and prosperity to the continent."

"Mr. Jäger, do you see the Americans presence as an occupation?"

"Whether it is or not is not my concern. It is that perception that is at the heart of this problem. The American President represents a population far larger than ours and he has the power to act decisively."

"Well, that is not entirely accurate, the President needs the approval of his Congress to ..."

"He is doing the right thing by removing his citizens from our continent. If we had one president, one government with unified policies to deal with our unique Pan European issues rather than the current combative committee, this unrest would stop."

"And you think you should lead this unified Europe?"

"Frankly, I don't see anyone else who is as capable as me. If I were at the helm, this disruption would end."

"Really?"

"I guarantee it. I am the only man prepared for the challenge to lead Europe in this new millennium."

CHAPTER 11

LOURMARIN FRANCE

Friday, 2:00 am

During the night, the terrorists struck again, this time they chose Provence and found their Americans in the tiny village of Lourmarin. Three couples who had rented houses were dragged from their beds, taken out into the street and shot.

By 2:00 am, the videos of the murders were edited to include more declarations to the American people from Rote Faust and were posted on the Internet.

OPPORTUNIST?

Saturday

A member of the White House press corps asked President Lake's Press Secretary what the President thought of Arnulf Jäger's assertion that Rote Faust was a continental movement.

The Press Secretary said, "I think the view of the White House is that Mr. Jäger is simply a political opportunist who doesn't fully appreciate the severity of the situation that faces the EU."

"What about his proposal for a single Pan European government?"

"I'm not going to comment on the statements of every crackpot with access to a microphone."

The Mounting Crisis

Tuesday March 23

Having worked nonstop since making his speech, Darcy Lake was devoting every minute to deal with the crisis. He directed his Chief of Staff, Bill Oakley, to postpone his trip to Japan.

At 4:30, his advisors from the NSA, CIA, FBI and HS, as well as the head of the Joint Chiefs, arrived to discuss possible military intervention. At 5:00, the Vice President, the Secretary of State and the Secretary of Defense joined them, and the session got heated.

Lake wanted to go in guns blazing. Thanks to the efforts of Secretary of State Joan Patella, cooler heads prevailed, and a post evacuation nuclear attack was taken off the table.

The discussion went on and while they decided not to declare war, they did find some common ground. There was a consensus to take over control of the antiterrorist efforts in Europe.

They also decided to ask Congress to approve the plan to give the US military the authority to take whatever actions deemed necessary to save American lives, including use of force. At 8:30, representatives of Congress met in the Oval Office and were informed of the plan. Two hours later, Congress gave their approval to move ahead.

Every agency with antiterrorist mandates was in the field hunting down the killers and not all of them felt inclined to work with their European counterparts. G-2, Brigadier General Wolfson of Military Counterintelligence, briefed the President on what the Army's Counterintelligence European Division was doing and was told to have his agents work more aggressively. "This terrorist group must be hunted down and eradicated by any means necessary," President Lake said, "Do you get my meaning General?"

"Yes Sir, loud and clear, loud and clear."

The same message was given to the other members of the DHS, JCS, CIA, FBI, NSA and HS. The message passed down through the departments to the people in the field was, 'Forget the ROEs (Rules of Engagement), just get the sons-of-bitches'.

JÄGER'S PRESS CONFERENCE

After a one-hour nap, the President went on television and radio again to address the nation. Americans across the country had already seen the new videos and were enraged.

They demanded that their government take immediate action. Some people even demanded that the US declare war on Europe. He didn't mention that his idea was nuking the continent, but he assured the nation that his government was taking direct action to save American lives, and he condemned the Europeans for allowing the rise of such an aggressive Anti-American movement.

European leaders were united in their condemnation of these acts of terror and promised to do everything in their power to bring the terrorists to justice.

Arnulf Jäger held his own press conference to say that measures taken by the EU were not sufficient to deal with the situation. He also said that the White House would do well not to dismiss him so lightly.

The Pan European movement was growing stronger by the hour. Jäger demanded that Europe immediately hold a referendum to give the people the opportunity to vote for a Pan European Government.

Demonstrators were in the streets with signs saying Yes to Paneurope and No to America. Some held signs that simply said No! There were clashes between the two sides.

Radical groups in the Middle East applauded the actions taken by Rote Faust, calling them freedom fighters, and their supporters all over Europe came out to protest the police and military crackdown.

Russian President Mikael Zokorev claimed that there was a similar threat to Russian tourists in Europe. He said he was going to send troops into the former Soviet Satellite States to assist in the protection of Russian citizens. President Lake immediately issued a statement saying that there was no evidence whatsoever to support his claim and his real purpose was to re-establish the old Soviet Block. Lake said any such action on the part of Russia would be viewed as unwarranted aggression and he was prepared to send American troops to support the governments of Latvia, Belarus, Estonia and Ukraine.

"Their governments complained that the Russians had no right to enter their countries and immediately put their armies on alert.

Thousands of the Yes people protested that that was just another example of American interference in European affairs. And Zokorev denied that, unlike the Americans, he had no intention of becoming an army of occupation. His only concern was the protection of ethnic Russians.

Tensions soared as Russian tanks began to gather along the borders.

International stock markets continued to react negatively. The manufacturers of weapons systems and munitions became very busy and those who bought into the whole doomsday scenario began digging bomb shelters.

EUROPOL H Q

Sunday March 28, 8:38 pm

Two Spanish investigators, Manolo de Sylva and Jorge Romero from the CNP (Cuerpo Nacional de Policía), were teamed with Kat and Devlyn to oversee operations in Portugal and Spain. The CNP agents had been in Madrid investigating the explosion that killed seventeen tourists and injured fifty. After two days spent sifting through the wreckage, they returned with evidence that connected the Rote Faust attack to another group.

"We found fragments of the materials used in the explosion that were found at bombings attributed to ETA. They were traced back to a bomb making facility that blew up in the Basque city Getxo," said Manolo. "We thought ..., perhaps I should say that we assumed, at the time, that the bomb makers had died in that explosion. Five bodies were recovered, but we have since heard a rumor that the one who designed the bombs was not there when it went up."

Jorge said, "The bomber of the hotel used the same components found in the bomb that destroyed a Spanish Socialist Workers' Party office in Durango."

"Exactly," said Manolo. "The interesting thing with the Durango bombing is that they were warned before the bomb went off and no one was injured. They said the man that called in the warning was

French."

Jorge added, "But there was no warning before Madrid's bombing."

"When you followed up after the Durango incident," Kat asked, "what did you find?"

"We were able to trace the call to a café in Durango. For obvious reasons, no one there that day remembers a Frenchman. But then we got an anonymous tip. The caller said that the man we were looking for was from Mauléon." He saw the blank looks on their faces, so he said, "It's the capitol of Soule Province in the French Basque Country. It is a nice, little coastal town. Our problem is they don't talk to the Spanish police there. We sent in an undercover agent and eventually he came up with the name Jesús Maria Etxebarria.

"Apparently, Etxebarria suddenly packed up and left town after the explosion in Getxo. Someone said it was because he was responsible for the accident. Others felt that it wasn't an accident and put a price on his head."

"So, he just vanished?" said Kat.

Manolo shrugged and said, "We haven't been able to find him."

"Maybe he's moved on to another cause and has decided to kill Americans for a change," Jorge said, finishing Manolo's thought for him.

Devlyn asked, "Is there a picture of this guy?"

"I wish. These people are not big on family photos."

"What about a description?"

"Sure, he looks like a Frenchman," said Jorge. He was sleepy and clearly growing tired of the conversation. He glanced at his watch, sighed then showed it to Manolo. It was almost midnight and Manolo rolled his eyes.

"If you were able to determine what components were used, maybe we could track down the source of the materials," said Devlyn.

Jorge threw up his hands, stood up and walked to the window where all he saw was his frustrated reflection, thinking that he looked as tired as he felt. "We have already thought of that, of course. The ingredients can be found almost anywhere. The trigger was a cheap cell phone. A partial serial number was found on a fragment. Our department of investigations has reopened the case and brought the evidence out of storage. They are now trying to match it up with a make and batch number. That might tell us where it was purchased."

"When will they be able to give us that information?"

"As you must already know, these things take time," Manolo said. "Listen, it is after midnight and I have to get some sleep."

"First, can I ask you a question off topic?" said Kat.

Not bothering to hide his frustration, he began to pack his papers back into his briefcase and said, "Why not?"

"What do you think of this Jäger guy, is he for real?"

Manolo stopped and turned to face her and then sat on the tabletop. "Do you think he's involved?"

Kat thought for a moment. "I don't know, but there's something not right about him."

"In Spain, we don't know much about him. But we hear stories."

"Oh? What kind of stories?"

"He is one of those people who wants to rule the world. There is always some crazy person who wants to be Emperor, Charlemagne, Elizabeth of Austria, Charles V, King Philip, Napoleon, Hitler, and the list goes on. The rumor is that he already runs the underworld, but there is absolutely no evidence that he does."

"And what about the Pan European Movement?"

"It is ..., how do you Americans say? Pie in the sky."

Jorge added, as he looked at his watch. "Miramis amigos, es tarde, vamos a recoger esto de nuevo mañana."

"Sure," said Devlyn, and gave the Spaniards a casual two finger Boy Scout salute as they disappeared through the door.

"What do you think?" Kat asked.

"I suppose there's nothing more we can do tonight. Do you want a lift to your hotel?"

"It's just across the mall. I think I'll walk, thanks."

"Right." He gathered his things and stuffed them into his case. "What are your thoughts on Jäger?"

"Like I said, I don't know, but the guy gives me the creeps. Perhaps it's just because of the way he looks.

"We all can't be beautiful."

"And truly he is not beautiful. That freakish huge head with that little cherub face, I mean he's kind of hard to look at."

"From what I hear that melon is filled with a remarkable brain. OK, I'm done here. See you tomorrow."

As Kat walked across Eisenhowerlaan to the Novotel she couldn't stop thinking about the deaths and wondered what kind of monster was behind it.

The Unwelcome

Tuesday, April 6

Restaurants and hotels all over France began to turn American tourists away, fearing that their presence would attract attacks from the terrorists. The tourism industry, shops galleries and theaters felt the immediate effect. Some restaurants that catered to America tourists, instantly lost their client base and closed their doors; some, perhaps, would remain closed forever.

As morning broke, Arnulf Jäger was in full campaign mode in a nonexistent election. He made several appearances a day as he made his way across Europe. Sweeping through every country, he showed up on morning TV programs, at street rallies, lunch time radio, and television news specials, spouting his vision for the new amalgamated Europe.

He insisted the only way to save the continent was to create an all-powerful Pan European Government and only he had the qualifications to be its President. The existing Pan European council tried to distance themselves from him, but it seemed pointless. He was too loud and too persistent to be ignored.

Jäger began an instant media blitz extolling his virtues, disseminating misinformation and lies disguised as real news. The campaign mobilized thousands of supporters across the continent. It wasn't long before a significant segment of the population began to believe there was an election campaign and that they were actually going to vote.

Another Link

Wednesday

Police in Paris were investigating a break-in at the office of a real estate company and were told that the only thing taken was their client list for country properties rented by Americans.

That gave investigators the link to the murders in Lourmarin. Agents of Europol received a copy of the list and sent it to Interpol, the French Internal Security and US Military Counterintelligence. The remaining Americans on the list were quickly evacuated.

At the same time, investigators with GIGN (Groupe d'Intervention de la Gendarmerie Nationale), the elite law enforcement and special operations unit of the French National Gendarmerie, were dealing with the shooting in the Paris restaurant. They were going over surveillance video taken from cameras on the street around the restaurant. Scanning the images of the gunmen through their newly acquired Israeli facial recognition software, they were confident that they would soon be able to identify the suspects and track them down.

In another investigation, two of the gunmen who died in the attack on the American Embassy in Lisbon were traced back to the Spanish town of Puente Mayorga, just north of Gibraltar. It was a dead end because the names and home addresses of the men were fake. That pointed to the possibility that someone inside the government was falsifying documents. Finally, their true identities were discovered through criminal warrants for outstanding crimes in several other European countries. Their last known addresses were in the same apartment building in Leipzig, Germany, a building that was owned by Zapf Industries.

Eventually, the FBI traced Zapf back from Delaware through several numbered companies, discovering it was just a mailbox in a suburb of Tucumán, Argentina. The principals listed were dead goat farmers and that search ended there.

A KEY SUSPECT

It was mid-afternoon as Kat was going through the list of the tenants in the Zapf owned buildings when she spotted something. "Hey guys, look who I've found here." She highlighted the name and handed it to Jorge. Manolo read it over his shoulder and whistled.

"I don't believe it," Jorge said, and handed it to Devlyn.

"What are the chances that this really is the same guy?" Devlyn asked. "You'd think a man on the run would change his name, I mean, how many people could there be with that name?"

"Well there is only one way to find out," said Kat. She picked up the phone and put a call through to GSG 9 to ask them to take Jesús Maria Etxebarria in for questioning.

Chapter 12

Laying the Foundation

In 1988, Hunter began laying the foundation for the moment when he would replace the criminal elite and become the ultimate leader in Europe. What he wanted was a place far enough away from the hell storm he would rain down on the continent. It had to be a place from which he could run his investment company, TALEN Equity. Talen was a lucrative business in Germany, but it had limitations, it needed room to grow. At the beginning of February 1990, he found an old monastery on top of a small mountain in Umbria. Sandwiched between the mountain and the lake was a picturesque little village named Peredicci.

As the Abbey di San Martino no longer held any historical value, Hunter was able to buy it from the Vatican without too much trouble.

The moment the transaction was finalized, work began with plans drawn up by the famous Spanish architect Rodrigo Hermida.

The result was an architectural abstract sculpture towering over the landscape. A monument to the pursuit of wealth and power, built almost entirely with energy efficient, gold impregnated glass on a black steel frame. The benefits were twofold, the gold made it impossible to see in from the outside and, at both sunrise and sun set and in the dark of night, it glowed like the fires of hell rising from the abbey ruins. The stunningly excessive edifice soon became known as the Golden Fortress.

When it was completed, Hunter brought in dozens of employees to work in his new base of operations, and he protected it with a well-armed security force.

They were kept hidden away, housed in barracks inside the compound. Hunter's business interests as well as his unique hobbies made security vital. To keep visitors away, he had a fence closing off the top section of the paths and signs suggesting very serious penalties would be exacted on trespassers. The ambiguity of that message was more than enough to warn off the casually curious. The regularly spaced skull and crossbones signs affixed to the fence reinforced that message.

The Silent Partner

1990

At the time Hunter was building his command center, another German crime boss was moving in on competition in Europe and Russia and rapidly taking over their territories. Hunter held back to give the man time to clear the way, then would move in to claim the amalgamated territory for himself.

Delph Petrus was keenly aware of Hunter's power, and the potential to become a problem. But as long as Hunter remained isolated in the remote hills of Umbria, Petrus thought he was safe.

It took Petrus twelve years to clear away his competition and while he was building his empire, Hunter was directing his energies towards political influence. Petrus thought his last bit of business would be the takeover of TALEN, then he would be unstoppable. At the same time, he was making his boldest move yet, attacking a corporation in Canada which would give him an open door to the US.

Feeling invincible, he communicated with Hunter and proposed a silent partnership, in essence a mutually beneficial truce. Hunter knew that crossing the Atlantic to attack the Americans on their home ground was a mistake and destined to fail. But he didn't say that to Petrus and agreed to discuss terms.

Hunter smiled as he signed the agreement because he knew he had won. His people were already infiltrating the Petrus organization. The corporate takeover of Dectron International was going poorly, so while Petrus was preoccupied with his problems, Hunter was taking over his organization without Petrus noticing a thing.

When Petrus was assassinated, what was left of his organization made it clear that it was up to Hunter to exact revenge.

Immediately after Petrus' death, Hunter's security service in Zürich retrieved a series of recordings made from exterior and interior cameras of the Petrus house. They showed everything that happened that day, from the Russian soldiers who eliminated the Petrus security force and the arrival of the assassin. The interior cameras captured Anita Franco's nearly perfect assault. After her death, the Russians returned and took her body away. The presence of the Spetsnaz, Russian Special Forces, was clear evidence that they were working for the oligarch Vladimir Mogilevski, a retired general of the Spetsnaz GRU.

As it happened, this too became an opportunity for Hunter to advance his schedule. Sixteen months of preparations followed and when he was ready, he sent hit squads to each of Mogilevski's properties with orders to kill him and destroy everything.

Mogilevski's resources were extensive and once he got wind of this plot, rather than fight back he simply disappeared.

Chapter 13

Retribution

5:20 pm

Hunter had been preoccupied with business, but when he found out that the two idiots in Istanbul tried to kill Kat, he was livid. He sent his personal bodyguard, Wilhelm Tag, to Istanbul to find out what happened.

Within hours Wilhelm phoned in his report. "It was a free-for-all. The detective's partner told me that Burakgazi was planning to betray us. He was going extort money from Franco and then kill her the moment she paid him."

"He had her in his control and yet she was still able to kill him?"

"She is very skilled."

"I hope she made him suffer," said Hunter sullenly. "You have eliminated the others involved with this fiasco?"

"Yes sir, they have all been dealt with."

"Good." Pacing back and forth by his desk he pondered the question carefully before he spoke. "I wonder if she was able to get any information out of the fool before she killed him."

"It is impossible to know, sir," said the Aryan giant. "But I am sure that he knew nothing that would lead her back to you. His only contact was with Zürich."

"Good. I need this woman, Wilhelm. I want her alive, I can use her."

"But the woman is lethal, sir. Bringing her to you would be very risky. It would be safer if you would let me kill her."

"No!" he shouted. He was thinking about his moment of retribution, the sexual stimulation and the pain he would savor. "Be patient, Wilhelm, I will probably let you have your fun with her eventually but, first, I want to see if I can force her to participate in a plan I am considering. Find her for me."

"Of course, sir."

Rubbing his bald scalp, Hunter walked to the golden glass wall to look out across the landscape. "It is going well, Wilhelm," he said thoughtfully. "The operation to destabilize America's presence in Europe is working beautifully."

"How long will we continue these assaults?"

"I'm not sure yet. It depends on how quickly it takes for the markets to realize that supporting the Americans is bad for business. Then the weaklings in power will finally agree to the referendum. Another month perhaps, maybe less. But by then, America will be on her knees. Only then will I stop the attacks. Before that happens, I will continue to fill my war chest. It is going well, Wilhelm; it is going very well."

Chapter 14

Behind This Door

Leipzig, Friday April 9, 3:45 pm

Officers of GSG 9 in full assault gear returned to the apartment building where Jesús Maria Etxebarria was listed as the tenant. They had been informed that he was at home, so they stood silently outside his door until everyone was in position. The plan was to smash in the door, toss in a flash/bang grenade and just like that, the man would be their prisoner.

As soon as the battering ram touched the door the apartment exploded. The devastation was horrific. A shaped charge blew out a section of the wall sending the door crashing into the men in the hallway, two officers were killed instantly, and four others were seriously wounded. The rest of the squad rushed to help their fallen comrades before the fire spread. The sprinkler-system began to rain down cold water throughout the building pushing down the dust.

When the water was shut off and the remaining officers entered the apartment it appeared that Etxebarria had left only moments before they arrived. There was a cup of coffee and a cigarette in an ash tray on the kitchen table. Remarkably it had not been disturbed by the blast, in fact, if it wasn't for the water from the sprinkler system the apartment seemed relatively intact.

In the bedroom, they found a work bench covered with tools and bomb making materials under the bench and on shelves above it. They found a box of cell phones with a packing slip inside. The phones' consecutive serial numbers linked them to the fragment found in the hotel in Madrid.

The commander had just phoned in his report when one of his men picked up the box.

The second explosion brought down two thirds of the building killing everyone inside. Forty more names were added to the growing list of victims of Rote Faust.

POLICE WORK

4:40 pm

Tracing the phones back to their source, the Joint Task Force found that a shipment had been stolen from an electronics store in Munich in January. Munich police had the surveillance video but couldn't identify the robbers.

The Munich Police had better luck with some of the other materials. Plastic coated wire purchased at a local hardware store led them to an archive of cc camera recordings. They watched as a man they would later identify as Etxebarria, make the purchase. Now they had a face to work with and the search for their bomb maker became the new priority.

DOCKED IN ODESSA

10:00 am

The heightened alert across Europe and the manhunt for Etxebarria seemed to slow down the attacks. In the calm that followed, the protection and evacuation of American citizens had become more effective.

Their investigation seemed to have stalled and Kat was feeling restless and trapped in her office. Other teams were out following up on the leads Devlyn had found delving into intel from home office and NSA. He traced a reference to Etxebarria in an email sent to one of the terrorists who died in the Lisbon attack. That led them to a man in Lebanon. He sent a team to arrest him but when they broke through his door, he detonated an explosive taking out three agents and flattening the building.

All they had were the apartment buildings in Leipzig and the info from that Mercedes SUV.

"I wish we had a satellite image of the freighter."

"We don't know for sure but it's likely that after Berdyans'k the ship went to Odessa."

"That had occurred to me." He casually tossed a few color 8 x 10s of ships onto the table. "Could you pick out the ship you saw?" asked Devlyn.

"Not a chance. All I saw was the blinking red light."

"That's a shame. It's a bit of a stretch but there is a red salvage vessel in the harbor. I'd tell you its name, but I can't read Cyrillic."

"I can," she said. "Let me see that." Kat looked over Devlyn's shoulder and said, "That means Red Star."

"OK, so there's a ship called Red Star and it's docked in Odessa. Now to me," he said, stepping back from the table, "that looks like a good candidate for our boat."

"I agree but ...," she said, and sat back down at her desk.

"Come on, face it, Katrina, right now we've got nada. Do you think there is any chance at all that this might be what we're looking for?" He paused. "Look at it again."

And again, she leaned over his shoulder then took the photo from his hand. "They couldn't have been too far out because they were watching the dacha from the ship." She closed her eyes and tried to recreate what she had seen in her mind. "It was after one and the lights in the house were off, so they must have thought Mogilevski was asleep. The ship signaled the guys in the truck to hit the house." Suddenly she opened her eyes and pointed to the tall mast on the Red Star. "The light seemed to be floating quite high and the Red Star's mast is really tall."

"So, do you think this could be the one?"

"I can't be sure. Let's compare it to the others." Devlyn spread the photos on the table and they studied each one. "*The Red Star* is the only one with a mast like that."

"Alright, so if this is the same one that was controlling the attack, where does that lead us? How does it lead us to Rote Faust?" Devlyn asked.

"I think we'll find that the owner is Zapf Industries. If we can trace who owns Zapf, then we'll find the person behind Rote Faust."

"Good point," Devlyn said. "Mercenaries carried out the first attack, right?"

"Yes. Paul, we've been through this."

"I know but wait a second." He turned back to the photos and stared at the Red Star. "My question is, who else had a reason to kill Vlad?"

"I wish we could ask Vlad, but I don't know where he is."

"I do."

Spinning him around to face her she practically screamed, "What?" Though he didn't show it he was surprised by the ferocity of her reaction. "Why didn't you tell me that before? I've been worried sick about him."

"I had my reasons," he said, keeping cool, "But I promise you, he's safe. He's with General Hershoff."

She took out her phone put it on speaker and dialed Ramsey's number.

"Hello?" The old general's voice was cold and distant, but it warmed up the instant he recognized her voice.

"Ramsey, it's …"

"Kat! It's great to hear your voice. How are you?"

"I'm better now knowing that Vlad is safe. Can I speak with him?"

"He's not here."

"Shit. Well then maybe you can tell me."

"If I can. What is it?"

"Someone still wants him dead and we're trying to figure out who. Would you know if Petrus had someone who'd want revenge, a relative with money maybe?"

"No relatives. It was rumored that he had a silent partner, but I have no idea who that was."

"Can you ask Vlad and get back to me?"

"How do I get in touch?"

"Call your buddy Devlyn, it looks like we'll be attached at the hip for the foreseeable future.

"OK. Kat, take care of yourself will ya'?"

"Always Ramsey."

As she disconnected, Devlyn said, "So we wait until we hear back from him."

"I hate this. There has to be something that points to this guy."

"What about the asshole who is running for president of the Pan Europe Movement?"

"No coincidence there I'll bet. The question about him is where does he fit with the organization?"

"Or is he just riding the wave?"

"Yeah, there is that. I looked up the Pan European Movement. It started back in the nineteen-fifties. The guy who started it died in the seventies. It's been a sort of back burner issue since then. But they aren't a radical group, hell Einstein was into it, Sigmund Freud too, and I understand that Churchill thought it was a good idea before the war. The only one I heard who was against it was Hitler."

"Besides the nutbar, who is involved in it now?" Kat asked.

"I have no idea."

"OK, so what do we know? Is there anything that might be able to help us find out who is involved."

"Alright, we think we have the ship, it's in Odessa which is basically a Russian port ..."

"That means military security and they're not going to let us in."

"Yeah. But I wonder if it would be possible to get someone else in there." she said, as she sat down again and stared at the picture, imagining how big this had become.

"You're thinking that if there was someone from the Red Star crew there, he could answer some questions."

"Yeah."

Manolo and Jorge had been quiet listening throughout their exchange but as the silence stretched on Manolo asked impatiently, "Do you Americans finally have something we can act on?"

"It's possible," said Devlyn.

"How's your Russian, Manolo?" Kat added.

"It is the shit, but better than my English," he said.

"Mine too," said Jorge.

"Do you think you could pass yourselves off as longshoremen?"

"Sure."

"OK good," said Devlyn. "I want you to go to Odessa and see if someone from the crew can enlighten us about Zapf."

"It's a hell of a lot better than sitting here listening to you two," agreed Manolo.

"Great, keep in touch. Let us know what you find." The two Spaniards left immediately and as Kat watched Devlyn fit his notes into a valise she asked, "What are you going to do now?"

"I have a theory I'm working on. I don't want to talk about it until I've done some research."

"So, what do I do, sit here and twiddle my thumbs?"

"You're a big girl. You figure it out."

GOING TO AMERICA

Sunday April 18

Ramsey Hershoff was a shrewd and resourceful man, well versed in the art of warfare and spy craft. He knew nothing about the Anita Franco cover until he took Vlad into his version of witness protection.

Since her first 'death' in Canada, Kat hadn't spoken to anyone she'd known before except Devlyn and Vlad. Perhaps all the publicity surrounding the Happy Widow of Ibiza had made its way to her friends at Eagle's Nest. Without making contact with them she might never know if they were aware that she had lived on with an alias only to die again. Knowing the business she was in, they might have understood what she had done. Or maybe not.

"Hershoff," he said.

"Ramsey hi, it's me."

Hold on while I put on the scrambler." He paused then said, "I haven't got that information from Vladimir you asked for yet."

"That's alright, I can ask him myself. I'm coming to New York."

"That's terrific. When?"

"I'm at the airport now. I just have to wait to get on a flight."

"Alright, call me when you know what flight you're on and I'll meet you at the airport."

"No, don't do that. But what you can do is book a hotel room for me."

"I can do that; I'll get you a suite at the Plaza."

PART 2

Chapter 15

An American Exodus

Monday April 19

Kat's only way back to America was to join the exodus at the airport and stand in line, just another frightened American trying to get home. When Henrick De Jonckheer dropped her off, she hurried in out of the rain, pulling a small suitcase behind her. The situation inside was less chaotic than she'd anticipated.

Her badge and ID folder was suspended from the belt of her jeans at the front, and her SIG was clipped on her belt under the US Army jacket. Her short hair was tucked back behind her ears and covered by the US Army ball cap the Field Office kitted her up with. It certainly wasn't subtle and made her feel like a duck in a shooting gallery, but if there was a situation that forced her to draw her gun it was important to make it abundantly clear to the authorities that she was one of the 'good guys'.

She joined the line for the KLM flight heading to New York and waited with the other escapees. Most weren't paying attention, but some seemed to notice the jacket. She couldn't tell if they were reassured by her presence or frightened by it. She stood behind a young couple from Boston with two small kids who smiled at her and said hi. It was really sweet, so she smiled back and waved. Their father pulled them closer and told them not to bother the lady.

She smiled and looked away. Time passed slowly and as new people joined the line, Kat casually scrutinized them looking for anomalies but expecting to find none.

Then she noticed someone about ten meters away, who didn't fit the profile. She was a tall, thirty-something, attractive blonde, wearing the dark sunglasses. The sunglasses were odd because they hadn't seen the sun for days. Her long, tan raincoat was open and bulged out on the right side and she had a backpack resting against her leg. Kat had a bad feeling about her.

The strap across her chest was a carry strap, something Kat was familiar with, having used one like it to secure a weapon at her side.

Perhaps she was a plain clothes cop. Just another layer of protection. But then, why the backpack?

The blonde made eye contact with a bearded black man standing near the gate behind her, shook her head then turned away. He was moving about restlessly. There was no way that he was with the police. Kat sized him up quickly and felt that something bad was about to happen.

He had a backpack just like the blonde's and began swinging it like a pendulum from his left hand.

"Oh shit!" she said aloud, "This is not good."

The woman noticed her making the connection and there was no doubt about whose side Kat was on. She looked at the man and nodded. Then looking back at Kat, her eyes seemed to be on fire. She reached down for the backpack and began to swing it back. Kat drew her gun.

"Gun!" screamed the young woman from Boston, and her husband grabbed the girls and hit the floor.

"Gun!" shouted a man passing by. He dropped his bag and ran. The people around her began to scatter as panic gripped the crowd. The young woman from Boston just stood there.

Kat aimed for the tall woman's head and squeezed the trigger just as the blonde's arm was at the back of its swing.

She fired off two rounds tightly grouped in the center of the woman's forehead while yelling, "EVERYBODY DOWN!"

Taking her own advice, Kat dove behind a pushcart piled high with heavy suitcases as the terrorist collapsed on the backpack. It detonated the instant it slammed onto the floor.

The explosion swallowed the screams. Her body practically disintegrated but absorbed some of the shrapnel it emitted. Even so, the bomb scattered steel balls and nails that peppered everything around it. The luggage protected Kat and the people behind her, absorbing the effects of the blast, but the young woman was not among them. Several other people out in the open were cut down. Many were dead. Several were wounded and dying.

The other terrorist was firing his weapon into the crowd with one hand while wind-milling his pack with the other. At the top of his swing Kat rolled over and pumped five rounds into him. The pack went flying up to the ceiling above him and exploded like a halo of fire on contact. Most of the projectiles from it went into the floor and the ceiling above, but two deadly arcs of metal bits spread out and more people fell.

In an instant, the terminal was filled with smoke, dust, scattered remnants of luggage, bits of structural material, bodies and blood.

Kat was caked with dust but otherwise unhurt. She reloaded her weapon before she stood up. And when she got to her feet, she surveyed the devastation. If there were any other terrorists in the terminal they had to be among the dead and wounded. The girls were huddled over their mother as the husband cradled the dead woman's head. "I told her to get down," he kept saying, "Why didn't she get down?"

The screams and cries for help welled up as emergency workers and survivors came back to the wounded.

A man shouted at Kat, "Are you alright, miss?"He was approaching her through the dust cloud.

"What?"

"Are you injured?" he asked, then he saw the gun and backed away.

"Jesus!" "It's OK, really, I'm security," she said, quickly brushing the dust off her jacket. "And no, I'm not injured. I'm OK, thank you."

"Are you sure?"

Just there on the floor, perhaps two meters away, was a woman covered in dust and blood with her lifeless eyes open and her cheek pressed into the ever-expanding pool of blood. Next to her was a man lying in that same pool of blood and his right hand was reaching out for hers but they didn't touch.

She shook her head. "No," she said, as she closed her eyes, "I'm never going to be alright again."

Walking around the bodies, a policeman approached her and when he reached for her arm, she wondered whether it was to steady her or himself? "I think you can put the gun away now," he said.

"What?" She hadn't realized that she was still holding it. His eyes looked haunted and his hands were trembling. "Oh. Oh ..., yes of course." She holstered the SIG. The action seemed to help relieve his anxiety a little.

"Are you alright?" he asked again.

"No. Christ, look what they've done."

"I can't believe anyone survived that. How did you know she had a bomb?"

"She just didn't look right, you know? Then I saw her make eye contact with that man over there and noticed that he had the same kind of backpack."

"More people would have died if you hadn't acted."

"You think so?" Looking back at the dead and wounded, she said, "Maybe if I acted sooner, we wouldn't have lost anybody."

"They'll want a statement."

"I expect so."

"Why are you carrying a weapon?"

"I am a Special Agent," she said, taking her badge from her belt, "with US Military Counterintelligence. Federal agents are obligated to be armed at all times."

"Like the FBI."

"Yes, something like that. My agency is working with Europol during this emergency." As she held badge up, she looked at her hand and was surprised by how unsteady it was. "I guess I am a little ..., shaken by this."

"We all are," he said, as he took it from her hand. He rubbed the badge with his thumb, a sort of automatic response as if he found the mottled cold surface reassuring. After a moment, he read the information on her card. "You are a Lieutenant Colonel?"

"Yes." She took the folder back and returned it to her belt. "What happens now?"

"We investigate. We find out who these people were and why they did this."

"They have to be Rote Faust. That's why I'm here," she said.

The blast area was relatively small and cordoned off quickly behind hastily fabricated construction walls. Beyond it, the airport began to function again under heightened security.

Hours later planes began to take off and land. New arrivals to the airport were stunned by what had happened and no one lingered.

Henrick returned as soon as he heard about the explosions and was relieved when he made his way through the devastation and found her alive. He put his arms around her, and she leaned on him. "Come on," he said, "there is nothing more we can do here. He led her back to his car, and they sat for a while so she could tell him about it. When she finished her account of what happened he drove her back to the hotel.

She called Devlyn to say she was alive. Then she called Ramsey to tell him that the trip to New York had to be postponed for now.

Chapter 16

Under The Gun

9:18 pm

While he was sitting in the lobby waiting for Kat to shower and change, Devlyn's cell phone began to ring. He snapped it open and put it to his ear. "Devlyn."

"Colonel, this is Special Agent Parr. We have a situation in Brussels, and I think you need to get down here right away."

Parr was standing up against the corner of a restaurant looking down an alley at the back of a theater in Brussels. Around the dog leg was the stage door of the Ancienne Belgique, a concert venue in the heart of the city. Inside the venue was the ABClub, the smallest concert hall in the building. And in that small concert hall, were approximately two hundred and fifty ex-pat American fans of the California hard rock girl band The Pink Boar.

After the concert began, a faction of Rote Faust congregated in the alley behind the concert hall and were let in through the stage door by an inside man. Four men stayed in the alley taking cover in the band's tour bus, fifteen came out onto the stage with AK-47s and hand grenades, while eight others went to the roof top to secure the perimeter.

The killing began immediately. The moment they moved onto the stage, the leader took out his pistol and shot the five women of the band, one by one. The rest turned their automatic weapons on the crowd.

The hall filled with screams and the rapid fire from fifteen assault weapons. Some people managed to rush to the back door and the side fire escapes, but many didn't make it before they were cut down. Those that did found the exit doors had been chained, and then the bullets found them. People were either shot or crushed to death against the doors. The bodies piled up and the remaining screams were drowned out by gunfire.

Dozens of people called the police emergency number 101, and several were cut down while their fingers were still poised above the keys of the phones. By the time the State Security Service arrived, most of the concert goers were dead. All of them would be dead soon.

CI Special Agents Chris Parr and Jasmine Sabiri were teamed with the Belgium Special Weapons Unit heading for the stage door, but gunfire from above had split them up. The point man took a round through the top of his helmet and fell dead under some graffiti exalting homosexuality.

Parr was at the back of the unit and took cover with three members of the VSSE tactical team at the end of the alley.

Sabiri was in the alley with five others. They were trapped and taking heavy fire.

Parr hadn't been able to reach her over the radio or communicate with his section chief, Warren Jobin. He could see Jasmine though. When he couldn't reach Jobin by phone he called Devlyn, the senior officer of the 66th Brigade.

"Parr, what's going on?"

"Terrorists have struck a concert hall in the center of the old city." The Special Agent explained that the main force was at the front of the concert hall trying to decide how to proceed. "We've been hearing a lot of gun fire inside, and we're taking fire from above and from the front. We can't move without taking heavy losses. We can't get near the place."

"Shit, have you heard from anyone inside?"

"We got a call from an agent inside a few minutes ago. She said they're just mowing everyone down."

"Holy Jesus, Parr," Devlyn said, overwhelmed by what he was hearing. "OK, where is Jobin?"

"He's in the command unit with Belgium State Security and I can't communicate with him. I don't know what's wrong. Sir, the situation here is all FUBAR (Fucked Up Beyond All Recognition)."

"No shit! What are the Belgians doing?"

"I don't know."

"Parr, where's the rest of your team?"

"They're inside. The call that got us here was from Special Agent Frances Gould, I think she's dead. She just stopped talking in the middle of a word."

"Oh Christ," Devlyn said, as his gut tightened. "How the hell did they get in there?"

"It was their down time, they wanted to take in a concert."

"You've got to be kidding me! You're telling me that Jobin let them go to a concert while all this crap was going on?"

"I know. It's just the way Jobin operates here. He thought that since most of the people in the audience were Americans our people could provide some security."

"Really, and I wonder how's that working out for him now?"

"Fuck, I don't know what to tell ya, it seemed to make sense to them at the time.

"Was Gould able to give you any useful intel?"

"No, she got cut off before she could give me any details."

After the attack at the airport Devlyn had thought that things couldn't get much worse, but what happened in Brussels just pulled the floor right out from under him. They were down to three agents. One was pinned down under fire, the one guy that could get to her was on the phone looking for a savior. And where was Warren-Fucking-Jobin? In the back of a command truck somewhere with no radio communications and doing sweet-fuck-all.

Hunched over with his elbows on his knees he buried his face in his hand. "Jesus Christ," he said quietly.

"Yes Sir," Parr said, in full agreement.

"You know as well as I do that the chances are pretty good that they're all dead now, or soon will be"

"I know," said Parr.

"So, you should pull back and regroup. Are there still snipers up on the roof?"

"Yeah, I guess the people out on the street are taking some fire too. I heard that they'd sent some tactical people up there. I don't think they made it. We're still taking heavy fire from there."

Sitting in a lobby, hundreds of kilometers away, Devlyn was feeling completely useless. "Chris, uh … Goddamnit Chris, I wish I could tell you what to do but …, uh, …, look, can you see Jasmine from where you are, can you talk to her?"

Devlyn had never used his first name before and the fact that he did now, was not encouraging. Parr looked around the corner and saw her looking back at him. She was in middle of the bunch. The six of them squeezed into a doorway part way down the dog legged alley Rue de la Chaufferette. He could see something in her eyes. He'd been with her long enough to know what she was thinking. "Oh fuck, Jasmine, no! Stay put I'll get you out of there somehow!" he shouted. She was saying goodbye. "Jasmine please … stay put! Sir, she's looking at me like she knows it's over for her. I can't let her …"

"Chris don't do anything stupid. Do you hear me? Chris?"

She was about twenty-five meters away from him and he thought he could go and get her, bring her back to safety. "

Aw, fuck it! I'm going to get to her."

"Chris, …, don't you fucking go out there! Chris …" The instant he stepped out a burst of automatic fire forced him back. Devlyn heard the bullets striking the brick. It sounded so damn close to the phone.

Parr looked up and saw the gunman leaning over the edge. He took a shot and the man's head exploded, he tipped over the wall and dropped to the pavement. Would she come back to him now? She wasn't moving, so he had to. He stepped into the alley firing up and the men with him gave supporting fire. He moved forward and was only meters away when the fire storm from above pushed him back. If he could get her back with him, she would be alright, he was sure of it. All of a sudden, the shooting stopped. The terrorists had moved back. He looked up and began to raise his hand, but before he could beckon her, she turned away. "I can't get to her. Oh shit, something's happening up the alley."

"What, what's happening?" Devlyn shouted into the phone.

"She's ..., they're taking fire from the alley now. I think the tour bus is backing up. Fuck this! Jasmine ..." There was an explosion in the alley and a half second later another. "God! They've tossed grenades into the alley!" Parr looked around the corner. "Oh, fuck no! Oh Jesus ..., Jasmine!" he screamed, as he dropped the phone. Devlyn could just hear him in the distance screaming, "You mother fuckers!"

"What? What's going on? Chris, can you hear me? Chris!"

Everyone tucked in by the door was dead, and the tour bus was backing up towards him. Jasmine's body was being crushed under its wheels. He stepped out into its path and began to fire into the bus.

The phone picked up the roar of the engine as it approached and the thud as it ran Parr down. Then it picked up the cacophony that erupted as everyone left standing in the street fired on the bus until it suddenly exploded into flames.

Devlyn closed the phone and stared blankly into space. That was when he noticed Kat was behind him. "Paul, what was that?" He didn't respond. "Paul, come on, tell me, what just happened?" Again, he didn't answer, so she put her hand on his shoulder. "Paul?"

"That was Chris, Chris Parr ..., in Brussels. I ..., I just heard the man die, Katrina." He closed his eyes and rubbed his face. He was crying.

"Oh God." She had known Chris only through conversations with his partner. "Paul, what about Jasmine?"

"Jasmine? Jesus ..., I can't believe this is happening. Jasmine, she's gone too, the whole unit is gone."

Feeling like her legs could no longer carry her weight Kat dropped to her knees behind the couch. "H ... How?"

"Rote Faust hit a concert hall."

"Who else do we have in Brussels?"

"Let me think," he said, pinching the bridge of his nose. He took a deep breath and sat up so he could concentrate. "Warren Jobin, he's the section chief there." He opened his phone and called him. "He's at the concert hall too." The phone rang twice, then Devlyn said, "Yeah Jobin, Devlyn. What's your status?"

"Paul? This is a fucking disaster. Grenades went off behind the hall and I just saw Chris Parr get run down by a bus. They ran him down with a bus ... and then it blew up in the street."

"I understand that Jasmine Sabiri and the tactical team she was with have also been killed."

"How do you know about that?"

"Parr called me. I heard it all over the phone."

"Paul, what the fuck was he calling you for?" asked Jobin, sounding angry and defensive.

Devlyn wasn't going to let him deflect the issue and said, "That's Senior Special Agent Devlyn to you, and he called me because he couldn't get through to you, Jobin. Now tell me, why was that? Can you do that for me?"

"I ... I was talking to the Minister of the Interior. I know. I ..."

"Where are you now?"

"I'm in the mobile command unit. They've sent a tactical unit in through the front and there's been heavy ..." A huge explosion rocked the command unit.

"Jobin! ... Jobin! Oh, for fuck sake. Are you still there?"

After a lengthy pause Jobin spoke again and his voice was weak and trembling. "They ..., they blew the place up. The whole fucking concert hall just ... blew up. Jesus Christ! I ah ... I ... holy fuck! They are all dead, everyone. Look ... I can't talk now. I'm going to have to call you back."

When Devlyn looked over Kat was no longer there. He heard sounds coming from the breakfast room. She was there in front of the large screen television and the news channel was replaying the recording of the explosion he had just heard over the phone. They watched as the front of the concert hall blew out. The roof of the theater and the buildings on either side of it collapsed and the walls tumbled in. Dust, stone, brick and steel flew up and rained down on everything as fire and smoke filled the sky.

There had been people standing there a moment ago, special terrorist units ready to go in, news people, fire fighters. When the dust finally settled, they were all gone.

Black smoke billowed from the wreckage while what remained of the block was just a scorched shell. The image cut to a live feed. Fire engines were arriving on the scene and setting up in the rubble to battle the blaze.

It cut away again to the anchor desk and the news reader visibly shaken, turned his attention to the attack on the Amsterdam Airport.

Surveillance footage showed people standing in the line for the KLM flight for New York. Suddenly a woman was swinging something and another woman in a ball cap drew a gun and shot her dead. The moment she fell there was an explosion, and the camera went dead. The whole attack was captured and was playing back like a nightmare that would never end. Devlyn turned up the sound. Kat just looked on in tears.

After comments from a reporter at the scene, the image switched back to the disaster on the Boulevard Anspach, which now resembled a war zone. The reporter on the street was telling her audience that there could be as many as a thousand dead and many more wounded. The screen cut to the burned-out hulk of the tour bus and the reporter said that they found the remains of two terrorists inside.

The phone rang again. "Oh God, what now?" asked Kat.

"Maybe it's Jobin again," Devlyn said.

"Paul, could this day get any worse?" Kat asked.

"I don't see why not. Yeah Jobin, is that you?

"This is a total disaster here. We have witnesses who said that while we were concentrating on the front of the building, they saw several gunmen escape through the alley just before the big explosion. They took off in a van that was parked up the street."

"Did anyone get the license number of the van?"

"No."

"Did they say how many there were?"

"Maybe seven or eight depending on whom we talked to. The point is they massacred hundreds of people and the bastards got away. The bastards got away. I don't know what to do now. Do you have any orders for me?"

"Yeah, I want you to hand in your resignation."

"What?!"

"You heard me; you're done, Jobin. I'll be coming down to head up this investigation and I don't want to see you when I get there, because I'm tempted to personally put you on that KIA list. Now pack up and get the fuck out of Brussels."

In Stunned Silence

They sat for a long while in the breakfast room with neither of them saying a word. Devlyn was staring at his hands, turning them over and over as if there was something on them, he couldn't quite see. Kat couldn't get the image from the airport of the couple and the family from Boston out of her mind. At last she had to break the silence. "OK, what are we going to do now, Paul?"

"I said we'd go down and head up our investigation." He didn't look up from his hands. "So, that's what we're going to do now."

Kat moved closer to him. "Sure, OK. What are you thinking?"

"Did you ever know them, Katrina, Chris and Jasmine?"

"I never met Chris, but I knew Jasmine, you introduced me to her at Fort Meade."

"I don't recall."

"It was before I went to St. Petersburg."

"Oh? You'd think I'd remember that."

"You set us up so she could teach me Farsi."

"Did I? I don't recall."

But Kat did, and looked at the floor as her memories flooded in. "Only she called it Persian because that's what her parents called it. She was distant at first, but after a couple of days we got to be good friends. I liked her a lot. I'm sorry that I never saw her again after that."

"Did you learn anything from her?"

"Yes, of course I did, she was a great teacher." Kat stared off at the television screen but was unable to take it in. "She was quite a woman."

"That she was. She and you were a lot alike, you know, the same kind of background and all."

"Are you kidding? We were nothing alike."

"Come on, both of you were from immigrant families."

"But that's where the similarity ends. She grew up with a family that loved her. She had a happy normal goddamn life ... without ..."

"Without?" asked Devlyn, wondering why she stopped.

"Look," she said, pointing at the screen. "He who would be king is on."

The image on the screen had changed to a studio shot with an interviewer sitting at a desk while the scene of the Brussels disaster played in the upper right corner. Sitting beside him was the now familiar face of the weird looking, bald billionaire. The interview was in German, so Kat translated it for Devlyn.

"He said, welcome and Jäger said he hopes he can be helpful. Sure he does. OK, the interviewer said people are talking about Jäger becoming the President of the Pan European Congress. He wants to know how he could prevent the attacks." She stopped to listen.

"Jäger says, 'With a very firm hand.' What an asshole. Then he says … blahdie - blahdie - blah."

"What?"

"It's not worth translating, it's that same shit every time he opens his mouth."

"I don't understand why they give that idiot air-time," Devlyn said. "Why don't you go up and pack a bag? I'm going to see about getting us a car."

"You want to drive there?" she asked, surprised.

"I sure as hell don't want to go near a goddamn airport any time soon."

It was well after 2:00 am when they arrived in Brussels. Day 15 of her trip into hell and it was just the beginning.

Chapter 17

Who Is To Blame?

9:40 am

Five agents arrived from Paris to join Devlyn's investigation team in the field office vacated by Warren Jobin. Their objective was to track down the van that drove away just before the theater was destroyed. They were trying to work with the Belgium authorities, but finding themselves increasingly isolated and the stress was getting to them. There seemed to be a growing sentiment amongst some of their European colleagues that the Americans had brought this on themselves and Europeans were suffering because of it. A sentiment Jäger brought to the conversation and it was spreading, although the leaders of the EU felt strongly about the value of a continued and strong alliance with the U.S.

Devlyn offered his own opinion. "What some of these people are suffering from is a massive case of the Stockholm syndrome. It's like having sympathy for the abuser while blaming the abuse on the victim." Kat couldn't disagree. Jäger was popping up in the media everywhere, openly saying that the Americans were to blame for what is happening. Those that agreed with him were becoming louder all the time. The purveyors of right-wing public opinion talked about Jäger as if he were a savior. Mobs gathered in the streets chanting his name and demanding that Europe hold that nonexistent referendum.

The CI team had to find something, anything, to lead them to the terrorists and the pressure from home was on to do it quickly.

The descriptions given of the van the terrorists used varied from one witness to the other, but eventually they isolated a few common details. It was dark blue or black and might have had a sign on the side which may have included the name Dunkirk, or some derivative of that name. The agents spread out, collecting video from the cc cameras throughout the area. Early in the afternoon of day 16 they caught a break.

A black van with Point Micro Dunkerque Sarl, Équipement Industriel Général printed on it showed up in the security video of a shop in the Rue du Midi, where it had been parked since close of business the day before the attack.

Due to the smoke from the explosions, the images of the escapees were unclear, but the consensus was that there were nine terrorists, two of them likely women, getting into the van. They were dressed in steel gray overalls. The van drove up to the Rue de la Bourse then turned right. The terrorists were heading north.

Concentrating on shops in that direction, an agent turned up another capture from a camera at the parking garage De Brouckére showing it turning left onto the Rue des Augustine. The pace began to pick up from there. The next bit of video showed them heading north again, following the river. Then it was spotted on the Avenue du Port.

What the agents didn't see, was that every few blocks, when they were out of the eye of the cameras, a couple of the terrorists would get out. The coveralls had been removed and they simply faded into the crowd.

The last image the CI team found was on a recording from a security camera on the wall of the pharmacy across the street from the Eglise Notre Dame de Laeken Cathedral. It gave them something that would lead them right to the terrorists' door.

Cars were stopped at a traffic light and that placed the terrorists' truck right next to the camera. There was enough illumination to see through the window of the passenger door. The driver even looked at the pharmacy window and the image was clear.

Now they had their first photo of a live member of Rote Faust. The picture was circulated, and a blanket search was conducted north of the city. Two hours later the van was found abandoned in a parking lot in front of an industrial yard in the little village of Nieuwenrode.

A Face, A Name

Because the van belonged to an industrial machine and welding supplier, it didn't look out of place there. No one had paid any attention to it until the police arrived and called in the CI team. The coveralls and the weapons were still inside, but everything had been carefully wiped down.

The photo of the driver was subjected to a facial recognition program and he turned up in a military data base. They began filling in a history of the man who would lead them to others in his cell.

His name was Emil Quebedeaux, a native of Rouen in Normandy. Since his birth, he had been a constant annoyance in his community. His pranks and misdemeanors rapidly escalated until he was finally caught breaking into a convenience store to steal cigarettes. The judge gave him a choice, jail or the Foreign Legion. He chose the Legion and eventually was deployed to Afghanistan.

After an incident in a bar, Quebedeaux was tried for attempted murder, found guilty, served two years of a ten-year sentence in prison back in France and given a dishonorable discharge. As soon as he was released, he moved to Marseilles to hook up with people he met in prison and quickly melted into the underworld.

While the Belgian police were investigating the stolen van, they came across a grizzly scene in Charleroi, south of Brussels. They found the original driver of the van, dead in an industrial unit along with the welding equipment he was to deliver.

Devlyn's team had taken point but the whole of Western Europe was on high alert and everyone was looking for Quebedeaux. The CI team from Paris caught a lucky break from the Marseille Police when one of their paid informants reported seeing him going into a hotel.

Fools Rush In

Based on that tip, Devlyn, Kat, S.A. Brad House and S.A. Josh Solomon, two of the agents from the Paris office, flew down to Marseille. Devlyn was practically apoplectic when he discovered that Quebedeaux hadn't been arrested yet. He couldn't understand what they were waiting for.

The Marseille police told him that he was spotted in a no-go zone, a particularly dangerous district in one of the most dangerous cities in the world, a district that police absolutely refused to enter.

"What the fuck are you saying? You've got whole communities that just fend for themselves?"

"Yes, exactly," said the police chief. "Very bad things happen when my policemen go in them. I will not risk their lives for this."

"That's it? Let me get this straight, hundreds of Americans are being butchered out there and you're afraid of some goddamn street gangs? This is unbelievable!"

"May I remind you that it is not just Americans who are suffering here. Nonetheless, that is my position," the police chief told him.

"Well fuck that shit! This guy has information that could end this, so if you're too ..."

"Special Agent Devlyn," Kat cautioned.

"OK then." He took a breath. "Fine, we're going in then."

"You would be a fool to try. You will never survive in there."

"Duly noted. But hear this. This is priority one. By executive order, there are no ROEs (Rules of Engagement), we will do whatever it takes to bring him out alive. If the Marseille police or anyone else tries to interfere in any way, I am authorized to treat them as hostile. I hope you understand what I'm telling you." The police chief looked at Devlyn and shrugged his shoulders.

"Do as you please, my friend."

A Floating Safehouse

When they arrived in the city, Devlyn checked in with G-2 requesting assistance with finding a safehouse. Wolfson contacted the American Consulate in Marseille and one of the options caught his eye. It was the Rebecca, a hundred and fifty-one-foot, Dutch built, luxury yacht owned by a friend of his Hector Pullman, a very wealthy and patriotic businessman from Fort Worth, Texas. When the trouble started, he docked his yacht, let his British crew go, handed the keys to the Consulate then beat it for home on his private jet.

It was a simple matter of contacting him in Fort Worth and appealing to his much-lauded patriotism. "Alright, providing they ain't going to sink my boat," the Texan said reluctantly.

The team took the news of their billet begrudgingly with thoughts of an old, smelly, fishing scow. Putting off the thrill of discovery they did a recon of the neighborhood the police were so afraid of. They found that there was some substance behind their reluctance to enter it.

"I suppose we'd better suck it up and see what G-2's set up for us," Devlyn said.

Pullman kept the Rebecca in the Marseille harbor, two slips down from a small naval vessel. After Devlyn picked up the keys, the four agents headed for the slip and couldn't believe their eyes. For a moment, they just stood there staring at the yacht.

"It's a bit bigger than the boat you wrecked in Ibiza."

"I did not wreck it, I set it adrift. There is a big difference."

"Sure there is. Whatever floats your boat, Paul," she said, as she led them up the gangway.

The men were dazzled by the tech and wandered all over the ship checking out the systems and House said it felt just like Christmas.

Kat wasn't interested in buttons, levers and machines, but when she opened the door of the forward cabin on the main deck, she whispered, "Hello gorgeous!" The men were in the wheelhouse, one deck up, so she casually called up to them. "Ah ..., guys, I call dibs on this cabin down here."

"Hey, no way," Solomon shouted, feeling that cabin assignments should be a democratic process.

"Tough nuggies, Josh, finders-keepers and the girl gets it," she said.

"But we ..."

"What did she say?" Devlyn asked.

"Something about claiming a cabin," Solomon said.

"Listen, she outranks you Solomon, and the last thing you want to do is piss that woman off. So, we're going to let her have anything she fucking-well wants, OK?"

"OK Boss," said House.

"Now, how do you turn on the radar?"

"But ..." Solomon began.

Devlyn practically growled, "Now what did I just say?"

"Yes Sir."

When they tired of playing with the boy-toys, the men went down to see what she'd found. "Holy shit," Devlyn said gently, "will you look at this place. Katrina, you realize that we aren't going to be on this tub long enough for you to get settled in."

"Well I'm going to enjoy every bit of it while I can. Where will you be sleeping?"

"Apparently, it's not going to be in here."

"C'est absolument exact, mon cher," she said, meaning 'no shit Sherlock' and closed the door.

The men divvied up the three suites on the deck below and stowed their gear. After everyone was settled in, Devlyn called a meeting in the lounge on the main deck and they began to plan the extraction. First, if they were to get into the neighborhood without being stopped at one of the gang's unofficial check points, they had to look like they belonged.

They spent the afternoon observing the activity in the community and came away with a good idea of what they needed to get in unnoticed. After commandeering two unremarkable cars from the police-impound lot they went into a second-hand clothing store where they found outfits that would help them blend in.

Mingling with the Algerian population in the north of the city, they worked on their Algerian/French accents for the rest of the day. Devlyn realized that although they spoke French, they spoke to each other in Standard Arabic.

Back on the yacht, they went over the plan with a map of the city. It was an anxious session, Devlyn and Kat were going in to apprehend Quebedeaux, while Solomon and House would hang back to cover their six. There was no guarantee that their guy would be where he was supposed to be, or that the street the hotel was on wouldn't be guarded. It was likely that he would not be alone and quite possible that none of them would get out alive. But they needed the information he had and, if at all possible, he had to be taken alive.

Chapter 18

To Apprehend

11:55 am

Their informant said their target kept a room at the Hotel D'Anjou on Rue Sénac de Meilhan. It was a narrow, drab little street in the district of Thiers in the 1st arrondissement of Marseille, just south of the train station. Their approach was difficult because of the seemingly random layout of the city and countless one-way streets.

Devlyn decided to go in around noon, while people were off the streets having lunch. It fell upon Kat to commit their route to memory so that they wouldn't be seen with a map. They would go in quietly. If he wasn't there they would leave, no fuss no muss. They had suppressors on their handguns. House and Solomon also had MP5 submachine guns under their jackets.

They entered Thiers from the southwest, threading though the confusion of one-way streets, some congested with parked cars on both sides and pedestrians ambling down the middle. They squeezed along narrow lanes bordered by iron barriers that separated the sidewalks from the traffic and yet people still insisted on walking down the middle of the road.

Shop fronts, restaurants and apartment building walls were all 'decorated' with graffiti, some of it was interesting and colorful art and the rest was ugly and threatening, markings of gang territory.

As they jogged around the east side of Place Jean Jaurès, they passed a few gang members. The police called them les jeunes, young men, obviously, they were armed and guarding their turf.

The agents rounded the north end of the plaza and Kat subtly pointed to the right. Devlyn broke away from the flow of traffic onto the Rue de la Bibliothèque, a shallow canyon of apartment buildings with barred windows, shutters closed tight and walls marred by gang graffiti. No one gave them a second glance.

House and Solomon were following a few car lengths behind and were being ignored as well. They made the turn and a block down they turned right again onto Quebedeaux's street, the only cars to do so. There was a solid line of parked cars on the left side and iron stanchions protecting the sidewalk on the right. "Fuck it," Devlyn said, and pulled up on the sidewalk between the thin poles right across from the hotel.

House and Solomon parked further back, then got out and found a spot between a car and a dumpster where they had some cover and a full view of the road.

Devlyn waited until they were in position before he nodded to Kat and got out. He stood in the middle of the quiet street and waited for Kat to fall in behind him. Holding her head down, Kat stepped into his shadow and followed him at a respectful distance.

He opened the door and stopped, holding Kat back with his outstretched hand. "What's the matter" she asked convincingly, reprising the Algerian accent.

"Quiet woman," he growled, as he peered into the unlit hall trying to get his eyes accustomed to the darkness. On such a baking-hot day, much of Marseille smelled of the sea, seasoned with vehicle exhaust, garbage, urine and feces. It was hard to imagine that it could be worse inside the hotel, but it was.

Kat immediately pulled the material up to cover her nose and mouth. The air was damp and smelled of mold and hot, sweaty, unwashed bodies with a pungent accent of stale cigarette smoke and piss.

The entrance hall was long and narrow. A stairway directly ahead of them on the right split the space with a narrower hall that stretched to the back of the building. At the end, a small amount of light filtered through a window, opaque with grime.

Devlyn moved forward cautiously, and as his foot crossed the threshold the door began to close behind him. Kat caught it with her free hand and followed him in.

The floor squeaked like an alarm system beneath their feet and their movement also tripped a sensor. A single, naked bulb illuminated the hall, bathing it in a gloomy, yellow light. Kat took in the decomposing wallpaper, cracked plaster and the cockroaches scurrying off towards the stairs. She tried holding her breath, but it didn't help.

Devlyn approached the window that was cut into the wall about half-way down the hall. Kat quietly floated behind him with her right hand on her gun in the folds of her dress. The clerk stirred but said nothing.

"Greetings," Devlyn said, sounding convincingly Algerian.

"What do want," replied a gravelly voice, with no hint of welcome. Kat subtly moved toward the entrance of the tiny room. Devlyn drew closer to the window to get a better view of the man.

He was perched on a stool partially hidden in the shadow, his left arm rested on a small shelf, his hand balled into a fist. Devlyn was about to say something but stopped short when a yellow light switched on behind the man.

The voice had sounded like the speaker was old, but in truth he was in his late thirties, lean and tightly muscled. His bald head was shaped like wedge and his skin was stretched tight, like parched leather, over his skull. A scar framed the corner of his eye. He squinted slightly as the smoke curled up from the cigarette that hung from his lips and said in Arabic, "Come closer my friend."

Devlyn put his hand over his heart and said, "May Allah be with you." It was the only greeting he knew, and the man accepted it with a slight nod. He showed no sign of recognition. It was just a trick of the light but Devlyn thought he'd aged since the surveillance picture was taken.

Reverting to his native language Emil Quebedeaux asked, "What is it you want?" Like a venomous snake, his dead eyes gave no hint of what was going on in his mind, but the tattoos on his arm and hand told a story of hate and violence.

Devlyn was certain that in Quebedeaux's hidden right hand was a gun aimed at his stomach. Would he shoot through the wall, or would he take the time to bring it up?

"Let's start by raising your right hand where I can see it," Devlyn answered, dropping the accent. His SIG was out in less time than it would take to clap your hands and he turned sideways as he aimed at the man's head. "And do it slowly."

That quarter turn was probably what saved his life. The instant he moved, the wall under the window erupted and the bullet traced a line across Devlyn's abdomen. He fell back, exposing Kat.

Her weapon was already up, and she fired before the terrorist had a chance to shoot again. Her bullet bore a hole through his right shoulder. He jerked back off the stool into the wall behind. Before he hit the floor, Kat was through the door with her gun pointed at his head. He reached for his gun and, without hesitation, she put a bullet through his hand. Flinching back, he screamed obscenities.

"Clear" she said, as she grabbed Quebedeaux by his injured shoulder and dragged him to his feet. He grunted and groaned, but she wasn't concerned about his pain and he couldn't resist. As she moved back into the hall, she looked at Devlyn. "Are you OK?"

"Yeah." Quebedeaux's shot was loud enough to raise the whole street. Devlyn was flat on his back on the floor when someone upstairs fired down at him. The bullet slammed into the floor by his head. Devlyn saw him reaching over the banister for a second shot and fired up hitting him in the face. The man crashed through the railing and tumbled down the stairs, bringing down a shower of wood and dust with him. There were no other sounds from above.

A moment later, the front door burst open and Devlyn rolled over to meet the new threat. House shouted, "It's me!" He entered with his machine gun ready, "Are you OK?"

Since House spoke English, Devlyn decided that there was no point in hiding the fact that they were Americans, so he dropped the French. "Yeah, check upstairs, see if it's clear," Devlyn said, getting up. House bolted up the stars and banged through the closed doors on the second floor.

"Clear," he shouted a moment later, and came down.

"What's happening outside?"

"Nothing, but if there is anybody at home on this street, they must have heard that. He saw the blood across Devlyn's abdomen "Is it bad?"

"It's nothing. Where is Solomon?"

"He's behind me, covering the door."

"OK, leave him out there. We've got our guy. Katrina has him, but she is going to need some help getting him out of here."

Kat shoved Quebedeaux out into the hall so House could take his left side. He twisted his arm behind his back sharply and they followed Devlyn outside and across the street while Solomon kept watch. Devlyn gingerly slid behind the wheel and started the engine. They had no idea if anyone was watching them from behind the shutters, but no one interfered.

Kat and House followed Devlyn with Quebedeaux between them and forced him down on the floor in the back of the Renault. Kat climbed in over him and held him down with her foot. He groaned, "I'm bleeding."

"That's not my problem," she said. She had only one thing on her mind and it wasn't making the bastard comfortable. House closed the door and slapped his hand on the roof.

Devlyn popped the clutch and swerved off the sidewalk, going through the gears quickly as they raced away from the hotel. House ran back to the other car where Solomon was waiting with the motor running, and in seconds they were on Devlyn's bumper just as he was about to charge into mid-day traffic. "Paul calm down we're OK," Kat said, "It's just Solomon and House behind us."

"OK." He slowed down and joined the traffic flow more cautiously. "Is that better?" he asked.

"Much, Are you OK?"

"It's bleeding, but I'll live. How is he doing?"

"He needs a doctor." Quebedeaux groaned again. "Shut up and grow a pair," she said.

Devlyn laughed and said, "Jesus, Katrina, you'll make someone a wonderful mother someday."

"Shut the fuck up," she snapped. Without knowing it, he'd hit a nerve with that jibe. She had been feeling nauseated since they arrived in Marseille and there was a good chance that what she was experiencing was morning sickness.

"Why didn't you just shoot him?" she said heatedly, hiding the true reason for her anger. "He could have killed you."

"Well he didn't, and you took care of him, so ..., just let it go, OK?"

Without another word, Devlyn navigated over to Rue des Convalescence, which seemed appropriate, and around the traffic circle at Place Sadi Carnot to Rue Méry, then down to the harbor and the safehouse. He sped through the gate of Marseille Fos with Solomon and House right behind.

Shielding Quebedeaux from the curious, the four agents moved him out onto the dock and up the gangway. Without wasting time, they carried him down to the crew's cabin at the bow of the yacht. Solomon ran ahead and covered the bunk with a plastic sheet, and they summarily dropped Quebedeaux on it.

Dockside Security

Kat had taken a short medic's course at Fort Rucker and it came in handy now. Devlyn called the Consulate to arrange for a doctor and Kat did her best to see that Quebedeaux didn't bleed out.

Devlyn was given a name; a man the diplomat said could be trusted and told that he would be sent to them immediately. "He'll want to be paid in cash. Will that be a problem?"

Devlyn knew Kat had a few thousand Euros in her purse and said, "Not at all. The man will need blood."

"I don't suppose you know what blood type."

"Not a clue."

"OK, I'll let the doctor know."

"Thanks."

House and Solomon took the cars away and dropped them off where they were sure to be stolen. Kat's prisoner/patient was unconscious, so Devlyn went up to the captain's cabin to lie down. On his way past the bar on the wheelhouse deck, he selected a rare and expensive bottle of single malt scotch, poured three fingers into a crystal tumbler and gulped it down, then took the bottle to bed.

After dealing with the cars, House and Solomon picked up some take-away for their lunch and hurried back.

They found Kat sitting with Quebedeaux and offered her some food. She wasn't hungry. Devlyn was asleep. They took the food out to the poop deck to keep watch for the doctor.

Fifteen minutes later, an old brown Mercedes pulled up on the wharf and parked in front of the yacht. House ran down the gangway to greet the driver. "Who are you?"

"Dr. Pascal, I was sent for."

Devlyn heard the car arrive and came out to the rail of the boat deck. "If that's the doctor send him up here to me," he said, then went back into the lounge, picked up the intercom and pressed the focsle button.

Kat answered, "Yes?"

"The doctor is here. I need to see him first."

A typical upper middle-class Frenchman, Pascal had House carry his supplies for him. The consulate employee shared a brief history of the doctor with Devlyn indicating that he was a deeply flawed man. Kat disliked him at first sight. "Do you speak English?"

"Of course," said the doctor.

"Bien, thank you for coming doctor," she said, while watching his every move. He had studiously tousled brown hair, a longish nose and a tight humorless mouth. Looking at the cases he brought, she asked, "Are you planning on moving in?" He didn't seem to be amused.

"I was informed that this was an emergency, so I have come with the appropriate equipment. They contain blood and delicate instruments, so be careful with them," he said, "Where is my patient?"

"Patients," she corrected him, and headed for the stairs.

"You said patients, I was led to understand that there was one in critical condition."

"Yes, gunshots to the shoulder and hand."

"Then I will see him first." He started to move away.

"No-no-no, we are heading up these stairs first."

"Ah, so he's up there is he?" Kat nodded without contradicting him.

Leaving his equipment where House had left it, he began to follow her.

"Way to plan ahead and all that ..., but ..." she said, with her arms folded across her chest. "... I'm not a porter, so you're going to have to carry them yourself." He stepped back and looked at his cases then back at her in stunned silence. "OK, good talk, but time is wasting doc, so let's get on with it, shall we? Follow me."

"May I know who the patient is?"

"My partner."

"Is he very badly injured?"

"I don't know how bad, but he's the one you are going to treat first."

"Young woman, this is not a decision you are qualified to make. I will treat the more serious case immediately. Your partner can wait. Where is the other one?" he asked. He turned to the stairs leading town to the guest suite and crew's quarters. "Is he down there?"

She quickly moved to block him and put her hand on his chest, stopping him in his tracks. "Oh no, that's not how we're going to play this. You're pushing all my buttons today, doc, so I'll just say this once." She had been in a foul mood since Devlyn was shot, now she was completely fed up. She took out her gun. "You will do what you are told, or so help me I'll end you right here." She held the gun by her side and the doctor stared at it. "I hope I have made myself clear."

He looked up at her, seemingly unfazed, and said, "Are you actually threatening me?"

"I'd like to think of it as a natural sequence of events. You do what I tell you to do, or you die. What's it going to be, doc? Quickly now, I have another doctor on call." He began to stammer. "Doc, I need to know right now. So, what are you going to do?" She raised the gun. "You've got till three. One."

"You would not dare to shoot me."

"Two. You would not be the first man I shot today." She pointed it at his head. "Right now, I'm happy to go either way, I just have to know now."

"Alright!" he said, picking up his equipment.

"That's better."

"I will see your partner first." He pushed by her and started up the stairs. "And please put that away."

He spent about twelve minutes cleaning and taping up the wound then gave Devlyn something for the pain.

"House, take the doctor below for me." When the doctor was gone, he said, "I heard what you told him down there. I appreciate it, Katrina, thanks."

"I've got your back, Paul, always. I have to go now." She went down below and found Pascal setting up the IV. "OK," she said, then turned around and found Devlyn standing behind her. "Jezzus, I thought you were going to take it easy."

"Now I've got your back," he said warmly.

Quebedeaux awakened briefly and his reaction to Pascal was disturbing. Kat thought she saw mutual recognition there. "Dr. Pascal, do you know this man?" she asked.

"What? No, of course not. It is just that I was not informed that his condition was so ..., so serious."

"Believe me, he's lucky to be alive at all," Devlyn said. "We'd like you to make sure he stays that way for now. Do what you can for him; he has to answer some important questions."

"The man is suffering from blood loss and he is in ... Here, what are you doing?" he said, as Kat opened his case and began looking through it.

"I'm doing what should have been done before you came aboard. Solomon, search him."

"I resent the implication."

"Resent it all you want, Doc. Anything Solomon?"

"No, he's clean."

"OK."

"Why don't you two go up and keep an eye out for hostiles," Devlyn said.

"You got it, boss."

"It's Sir, not boss, now get upstairs."

"Yes Sir, sorry," House said, and they left.

Kat moved over to the other case and started shuffling through it.

"Arret! That equipment is sterile."

"That's an obvious lie. Now, why would you lie to me, Doctor Pascal? Is there something in here that you don't want me to see?"

"I don't like my instruments manhandled."

Kat stared at him for a few excruciating seconds, trying to determine if they should continue to trust him. Her conclusion was no. Remembering the case with the false bottom she took with her to St. Petersburg, she rapped on the floor of the case and looked for a way to open it. Having found nothing she sat back and said, "Alright, I'll accept that for now."

"I am so relieved," he said, with obvious sarcasm. "Now may I continue caring for my patient?"

Kat looked to Devlyn for his opinion. "OK, he said, "but if you do anything that doesn't look kosher, I won't hesitate to shoot you."

His voice held none of the lightness it had when talking to the others, which made Pascal blink; he swallowed hard and nervously turned his attention back to Quebedeaux. "He's in shock. I don't think he'll be answering any questions for you quite yet." He looked at Kat. "Mademoiselle, is it possible that you could assist me?"

"I'll do what I can," she said.

"Very well. You," he said, pointing at Devlyn, "get out."

"You keep pushing your luck like that and it'll run out," Kat warned. "He'll leave when he's good and ready. Just do you job."

"Very well, towels and hot water."

Kat handed her gun to Devlyn and left the room. Minutes later she returned with water. She placed her materials on the floor beside the doctor and then took back her gun. "OK Paul, I can handle it down here, why don't you go to one of those cabins back there and lie down."

"Who's in charge here?"

"If you have to ask then ..."

"Yeah, it's not me. How could I forget that? I'll be up in the wheelhouse. Call me if you need something." He went to the captain's cabin to do some reading.

His material of choice was a check list he requested from the owner, which had just arrived by fax. It was a short stack of papers Pullman had written for him, titled, How to Operate the Boat for Dummies.

The bottom line was, Don't sink it!

When he finished, he called House and Solomon up to make ready to cast off. Below decks, Quebedeaux was stabilized and sleeping. "That is all we can do for him. Now, you may go," Pascal said.

Everything about the man seemed wrong and she couldn't wait to get away from him, but she said, "I'll just stick around until someone replaces me."

"Mon Dieu, c'est tout!" he said, throwing his arms out in front of him in frustration. "You people are unbelievable. He will be sleeping for hours now. I assure you that I am perfectly capable of keeping him quiet."

"I'm sure you are, that's what I'm afraid of."

"What do you mean by that?"

"It's simple, Pascal, I don't trust you, so park it on that chair."

"How dare you speak to me like this!"

For the second time, she felt it necessary to point her gun at his head. "Sit," she said, with a calmness that felt more threatening than a scream.

Just then they heard the generator start up and then the engines roar to life. Kat reached for the intercom and called up to the wheelhouse. "Are we going somewhere?"

"I got a radio message from Maryland. It seems that now that the French know we have him, they want him back. G-2 ordered us to get out of the country. We're heading for Monaco. You can kick the doctor off now, there will be a medical team and agents waiting to take our friend off our hands."

"Fabulous, what time is it?"

"It's ah …, 5:40, what's going on down there?"

"He's on an IV, stable and sleeping. I don't know how long he'll be out. Can you ask one of the guys to come down and take over?"

"Yeah, as soon as we cast off."

"Thanks," she said. She tucked the phone between her cheek and shoulder as she looked over at the doctor. "OK Doc, the boss wants you to take a hike, so let's get you packed up and off the boat."

"No, I will not leave my patient," Pascal said, then looked back at Quebedeaux.

"Hold on a sec, Paul," she said, glaring at Pascal. "You have a problem?"

"He may need something when he wakes up. I cannot leave him."

"I think I can deal with whatever he needs. Just leave me something for pain and …"

"No!"

"You are a strange little man, Dr. Pascal." She lifted the phone to her mouth and said, "Paul, the guy wants to stay with us." She looked at Pascal, thinking there was definitely something wrong with him. She just couldn't put her finger on what it was.

"OK, we haven't got the time to argue with him."

Sailing For Monaco

Solomon arrived to relieve Kat. "House said he could handle the lines by himself, so I'll spell you here for a while."

"Thanks, I'll be in my cabin if you need me. Don't leave him alone with Pascal."

"Your cabin?"

"Eat your heart out Solomon. You heard what the big guy said, the girl gets what the girl wants."

"Gotchya."

By the time she reached the main deck, House had already unplugged the shoreline and phone lines and stowed them away. She watched as he lifted the last of the slackened mooring lines off the bollard, let it drop into the water then ran to the gangway. Kat helped pull the line aboard and House shouted, "All clear."

Devlyn pressed the control on the console to winch up the anchor and another to retract the gangway, then he pushed the throttles forward. The Rebecca slowly began to move out into the channel.

House asked him, "Where did you learn to drive this thing?"

Pointing to Pullman's manual all Devlyn would say for the moment was, "I read the book."

He maneuvered the big boat around the breakwater. "OK now, keep an eye out and tell me if I'm getting close to anything."

Running at about five knots the Rebecca slipped gracefully by the old fort that guarded the harbor on the western shore. House said, "That's impressive." Devlyn wasn't interested.

A couple of minutes later they passed the Palais Du Pharo on the east side and cleared the seawall.

Even though his abdomen was hurting like hell, Devlyn had to smile. There was something about being in control of a thing this big and expensive, that gave him a huge rush. It was unbelievable that G-2 had arranged for them to use such an exotic, over the top, toy as a safehouse. The smile broadened into a full grin as he pushed the throttles forward and the breeze tugged at the small triangular flag on the short staff at the bow. There was a satisfying sound as the bow cut through the light swell and the bow wave rolled back into the sea. He leaned back on the pilot's rest and sipped his scotch as the Rebecca put some distance between it and the city with satisfying authority. A squabble of gulls circled and squawked above the following wake and Marseille began to fade into the background like a bad dream.

Kat had stopped in the main lounge to take a bottle of Perrier from the bar fridge on her way to her cabin. After stripping out of the drab clothes she bundled them up and stuffed them in the waste basket, then headed for her private spa. She lingered in the rain shower hoping that the hot water would release some of the knots in her neck and back.

House joined Solomon down below to sit with Quebedeaux and the doc, while Devlyn settled pleasurably into his new-found solitude in the elegant wheelhouse with his bottle of scotch. The world, at least their little part of it, was at peace for a while.

Kat walked out through the dressing room to the suite's study wrapped in a plush towel, a second towel was wrapped round her head like a turban. She luxuriated in the delicious feeling of the deep pile carpet between her toes.

Curious about a panel of buttons by the desk she went to it and spotted one marked 'Forward Window'. She pressed it and what happened next was like the opening of a one act play. The wall of curtains drew back revealing the bow of the yacht, and the Med spread out before her like a sparkling, rolling stage.

In that moment of tranquility, she allowed the violence of the recent experience to slip from her mind. The burgee snapped in the breeze and the yacht seemed to be all alone heading south. The next bit of land was Africa and, for whatever reason, the idea of that was magical. The foreword deck was empty, so she let the big towel fall to the floor and standing in front of the window like an erotic Art Deco statue, she let the last of the waning sun warm her.

There were photos of the young mistress of the yacht, one autographed, With all my love, Rebecca. There was another that showed Rebecca with her much older husband. Obviously, she was not the first Mrs. Pullman. Who knew how many there were before her? It didn't matter, she was probably determined to be the last. Another showed the tall, slim and elegant woman in a long dress with a bouquet of roses and a Miss Texas 1997 sash across her chest, a crown on her head and a big old Texas smile. Rebecca was a winner alright.

Kat began to think about her own life and what she wanted. She put her hands on her belly gently moving them clockwise. What had earlier been just a feeling that something was happening inside her, had become a certainty. She was going to be a mother.

She could feel the life growing inside her and wondered if she should share the pregnancy with Devlyn. Putting that question on hold for the moment, she continued her inspection of the room.

Entering Rebecca's dressing room, she found some warm and comfortably elegant clothes. She dried her hair and put it up in a French bun, dressed and then climbed the stairs to the wheelhouse.

The REBECCA was cruising on auto pilot, heading for Monaco at twenty-five knots. Leaning back comfortably against the padded bar that substituted for the captain's chair, Devlyn looked relaxed with his eyes fixed on the horizon.

It was the first time she had visited the impressive wheelhouse. "Now this is really something," she said.

Startled, he twisted around. "Damnit woman, why do you have to sneak around all the time. It's spooky."

"Sorry." She made her way over to the bench behind the chart table and sat down. "Where are the boys?"

"Below," he said. "They won't come up unless I call them."

"Then there's no need to disturb them."

Up The Coast

With the sun disappearing behind them, the evening quickly cooled, and the breeze was becoming a gusty wind. The Rebecca began to roll gently in the beam sea.

"Where are we now?" asked Kat. "Ah..." He looked back at the radar. "We're coming up to Îles des Embiez," he said, "we'll be crossing some ferry routes out of Toulon soon, so I'll have to keep an eye on the radar."

"Oh, here it is," she said, leaning over the chart table. "Are you going to go through the channel between the coast and the Île Marie?"

"I thought it would be safer to go around. I'm thinking the French might be looking for us, but there may be some rough water out there, so ..."

"Does your wound feel any better?"

"It stings, but I'll live."

"I'm glad to hear that. I guess it's going to slow you down a bit."

"Speaking of that," if we're running into rough water then I'm going to slow the boat down a bit."

"Will it help?"

"I don't know, he didn't cover that in the instructions. Katrina, I was just thinking that I should leave Quebedeaux's interrogation to you." He looked back at her.

"Not a problem."

"Good. Do you need me there with you?"

Kat thought about that question, putting it in the context of the long term. Did she need a man in her life? Perhaps the better question was, did she need this man in her life? "No," she said. He had served his purpose and that was the end of it. "Unless you'd like to sit in, I think I can handle it from here."

"OK."

"Then I guess it's time to see what he has to say," she said. The deck began to pitch and roll. Moving carefully, she headed for the stairs. "Whoa it's getting rough. You weren't kidding about going around. Can we change our minds?"

"What's the matter, seasick?"

"No, but I can't say I like this."

"It shouldn't last too long," he said.

"Glad to hear it," she said, and went down the stairs.

The yacht was being tossed about, pitching and rolling in a following quarter beam sea. Waves began to jar the yacht as they broke against the hull, throwing up spray that reached over the top deck. At times, it looked like the Rebecca was just going to nose into the sea in the trough of a big wave and never come up.

It was amazing, she thought, how quickly the sea could turn ugly.

Angry Seas

As sore as he was, Devlyn was thinking about Kat. She had never been an admirer of his, but he thought that after their roll in the hay in Madrid, there would have been some sort of thaw. Not only was there no thaw, she seemed to be growing more distant every day. Maybe the stress was getting to her. Maybe he should have gone with her to question the prisoner. He reached for the intercom on the console and pressed the button for the crew's cabin.

"Solomon."

"How is our guest doing?"

"He's still out, but the doc says he's not in any danger. Katrina is here now."

"OK, I'm coming down to join you, so I need House up here to take a watch at the helm."

"Copy that." Solomon replaced the receiver. "The skipper's coming down. He wants you up there to steer the boat."

"What? I don't know anything about boats," said House.

"Tell it to the man."

While he was hanging on to the console in the wheelhouse trying not to fall over, he repeated his issue.

"What's to know? You just stand here and try not to hit anything. I promise we'll be done before we have to make a course change."

"Yes Sir. Why are we getting waves like this now?"

"The sea gets bumpy, what can I tell you? I think it'll calm down soon."

"What if I see another ship?"

"If something gets in the way pull the throttles back and call me," Devlyn said.

As he reached the stairs the intercom buzzed. House picked it up. "Sir, ... it's Solomon, he wants to talk to you."

"Shit!" He staggered back and with his feet planted far apart he took the phone. "Yeah."

"Quebedeaux is awake and talking."

"OK, I'm on my way."

"Is there any way you can stop the rocking, Sir?" House asked. "I don't think I can do this; the waves are making me sick."

"Fuck!" he said and returned to the wheelhouse. "Dammit, let me see what I can do." Devlyn reached for Pullman's notes and reread the instructions for the flopper stoppers, found the control and the large stabilizer fins extended from the hull below the water line, reducing the roll.

"That's better now," House said.

"Good, alright, stay on this heading and keep an eye on the radar for other ships. If you have any serious problems call me."

He found the doctor sitting in the small common area outside the focsle looking angry. Solomon was standing in the doorway of the forward head, hovering. Held together by copious quantities of bandage, Quebedeaux was sitting up. Still hooked up to the IV he was very pale. Devlyn touched the IV bag hanging from the bunk above and asked, "Is he on something for pain?"

"Of course," said Pascal.

"Too bad. Is he lucid?"

"Apparently."

"OK, take a hike; we've got it from here."

"No! I insist that I remain with my patient."

"Not possible, leave now. Go to the cabin at the other end and I'll call you if we need you." The doctor refused. "That," he said, picking him up by the arm, "was not a request," and he practically threw the smaller man down the hall.

"C'est la merde du taureau !" 'This is bull-shit' he said, stumbling. Devlyn just jerked his head aft. "Merde!"

As he turned back, Devlyn saw Kat watching approvingly. Pascal gave her a murderous look and went on his way.

"Have you got a problem, Doctor?" she asked.

"Putain stupide," he said, as he hurried away to the cabin and slammed the door.

"There is something seriously wrong with that guy," she said, to Solomon and Devlyn.

"Hold up a sec. Did he call you what I think he called you?"

"He called her a stupid whore," Solomon said.

"Yes, thank you Solomon. I really needed to hear that twice. Forget him, he's not worth the bother."

"Alright, let's start the interrogation."

"Hang on, Paul. Honestly, you look like you're about ready to drop. Why don't you sit this one out and let me do it?"

"Are you sure?"

"Yeah, I've got this. Let me by." Devlyn stepped out of the way and let Kat re-enter the room. The moment Quebedeaux realized that she was going to do the interrogation he became agitated. "I promise I won't shoot you again," Kat said, then looking at Solomon, asked quietly, "Did the doctor say anything to him about me?"

"He whispered something, but I didn't hear what it was."

"OK." She stood over the bunk and down at her subject. "It's time we had a little talk. I promise I won't shoot you," she said in French.

He looked at Solomon and in English said, "I won't talk with this bitch. Get her out of here."

"So, you speak English. OK then, here is how it's going to work. I will ask you a question and you will answer me, or I may forget my promise."

"What promise?"

"About shooting you." Her tone was even but there was no doubt about her intentions. His eyes were darting from her to Solomon as if he expected Solomon would save him. "Don't look at him. Focus on me."

Quebedeaux was a miserable looking specimen, wide eyed and trembling. "OK."

"That's better," Kat said. "Now let's begin with something simple. What is your name?" She waited a few seconds and then sounding bored and impatient, she took his chin between her fingers and said, "Come on, give me your name."

"Eat shit."

"Wrong answer." She let go of his chin and punched him in the mouth.

After he finished spitting out blood, he said, "OK ..., OK. Emil Quebedeaux."

"There ..., you see it's very simple, I ask a question, you give me an answer. Where do you live?"

"The hotel where you shot me. I..., I know who you are! I recognized you the moment I saw your face."

"Really, so you got the memo from the boss man too."

"Yes."

"Sure, these things get around. What I want to know is who gave you my picture?"

"We were all told to watch out for you."

"I got that part, what I asked you was ..., who gave you my picture?"

"They will find you. We have people everywhere, you can't hide. No one can hide from us."

"Someone else told me that and I killed him. Emil, listen to me carefully. For you, there is no 'us' anymore, no 'we' no future. As far as they are concerned, you are a dead man." She reached forward and pinched his bony chin again and held his face still. "There will be no trial for you. If I let you live, then you will rot in a cage in Guantanamo for the rest of your natural life. Do you understand me, Emil? Tell me what I want to know. Who told you about me? Who gave you the picture?"

He said nothing and she waited for a few seconds.

"You know, it is quite possible that you will not survive long enough to get to Guantanamo. I understand that there are lots of sharks in this channel and you are bleeding. Tell me, who gave you the picture?"

"I have told you too much already."

"Oh, I don't think so," she said, keeping her voice low and calm. Looking back at Solomon she said, "Perhaps we should take him up, tie a rope around his waist and troll for fish." There was an edge to what she said that made Quebedeaux back away from her again. "Do you think I might catch something if I do that?"

"It's possible, they say they hunt at night," Solomon said. She smiled, but there was no humor in it and her eyes were ice cold.

"You would never do that," said the prisoner.

"You have no idea what I am prepared to do to you, Emil. Cooperate with me, or you will be fish food." She waited for a few seconds. "Talk!" A few more seconds passed in silence. "No? Well then, I think you just need a little persuasion. Solomon, would you please help me take him out to the diving platform?"

Solomon nodded and took one arm, Devlyn took hold of the other and they hauled him off the bed.

"Wait!" They stopped. "You can't do this!"

"Oh, but I can. Gentlemen, if you please."

"No!"

"You," she jabbed him with the tip of her finger, "have murdered hundreds of my people. You and your kind slaughtered them, as if their lives meant nothing. But, Emil, the reality is that you are nothing, you are a waste of space. The people were good people, with families, they were contributing to society. You have never contributed anything in your entire life. Maybe, if I throw you to the sharks, you will finally be able to contribute something useful."

Solomon began to pull him away from the bed. "When we get him up top, make sure the rope is nice and tight, so we don't drop him too soon. He may have something to say before we start trolling."

"No, no. I'm sorry, OK? I'll tell you anything you want to know, just don't do this to me."

"This is your last chance. Am I clear?"

"Yes, yes," he said. Solomon set him back on the bed and the answers began to flow. "His named is Helmut Kroner. He is in charge of a large private security company in Zürich. He distributed the photos. He said that there was a hundred thousand Euros to the one who could capture you alive and bring you to him."

"Very good. Now, where were you supposed to take me?"

"To his private estate."

"I don't believe you. Why would he let someone like you visit his private estate?"

"That is where he gave us our assignments. It is very secluded; we could come and go without being seen."

"Alright, tell me about the estate." She imagined something like the Petrus estate, but what Quebedeaux described was a comparatively modest glass house in the forest on the side of a mountain.

"What mountain?"

"I don't know the name of it, but it is just outside of Albisrieden in District 4, off the Albisriederstrassa. I have been there twice. It is hard to find, but I can take you there."

That sparked a memory. She'd seen pictures of a house that sounded just like that, but she couldn't quite place it. Running her fingers through her hair it came to her. The article in Architectural Digest at the hairdresser's in Madrid. It was an amazing house, made almost entirely of glass and steel.

She asked him about the attacks on the Americans and his story carried them through every detail of what his gang had done. While Quebedeaux spoke, Solomon recorded everything on a small digital recorder and the story was so disturbing that Kat actually considered going through with her previously empty threat of tossing him over the side.

His gang had committed most of the murders claimed by Rote Faust in France and Belgium, beginning with the murders of the young women on the Golden Fox soccer team bus. The leader of the gang, the man who spoke in the video, was the man Devlyn killed at the hotel in Marseille.

On Kroner's orders, they joined with two other gangs from Belgium and Holland to massacre the people in the theater in Brussels. Their instructions were to make sure that no one came out of there alive, including the members of the other gangs. They had to demonstrate to the world that they would stop at nothing to drive the Americans from Europe.

What Quebedeaux didn't know at the time was that the other gangs had received the same instructions.

He began to name the others in his cell, eight low level criminals who became instant terrorists. The names came out so fast, that Kat had to ask him to repeat them, so Solomon could make sure the recording was clear. Devlyn decided they would let the Belgians and French deal with them. He wanted to go after Kroner.

"OK, the big question is, is he the man at the top?" Kat asked.

"He is the only one I know. There may be others higher up, but I have never heard anything about them."

"Where does he work during the day, what is the name of his office?"

"I told you, I don't know."

"Does the name Zapf mean anything to you?"

"Zapf?" he said, sounding it out as a question, but it was clear that he knew the name.

"Solomon," she said, taking her KA-BAR from her pocket and opening the blade, "hold him still while I cut him a little."

"Wait! Yes, alright I know this …"

The words were just leaving his lips when the door burst open. Kat was knocked to the floor as Pascal barged in and started firing. He got off three rounds before Kat lunged from the floor and buried the blade of her knife in his skull. Pascal's knees buckled then flopped back into the companionway. Solomon had been hit in the throat and died seconds later. Quebedeaux died immediately, with two rounds in his chest.

"Jesus Christ, what the fuck was that?!" shouted Devlyn.

House came running down the stairs with his gun in hand and stopped at Pascal's body. "Holy fuck! What just happened? I thought this asshole was on … Solomon?" He saw his partner down.

"He's gone, House, he's gone."

The three agents sat together up in the wheelhouse while Devlyn called the task force to report what had happened and pass along the substance of Quebedeaux's interrogation. They were redirected to the April Marine in the port of Cannes. A cleaning crew would be waiting for them.

Kat curled up on the bench in the wheelhouse and watched Devlyn turn the Rebecca into the wind, setting the new course for Cannes, the Jewel of the Riviera.

The change in course brought them into calmer waters, a relief of sorts to House. The loss of Solomon hit him hard and he asked to return to Fort Meade for reassignment. Devlyn said he would take care of it.

House thanked him and moved a lounge chair out on the boat deck with Devlyn's bottle of single malt for company. He stayed there, staring out into the dark.

Kat decided to go down and stretch out on the huge bed. "Hold on a second, Katrina."

"What?"

"That stuff with Quebedeaux and the doc, you weren't kidding, were you? Where did that come from? I mean damn, when did you get so nasty?"

"You heard what Pascal said, Paul. I'm a whore, Anita Franco, a vicious predator, an assassin, and I owe it all to you." As she walked down the stairs, she said without looking back, "I'll come up after we dock."

CHAPTER 19

SHORT LEAVE IN PARIS

As they were finishing up with the cleaners, Devlyn told Kat that the National Security Police in Paris had requested that he come in for a debriefing. "Paul, there's something I need to deal with in Paris, so why don't I take care of the debriefing for you?"

"Great, I'll go ahead and set things up in Zürich and you can meet me there."

She took a flight up to the City of Lights and made a quick stop at the NSP headquarters and gave them the recording Solomon made of Quebedeaux's confession, which identified the members of his cell. They were impressed by the way she handled the interrogation. After about an hour's debriefing, she left and found a five-star hotel in the heart of the city and looked through the phone book for a gynecologist.

The names of the terrorists were put on a list with the heading, Le Plus Voulu (Most Wanted).

All were known criminals; their photos were circulated, and an intensive continent-wide search began. Within an hour of the publication the two women, Selina Josserand and Adrianne Isabelle, were found at a café in Paris. They didn't expect to be identified so they hadn't bother to hide. Their arrest was carried out without violence.

Vogelgrun, France

Four days later, the police were patrolling the D145 highway through Alsace and thought they recognized the male suspects in a group of bikers heading toward Germany. A roadblock was quickly set up at the traffic circle at Vogelgrun, just before the bridge over the Grand Canal d'Alsace, manned by both French and German police.

As soon as the bikers saw the roadblock, they wheeled around and ran straight into a wall of heavily armed police who had assembled to take them from behind. Something the Vietnam vets used to call a Mad Minute ensued and, when the fire fight was over, two French officers had been wounded and all 12 bikers were dead. All the names on Quebedeaux's list had been accounted for.

Paris

Hoping that the women might lead them to other Rote Faust cells, French Internal Security arranged to have them released. A team of plain clothes agents followed them, but, predictably, the women spotted the tail and tried to shake them off. It quickly turned into a car chase through Paris in heavy traffic. Racing through the crowded city, both the women and the police caused a number of collisions. Several people were hurt before the chaos ended in a big pile up. The driver of the police car was injured, and the women got away.

Another police car picked them up again a few minutes later and followed them to an apartment on the Rue Etienne Marcel in Pantin. The detectives watched as the women went into a graffiti covered building then called for backup.

Hours went by with no activity and, during that time, the agents back at HQ did a name search on the residents of the building. They came up with the name Darvell Debroux and alarms went off. Debroux was one of the men on the list who died out on the highway. The agents at the scene were ordered to move in and retake the women.

Using a battering ram, they knocked down the door and ran into the building expecting gun fire or, at the very least, some screaming. But there was none of that. They initially thought that the women had escaped.

But no, it did not end well for the women. They were found stuffed in a closet; their throats had been slashed. Their killer or killers probably left by the back door while the agents were waiting for backup.

Chapter 20

Paris

Monday, April 8, 1:45 pm

Kat found a very pleasant doctor who checked her over and assured her that she was both healthy and pregnant. It was a great relief to have her feelings confirmed. "You are about four to five weeks along and everything looks perfect."

"So it's going to be mid-December."

"That sounds about right, yes," she paused, considering her next question carefully, "You seem to be very tense. Is the something troubling you?"

"Work is… a little hectic just now."

"Must you continue working? Perhaps you should think about leaving your job for the sake of the child."

"You're probable right. I'll have to think seriously about that."

"Good. One more thing, will you be staying in Paris? You should be scheduling regular appointments to ensure that you are both healthy. I would be happy to see you right through until the birth."

"Honestly I'd love that, but it's not going to be possible."

"That is a shame Well, if you should change your mind… just give my office a call and we will fit you in."

While she was in the capital, Devlyn moved to Switzerland taking over a CIA safehouse in Zürich's District 4. He began assembling a new team from all over Europe.

As soon as they arrived at the safehouse they immediately began collecting intelligence on Helmut Kroner.

Devlyn asked the liaison at Europol to send him copies of Architectural Digest dealing with properties in Switzerland. They soon found the article Kat had mentioned and cross-referencing the property and the name Kroner they matched that with the address Quebedeaux had given them.

Kat stayed in Paris for a week shopping. It eased the stress she was suffering, and it was easy for her to stay off the terrorist's radar. But she had to set it aside and get back to work. Traveling first class to Zürich by train, she contemplated what lay ahead for her. If she remained with the Army, it would be a short life. Under the circumstances, it was likely to end long before her due date. Was there the slightest chance, any possibility at all, that she could leave it now?

A light rain had been falling on and off all day, making it feel more like late fall rather than spring. She was prepared for the weather with a warm sweater and a blue semi-transparent plastic hooded raincoat.

Lifting the hood over her head she ventured out and found the shower had become a downpour. Unconcerned, she opened the huge red, white and blue umbrella she found in Paris. It was able to protect everything but her new shoes.

Looking out at the dreary vista and listening to the rain beating down on her umbrella, she continued to reflect on how her life had changed so drastically, especially over the past two years. It was like she'd been strapped to a metronome that was gradually speeding up as gravity dragged it down. Would it stop before she hit the bottom?

She was almost certain that it would. It had to. Having the baby would save her and that gave her hope, something to celebrate.

Holding the umbrella as close as possible, she hurried across Bahnhofplatz to the platform shelter in the center of the street. Even under the shelter, she still needed the umbrella's protection while waiting for the number 3 Tram. That would take her north to the CIA safehouse where Devlyn's team was waiting.

It wasn't hard to maintain a celebratory mood even in a downpour. She was going to have a baby, so let it rain. While others competed for cabs, she was happy enough to wait for the tram. She had good news and she was going to hold on to it.

After checking the schedule on the glass wall behind her, she looked at her watch, calculating that the next tram would arrive in about five minutes.

The buoyant mood was tested when a tiny old man in a rumpled canvas coat and a knockoff Tilley hat, drew uncomfortably close. She looked down at him out of the corner of her eye and tried to warn him off with a glare.

It had no visible effect whatsoever.

The gnome-like creature barely came up to her shoulder. She marveled at the way nature took its revenge on some people as they grew old. She wondered what sins he had committed to be so callously disfigured. His body had obviously shrunk, but certain facial features had kept on growing long past the point when enough was enough. His long, wrinkled face was overshadowed by a disproportionately large nose. His ear lobes hung over his rumpled collar and his stubble covered chin hid most of his food-stained tie.

He kept looking up at her through cloudy basset-hound eyes and bushy eyebrows in desperate need of a trim. He was bringing her down and that ticked her off. She wasn't sure whether to pity him or just push him away.

He turned his whole body to face her, and she wondered if age had fused his neck so that he couldn't turn his head. He shuffled closer until he was pressed up against her. She glared at him again. That didn't work, so adopting the formal speech Germans seemed to reserve for lesser beings, she said, "I do not like being touched. Remove yourself."

He didn't move, but, instead, pointed to the umbrella. She realized that the gnome was trying to use her as a shield against the weather. He smiled and surprisingly spoke English to her and said, "You sound like you are from Berlin. The accent is very tricky, so well done Señora, it's a nice touch." His use of that title sent a twinge of electricity running up her spine. She took a few steps to the right. He followed her. "You are also very tall. Taller than I expected."

She glared again and said, "Go away!" as she took another step to the right.

"It is unusually cold today," he continued, and she looked around to see if anyone was watching.

The other people on the platform were diligently pretending not to notice, so she tried to ignore him as well. "It's because of the wind that comes up off Lake Zürich. Most people think it comes from the mountains, but no, it is from the lake. I know this."

She looked the other way. He tapped his foot on her suitcase and tugged on her coat. "Is this your first time in Zürich?"

She flashed on the image of throwing him under the approaching tram and almost smiled. Instead, she repeated, "Go away," and gave him a quick bump with her hip. It moved him, but he returned as if she was a magnet. He would not be put off. "I am getting very angry now", she said. "Go away."

"Uh hah," he said, as he touched the side of his nose with his finger, "I was warned about your temper."

"Excuse me?" she said. You have no idea, she thought. He tapped the side of his nose with his index finger again. If the movies were to be believed it was a signal from one grifter to another. "You are a delusional old man, now go away."

Thankfully, the tram screeched to a stop in front of the shelter and she closed the umbrella and hurried up the steps. He said nothing more for the moment but followed her on board like a miniature shadow.

Pulling off the hood, she sat on the outside seat on the right side of the car and placed her suitcase on the seat beside her. Clearly, she thought, this would end his game. It became painfully obvious that it hadn't. He was stronger than he looked and pushed her up against the suitcase. When there was just enough space, he hopped up beside her. She was forced to move the case to the floor to gain some distance but now she was stuck between the window and him. He had short legs, so his feet only just touched the floor. Turning his body, he looked up at her through those dog-like eyes and staring at her intently, he said, "Now, isn't this cozy?"

In exasperation, she felt she had to get it over with and said, "Alright, what is it? What do you want from me?"

"I wondered how long it would take."

"Well bravo, now you know. What do you want?" she said, but she knew that he was after the bounty.

"I must say that I almost did not recognize you with this new hair do.

I would not have thought it possible, but you are even more attractive. "Kat rolled her eyes and stepped away. He followed. "This style, it makes you look more... Uh, what is this word I'm looking for?" He paused. "Sophisticated? Yes, you look quite sophisticated."

"Oh, for God's sake. Listen to me, you ugly little man, if you persist with this harassment, I promise that this will not end well for you."

"On the contrary, Señora Franco, I think it will go very well for me." She felt the barrel of a gun against her ribs. "I know a man who is extremely anxious to meet you. It is worth a great deal of money to me if I take you to him. And I'm going to take you to him right now."

She focused on him, and quietly said, "Trust me. You really shouldn't do this."

"You think perhaps that someone will intervene on your behalf? My dear, this is Switzerland, no one would lift a finger to save you." When he looked about, people averted their eyes. "You see? You are completely alone on a crowded tram." He was right.

"I am getting off at the next stop."

"No."

"Are you going to shoot me here, in front of all these people?"

"You will do exactly what I say, or I will be forced to shoot you. It would be a shame to put a hole in such a beautiful creature as yourself." He prodded her with the gun. "Do you understand me now?"

"Oh yes," she said, as the tram was approaching the stop, "I understand perfectly, but I am getting off now." She looked down and saw that the gun was in his pocket. "This is your first kidnapping, isn't it?"

"What?"

"Just an observation, that's all." The tram stopped. "Shall we go?" she said, and stood up nearly causing him to fall to the floor.

Irritated, he hopped out of the way and looked up at her. She appeared very calm and unconcerned by the threat. He nervously backed out of the way. She then put her suitcase down and extended the handle, which in turn extended the distance between them and walked to the exit. He was forced to quicken his pace to follow her down the steps to the street.

As she opened the umbrella, he rushed to her side again and took the gun out of his pocket. Pressing it into her side. "Put that thing away, I know you won't shoot me. He wants me alive."

"Dead or alive the notice said."

Unimpressed, she shrugged.

He signaled that they should walk to the pedestrian crossing and then cross to the far curb.

Kelkbeirtestrasse and Badenerstrasse met at an acute angle, and on the apex was a newly restored building with the name Rosengarten painted high up on the stucco wall. Before the renovation, it had been a restaurant and it still had the appearance of one. That gave her an idea. She said, "Are you taking me to dinner Herr ..., what is your name?"

"Karpp, Colin Karpp," he said. He seemed flustered now and a little out of breath. "Why would I take you to dinner?"

"You expect to receive one hundred thousand Euros from Kroner for me."

"How do you know this?"

"You are not the first man to try."

"What happened to the others?"

"I killed them of course. You must know that if you survive and manage to turn me over to him, he will kill me. I should think that you would experience some guilt because of it. Perhaps you could ease your conscience a little by buying me dinner. Think of it as my last request."

"You killed the others?"

"Oh, please. Who do you think you are dealing with?"

"You are a cool one, I'll give you that. Alright, I like your attitude, I'll buy you dinner. But the Rosengarten is no longer a restaurant, it's a real estate agent's office."

"Ah, a pity. Perhaps there is a restaurant close by?"

"Perhaps."

"I'm getting tired of holding this thing, couldn't we get out of the rain first. Look, we could stand under that little roof at the end of the building while we look for a restaurant."

"Alright, fine." Traffic stopped for them as they hurried across the street. When they stepped up onto the sidewalk he said, "How did you know about Kroner?"

"We can talk as we walk there, it's so close. Tell me, Herr Karpp, you said that my hair style has altered my appearance."

"Yes?"

"Then how did you recognized me; I'm dying to know."

"But ..."

"I'll tell you how I know about Kroner in a moment, but first you must answer my question." She waited. "Come on, my shoes are going to be ruined."

He looked puzzled that she would worry about her shoes at a time like this but shrugged and followed along. "Well, you see my dear," he said, eager to demonstrate his powers of observation. They climbed the few steps up to a back door facing onto Kelkbeirtestrasse and stood under the overhang. "I never forget a face, especially a pretty one like yours. I read about you some time ago when you were traipsing around Europe. Remember that?" His face twisted into a gloating grin. "I knew him you know, Herbig. He needed my expertise every so often, so over the years I did quite a bit of work for him. It was a great loss to me financially when you ended his life."

"So, you know all about me then," she said, turning so that her back was against the door.

He faced her and smiled. "Most assuredly. Now, it is your turn."

"Well," she said, as she casually looked around. "Before I killed them, I persuaded them to tell me about Kroner." The intersection was quiet, there were no other pedestrians in sight and a three-sectioned trolley bus was just crossing Badenerstrasse, making the turn onto Kelkbeirtestrasse.

"You tortured them?"

"Tortured them? Well, perhaps a little." There was a stop a few yards behind her. She let go of the suitcase and looked behind him as if she had spotted something of interest. He turned to look. Lowering the umbrella to rest on his shoulder, effectively hiding him from the passing bus, she said, "Since you know me so well, this shouldn't come as a surprise."

"A surprise?" He turned back. "But I can't see with that in the ..." he began, but it was already too late for him.

Her hands had gripped him around his chin and the crown of his head and in that instant, he understood and was terrified. "No."

"I'm afraid so. Goodnight." With a sharp twist to the left and back, she snapped his neck. It was mercifully quick.

The gun fell from his dead hand and clattered to the concrete floor. She caught him before he fell and lowered him carefully onto the landing. She placed him so that he looked as if he was just sitting there. A homeless man sleeping on the steps. She scooped up the gun and put it in her purse, folded the umbrella, and dragging the suitcase she hurried down the steps.

Her timing was perfect, arriving at the stop just as the bus doors opened. She stepped on at the front just as a man exited by the back. Tensed she watched him, wondering how he would react when he discovered the body.

She needn't have worried, the old man was quite right about the Swiss, he paid no attention to Karpp. Apparently, they didn't care to get involved. No one on the bus paid any attention to her either. Calmly she found a spot at the back, settled into her seat, and closed her eyes.

An estate agent opened the door of the Rosengarten and bumped into the man. "Oh God." The smell of feces caught his breath. "Hey, you. You have to move. You can't sleep here." He gave him a kick to wake him up. "Hey! Old man, you ..." Karpp's hand dropped from his lap and it was obvious that he was dead. Angry that a homeless man had the effrontery to die on his doorstep and ruin his day, the agent leaned in the doorway and shouted, "Clara, there is a tramp at the doorway, dead. Call someone to clean it up, I'm running late."

Kat was far away by then and wondering what had come over her. How could she be so calm after what she had just done? She should be feeling some remorse, something. But she didn't ..., not a twinge. Maybe it hadn't hit her yet. It was possible that it never would.

It had been 28 days since the attack on the dacha, and the trail of bodies she was leaving behind was growing longer all the time. Staring at her reflection in the rain spattered window, she felt confused, how had this happened to her?

She remembered the first time on that mountain in Honduras when she felt so revolted and ashamed. How had killing people become such an easy thing to do?

Zürich, District 4

4:40 pm

It took some time to work her way back to the safehouse on Zypressenstrasse. Turning onto the short walkway, Kat stopped and tilted the umbrella back to look up at the white stucco facade and count the floors. The CIA's facility was known locally as an apartment hotel for business travelers. The neighbors were used to seeing different people come and go all the time, so her arrival with a suitcase was unremarkable.

There was a man staring at her from a fourth-floor window. She was going to acknowledge him, but he disappeared. Devlyn said they would be waiting for her. She folded the umbrella and stood before the camera over the door.

There was a buzz and the door clicked open. The tiny lobby was dark, lit only by the light that came through the glass door. There were apartments on either side and a stairway at the back to the right. The stairwell had a landing between each floor and was open to the ceiling above the fifth floor.

A door opened on the second floor as she made the landing, and a young couple came out. The woman approached her smiling, "You must be Katrina," she said. Kat recognized her accent from her time at flight school in Alabama. She was in her late twenties, shorter than Kat, very slim and attractive with an intelligent face, and keen blue eyes. She tucked her medium length blonde hair back behind her ear and extended her hand in greeting. She couldn't be a field agent, Kat thought, she seemed too open for that.

"Yes, hi," said Kat.

"I'm Meadow Fields. Awful isn't it, Meadow Fields. I mean, like what parents in their right mind would do that to a kid? It says a lot about my parents. Oh, and this is Conner Downs, my partner. We came from Copenhagen for this little party." She sounded so enthusiastic.

"Hi," said Connor, without a smile. He reached out from behind Meadow to shake her hand. "Pleased to meet you." He was about six feet tall and very fit. A good-looking prep school jock, with soft hands. Kat pegged him as an analyst as well. "That's quite a grip you have there."

"I've heard that. Hello Conner."

"Devlyn is in the ready room, why don't you leave your suitcase here and head on up? Conner will take it to your room later."

"OK, thanks."

The door on the other side of the landing opened and Kat turned to see another couple "That's Maddix Quinn and Samantha Carpenter," Meadow said. "They're from Rome."

They waved and said, "Hi." Kat smiled back.

"Samantha added, "We've heard a lot about you from House before he left. He said you play a rough game."

"I don't play games."

"Uh huh. Yeah, well it's a pleasure to finally meet you."

"Thanks." They didn't look like field agents either. What was Devlyn planning to do with these people?

On the third floor, two more stepped into the procession. "The pretty one is Le-Ann Joyce," said Meadow, "and the homely one is Ted."

"Hey!" Ted protested.

"Hi Ted, do you have a last name?"

"Actually," said Meadow, "he has two. It speaks volumes about him."

"It's Scott-Buckner," said Ted, "and don't you pay any attention to Meadow, I think she was dropped as a child."

"His name makes him sounds like an author, doesn't it?" Meadow said. "He's moody like an author too. They're from Madrid. You spent some time there recently I hear."

"I did, and Rome for a while too. Hola Ted and Le-Anne," Kat said. Le-Anne was put together like an athlete. Ted was harder to peg. Then she saw the calluses on his knuckles and realized he was a fighter. Now, they were field agents.

"Yo! People, wait-up I'm coming too," said a voice from two flights below.

"Oh, that's Al Jordan. She's from Wichita, Kansas, so when she tells you anything, consider the source."

"Oh, well fuck-you-very-much, Meadow. And I agree with Ted, it's brain damage for sure," she said, as she caught up to them. Al was a nice-looking farm girl with a build like a wrestler. She had a round freckled face, framed with curly red hair and green eyes. "And there's nothing wrong with Kansas, Meadow."

"Did I say there was?"

"Hi Katrina, I'm Alexandra and you'll meet my partner in a second. The big lug is upstairs."

"She's a real cowgirl. I've known her since freshmen year at UCLA Berkley," Meadow said, "so I know whereof I speak."

When Kat reached the fourth floor, the man from the window was standing in the open barring her way. As advertised, he was large and thickly muscled, making Kat think that he and Al were well matched. He stared at Kat angrily as he gripped both sides of the door jamb with his big vice-like hands. "You must be the infamous Katrina Fernando," he said, looking her up and down. "You're late."

"Make that, you're late, Ma'am. And who-the-fuck are you?"

"Kat, that's my partner, Jamie Nunez," Al said sheepishly. "What's the matter with you, Jamie?"

"Tell me, Special Agent Nunez, are you going to get out of my way?" When Kat put the tip of her umbrella against his chest Nunez looked as if he was going to explode. She smiled and firmly pushed him out of the way. "Thank you. Oh, just so you know, my friends call me Kat, but to you I'm Senior Special Agent Fernando."

"Yes Ma'am." He was something else before he came to CI. With that attitude, she guessed, he was a Marine. Once a Marine always a Marine.

She walked in leaving her umbrella by the door. The war room, if one could call it that, had the feel of a high school computer lab and conference area. The fabric clad cubicles were covered with research notes. Laptops and reference material filled the space on every desk. Devlyn stood in the far corner with a cup of coffee.

"How was Paris?"

"It will never change."

Beside him on the left was a counter with a sink and a coffee maker. On the wall behind were the security monitors linked to cameras inside and outside the building front and back. The long wall on his right was covered with notes, photos and diagrams of the subject's estate, some of them were connected by colored string to an enlarged map of Zürich's District 4. Kat recognized some photos from the article in the Architectural Digest.

"Vacationing in Paris in the middle of a mission?" said Nunez.

It was a challenge that Kat ignored, but all the same Devlyn intervened. "You don't want to be messing with Col. Fernando, Nunez, she'd eat you for breakfast." With that warning and Kat's remark about not playing games, the others filed in quietly and went to their workstations. Devlyn said, "But you know, he brings up a good point, what kept you?"

"You can't rush Paris," she said simply, and sat down at the long rectangular table. "Actually, there was something else. When I arrived this afternoon, I was met by someone at the train station."

"Oh, more paparazzi?"

"No, a bounty hunter." She set her handbag on the table. "He wanted to take me to our friend Kroner."

Everyone stopped and stared at her. "It was a mistake he's not coming back from. I took a tour of District 4 to make sure I wasn't followed."

"You killed him?" Devlyn asked.

"He recognized me, called me Anita Franco, put a gun to my ribs and told me he was going to collect the reward for me dead or alive. So, yeah, I killed the son-of-a-bitch. Is there any coffee in that pot, Nunez?"

Nunez suddenly decided that it would be a good idea to follow Devlyn's advice. "Sure, how do you take it?"

"Black," Kat said.

"What did you do with him?" Devlyn asked, as if he were only mildly curious.

"I broke his neck and sat him up against a building like a homeless man."

"I don't think they have homeless men in Switzerland."

"Well, let's just pretend that they do now."

"Were you able to find out who he was?" Devlyn asked, as Nunez carefully put her coffee down beside her and went to his cubicle.

"Colin Karpp, I think he was a grifter, said he knew Herbig and Petrus."

Devlyn poured himself another cup and joined her at the table. "And nobody saw you?"

"No one." He leaned back and took a sip and then held the cup between his hands for the warmth. The others were paying attention as she continued, "I also think that the incident pretty much tells us that I'm not going to be much use to the team. Not if I can be recognized by their people wherever I go."

"That is a problem," Devlyn said quietly, and asked Quinn to check the police radio traffic to see what, if anything, was being said about Karpp. He tasked Carpenter to dig up whatever she could about the old man and then told the rest to get back to work.

Quinn said that the police had found the body very quickly and started going door to door trying to find a witness. So far, their canvasing had turned up nothing.

Within minutes they had identified the victim. Kat had pegged him. He had been a con artist, but his file said that he had either reformed, or retired from the game.

Quinn said, "The police are saying that the killing appears to be a professional hit. They're saying his past has finally caught up to him and they don't sound terribly interested. The lead investigator said that the killer has probably already left the country and they weren't going to waste time trying to find him. So, I guess that means you're in the clear, Special Agent Fernando."

"Paul, can I speak to you in private?"

"Sure, out on the landing." They left the room and Devlyn closed the door behind them.

"Since I can't be part of this mission anymore, I'm going to resign my commission and go back to the States."

"No, that doesn't work for me."

"Tough nuggies. Listen, I'm tired, where do I bunk down?"

"Main floor across from Jordan and Nunez. The key is in the door."

She opened the door and said, "Goodnight everyone."

"Aren't you going to eat something?"

"No, I'm done for the day," she said. Devlyn watched her from the rail until she disappeared on the main floor dragging her suitcase.

"God-fucking-damn," he said quietly, then went back inside.

No Sacrifice Too Great

4:32 am

As he lay on his bed that night, Devlyn tried to come up with a way to keep Kat involved. The last thing he wanted was for her to leave. It suddenly occurred to him that the very thing that made her appear to be a liability was an advantage.

Since Kroner wanted her so badly, she should give herself up. With that problem solved, he fell asleep. He was awakened by a quiet alarm that told him someone had gone into the war room. He looked at his watch, 04:30. "Who the fuck is that?" He jumped out of bed, threw on some clothes and headed down the stairs. The door was open and there she was, dressed for work and making coffee.

"What's the matter? Couldn't sleep?" he asked.

She barely turned her head. "I've got too much on my mind," she said, picking up her cup.

"Is there enough in that pot for two?"

"Knock yourself out," she said, as she walked back to the table. He filled his cup then joined her.

He concentrated on his coffee in silence for a while and she wasn't going to interrupt him. At last, he put his cup down and said, "I've been thinking about how to get at Kroner. The thing is ..., you are the key."

"Me?! Paul, you know if I can contribute, I will, but ..."

"Hear me out. The way we can get this guy is if we send you in."

She sat up straight. "What, alone?" she said.

"You've done it before."

"Yeah, your Trojan Horse gambit. I got knifed doing that."

"Kat, we need to know what role Kroner is playing in this, and, like you said, he wants you delivered to him alive."

"Sure, so he can kill me himself."

"We don't know that. As far as we know he has no reason to want you dead."

"As far as we know."

"He thinks you are an assassin, maybe he just wants you to kill someone for him. Maybe he has a higher up who wants you alive because he wants you to kill someone."

"That's a lot of maybes for me to put my neck under the blade, don't you think?"

He sat back and ran his fingers through his hair. "Do you remember that research I started when we were in The Hague?"

"Yeah, the first one to jump back into the market."

"Right. I've been watching it very carefully, waiting for someone to start buying when things hit rock bottom."

"And ...?" She paused, waiting for him to fill in the blank.

"After the soccer team massacre, just before the President gave his speech, someone bought a shit load of gold. Tons of it! He bought more than some countries keep on reserve. Then a couple of days later he sold it all, causing a huge negative wave.

"I told you that all it would take was one guy to start the buying and the market would recover. After the Quebedeaux gang was taken down, a German broker was buying in New York, London, Paris, Stockholm, Hong Kong, Shenzhen. You see where I'm going with this? It's working just like it did after 9/11, and the guy behind it is spending billions and stands to make trillions in the recovery."

"I can't even begin to comprehend a number that big. Your point is?"

"My point is, that guy is not Kroner. He's up to his neck in it for sure, but, Kat, he isn't remotely on the same level as the guy who started this. My gut tells me that the guy at the top needs Anita Franco to do something for him, something only Anita can do."

"So, you're saying Kroner won't try to kill me, he'll just hand me over to some super villain who wants to use me."

"Exactly."

"And then he'll kill me."

"Look, if we get Kroner to talk to us then we'll find out who he works for and this whole thing will be over."

"And that would be worth sacrificing my life?"

"You swore an oath to protect America with your life."

"I've heard this speech before."

"Americans are dying here, good decent Americans who never did anything to deserve what's happening to them."

"You've said that too."

"I believe that the only reason this is happening is so that this son-of-a-bitch can get richer and more powerful than he already is. The world doesn't need another Mad Fuck calling the shots."

"You're talking about a man like Arnulf Jäger, the guy who wants to be Emperor of Europe."

"Yeah, a fruitcake just like that. We have to stop him! So, Kat ..., you tell me. Is there any sacrifice too great?"

"OK, you've made your point, but I'm not going to just walk up to his gate and say take me, I'm yours."

"Have you got a better plan?"

"No, but I'll try to think of one."

The Glass House

5:45 am

Kat stewed about it in silence and then she looked at the picture of the glass house pinned to the wall. Kat asked Samantha for a copy of the article. The house was designed by Spanish architect Rodrigo Hermida, known for his extreme and exotic designs with glass and steel.

The architectural tour de force was a series of stepped glass clad platforms that seemed to float above the earth on gracefully curved struts of welded steel. The house was set in the center of forty acres of rugged, forested land on the gentle slope of a mountain overlooking Zürich. The photos conveniently showed every aspect of the structure and much of the landscape.

"It wouldn't be a problem to locate him in that," said Quinn. "We'd also have a pretty good idea of who was with him."

Downs added, "With that landscape to cover us, we could get close to the house, blow the door and take him."

"Kat and I have been working on a different plan," said Devlyn. "He wants Kat alive, so she is going in alone."

"What's plan B?" Meadow asked.

"There is no plan B. We have to keep this as quiet as possible if we are going to find the man at the top," Devlyn said.

"But Sir, it would be suicide. You can't let her do this."

"Look guys, I appreciate your support, but bottom line is they're after me," Kat said. "Inevitably they're going to get me, so I'd sooner do this on my own terms. I'm not going to just walk up to the gate and give myself up. There is another way in. Devlyn agrees that this is the best option we have."

"This is insane," Alexandra said. "We have to ..."

"OK, shut it! All of you!" Devlyn said, banging his fist down on the table. "I'm not running a democracy here. This is the way it's going to be. Fernando does a solo insertion and that's the end of it."

Kat waited until they calmed down, then said, "Alright, I've made a list of the things I'll need to take with me." She tossed it in the middle of the table. "Can one of you source these things for me ASAP?"

Leigh Ann snapped up the paper and read it over. "Yeah, I can fill this out for you. Thanks to our CIA hosts we have most of it here in the armory."

"OK then, if there's nothing else I'll get myself ready and go in tonight," she said, stood up and left the room.

Chapter 21

This Is Death Calling

10:00 pm

The voice said, "Hello? Who is calling please?" in crisp Swiss German.

"Good evening Herr Kroner, this is Anita Franco. I understand you have been looking for me."

"Anita Franco?! How ...?"

"Let's not waste time, Herr Kroner. There isn't anybody I can't get to if the price is right. I understand you have a contract out on me. Can anyone kill me for you, or just professionals?"

"No, no. There has been a misunderstanding, that is all. It's not a contract in the usual sense, I merely wish to invite you here to respond to a request. May I ask how you became aware of this invitation?"

"Oh, so everyone who has tried to kill me simply misread your memo? Herr Kroner, do you honestly expect me to believe you? Come on, humor me, why do you want me dead? Have I done something to offend you?"

"It is true that I am deeply troubled by the way you have been killing my employees but, I assure you, I never wanted you dead. As a matter of fact, I have a client who wishes to avail himself of your services."

"It seems like an odd way of going about it. Usually, all it requires is an ad in the International Herald Tribune saying, 'Darling daughter, all is forgiven, please come home', and a phone number. It's all there on the website."

"What website?"

"What web ..., my God, who put you in charge? Never mind, it's been taken down now. I'm sure the people who tried to collect the reward might have saved themselves a great deal of pain and suffering and ..., of course, death if you had followed procedures. Water under the bridge as they say. Oh, I've taken the liberty of adding your grounds security to the list of the dead."

"Don't be absurd, you can't kill my bodyguards." he said, as his illusion of safety crumbled.

"You misunderstand me. I'm telling you that they are already dead. The men inside with you will be joining them in a moment."

"You can't be serious. I don't believe you."

"You can't possibly imagine how little I care about what you believe, Herr Kroner. We will have our little face to face chat very soon. But I insist that you be alone for that. I'd hate to be interrupted."

He laughed. "You are deluding yourself if you think I can be intimidated so easily. I can't fathom why he wants you alive, but those were his instructions. So yes, we will have that conversation but, on my terms and conditions. You will arrive at my gate in one hour unarmed. You will hold your hands up and peacefully surrender yourself to my guards."

"That would be impossible. As I told you, they are all dead."

He covered the mouthpiece and gave some hasty instructions to the guards in his office. One of them picked up a radio while the other went to the window. Then Kroner said, "You don't even know where I live."

Two bullets from her M24 SWS sniper rifle pierced the window in rapid succession. The first slug deformed slightly when it hit the tempered glass, so when it struck the man at the window his head exploded like a pumpkin. The second bullet had no resistance and caught the man with the radio before he could duck, leaving a hole in his head the size of a silver dollar.

Kroner sat frozen in his chair. When he realized that there wasn't going to be a third bullet, he dropped the phone and collapsed to the floor. He recovered his senses, reached for it, and screamed, "Where are you?!"

Answering calmly, she said, "I'm just outside looking at you Herr Kroner. I have one or two other little details to attend to just now. It would be safer for you to remain in your office. I don't want you to be in the way when I enter."

The guards at the front heard the breaking glass and came running out into the open to investigate. They had no idea what was happening and put themselves right in her line of fire. Two more shots and they were down.

Maddix had told her that Kroner had eight men in his protection detail. Counting the four security men in the forest and the four she just eliminated, she thought that Kroner might be alone now.

"Herr Kroner? Ah ..., Herr Kroner?" she called from the door. "Are you still in there, Herr Kroner?" Her voice was menacingly calm.

She entered very carefully in case there were other security people lurking about that were missed in the count. There were none, but as she reached out and turned the handle of his office door, bullets from an automatic weapon shredded it. He kept pulling the trigger even after the magazine was empty.

The moment she heard the clicking of the empty chamber she pushed on the door with the barrel of her SIG and lobbed in a flash bang grenade.

The explosion disabled Kroner. She found him on the floor crying pathetically. When her boots stopped in front of his face he said, "Please ..., don't kill me," In that moment as he begged for his life a terrible irony dawned on her that she was no better than the men she was hunting.

"Please," he said, with his eyes shut tight, weeping, and unable to stop. She towered over him.

His cries filled the room. He was crouched down on his elbows and knees with his fingers laced over his head. As if that would protect him, she thought. He looked so small and pathetic in the center of the big room. She was in no hurry. She would wait until he gave some sort of sign that he was ready to talk.

Eventually he stopped sniveling. He unlaced his fingers and looked up slowly, like a tourist taking in the Statue of Liberty. Her eyes were cold and black, completely devoid of feeling. She was not Liberty, she was Death. Her beautiful face made the vision all the more horrifying.

He closed his eyes again and waited for what was coming next. "Open your eyes," she said quietly, and he did. "You know what I came for."

"Please ..."

"No! You don't get to ask for mercy. Who is that client you mentioned?"

"Can I at least get up off the floor?"

"No, I want his name," she said, as the mouth of her gun moved forward slowly until it kissed his forehead. "Give me ... his name."

"He will kill me."

"You say that as if you think you have a future, Herr Kroner ..., you don't." Her beautiful mouth formed those cold words slowly and quietly, like daggers of ice. "It's just a matter of how long it will take and how much pain I will make you feel before I put you down. It's entirely up to you."

His mouth went dry. "Please ...," he rasped, "I need some water."

She lost it. The ice Queen suddenly vanished as she shrieked, "NEED?! You need something? The young women on that bus needed to live, to go home to their families! The couples dragged from their beds and murdered in the street needed to live, the hundreds of people you slaughtered in that theater, they needed to keep on breathing. It's because of you and that man you are protecting ..., that they are all gone. So, tell me his name!"

"Please!"

"No ..., I need his name, Herr Kroner! I need his goddamn NAME!" She began poking him with the gun leaving small, red, doughnut shaped welts on his shiny bald cap. "I will ask you one last time. Give me his name!" Her voice went quiet again as if the Ice Queen had returned. "But trust me Helmut ..., this is the last time I will ask you before you begin to bleed."

Any thought he may have had of resisting her, instantly evaporated. "It's Hunter, his name is Arnulf Hunter, he is a German."

"But Hunter is an English name not German. Where does he live?"

"In Umbria, he runs an Equity Fund out of Italy; Thecla, Alcon, Lawton, Echart & Norden."

"That is a mouthful, they wouldn't use that on the letterhead," she said.

"No, they use the first letter of each name."

"TALEN," she said.

"Yes."

Then something inside her clicked. "Wait a second, Arnulf Hunter runs Talen?" Her brain shifted gears and she remembered something. "And Arnulf is a combination of the German words eagle and wolf. It's not a common name, is it?"

"I don't know, I suppose not."

"Holy shit! And Hunter in German is Jäger. This is incredible, don't you see? Arnulf Jäger runs Talen and Talen is Rote Faust. You're working for Arnulf Jäger? Of course, the man who would be king. Where is he now, in Italy or Germany? Tell me everything about him. We have plenty of time, so don't leave anything out."

THE JÄGER STORY

It was as if the flood gates opened and the history of Jäger and Rote Faust spilled out of him.

"Jäger is an East German," Kroner said, "He is the son of a Nazi war criminal, SS Colonel Felix Jäger. The senior Jäger evaded capture for a while hiding in Stuttgart but was never able to get his hands on his looted fortune. Thanks to the efforts of his banker, my father, it remained safe here in Zürich until his youngest son was able to take possession.

"Arnulf is an awkward, ugly man but he is brilliant. He took that modest fortune and made it swell into the billions. Publicly, he is a benefactor to many worthwhile charities. People admire him because he is an engaging host, a shrewd businessman and an advisor to the leaders of Europe.

"Like his father, he has dedicated his life to the acquisition of unlimited power and wealth by any means. His ultimate goal is to hold the highest office in Europe.

"Jäger is like a giant jellyfish with thousands of poisonous tentacles that reach deep into government agencies and corporations. His touch is either paralyzing, murderous, or completely corrupting."

Kroner told her about the Golden Fortress Arnulf built on the ruins of an ancient monastery in Umbria. As he told the story he began to relax, as if he had forgotten how perilous his situation was.

"Jäger's interest in the Spanish architect influenced me to buy this house."

"I'm not interested in your house. Tell me about the security at the Golden Fortress."

Kroner's security service had created it, so he knew all about the extensive security force Jäger kept and the defenses of the fortress. Including the network of explosives around the perimeter set up by Jesús Maria Etxebarria. "There are only two ways up to the fortress," he said. "There is a narrow road that winds up the mountain and no one gets beyond the gate without an invitation and a retinal scan. The other way in is from the air."

"Do you know where the bomb maker is? Does he stay in the fortress?"

"No, he has a house in Peredicci."

"Does Jäger want to kill me?"

"He will ask you to kill Mogilevski for him first but, yes, when that is done, he will kill you. You can't get to him and you won't stop him."

Chapter 22

The New Mission

Wednesday

Devlyn took charge of Kroner and immediately informed his contact at Europol that Jäger should be arrested. They took Kroner back to the safehouse and kept him confined while Devlyn checked in with G-2. On orders from Fort Meade, Devlyn borrowed a CIA jet to take he and Kroner to the States.

As the senior agent now, Kat remained in Zurich to shut down the operation. For the remainder of the team, the situation seemed to be under control, the terrorism would stop, and everything would go back to the way it was. But that only lasted about four hours. They had all underestimated Jäger's political influence and his hold on public opinion.

Jäger denied having anything to do with Rote Faust and there were millions of followers who believed that he could do no wrong. It was generally viewed that the Americans had trumped up these ridiculous charges against him because of his growing anti-American rhetoric

Back in America, by 7:00 am the twenty-four-hour news cycle picked up on the redacted story of the arrest of Kroner and was demanding Jäger's arrest.

The European media was unevenly split. The right was sympathetic to the demonstrations in the streets for a Free Europe. The loudest voices were Jäger supporters. They said the only evidence to support the American claim was the fabricated story from a man the American's had in custody and refused to identify.

Jäger continued to appear in the media, and no matter what the media said about him, he said they were all lies, and his supporters believed everything he said. Detractors were abused and beaten, critics received death threats and the attacks on Americans continued.

An attempt was made to go after Jäger but the American's met with roadblocks and red tape at every turn. It became increasingly apparent that in Europe it would be political suicide to oppose him. He remained a free man and apparently destined to run a new and more powerful Pan European congress.

Kat received orders to remain in the safehouse pending a new assignment. What that assignment would be was still in the development stage.

CIA Safehouse

The following day was quiet in the safehouse. Kat was unaware that Devlyn's plane had not yet reached Maryland. Her team was getting ready to move out of their temp quarters when she called a meeting.

"We are all done here, Special Agent Fernando," Nunez said. "What are you going to do now, give us a goodbye speech?"

"Have you always been an asshole, Nunez, or is this a new thing with you?" Kat asked.

"Hey, you can't ..."

"Oh, but I can, so shut the fuck up and listen for a change. I've been thinking of a plan to go after Jäger in Italy and I need to go there to do a little recon work."

"Have you received new orders?" Nunez asked.

"No."

"Well then you can't just take off and start your own mission," he said.

"In the absence of Special Agent Devlyn, I am the acting commander of the 66th Brigade, so I direct our operations in Europe. Do you have a problem with that?"

"Some of us do, yeah. You were out of control when you stormed the

Kroner house."

"You think it was excessive?"

"Yeah, I do. You killed a lot of people."

"Anybody else feel that way?" No one said anything. "No? OK look, I'll be straight with you, I'm going off the reservation on this one. I'm prepared to go it alone; however, I could use some back up. So, I'm asking for volunteers to come along."

"Going rogue could end your career," said Alexandra, "and anyone who goes with you is putting their head on the block right next to yours. I'm sorry but I can't do that."

"I understand. Anyone else want out?" She wasn't a bit surprised when Jamie Nunez agreed with his partner. Le-Ann and Ted were out as well.

Meadow said, "It is going to cost money to get there and get supplies. If you go off on your own who is going to pay for it?"

"Money is the least of my problems, so you let me worry about that."

"Oh, well OK then, I'm in."

"If she's going then so am I," Conner said.

Samantha and Maddix talked it over quietly, then said they were in too.

"Thank you, guys. OK the rest of you can return to your previous stations with my thanks, it's been a pleasure."

As soon as they left, she sat down with her new team and told them how the plan was going to work.

PART 3

Chapter 23

Meeting in Rome

11:40 am

Traveling separately, they met at Kat's hotel in Rome and assigned tasks to get the mission under way. Samantha was to find out what she could about Peredicci, Maddix and Conner were responsible for procuring the weapons and transportation and Meadow was to find a hotel in the general vicinity of Peredicci. The cars were left in the underground parking with the weapons stashed in their trunks. After dinner, they all met in Kat's room to go over the next phase of her plan. Samantha read from a brochure describing the village of Peredicci and the abbey that once occupied the top of the mountain. "There was a monastery there once, the French blew it up leaving a foundation. I gather Jäger built his fortress on that. This part might be useful, the monks had built paths all over the mountain with lookout and rest spots. Lots of tourists use them so that could be a way to get close to the top."

"Does it say anything about the fortress building?"

"No, that's it."

"I read that many abbeys had their kitchens and storage rooms in the cellars," said Maddix. "I wonder how much if the original foundation was saved."

"Interesting information. Good job, guys, I think we're all set to go. Meadow found a place for us to stay at the Hotel San Francesco in Poggio Bustone, it's not too far from Peredicci. We'll drive up to Umbria this afternoon and check in. I'll start my recon tomorrow."

Poggio Bustone

Few tourists realize that April is such a wonderful time to visit Umbria. The sun was shining, the days were warm, and everything looked pristine. At first light, it was cold and there was a heavy mist that covered the valley. Kat dressed for birding and hiking with good boots, a warm vest, a hat and gloves. She also had a pair of birder glasses, a book of African and Southern European birds and a guidebook of Umbria. She left the hotel without speaking to anyone and headed for Peredicci.

It would have been a lovely drive to the village from her hotel. But the view from the narrow, winding roads, through stunning farmland and small villages was obscured by fog. The road dipped and curved up and down small mountains and valleys and even though she wasn't able to enjoy the scenery, it gave her time to get familiar with the route. When the time came, and she knew it would, she could get away from there as quickly as possible.

She arrived at the foot of the mountain and parked on the lake side of Via Panoramica, a narrow road with a scenic viewing area overlooking the Lago Peredicci. In case she was being observed, she spent some time looking out over the lake. The entrance to the web of paths was easy to find, and she hiked up casually looking around for signs that she may be observed. After an hour, she thought it best to move on.

She drove by the house where Kroner had said the Basque bomber lived, but there was no sign of life. She would check on him again later. Leaving the car in the lot at the side of the Hotel Lido, she walked around the village like a tourist, taking pictures and looking around.

The people were younger than she expected and looked more like tourists than locals. They looked like office workers. She drove back to her hotel wondering what brought them all to that little town. She sat in her room thinking about what she had seen and whether her plan still made sense. Where were the old people? Did Jäger control the village? He's a control freak so is it possible that he bought up the place and got rid of the villagers?

She ate dinner alone in the hotel dining room and didn't see the others before she retired for the night.

Back to Peredicci

Acknowledging her team with a quick smile from across the room at breakfast, Kat exchanged some comments about the weather in the lobby. Then they met again outside as they walked to their cars to talk about what they had learned so far.

Kat returned to Peredicci and explored the small mountain roads, looking for the one that led up to the abbey. Eventually, she found it after passing through a small community of big houses. The road wound up the east side of the mountain and ended at the abbey gate. She parked the car, got out and began snapping pictures.

Two machine gun toting guards appeared at the gate moments after she arrived. There had to be a camera watching the entrance and she wondered if there were cameras everywhere. Smiling brightly, she said hello, but they weren't interested in being friendly.

"You can't be here, signora. Go now."

She kept the smile as she said, "My, what big guns you have. I'm sorry for the intrusion, gentlemen, but I've heard so much about the abbey and the birds that nest around here. I thought I should make a point of coming to see it. I was hoping you would let me take some pictures up there."

"Not possible," the guard said. "It is forbidden," he said, and became more threatening when he chambered a round. "Get in your car and go now."

She quickly raised her hands and demonstrated a very convincing look of alarm. "Of course, I wasn't ... ah ... well, if it's all the same to you, I'll just go then."

She couldn't turn around on the narrow road, so she had to back up until she came to a driveway some distance down the road.

She finished her tour by driving all the way around the mountain and then around the lake, looking for a better view of what was on top.

From the best spots, what she could see over the treetops could only be described as a fiery golden beacon, glowing in the sun. She couldn't see anything other than the points of the unconventional golden towers. She took her time snapping pictures from every location while looking for other security cameras.

In the process, she found a foot path leading up the side of the mountain from the Via Panoramica.

Remembering what she was told about the mountain being a mine field, she decided to explore it when she had more time. She found a good spot to step off the path undetected. After marking it with a piece of wool pulled from her sweater, she returned to the hotel in Poggio Bustone.

Chapter 24

Enemy Territory

4:30 pm

Kat sent Meadow and Conner to Peredicci to get a room at the Hotel Lido. Their job was to spot Etxebarria and keep him under surveillance. "If you have an opportunity to eliminate him take it, then head to Rome and fly back to the States."

"We can't just kill the guy," said Meadow. "We're analysts not assassins, Kat."

"Meadow, listen to me. Our mandate is to stop the terrorism. There is a time for gathering intel and assessing the enemy's intelligence capabilities, and that part of the job is done. Now the job is to neutralize the enemy and there is only one way we are going to be able to do that here. Are you following me?"

"Colonel ..."

"No, listen, Meadow. We are front line soldiers now, boots on the ground. At the risk of sounding like Devlyn, we are at war. What we're doing here is in the defense of our country. Jäger must be stopped and it's up to us to get the job done. Have I made myself clear?"

"Yes Ma'am."

"Can you do this?"

She looked at Conner and said, "Yes Ma'am."

Establishing Her Cover

10:35 am

Kat stayed in Poggio Bustone birdwatching while Maddix and Samantha checked out and drove to Peredicci. After scouting around, they checked into the Hotel del Lago, a nice hotel across the small bay from the mountain. Maddix's job was to park on the Via Panoramica and keep a lookout while Kat made her second probe up the mountain. Samantha was on the radio keeping the team up to date on each other's movements. Kat arrived at noon and started bird watching on the far side of the lake gradually making her way around to the Via Panoramica. While taking pictures of every bird that flew by, mostly sparrows, she looked around for hidden cameras. Her second hike up the path would take her to her wool marker and then off the trail into the minefield. Maddix had been dropped off by Samantha earlier and was leaning against the rail overlooking the village, sketching the scenes in pencil. They studiously ignored each other.

The celestial powers all seemed to be in sync that day. Her mood was good; the day had warmed up considerably. A dog lay in the shade of a parked car with its eyes closed. It seemed that only the birds and Kat felt the need to move about. She made a show of looking out over the lake and to her surprise she spotted a great egret flying in her direction. According to the bird book, this was a rare sighting in the area. They were generally found further north in the Emilia - Romagna region. She noted it in her bird book in case someone was watching. As she followed its progress, she also noticed of two members of her team approaching from the west.

Meadow and Conner were taking a walk along the Via Panoramica holding hands and paid no attention to her. They were admiring the village and the conical mountain on the other side of the lake. Conner pointed out a small boat being rowed away from a dock at the foot of the mountain and Meadow expressed that it was all too romantic for words. They disappeared down the path to the village talking quietly.

The egret flew right over Kat and up the mountain where it settled in a tree and was lost from sight. Casually she crossed the road, looked up in the direction of the bird with her binoculars and began walking up the path.

The tree cover was quite dense and only a short bit of the path could be seen from the road so, in a matter of seconds, she was out of view. A few minutes later, she found the wool that marked her point of departure and stepped off the path heading up the mountain.

LIDO HOTEL

1:00 pm

Samantha stayed at the hotel until 1:00 pm then drove into town and sat on a bench in the park next to the Lido Hotel. Meadow and Conner were up the street sitting on a low retaining wall next to Etxebarria's house. Conner lifted his camera and focused his telephoto lens on the rowboat that was now making its way back to the dock. "Meadow, have a look out there and tell me what you see," he said, as he handed the camera to her.

"Jesus, is that the Frenchman?"

"I believe it is," he said.

"Fuck. What do we do now?"

"If he's out there then his house is empty. Maybe we just let ourselves in and wait for him."

"Can you pick the lock?" asked Meadow.

"Sure, I think so." He stood up and stretched. "Do you think anybody is watching us?"

"Well, I know people can see us, but I don't know if anybody is watching."

"OK, he's heading back, so we have to do it now. We'll walk up to the house, pretend to knock and then just go in."

"You can pick a lock that quickly?"

"Yeah, I've got this."

She touched her mic. "Samantha, Maddix, can you hear me?"

"Go ahead," said Samantha.

"We've spotted our guy and are moving in to take him out. We'll keep you informed."

"Did you receive that Maddix?" Samantha asked.

"Yes. From now on everybody stay dark until the Frenchman is terminated, or we hear from Kat."

"Copy that," said Conner, and they got up and moved to the door. They moved in as if they were speaking to the man inside. The main room was dark and sparsely furnished, several books were piled haphazardly next to a well-worn armchair, a small pedestal table stood next to it holding an ash tray and an empty beer stein. Another chair was pressed against the wall by the fireplace. The kitchen was neat but tiny, and at the far end there was a staircase to the cellar. Ancient crates gathered dust on the dirt floor and at the back of the house was a rough plank door. Conner opened it just a crack and saw the pathway to the dock. "Etxebarria's rowboat is close now, we should get ready," he said.

"Where should we do this?"

"This is as good a place as any. We'll hide back there and hit him after he closes the door." They screwed silencers on their SIG and crouched down to wait for him.

On the Mountain

1:00 pm

Kat had only gone three or four yards from the path before she encountered one of the APMs Kroner had mentioned. It was an M18A1 Claymore mine with a trip wire. She was familiar with this type of explosive and knew how to deactivate it. It had an effective range of about 50 meters, but the thing could do serious damage up to 250 meters away. It would probably set off a chain reaction the moment it went off and, if that happened, it wouldn't matter where she was, it would be game over.

With great care, she traced the trip wire over to a small tree and found another mine, which also had a trip wire going to the next mine and so on. Presumably every 50 meters or so there would be a mine and the pattern would be repeated around the mountain all the way up to the top. If she was going to get off this mound alive, she had to clear a path to the top.

The Claymore is helpfully marked on the dangerous side with the embossed words, **FRONT TOWARD ENEMY**.

It was 1:34 when she crossed over the wire and approached the mine from the firing position. She moved the 'Safety' switch to 'On' and then disconnected the M57 firing device from the blasting cap wire on the side and tossed it away behind her. It took her almost two hours to work her way up to the edge of the plateau where the monastery stood. In that time, she had found and disarmed thirty Claymores and marked a safe passage, 60 meters wide, back to the path. She took some time to rest before she moved closer to the edge of the field.

The structure Jäger had built was on her left and, yes, it was a fortress, just as Kroner had described. Designed to impress, its five free form towers framed with a network of black steel girders was clad with gold impregnated glass. They rose from the stone foundation like the flames of a forest fire. A lookout on the tallest tower could see almost everything that surrounded the mountain.

The shimmering, golden glass caught and distorted the reflection of the stone out buildings, making them look like they were on fire as well. Together they formed a sort of horseshoe partially enclosing a large flag stone courtyard. A spreading fig tree had been planted at the center of the courtyard and its reflection also played across the irregular shapes of glass like a burning bush. Three of buildings looked like cottages, handsomely executed in stone and timber under slate roofs. She thought they must be staff houses. The fourth building looked like a chapel and she wondered how religious a megalomaniac like Jäger could be.

She heard voices coming her way, so she crouched down and froze.

Two men in uniforms, like the guards at the gate, approached from her right. They were within a meter of her when they stopped, close enough that she could reach out and touch them. The first man took out a pack of cigarettes and offered a smoke to his partner. The shared match was tossed into the bush landing close to Kat.

"Be careful, Toller, do you want to start a fire?"

Toller turned slightly. "Do you want me to go in after it?" he asked.

"Never mind, I hear the helicopter coming."

"Fuck, isn't it always the way?" he said, dropping the cigarette on the ground. "You light the fucking thing and the bus comes."

"Always." They crushed the butts out under foot and ran to the center of the field.

Kroner had said there were only two ways to get up there, by road or by air. Jäger's helicopter rose theatrically into view on the far side of the mountain. It hovered for a moment while the guards congregated at the helipad to form an honor guard. "God," she said, "It's like he's already the president." When they were in two perfectly dressed lines, the chopper rotated, aligning itself to a proscribed landing position. The big machine settled gently and, as soon as the door opened, his security guards snapped to attention.

Jäger emerged and saluted the guard as he stepped onto the grass. Luckily, she was positioned to get a perfect view of the man. He looked relatively normal on TV, behind a desk or a podium, but in person he was quite different. Maybe that's why he always surrounded himself with guards, so people couldn't see what a freak he was. His bald head was unusually large for his slight body, as if he'd undergone an extreme weight loss program. Or perhaps he had a body transplant that had gone horribly wrong. She almost laughed out loud with that image in her mind. His movements were awkward as he walked, tilting back as if his legs were moving quickly while his head was trying to catch up. It was hard to imagine this clown as the evil genius.

The ceremonial entrance was a joke, but obviously Jäger took it very seriously, passing down the line with his beak-like nose in the air. It was a bit of a hike for him to cross the yard. Right on his heels, like little ducklings, were two men in dark suits, office workers she guessed. Following them were two heavily made-up women, dressed to party. As they crossed the courtyard, a doorway materialized, like a portal to another universe, and a very large man stepped out. He moved to one side to allow Jäger and his entourage to enter without breaking their stride. When they were out of sight, he scanned the field making sure there was no one else tagging along. Satisfied that he'd done his duty, he too disappeared inside, and the portal vanished.

The guards returned to their patrols and the pilot emerged, spoke briefly to one of the men, then headed for the cottages. She had counted twenty-two armed men and the pilot made twenty-three. Then there was Jäger, his four minions and the giant at the door, totaling twenty-nine people. It was anyone's guess how many there were inside. The place was huge. There could be hundreds of people in there.

Clearly, there was no way she could sneak in. She had to admit that the plan she had in mind was impossible. There was no sense in wasting the effort though. Since she was there, she would collect as much intel as possible. She sketched a picture of the house and outbuildings in her birder's book. Then moving very carefully around the edge of the field, she made a detailed plan of what she could see. She marked the spots that could provide cover and noted all the security cameras. When she was done, she went back down to the path and returned to the Via Panoramica.

CHAPTER 25

Alarm Bells

4:12 pm

Kat stepped out of the woods and saw Maddix sitting on the brick column with his feet on the guard rail diligently sketching away. He had a pencil behind his ear and a thermos and cup beside him. She felt a little guilty leaving him out in the sun for hours and wondered what he had drawn. She looked to her right and saw a few cars parked by the rail, one was occupied.

Alarm bells went off in her head. "Oh Christ!" The tiny Fiat was occupied by the big man from the magic door. What had she done that tipped them off? "Listen up everyone, I'm blown." It didn't matter now because here he was waiting for her. Maddix horror filled eyes suddenly lifted from his drawing. "Cool it Maddix! Just keep on drawing as if nothing has happened." She hoped that he hadn't been linked to her.

"Shit," he said, and did as he was told. "Good luck, Kat."

Raising her field glasses she scanned the sky tuning away from the giant in the Fiat as she spoke. "We're fresh out of luck guys, abort mission, repeat, abort mission. Everyone, bug out now, get to Rome and take off."

"Are you sure?"

"Oh God, don't question me, just go, now."

He stretched and yawned then hopped off the column and headed for the path to the village. Kat waited until he was out of sight before she stepped out onto the road.

Still scanning the sky Kat casually glanced in the direction of her car, the car that was parked out of reach behind the Fiat.

Does he know it's mine?

She was tempted to leave it and follow Maddix.

Jesus! Don't be so stupid, that would be a tip off that we're together. What if he doesn't recognized me? What if his being here is just a coincidence? What if I could sprout wings and fly the fuck out of here? Come on Kat, there is no such thing as a coincidence you're done.

She took a deep breath and headed to her car.

His window was open, and the giant was pretending to be reading a map as she walked by. He looked up at her. "Excuse me, signora."

"Si?"

"Do you live here?" he asked, and though his Italian was good, visually he was all German. Everything about him spelled trouble, the square jaw, blue humorless eyes, short cropped white-blond hair, and short, thick beard. He was the poster-boy for the Aryan master race, the only thing missing was the brown shirt with the swastika arm band.

Oh crap, she thought. "No," she said, "I am just visiting from Rome. If you want directions, I'm afraid you will have to ask someone else."

"Grazie. I'm sorry to have disturbed you.

"Not at all," she said, and moved on. When she heard the door of the car open behind her, she turned defensively and there he was ..., close up, he was huge. She couldn't imagine how he managed to get out of that tiny car so quickly. There was nothing but muscle beneath the suit and the other thing that impressed her was his Luger equipped with a silencer. "I'm sorry, did I say something to offend you?" she asked.

"My employer would like to speak with you. Please get in the car, Señora Franco."

She raised her hands from the elbows. "And what if I don't want to talk to him?"

"Then you would die right here. Which will it be, Señora?"

"In that case, I'd love to talk with the man." She looked down beyond the rail and saw Maddix disappearing into the village.

She closed her eyes for a moment as her heart contracted so tightly that she thought it might implode. "Let's not keep him waiting." After she took her seat in the tiny circus car, she watched as he got in behind the wheel with a miraculous lack of effort. She was about to comment on how impressed she was by his agility, but the blow he delivered stopped her cold.

Chapter 26

When Things Go Wrong

4:16 pm

Maddix had to find the others. Kat's standing order was that if she was caught, they were to leave her and get out of Italy fast. Samantha was supposed to be waiting for him at the park beside the Lido Hotel.

Their car was there but where was she? He thought perhaps she had already hooked up with Meadow and Conner. "Samantha, what's your 20?" He listened counting off the seconds of silence then repeated, "Samantha, where are you?" Nothing. "Meadow ..., Conner? Someone, answer me!"

He headed to Etxebarria's house, but there was no sign of them. He went back to the Lido, got in their car and headed back to their hotel.

Samantha must have walked back. He kept saying that over and over to himself as he sped round the lake to the hotel. He ran in through the lobby to the bar, she wasn't in there, so she had to be up in their room.

When he opened the door, he saw the nightmare that had taken over his mind when she didn't respond to his call. She was gagged and tied to the desk chair. He dropped his sketchbook, "Jesus, Samantha."

There was a man sitting in the armchair, pointing a gun with a silencer at her. Another appeared from behind the door and prodded Maddix with the business end of his Luger and told him to go in and sit on the bed.

Trying to maintain his cover as a French tourist he asked, "Que faites - vous ici?" There was no need to pretend to be afraid at this point, Samantha was bleeding from a cut over her eye and there was blood on the gag from her split lip. "Nous n'avons pas beaucoup d'argent, si c'est ce que vous êtes après."

"It is pointless to try to keep up with the pretense, Mr. Quinn," the standing man said, "we know you work for Señora Franco. Tell us, where are the others?"

Maddix wouldn't give up on his cover and continued in French, "Je ne parle pas anglais. Pour l'amour de Dieu nous laisser aller, nous sommes juste ici en vacances !"

"Really? Have it your way." The man raised his gun and placed it against Samantha's forehead.

"No! No, wait!" he said, breaking into English.

She looked terrified but she shook her head vehemently, mumbling through the gag.

"I ..., I don't know where they are. I thought they would be here," he said. She was crying now. "Please don't hurt her."

"What are their names?"

"Jesus, Samantha I'm so ..."

"I want their names!" the standing man said, and the other man pressed his gun against her temple.

"Alright! Alright," he said.

She screamed a muffled, "No!" but she couldn't stop him.

"Fields and Downs, Meadow Fields and Conner Downs."

"And, where are they?"

"I don't know. They were watching Etxebarria's house," he said, and she groaned. "I'm sorry, but I can't let them hurt you." She looked at him with an expression he had never seen before, just as the gunman pulled the trigger.

He watched the bullet exit from the other side of her head and she slumped off the chair with her eyes open. "Thank you, Maddix. That's all we wanted to know," the standing man said, as he fired his gun.

Chapter 27

A Captive Now

Even before Kat opened her eyes, she was overwhelmed by an incredible headache and nausea. She tried without much success to focus on the piercing eyes that stared out from that disturbingly large bald head. He was so close, stooped over so that all she could smell was his breath. She closed her eyes again. He'd eaten liver and onions for lunch, and she turned away, fighting the urge to vomit.

"I'm afraid that my man Wilhelm, may have hit you a little too hard. I do hope there is no permanent damage," he said, speaking to her in English

She opened her eyes then closed them again as he placed his cold hand on her cheek. "You are an extraordinary creature, Señora Franco. May I call you Anita?" he said. She wondered if he knew the truth about her. When her eyes opened again, he was even closer.

He noticed her distress, so he backed off and removed the gag. She sucked in a prodigious amount of air very quickly and began feeling dizzy. She closed her eyes again, slowed her breathing and sat still for a moment. Opening her eyes, she looked around.

She was inside a glass pyramid and, surprisingly, the glass was clear. The furnishings were few, minimalist and sterile, set up like a tiny island in the center of a vast and otherwise empty space. She caught a glimpse of a glass topped desk with stainless-steel legs. The only thing on it was an Apple laptop computer, it was open, but she couldn't see if it was turned on.

The terrazzo floor was highly polished and the mirror image of the stainless-steel furniture, a couch and two armchairs, seemed to sink into the depths. She assumed that the uncomfortable thing she was tied to was not part of the set.

"Not only are you an exquisite looking woman, but you are as deadly as anyone I have ever met. And that's saying something, believe me. How many of my people have you killed so far?"

She looked at him coldly and said, "I've lost count, but I could always add a few more. You for instance."

He laughed. "When I saw the surveillance video from Kroner's house I was mesmerized. I watched you question the man and it gave me chills. Oh, and then when you stacked the bodies in the entrance hall, I mean that was fabulous to watch. To think that single handed, you cut the throats of four without a sound then shot the rest of his security team. It was simply amazing. How far away were you?"

She just stared at him.

"Not going to tell me? Well, never mind. I look at you now and all I see is a young woman, so soft, so feminine, so exotic. One would never expect that you would be capable of such a slaughter. I told Wilhelm here to be careful of you. I warned him not to be fooled into complacency. I assure you, hitting you was an act of self-preservation." He lifted her eyelid and studied her pupil. "Perhaps you have a slight concussion. You may experience some nausea and a headache for a while, but they will pass."

"Are you a doctor as well?"

"A doctor, me? Heavens no, but I know the signs. Would you like some water? Wilhelm, give our guest a glass of water." The big man must have been standing right behind her because when he moved her back grew cold. She hadn't even known he was in the room until he handed the glass to Jäger over her shoulder. Jäger crouched down again so he could lift it to her lips. "Have a drink, it will settle you." He tipped the glass into her mouth and forced her to take it all. It tasted strange and bitter. "There now, do you feel better?"

"Just so you know, you have really bad breath ..., I mean it, it's really bad." She began to feel like she was going to fall off the chair. "What, wha - t, what was in that?"

"Oh, not to worry, it wasn't poison. Just a little something to help loosen up your tongue. It's surprising how little it takes to have an effect."

"Oh, shit," she said, terrified that she might give it all away.

"I see that you are concerned, so let me put your mind at ease. It is just a touch of sodium amytal. I assure you that it will not harm the baby."

"What?"

"And I told Wilhelm not to hit you in the belly. We can't take any chances, now can we?"

"What did you say?"

"Oh, my dear, you thought I wouldn't find out about that? The doctor in Paris mentioned it before she died."

"How could you possibly know that I saw a doctor?"

"After Devlyn told us that you had gone to Paris, my investigators traced your movements. It wasn't that difficult."

Jesus, she thought, when did he talk to Devlyn? "Is he here? Is he alright?"

"Oh, no my dear, he isn't here. But I touched a nerve, didn't I?"

Again, she said nothing.

"Well look at you. He said he didn't know what you were when you joined his little army. But really, I think he knew all along. You must tell me, what hold did you have over him to force him to keep your secret?"

"I don't know what you're talking about," she said, looking at him and thinking that the man must be completely insane.

"Oh, come now. You must tell me; I'm just dying to know."

She had no idea what Paul had told him to create this warped version of reality, but there was no way she was going to poke holes in it if it would give her some advantage.

"My dear, you are amazing. Most people would be blabbering by now. We try to keep our little secrets, don't we? But I got all I needed out of Devlyn and I'll get the truth out of you too, I always do."

That was another shock. "What have you done with him?"

"Well, he's dead now, isn't he? He and Kroner never made it to the airplane. We had a bit of a conversation here and he told me a great deal before I shot him. Here's the thing that I am curious about.

"I can't imagine what you could have done to convince Special Agent Devlyn not to give you up to the Americans. My suspicion is that you controlled Devlyn with sex. Am I right?"

"You are insane, you know that, don't you?"

"You know what I think?" he asked, but she said nothing. "Well, I'll tell you anyway. Devlyn warned me not to hurt you, now wasn't that sweet? It was as if he thought he could do something about it. Here's what I think, I think that he was the father of your child. Am I right? I know I am. And here's something else that might interest you," he said, clearly enjoying himself. "We found your team down in the village. My men found the Carpenter woman and took her to her hotel room. Then her boyfriend, Maddix Quinn, did us a favor by walking in and telling us all about the others."

She turned cold and her stomach felt like it turned inside out. "How did you find them?"

"This is Italy, my dear. You have spent enough time in Italy to know that the villagers see everything..., and the thing of it is, everyone in the village works for me. Soon you know, all of Europe will belong to me."

"What have you done with them?"

"I understand that the Carpenter woman was very brave and wouldn't talk. Quinn must have been very fond of her. He tried to save her by telling my men about your people."

"Where are they now?"

"Dead. They were both executed in their room."

Her head felt like it might explode. "You killed them?!" It took a few moments for her to find her voice again. "You really shouldn't have done that."

"Why not? You certainly would have. And just before you arrived, I was informed that my people found the other two hiding at my friend's house."

"Have you killed them too?"

"No, I have other plans for them."

"They don't know anything, so there is no point in torturing them."

"Oh, I know that," he said, with a dismissive wave of his hand. "But as you know, torturing can be so much fun. Enough of this preamble, there is business to be done. I have brought you here to do a job for me."

"You want me to kill Vladimir Mogilevski."

"So, Kroner told you about that as well, did he?"

"Believe me, if you hurt them, then you may as well kill me now, because I won't be doing anything for you."

"I suppose that shouldn't surprise me. You are loyal to your people. As it should be, until they prove unworthy. Case in point, I was under the impression that Kroner was a force to be reckoned with. But as you so ably illustrated for me, that was an illusion."

"Before you take this any further, I have to have your word that you won't harm those two."

"If I must. You spared Kroner; I suppose I can be equally magnanimous."

"Thank you," she said, hoping that he would keep his word.

"Look at me doing all of the talking and you were the one who drank the sodium amytal. Maybe I got our glasses mixed up. Now wouldn't that be too funny?"

Reining in her emotions she said, "You are nothing like I expected you would be."

"Really?" he said, stepping back and performing a pirouette with outstretched arms and palms up, "And, how did you expect me to be?"

"From what I saw in the media I thought you would be serious, intelligent and..."

"Yes ..., and what else?"

"Manly. I hadn't expected you to be a raging queen."

"Tsk, tsk, Anita, now you are just trying to make me angry. Nice try but it's not going to work." He turned away as if he had something to do, then turned back with his finger on his lower lip. "But honestly, do I look like a queen to you?"

"Definitely. A bobble-headed queen. I bet you do drag shows."

"You are trying to hit all my buttons, aren't you? Payback for killing your friends I suppose. Well good on you. I'm a big man, I'll overlook it this one time. What it tells me though, is that the drug is working. I don't mind telling you darling, it's all me. Everything they say about me, it's all true. But I don't care. I am going to be the richest, most powerful man in the world soon, so I can do whatever the fuck I like."

"You'll fail, just like all the other megalomaniacs before you."

"I don't think so. The thing is, Anita, I have already won. I have the world's greatest superpower on the run. Officially taking over control of Europe is just a formality now; I'm already calling the shots."

"Then why are you still having people killed?"

"Why? Because I enjoy killing people. You know, Lenin once said that it would not upset him in the slightest to shoot his people by the thousands. I feel the same way, especially Americans. Isn't that outrageous? One at a time or by the thousands, I don't care, it's all the same to me."

"You are a monster."

"Of course, I am." The smile and the musical voice returned, "That's why I am so taken by you my dear. We talk the same language, you and I. Kindred spirits." She couldn't hide her resentment. "Oh yes, you are a monster too. You can't deny it, so don't even try. You are the Medusa, a black mamba. If Oppenheimer were here today, he would say that you have become Death, the destroyer of worlds."

"That is a ridiculous thing to say."

"When you lock eyes on your victim he is as good as dead. That is why I wanted you alive. You will find and kill Vladimir Mogilevski. If you do this for me, then I'll see to it that you receive enough money to retire and raise your little bastard in peace. Do we have a deal?"

"You realize that Mogilevski is a friend."

"I do ..., I do, but that won't be a problem for you, will it?" She stared back unblinkingly. "I see that we have come to an understanding."

"I have one condition."

"Yes, and what would that be?"

"If I do this, I'll need my people with me to back me up."

"Oh, very well, Wilhelm bring the Americans."

"Unharmed," she said.

"And what if they've been bruised a little, will you kill me? Please. They are alive, be satisfied with that. I must say Anita, your attitude towards your underlings surprises me," he said, looking down at her. "You shouldn't coddle your people, my dear, it shows weakness."

Kat was overwhelmed when she saw them, Meadow and Conner arrived bruised, bleeding and shaken and but they were alive. She turned back to Jäger, "We'll need transport to New York."

"Certainly. I will have the helicopter take you to Rome. Wilhelm will arrange the flight to New York for you. And Wilhelm, see to it that they have a suitable escort."

"I'll need weapons to do the job."

"I'm sure that a woman of your abilities will be able to take care of that yourself." He signaled to Wilhelm to remove them and then left the room.

CHAPTER 28

DESTINATION NEW JERSEY

Their escort met them at the entrance, two extremely large and serious looking men in dark suits. Wilhelm gave them their instructions and went back inside. The chopper was warming up as they crossed the field. With her head down and her hands trembling, Meadow walked as close to Kat as she could. Conner kept a distance between them.

The trio was flown to Rome where they boarded Jäger's business jet and took off for New Jersey. Kat, Meadow and Conner sat up front while their goons had seats at the back. Kat wondered if they were there to kill them when the job was done. She thought it might be a good idea to have them arrested as soon as they arrived.

Kat told Meadow and Conner that the mission was over, and they had to get away as soon as the plane landed. There was little she could do on the flight except promise them that she would do everything she could to avenge Samantha and Maddix. "Kat, we all understood the risks when we came with you," Conner said.

"He's right, this wasn't your fault, Kat," Meadow said quietly, "Just get the bastard and end this."

"I'll do my best. I can't thank you both enough for what you did."

"But we didn't get Etxebarria."

"I know, but that wasn't your fault, it was mine." The conversation ended with that, and she sat for a while contemplating the phone on the desk. She picked it up then realizing it was probably bugged, she put it back, folded her arms and tried to sleep.

Reporting In

The Gulfstream stopped on the apron of Teterboro Airport in New Jersey, and the pilot opened the door at about ten past one, New York time. The goons stayed on the plane, which lead Kat to believe she was free to move around. After going through customs, Meadow and Conner left the terminal saying they were going to get a cab to Kennedy and fly to Washington.

She watched them go then Kat headed for the restroom with her suitcase. She had a phone hidden in a secret compartment at the bottom and was delighted to find that they hadn't discovered it. She dialed her assigned number and it was picked up on the first ring. "Maryland heating and air conditioning," the voice said.

"My furnace isn't working, I'd like to speak to the manager please," Kat said.

"Serial number please."

"MI 55-31-86."

The call was immediately put through to the G-2, Gen. Wolfson answered in a sleepy voice. "I was expecting to hear from you sooner than this. Where have you been?"

"After Devlyn left, I took a small team to Italy to follow up on Kroner's lead."

"Damnit Fernando, you were not authorized to go off on your own!"

"I know, Sir. But we found the man behind this in Peredicci, Italy. I thought I could deal with this the same way I handled Petrus, but I was wrong, and I failed."

"Jesus. OK, tell me what happened."

"Jäger's agents made us as soon as we arrived. The whole town surrounding his base is occupied by his people. I was taken first, then his men killed Special Agent Samantha Carpenter and Special Agent Maddix Quinn before they took Agents Meadow Fields and Conner Downs prisoner. I don't know why they weren't executed right away like the others. We were released a few hours ago and flown right to New York."

"Why did he release you?"

"He still thinks I am Anita Franco, the assassin. He sent me here to kill Vladimir Mogilevski. I demanded that he release Fields and Downs with me. They just left here for Kennedy and will continue to Fort Meade today."

"Well at least that's something. You know that Devlyn is dead?"

"Yes Sir, I was informed yesterday. I thought he was going to live forever."

"He was a hell of an agent. He saved your ass more than a few times."

She swallowed hard. "Yes Sir, he did. We were ...," she struggled to get the words out. "We were a good team."

"I'm sure you were. OK Fernando, what the fuck is going on over there?"

"Sir, you probably have a better handle on that than I do. I haven't seen any news since I was taken. He truly believes that he has already defeated America and will be elected President of Europe. I think we can stop him, but I need to set it up first with your help." When she finished giving him a full report of what had happened since Brussels and what she intended to do, he didn't say anything for quite a while. "Sir, are you still there?"

He cleared his throat and said, "Do you think going back alone to kill him is the best plan?"

"Yes sir, I do."

"I don't agree but, for now, I don't have any alternatives. Alright, I'm going to try to figure out how we can make this work. The plan will have to be presented to the President and I don't think that he's going to sign off on what you've worked out, I'll tell you that right now."

"Sir, what Jäger is doing right now is only the tip of the iceberg compared to what he's planning to do if he gets what he wants. I think all the leaders of Europe are in his cross-hairs so I'm willing to bet that they will support whatever we can do to stop him."

"I can't argue with that."

"It's imperative that Jäger believes I have completed the assignment. It's the only way he is going to let me back in. I don't know what kind of reception I'll get after that, but I guarantee that he'll want to deal with me in person."

"America does not use suicide bombers, Fernando. There has to be another way. I'll call you in the morning. Get some rest and keep your phone charged."

A New Plan

She leaned against the sink for a long time while trying to convince herself that she could do this. She had to do this. Kat called Hershoff to say that she was in New York. "Sorry to be calling you so late but I just flew in to Teterboro."

"There's something wrong, isn't there?"

"Jezzus, Ramsey, everything's all fucked up." During the short conversation, she told him what she had to do. He had a hard time processing it. "I need a place to stay. Can you help with that?"

"I'll make a reservation for you. Take a cab to Manhattan, The Grand Hyatt. I'll see you there."

"Thanks, Ramsey."

"Kat, I hope you know what you're doing."

"Yeah, me too," she said, and ended the call. She set her suitcase up on the sink and looked at herself in the mirror.

Turning her head, she lifted the hair away from her left ear to examine the bruise where the troll had planted his fist. "Holy shit." It still hurt like crazy and her ear was still ringing. Luckily, her hair covered it.

Her birder's outfit made her look like a tree-hugging fanatic from the wilds of Maine. She stripped off the khakis and stuffed them in the garbage bin and unpacked some things she bought in Paris. At the bottom of her jewelry pouch she saw her wedding rings. They were a little tight. She was gaining weight just like the doctor in Paris said she would. That almost made her break down, but it was short lived. She looked deep into the mirror and said, "Pull yourself together, Kat."

She took a lipstick from the bag and applied it to her dry, chapped lips, put a brush through her hair a few times and dabbed on some perfume. When she was satisfied with the transformation, she gathered herself together, repacked her suitcase and walked out to face the world as a softer, kinder version of Anita Franco.

Taking Manhattan

While making her way over to the waiting cabs she was thinking that she'd have to decompress in New York before she could do anything about Vlad. She approached a cabbie and said, "Are you working?"

"Where are you headin'?"

"Manhattan."

"OK, you got it," he replied, and opened the car door. She slipped in leaving her suitcase on the curb. He swung it into the open trunk, got behind the wheel and turned on the meter. What part of Manhattan are we going to?"

"East 42nd at Lexington."

They pulled up in front of the Grand Hyatt and the driver said, "OK lady, here ya are. That'll be sixty bucks." She handed him seventy. "Thanks," he said, and he got out to get her bag.

It was a very cool night, so she hurried to the door. She passed through into a predominately black lobby, a veritable forest of thick black columns. There was one receptionist on duty, an attractive young Chinese woman with jet black hair wearing a black skirt and white top. She had been sitting cross legged at the low, white stone desk but stood as Kat approached. Kat wondered if she was hired because she went with the decor.

"Good evening, welcome to the Grand Hyatt. How may I help you?"

"Hola," she said, speaking with a light Spanish accent. "I have a reservation; the name is Anita Franco."

"Thank you," the receptionist said, as she keyed in Kat's name. The information came up on her screen. "Here you are, Señora Anita Franco. Welcome to New York. May I see your passport please?" Kat handed it to her. "Thank you, Señora. And may I also have your credit card, thank you." She entered the data into her terminal. "Perfect," she said, handing back the card and passport. "All I need from you is your signature." Kat signed the registry. "Perfect. We have you booked into one of our Premier Suites and the room is ready for you."

"Wonderful. Is there somewhere I could get something to eat?"

"We have a 24-hour gourmet Grab and Go service in the Market room, it's just over there. You can get something hot in there whenever you want. How many keys would you like?"

"Ah ..., oh, just one, thanks."

"Here you are, Señora." The receptionist handed her a key card. "And there is a gentleman waiting for you in the Grand Club Lounge."

"Is there? Did he give you a name?"

"Yes, Mr. Hershoff. He said you were old friends. The bellman will take your case to your room for you and have a pleasant stay with us."

Kat smiled and headed for the lounge wondering what he had to tell her that couldn't wait until the morning.

Chapter 29

Old Friends

He was sitting alone in the room at a small table reading. There was a cold cup of coffee in front of him that he'd been ignoring, for God knows how long, while he skimmed through a magazine that didn't interest him. It was the first time she had seen him out of uniform, and he was looking old, anxious and tired. "My goodness if it isn't Mr. Hershoff."

He spun around in his chair. "Oh, there you are at last. Hello Anita, I was beginning to think you weren't going to make it," he said.

"Funny, I had the same feeling a while ago. Thank you for the reservation, I'm sure it will be lovely, but I thought we were going to meet for breakfast."

"Girl, this is breakfast."

She shrugged. "I suppose so. Have you retired, Ramsey?" She came close and put her hand on his shoulder.

"I wouldn't think of it. I've just gone native while I'm in New York," he said, quickly dropping the publication on the floor, with several others he'd skimmed, and stood up smiling.

"Ramsey, it is so good to see you," she said earnestly. She put her arms around his neck and hugged him, as if he'd just saved her from drowning.

"Let's sit down and talk, Anita." He pulled a chair out for her. "I haven't seen you since the transformation. Did Harm ever see you looking like this?"

"You mean dressed like a Euro trash jet setter? No."

"Don't sell yourself short, you look wonderful. Damn, what happened to your ear?"

"I met a troll and we didn't get along."

"I suggest you stop going to bars where trolls hang out."

"I'll keep that in mind. What's up, Ramsey?"

"OK, Wolfson just called me about you. We agreed that we couldn't waste a second. He spoke to the President by phone right after you called him and POTUS invited him to appear before a special meeting at the White House to brief the Secretary of Defense and Joint Chiefs later on this morning."

"That was quick."

"What you laid on him was some serious stuff, Kat. Do you want a coffee?" he asked.

"Ningunos gracias, Ramsey. Would you mind talking in my room? I'd feel a lot better if I could get these shoes off."

"No, not at all."

As the elevator arrived at her floor, she opened her purse. Ramsey said, "If you're looking for your key it's in your hand."

"Oh right, thanks." She took out a tissue instead and dabbed her eyes while they walked to her room. "Isn't it ridiculous, I look at you and I just seem to tear up."

"Here you are, room 1215."

"Right." She inserted the card and let him go in first.

The accent disappeared as soon as the door closed. "Sit down Ramsey, please. Would you like a drink?"

"No thanks."

"OK." She kicked off the heels and sat down to rub her feet. "When this mission is finished, I'm resigning from the Army and I'm going to buy a house in the country so I can sit alone and read trashy romance novels."

"I'm sure you think so now, but how many times have you ..."

"Ramsey, I'm pregnant," she said.

"Oh Christ, Kat. Is the father included in your retirement plans?"

"No, he never was. I just wanted to start a family on my own. Anyway, I just found out yesterday that he was murdered. I'm still finding it hard to accept."

"You're not talking about Paul Devlyn, are you? Oh, Kat, I am so sorry. Wolfson told me. It's damn hard to lose people close to you."

"Thank you. I don't think you ever met him."

"I did as a matter of fact, at the White House when the President hung that medal around your neck."

"I didn't know you were there."

"I didn't want to intrude, but Harm was so proud of you he invited me." They sat for a moment both trying to deal with the situation. "Kat, I'm trying to get my head wrapped around the idea of you being a stay-at-home mom."

"I know, but it's all I want now. If I survive this, it's the only future I can see for myself."

"I wish you all the best, you know that."

"I know." She stood up and walked over to the bed, set her suitcase on it, and opened the zipper. "What did Wolfson tell you about why I'm here?" she asked, as she started to put some clothes away in the bureau.

"He said you were here to kill Vlad and he wanted me to set it up. I told him you were both out of your fucking minds if you thought I would let you do that."

"But then he told you my plan."

"Yeah, well just the gist, but I get the idea and you can count me in."

"I'm glad. He's got to do some acting to make it work." She sat down again and told him what she had in mind.

"That's a hell of a thing, Kat, but he'll go along with it, no problem."

"That's perfect. How is he?"

"He's about as good as you'd expect considering." She stood up and went over to the window, but there was nothing out there to ease her grief. She turned to face him, feeling so alone. "God, I wish for so many things that I can't have." She turned and leaned against the windowsill. Sensing that she had something else to say, Ramsey waited for her to speak.

"Thanks for coming Ramsey. I really needed a friend right now."

He got up and hugged her and gave her a kiss on the cheek. "You can always count on me, Kat, always."

"Thanks. I'm sorry but I'm exhausted, can we talk tomorrow?"

"Sure, I've taken a room upstairs, 1423. Why don't we meet for brunch at eleven-ish?"

"Perfect." As soon as he left, she had a shower, dried her hair, and went to bed.

CHAPTER 30

FORT MEADE

The moment he put his phone down after talking to Kat, Gen Wolfson called the President to give him the substance of Kat's report and her plan for dealing with Jäger. Then he added his take on how the plan could be modified.

The President then called an emergency meeting of his executive staff to discuss the plan. Then at 3:00 am Washington time, President Lake called the President of Italy, Angelo Bionesca, and the heads of government in England, Germany and France, and told them what he would like to do. The President of Italy was adamantly opposed to President Lake's plan at first. When Lake pressed his case, Bionesca finally agreed on one condition, that if America took such a drastic action, they would provide adequate compensation to restore the area. The other leaders agreed that there seemed to be no other solution.

By 5:00 am, Wolfson was given the go ahead and began calling his command team to come up with ideas that would make the plan work. "My operative has informed me that there is a seventy-two-hour window. That gives us seventy hours to come up with an action plan and execute it.

"What I want are solid ideas to get this job done. The President has given us the order to eliminate the top of the terrorist organization. The only things he took off the table were the nuclear solution and a full-scale military assault on Europe."

The President wanted to drop a bomb on Jäger, The most efficient way to achieve that was to have Kat to return to the fortress to light a beacon. That was a very big ask.

G-2 called in his staff to get it going. What Wolfson wanted to know, was how she would paint the target; what they would use to track their agent and what ordinance would they deliver to their target. His staff worked with the information Kat supplied to come up with the answers.

The second meeting began promptly at 9:00 am.

"Good morning ladies and gentlemen, take your seats. Alright, as I said last night, this issue is time sensitive. So, let's get right to it, what have you got for me?"

Lt. Colonel Elizabeth Davis opened the folder she had prepared and said, "Sir, we have a new item that we can use for this operation."

"Our agent is going to be carrying this in with her and it has to be undetectable. Is what you are proposing undetectable?"

"Yes Sir." Davis headed up the tech department at Fort Meade and was an expert in surveillance, tracking, and detection hardware and software. For fifteen years, she had been responsible for providing the equipment and support for operatives in the field. "It's called a 'Radar Responsive' tag, which is like a long-range version of those stick-on RFID tags used to mark items in shops.

"The 'Radar Responsive' tag is dormant until woken up by a radar pulse and then undetectable without the specific code to track its signal. When these tags light up, they can be located by radio waves that penetrate buildings, so we could use it as a search and rescue device as well as a target. The system can be picked up from 16 to 20 kilometers away with a geolocation accuracy of one meter. We have this material embedded in a variety of objects, which are ready to be deployed right now."

"That sounds perfect. My agent said the target would be given a DVD. Can you make up a label to stick on a plastic jewel case?"

"We've already produced R/W DVDs and CDs with the fibers embedded in the disk that are untraceable." She took a sample disk from her attaché case.

"That has the RRT in it?"

"That is correct."

"And it's ready to go?"

"Yes Sir."

"Outstanding. And can you also put that tech into something the operative could wear?"

"Yes, I have a number of objects here, a wristwatch, a shirt button and a silver cross on a necklace."

"Let me see the cross."

She opened a small box and removed the necklace to show him. "The operative could wear this in the field and be picked up even if she is underground."

"The radio that picks up these emissions can distinguish between signals?"

"Sir?"

"If we had one for the target and one for our agent, could the radio waves tell the difference?"

"Absolutely Sir."

"Outstanding, I'd hate to have our ordinance zero in on the wrong target."

"Not a problem, Sir. All we have to do is sync the DVD up to the smart bomb's guidance system and the other to a tracker."

"Right, you move forward on that, I want to be able to get them to the agent ASAP. Now, I want the details on how we deliver the kill shot."

"Sir," Major Jason Park said, after typing in the subject of a search on his laptop. Park was pushing forty, but still looked like he had just graduated from West Point. He had transferred from the Air Force to operations at Fort Meade.

"Yes Major."

"We could send in an MQ-9 Reaper with your pick of munitions once we have the stats on the target. We have four payload options, a couple of Hellfire missiles, the GBU-12 Paveway, the II laser-guided AIM-9 Sidewinder, or the GBU-38 JDAM".

"Major, it's been a while since I had anything to do with that type of ordinance, so remind me again what the fuck GBU and JDAM mean."

"GBU means a Guided Bomb Unit, Sir. The JDAM stands for Joint Direct Attack Munition. It's a guidance kit that converts unguided bombs or 'dumb bombs', into all-weather 'smart' munitions. It can also have a laser-guided system attached to that."

"How accurate are those things?"

"Sir, the CEP or Circular Error Probable, is about a meter and it doesn't care about the weather. That would pretty much guarantee a kill."

"Alright, let's go with the GBU-38 JDAM. Where would we launch the drone from?"

"The target is in central Italy, so the nearest base would be Aviano Air Base, Naples."

"And they have what we need?"

"I have just logged into their site and put in a request, Sir. It will just take a minute to confirm."

"Very well, let me know when you have confirmation, and we'll go ahead with that plan. Next, the agent has requested some special effects to make the plan viable, so I am sending the 'Hollywood FX Bunch' up to New York today to deal with that issue. Get your devices to them Colonel Davis, and they will deliver the tracker and target to her."

"Yes Sir," said Davis.

Maj. Park spoke up, "Sir, it has just been confirmed, Aviano has the ordinance we requested, and I have asked them to set it up for us. They are dedicating a Reaper as the delivery system."

"Good."

"I'll get the target code to them right away," said Davis.

"Perfect. Is there anything else?" No one spoke. "OK then, good solutions everyone, thanks. Davis, I want you and Park in Italy to coordinate the delivery and I'm requesting a Special Forces team to head over there now to assist in recovering the agent. The clock is ticking people, so let's get it done."

Chapter 31

Pre-Show Jitters

Kat tried her to turn it off for a day, but that proved to be impossible. Between the deaths of half of her team, her pregnancy, Vlad's situation, and the likelihood that by Sunday she would be dead, her anxiety was nearly unmanageable. When she put in a call to Gen. Wolfson and was told simply that he was unavailable, she wanted to scream.

After she had brunch with Ramsey, she went for a walk heading along Lexington with no particular destination in mind, just needing to get out of the hotel. It was a cold morning, and she didn't have a coat, so when she arrived at East 57th St. she wandered into Saks Off 5th and looked around for something warm. It was a successful divergence, and she continued her walk bundled up in a new long, white, down filled coat that reminded her of the one she lost in Ukraine.

After some aimless exploring she wound up at MoMA. She thought it might help to take in the art but, for her, most of it was incomprehensibly obscure, but it was enough to distract her. At ten past one her cell rang. People were looking at her as if she'd slashed a painting, so she hurried to the stairs.

"Hello General, I'm sorry but I'm in a gallery," she said, heading for the ground floor. "Can you hold for a moment while I go outside?"

"Take your time."

She moved to the corner of the alcove just outside the door and stood there out of the wind. "Sorry, General, I can talk now."

"I'm guessing that you want to know what's going on."

"Yes Sir. And thank you for calling me back. I'm finding it difficult waiting for this to get started."

"I understand. We are moving as quickly as we can. I have sent members of my staff to Aviano Air Base near Naples. The Navy is helping us out with the ordinance, so it will be ready to go as soon as you are in place. The FX team should be in New York now. They will rendezvous with Mogilevski and Hershoff at Mogilevski's apartment. It took a while for them to put together the gags, as they call them, and will be ready for you at 15:30 hrs. They say the set up will take a few hours.

"Listen Katrina, I can only imagine what you're going through, but it's all coming together. You'll have everything you need to get the job done by tonight."

"Thank you, Sir. How will I let you know when it's time to light it up?"

"We are putting a tracker on both you and Jäger, so we'll be monitoring you all the way through this. Jäger's marker is in the DVD you requested. It that will paint the target for you. You'll wear yours on a chain around your neck. It's a cross, I'm assuming that you're a Catholic."

"Ah ..., no, but he doesn't know that," she said, she had never in her life set foot in a cathedral or church with the intention of praying.

"Fine, we'll be tracking you with that. When you are out of the way, we will detonate."

"Sir, there is no telling what he will do to me after I deliver the proof of death. The moment he believes Mogilevski is dead, I'll probably be dead too, so don't wait."

"This isn't going to be a suicide mission," the G-2 said. "I have asked to have a team from Delta Force sent in to back you up. They are being deployed now and will be in place before you get there. They will be in control of sending in the signal to light him up. All you have to do is deliver the disk and your job is done. They're going to do some recon to find a way of getting you out of there before the fireworks."

"Sir ..."

"We'll get this done; I promise, Katrina. I have to go now but I will be talking to you after the mission."

"Yes Sir, thank you Sir."

It was good to know there was a concrete plan in place, but it didn't ease her anxiety.

SF in Naples

The team from 1st Special Forces Operational Detachment-Delta arrived in Aviano Air Base late that evening. A small tour bus carried them to Umbria in the rain and drove directly to the base of the mountain. They found the Vocabolo Colle die Frati, a small road that serviced the farms on the north side, away from the village. They drove down and parked out of sight, a kilometer from the farmhouse.

The rain was going to be a serious problem, but the bigger issue were the people in the farmhouses. The team was warned that Jäger controlled everyone in the village. It was likely that his circle of influence included those people as well.

The men entered the buildings quietly while the residents were sleeping. Finding weapons and other evidence that proved that the four men inside were hostiles, it became necessary to take them out quickly before they could raise the alarm. With that done they moved on to the mountain.

As expected, the mountainside was treacherously slippery, so clearing the mines from their path was going to be dangerous and time consuming. It also meant that their surveillance equipment might not be as effective, the intel they gleaned from it less reliable. The team spent the night in the bush, taking turns standing guard.

Chapter 32

71 Street

The special effects team arrived with all the necessary equipment and began their set up in Vlad's apartment at 3:00 pm. When Kat called the phone number G-2 had given her, the FX coordinator said she could come over any time, but he wouldn't be ready for her to shoot the scene until later in the evening.

She entered Vlad's building on 71st Street at 5:05. The doorman who let her in was a special agent she recognized. She took the lift to the 14th floor and was greeted by two more special agents in the hall. Vlad's door was standing open and there was a great deal of activity going on inside. "Knock, knock," she said loudly, and walked in to find the apartment's main room sealed off with plastic sheeting like a quarantine zone. There was an opening marked with red tape and she peeked through. "Hello."

"Special Agent Fernando?"

"Yup, that's me." There were five technicians hard at it, installing the special effects devices to simulate the shooting. The FX coordinator came over to greet her. "Where are Mogilevski and Hershoff?"

"They were beginning to drive us nuts, so I gave them a buck and sent them out for ice cream." For the first time in days Kat laughed. It was hard to imagine a general and an oligarch being treated like annoying kids. "Yeah, well I was polite about it anyway.

"Look, we've set up for this gag like General Wolfson laid it out to us, but without a script I've left it flexible in case you want to make some changes. So why don't I run it down for you and you can tell me how to tweak it."

"OK, show me what you've got."

He began walking her through the set up. "This is supposed to look like an execution, so I thought your guy could be sitting down and tied to this chair. We'll use an air squib device for the effect on his chest. We'll place a tube with a special nozzle on the inside of his shirt, where you want the bullet to hit. There will be a thin steel plate glued to his body with a tiny explosive on it to blow a hole in his shirt. The blood is sent up from a radio-controlled air ejector we've fixed under the seat."

"What's that going to look like?"

"It'll be messy. We're going to use a battery powered toy called a Bullet Hit Nonpyro Splatter Blood Hit system."

"Nice name."

"It's super reliable. We picked one of his dining room chairs so the blood can exit through the open space on the seat back and we don't have to use explosives. The whole thing is going to be messy, so we only have one shot at it. Everything's gotta be coordinated so we'll do a few dry runs with you and Mr. Mogilevski. He'll have to rehearse his reactions before we film it.

"One of the techs will control a wire hooked up to a strap around his chest and he'll give it a little tug when the squib goes off. Your vic just has to react to that. It'll be an involuntary reaction because it might hurt a bit. Then it's up to him to die convincingly. Unless you have some major changes in mind, we should be finished the set up in just a few minutes."

"It sounds extremely complicated. What are you going to use to film it?"

He pointed to the heavy tripod and walked her over to it. "I've got a Canon XL2 digital camcorder here, that features a 3X 1/3" 680,000-pixel progressive scan CCDs for the high-resolution 16:9 aspect ratio..."

"Hold it right there, you're giving me a headache. I have no idea what you just said. What is the bottom line?"

"Good picture quality and it records on a Mini DVD video cassette."

"How are you going to put that on the DVD I present to Jäger?"

"That part's dead simple, I'll do the transfer for you before we leave.

We'll put it in a jewel case for the presentation."

"Great. How much recording time does it have?"

"More than enough for what we're going to do. You'll be able to play it back on any computer with a DVD drive, it's very portable. What gun did you want to use?"

"I use a SIG P226 with a silencer."

"The Navy Seal gun, yeah, I was kind-a counting on that." The man opened a large foam filled box. "We brought along a selection of funny guns, but I made sure we had a P226 with a silencer in the box. It does everything the real one does except throw lead."

"Perfect. I wonder," she said hesitantly, because she really wanted to sell this bit of theater but didn't want to make things any more complicated than they already were. "Would it be a problem if I wanted to shoot him more than once?"

"Ah ..., yeah, not a problem, we've got the equipment. All we do is add a few more tubes and nozzles. How many times did you want to hit him?"

"Three times would do it. And if I could put one in his head that would be great."

"One in the head? Well yeah ..., OK, we can do that too. We'll mount a low powered squib on a thin metal plate. My makeup guy will take care of that.

"We'll use the same system on the back of his head, run the tube up his neck from his shirt and have a little squib on the plastic behind him to blow a hole in that. It'll all be synced up and work.

"We could do a close-up on the latex appliance and it will be virtually undetectable. Your viewer won't see a thing. We've done this a thousand times without a problem."

"It sounds complicated but ..., great."

"As soon as the old geezers get back, we can start rehearsing."

"Well breathe easy boys and girls," Hershoff said, from the door, "the old geezers are back."

Kat sun around and ran to Vlad, throwing her arms around him. "Jezzus, Vlad, I was so worried about you." She began to cry.

"I am fine, Katrina, I'm fine."

"I kept calling and you never called back."

"Ramsey took my phone. He thought it best if I disappeared for a while. I had no idea that they went after me at the dacha. I am so sorry, Katrina. Thank God you are alive."

She slowly released him but held onto his shoulders. "And now I have to kill you. Can you ever forgive me?"

"I will forever be in your debt, my little tiger."

"OK people, enough with the reunion we have work to do," said the FX coordinator.

Vlad looked at the effects boss and said, "So, our little shop of horrors has conjured up a real show for us."

"You'll hardly feel a thing."

"Are you OK, Vlad?"

"Yes, of course. I am not the one who is in danger here, Katrina."

"Yeah, yeah, great. OK people," said the FX coordinator, "rehearsals now. We're burning daylight."

"Say, I meant to ask you before. Have you got a name, son?" Hershoff asked.

"Not on this job I don't, dad. So, Mr. Mogilevski, if you would be so kind as to come over here into the line of fire and take a seat, we can hook up the gags, tie you up and get started with some rehearsals. And Mr. Hershoff, you can stand at the back there by the sound tech, so you don't get splashed."

It was about ten to eight when the rehearsals were done. Vlad was tied to the chair in the center of the 'kill room' and by this time he was so tired that he looked like he'd been tortured. The lighting was perfect to capture the shot without looking like a lighting expert had done the setup. All the systems were turned on and checked out. "OK, we're good to go."

Kat turned on the camera, recorded the shooting ..., Pop-Pop..., Pop. She ended the recording. The performance was simple.

"That was a good take people," said the FX coordinator. Kat couldn't find fault with it, nor could the general.

"That is a chilling bit of make-believe," Hershoff said.

"I think I died rather well, all things considered," said Vlad. "Now what do we do?"

"Now you have a shower, then we pack up and get the hell out of Dodge," said Hershoff. I have an apartment on the 5th floor where we can stay until tomorrow, just in case there is someone watching the building."

"That sounds perfect, thanks Ramsey," Kat said." She hugged him and then Vlad. "You were perfect."

He kissed her on both cheeks and said, "Katrina, please don't die." Then they left the room.

"Alright people that's a wrap, let's get all this crap stowed away." He stepped away from his crew and approached Kat. "Special Agent Fernando, I have one more thing for you."

"Oh?"

"It's your tracking device. They'll be tracking you as soon as you get to Italy. G-2 said when this is separated from that disk by a kilometer, he'll drop the ordinance."

"Got it." Her response was all business showing none of the emotion of a moment ago

"OK," he said. Before he handed her the cross he paused to really study her face intrigued by her apparent utter calm. She had to know that she was going on a suicide mission, so what she was thinking? He hadn't intended to do it but her suddenly felt the need to physically connect with her. Instead of handing the necklace to her he fastened it around her neck. He wanted to see that spark of humanity return, but she had already closed herself off.

"Was there something else?"

"No. Just..., good luck Special Agent Fernando."

Chapter 33

Sunrise on the Mountain

While Kat was still asleep in New York, the SF team in Peredicci rose with a hint of the sun rising through the overcast sky. There was more rain forecast for the day so working up to the plateau would be difficult and dangerous. The men moved quietly up the side of the mountain and almost immediately encountered the first line of Claymores Kat had mentioned. It was a job made a little easier because the mines Etxebarria had used were American made.

Working as quickly as they could under the conditions, they began clearing a wide path, collecting the explosives as they went, all the way to the top. There were more on the north side of the mountain than where Kat made her way, so the going was slow. But there were no cameras to interfere with their progress.

Around mid-afternoon they hit a snag when they discovered a field of 'Bouncing Betty' mines mixed in with the Claymores and they were not American made. These were the kind of antipersonnel mines the VC used in Vietnam, about the size of a large can of tomatoes, buried in the ground with a post sticking up and small wires that protruded on the surface. They would be armed when the person stepped on them, then the mine would spring up to about torso level after the person's foot lifted and detonate, sending out steel balls or bits of metal. There is nowhere to hide when that happens. Clearing those mines took much longer.

A little way up from the first narrow field of Bouncing Betties they discovered an ancient path cut into the mountain stone. "What do you think of that, Cap?" asked Lt. Ray.

"Who knows? It could be a way up the mountain, or it could lead to a tunnel inside it."

"What if it's a tunnel, would that go up to the top?"

"This was a monastery at one time. A lot of those ancient places had secret passages so people could get out if they were under attack, so yeah. But it could have been buried when the monastery was destroyed."

"But what if it does go up to the top and it's open?"

"Gordy, it's going off that way. We're going straight up there," he said, pointing up hill. "We haven't got the time to waste on a long shot."

"Cap, I've got a feeling about this. Let me take one guy with me and see where it leads," Ray said.

Captain Holt took a moment to consider the request. He looked at his watch and said, "Alright, take Sergeant Allen along to make sure you don't get lost."

"Oh, thanks a bunch, Cap."

"And Les," he said, pausing long enough to get the sergeant's attention, "I'm relying on you to keep Gordy out of trouble."

"Always, Sir," said Allen.

"We'll be on com at all times. I'll let you know what we find."

"OK take off. Good luck."

Lt. Gordon Ray and 1st Sgt Lester Allen peeled off to follow the path and the others kept working their way up. Ray and Allen took care to stay on the stones, secure in the knowledge that you can't bury a BB in rock. They quickly moved away from the team as the path traversed the mountain and switched back. The rain was heavy, but they could pick out the glistening wires that stretched across the ground and cleared the Claymores as they went.

As the team neared the top Capt. Holt was getting concerned that Ray hadn't checked in, so he raised him on the radio. "How are you guys doing?"

"It looks like there is a tunnel entrance in the rock wall just up ahead."

"Good, report when you're inside."

"Copy that."

TETERBORO AIRPORT

8:35 am

The same goons that had escorted them to America met her in the terminal at Teterboro Airport. They snatched her the moment she walked through the door causing a bit of a stir with the other travelers in the terminal. That set the tone for the whole trip. They were big men, humorless, strong, blond and stupid, like a pair of Nazi Brown Shirt characters sent in from Central Casting.

She had no idea why, but they escorted her to the women's washroom, and it was obvious that the biggest one was going to go in with her. She tried to brush him off and said, "You know, I'm OK, I went before I left the hotel."

His big, meaty, and disturbingly calloused hand clamped down hard on her arm again. "Shut up and go in," he said, and began to push her sideways.

"Whoa-there cowboy, if you want me to go in there then I'll go in, but I can do this myself you know. I've been doing it since I was, oh I don't know …, two! So ..."

"Shut up and go in," the man said, shoving her through the entrance.

She pushed back saying, "Look Manfred, or whatever the fuck your name is, if you want to be useful you can stay out here and play with your little friend."

"I said, shut up." Gripping her by the back of the neck even harder this time, he forced her into the ladies' room.

"You do know what I do for a living, don't you?" she said helpfully.

It seemed like a valid threat to her, until he countered with, "Ya, me too. Now shut up." There was a woman just coming out of one of the stalls and another one at the sink. "You," he growled, "get out now, both of you. This room is out of order." Terrified, they scurried out passing his partner who made sure that no one else entered until Manfred was done. "Take everything off."

"What?!"

"You heard me, everything." After he completed a pointless, excessive and brutal cavity search, he allowed her to dress and, from that moment on, they stayed so close that she felt like sandwich meat.

"Manfred, I promise you that I will remember what you did back there."

"What of it?"

"I'm just saying, payback can be a bitch."

"Shut up."

The flight to Rome took nine hours-and forty-five minutes and they arrived to find that storm clouds covered most of central Italy. The five-hour time difference had stolen the rest of the day and she was sick to death of the men who pressed against her during the entire flight. It was as if they thought she could somehow slip away. *Hello!* she thought. *Where could I go?*

It was all she could do to keep up the illusion of confidence. It would be so easy to just give up and accept that she had no hope of survival. But she stood up and straightened her shoulders, determined that she would not give them the satisfaction. "OK, which one of you lovely gentlemen has my umbrella?"

"No umbrella for you. Go now." They were not bothering with her suitcase either. She held her coat over her head with one hand and they ran from the jet a hundred meters to the helicopter. She managed to keep her hair relatively dry, but her coat was soaked, and she had to endure another half hour sandwiched between the two, damp and smelly thugs.

THE TUNNEL ENTRANCE

They found an entrance to the tunnel and Lt. Ray called it in. It had also been booby trapped, but they defused three IEDs and moved inside relying on their helmet lights.

The tunnel floor was smooth and dry with a bit of an incline as it went deeper into the mountain. Les left little transmitters to boost their signal. The path looped a couple of times, like a corkscrew, and took them up to a set of stairs. Ray called in again. "Cap, we found stairs and from here on it looks like the tunnel is lined with brick and I think it goes all the way up to the top."

His captain's voice crackled in his earpiece. "Any sign of recent traffic?"

"Just some IEDs at the front then rodents and spiders so far. I don't think anybody's been in here since the abbey was destroyed."

"Does it seem secure?"

"Not a crack anywhere, Cap, it's just old."

"Copy. OK, let me know how it ends."

"Spoiler alert, it ends at the beginning."

"Fuck off, clown. Call me when you get there. Holt out."

Sgt. Allen chuckled, "When did he start calling you clown, Gordy?"

"There's a first time for everything, Les," said Lt. Ray. Les placed another small signal booster at the foot of the steps and then they began to climb.

They thought they were probably three quarters of the way up and they had left five signal boosters so when Capt. Holt's voice crackled in their ears again it came through quite clearly, "How's it going in there?"

"It keeps on going up, Cap. How tall is this mountain again?"

"Fuck, it's only 544 meters, Ray, you should be at the top by now."

"You wouldn't believe what they have done in here. There are about a million steps and they go through a big cavern half-way up. They built a freestanding circular staircase that goes up through the roof. I mean how the hell did they do that? We should be near the top soon."

To Umbria

It was an 85-kilometer trip from the airport to the fortress. Kat watched the sparse groups of lights flash by on black landscape below while her two escorts pressed on either side of her like giant, pathetic, wet dogs.

Inside Kat was utterly numb. With Meadow and Conner suffering God-knows-what, all that planning and effort had been wasted. Her future, her baby's future, the futures of Meadow and Conner gone. They'd be blown to hell like Samantha and Maddix the moment she faced Jäger.

She had no choice now, finishing the mission was all that mattered. She would destroy the cross; her signal would disappear, and they would assume that she was dead. That would ensure that Jäger would die.

The rain eased off as they arrived. It was 11:45 and the light from the fortress shone like a golden fire bathing the plateau in gold. Jäger was waiting just inside the mysterious portal, as her minders practically carried her to him.

"How nice to have you back with us, Señora Franco. Did you have a pleasant flight?"

"Not particularly," she said, deciding to act like she was in complete control. "The food was just so-so, and I thought the cavity search in New Jersey was totally unnecessary."

"They violated you?" he asked, sounding genuinely horrified.

"Not your idea I take it. Well perhaps Manfred here …"

"That is not my name," the big man said.

"Nobody fucking cares, Manfred! Perhaps Manfred here just wanted to get me naked and have some fun. Say Manfred, remember when I told you that payback was a bitch?" She promptly kicked the big man in the balls as hard as she could, and he dropped to his knees. "There's some payback, asshole."

Jäger immediately took a step back while Manfred's partner moved to retaliate. He was shocked to discover that she could kick well above her head without any trouble at all. She planted her high heel on his jaw with enough force to snap his head back and open a nasty hole in his chin. He was down for the count before he had a chance to raise his fists.

"Thank goodness I wore jeans," she said with a casualness that she didn't feel. She turned back to Jäger, "Can you imagine me doing that in a skirt?"

"Vividly," Jäger said slightly awed, and then it dawned on him that she could have done that to him any time she wanted. He produced a gun from his coat pocket. "Now if you are through playing with the help, I would like you to come inside. Wilhelm, clean this up for me."

Kat began to go with Jäger, but the moment she went through the portal Wilhelm fired two shots. She turned slowly and saw that both men had been shot in the head. "That was a bit excessive don't you think?”

“Not at all. You do remember that I told you not to coddle the help. Believe me, it never hurts to occasionally set an example, so that the rest will stay in line. Oh, I’m not faulting you at all, Anita. It’s just a different management philosophy that works for me. Believe me, they wouldn’t have died if they had been able to defend themselves against you.” He resumed his journey inside, and she followed. “I doubt that the others will make the same mistake.”

“You will be the Emperor soon, and they are after all just your minions, so I suppose you can do whatever you want.”

“Exactly.” With a wave of his gun, he signaled her to go into the great room. It was much the same as it was the last time she visited. The only difference was that the chair to which she had been tied before was gone. Jäger motioned to the white love seat. “Please be seated.”

She took off her damp coat, dropped it on the floor and walked over to the couch. Half expecting that he would want to sit beside her, she sat in the center with her arms spread out on the cushions like a tripod, then crossed her legs. It was softer that she expected.

Showing some irritation, he went over to his desk and turned to face her, “You aren’t going to try to kick me, are you?”

“Not from here, no.”

He raised an eyebrow as he considered her answer, smiled and said, “Good.” He put the gun down, then, with a pensive expression, he walked to the armchair next to her and sat down. Steepling his hands as if to pray, he said, “So, you said that you had no trouble eliminating your friend. Do you have any proof that you completed your task? A finger perhaps, or his heart in a box?”

On the Mountain Side

Five minutes after his last transmission from Ray, Capt. Holt heard a helicopter in the distance. He changed the frequency on the radio. “Sea Gull, this is Fox 1.” He and two men began to run up the mountain as the rain eased off.

A Navy Reconnaissance plane was flying a pattern over the mountain. “Go ahead Fox 1,” said the radio man.

"Sea Gull, we've got incoming. Request you send down that pulse." He looked at his watch. It was 23:44. "ETA three minutes."

"Roger that." Lt. Col. Elizabeth Davis was directing the mission from the air. "The devices have been activated. We have them on our radar now. Can you see if our agent is in the chopper?"

"It's too far out, Ma'am. I'll confirm in a moment." They were almost at the top when he checked the device that picked up the signals. Hers was identified as a green blip, the target was red. The chopper was just rising over the lip of the mountain. "Sea Gull, I'm getting a green tone from our agent." He checked his watch again, it was 11:45:30. "It's making its approach now."

"Fox 1, we need a visual confirmation that the agent has entered the building with the package."

"Copy that."

The moment it touched down, the field lit up and the chopper door opened. A woman in a white coat stepped down between two large men. Holt checked his photo of Kat. "Identification of agent confirmed."

"Roger that Fox 1. We've got good tone from target and agent."

"She is walking to the glass structure."

"Copy that. We can see her. Sea Gull standing by."

He watched as she was taken to the front of the fortress and was amazed when she dropped her guards with a couple of kicks. "That is one ballsy lady," Holt said. Then the two men were shot in the head. "Holy shit! I did not see that coming,"

"What just happened?"

"Ah ... nothing, Sea Gull, the asset has entered the building."

"Copy that."

"OK, let's head back down now."

Chapter 34

Inside The Fortress

She forced a smile. "I'm sorry, customs would have had kittens with that sort of thing so, no fingers or hearts. But I knew that you wanted a memento, so I created one."

"Now I am intrigued, what is it?"

"First, I want to see Meadow and Conner."

"But my dear, that is not the way things works here. As Emperor, I make the rules and my man Wilhelm sees to it that people follow them ..., or they die." Once again, the big man had come in so quietly that until his gun was pressed against her head, she had no idea that he was there. "I assure you that your people are still alive. Your cooperation will ensure that they stay that way." She looked skeptical. "Don't worry, Wilhelm will take you to them soon, but I want that proof now." She hesitated. "Show me something right now, or I will send you down to watch them die. Wilhelm is aching to have some fun with them, aren't you Wilhelm? His father was a butcher back home in Leipzig, he's an expert with the knife."

The thought of that was beyond disturbing, but she managed to maintain her composure. "It is in my coat pocket."

"Wilhelm, bring me whatever it is in the coat." The huge man nodded, picked up the coat and found the disk. "I'm anxious to know what is on this. Can you give me a hint?" he asked, as Wilhelm put it in his outstretched hand.

"What, and spoil the surprise?"

"Oh, I insist," he said. "Spoil the surprise."

"Alright fine, I made a movie, then transferred it to that DVD."

"Really, you brought me a video? How very theatrical of you. What is the quality like?"

"I believe that it is excellent. You will feel as though you were right there behind me."

"How wonderful."

"I'm glad you approve," she said, as he opened the case and examined the disk. "Does your computer have a DVD player?"

With a look disgust, he raised his voice, "What a stupid question, of course it does," Turning around he lifted the screen of his laptop and pressed a button on the tray at the side of the machine. The tray slid out, he placed the disk in the cradle and pushed it closed.

When it closed and Kat started to get up, Wilhelm clamped his massive hand on her shoulder and pushed her back down, "Whoa! OK, Jesus! Could you tell your troll to lighten up? I just wanted to watch."

Jäger nodded at Wilhelm. The man squeezed her shoulder until she thought she heard a crack and was sure the troll had broken something. "That's enough Wilhelm!" The man lifted his hand and stepped back. Rubbing her shoulder, Kat got up and went over to stand beside Jäger. Wilhelm was right behind her, pressing his gun in her back.

"Back off, Lurch." With a jerk of his enormous head, Jäger signaled his bodyguard to move back. "Much better, thank you. It has sound too, so you should turn on your speaker." Jäger touched the speaker then clicked play and the recording began. They watched as she adjusted the camera to put Vlad in the picture.

"What is all this plastic for?"

"It was just a little prep work. Shooting people at close range gets very messy. I wanted to keep the room clean."

The view changed to white when Kat moved in front of the camera wearing her hazmat suit. Suddenly there was a clear image of her face peering into the lens. Her plastic visor was up, but the hood covered her hair and forehead. Off camera, Vlad could be heard trying to speak with the gag in his mouth.

Kat said, 'I'm sorry, Vlad, but I have no choice.' The view changed suddenly, blurring the image as the camera was turned and focused on the victim, bound to a dining room chair.

She said, 'There, that should be about right.' She came back into the picture frame, standing to the left, close to Vlad. He looked terrified as she stood before him, his eyes were almost closed, and his face was tense with stress.

"OK, now I am enjoying this," Jäger said, looking at her over his shoulder.

"Here it comes," she said, bringing his attention back to the screen.

The video showed her picking up the gun and fitting the silencer. Vlad tried to say something, which sounded to Jäger, like a plea for his life. "Oh, I love it when they do that."

'Goodbye Vlad,' she said in the recording, and fired two muted shots. Pop, pop. His body reacted to the impact, jerking back in the chair as blood sprayed the plastic curtain behind him and two holes appeared. She fired a third bullet, pop, which struck his forehead; his head jerked back, and it was over. His blood was everywhere, some even landed on the camera lens.

She lowered the gun and left the screen so that all that could be seen was Vlad, slumped in the chair with his eyes open. After a few seconds, the camera shook slightly, and the image went black.

"There you have it."

"I must admit, you put on an exceptionally good show, well done, Anita. Now I can scratch that off my 'to do list'."

"Do you mind telling me why you wanted him dead?"

"Not at all, Petrus had some value, admittedly it was limited, and I was preparing to eliminate him, but your friend Mr. Mogilevski stepped out of line when he arranged for his death. As I have said before, it was a lesson to others to play by my rules. Everyone must play by my rules now."

Kat thought about reaching for the gun on the desk. She wondered if she could use it before Wilhelm blew a big hole through her spine. Nope, she didn't have a hope. "I'm glad you are satisfied. Now I would like to be paid. Release my people to me so we can get out of here."

"Oh, I have other plans for the three of you before you leave here."

"What plans?"

"A man in my position must be obeyed in all things, Anita. It makes things so much easier when people can grasp the logic involved in maintaining control."

"I see where this is going," she said, wondering if it was going to be quick, like the gorillas outside.

"Ah, I thought you might," he said, then he noticed her necklace and suddenly his expression shifted from patronizing to fury. "Excuse me! What is that thing around your neck?"

"It's just a chain."

"Show it to me." She was about to protest, but Wilhelm gripped her by the arms and Jäger moved in then backed up a bit. "You would be ill advised to try to kick me my dear. Wilhelm would snap your neck if you did."

"I wouldn't dream of kicking you."

"Good." He grasped the chain between his fingers and lifted the crucifix into view. "You weren't wearing this the last time you were here."

"I always wear it; you just didn't notice."

"No, I have always admired your full bosom. Believe me, I would have remembered a cross nestled in that cleavage." He snapped the chain from her neck and held it in his hand. "I had no idea that you were religious."

"I ..."

"Don't bother to lie to me again." He studied it. "What does it do?"

"It wards off vampires. What do you think it does? It's just a cross."

"I think not." He looked at the foil label on the jewel case. It hadn't meant anything to him until now, but he remembered reading about tracking devices in labels. He picked up the case and held it next to the cross. "Well, aren't you a clever little minx? You have put something in these little items, haven't you?"

"Now how the hell was I supposed to do that?"

He dangled the chain from his fingers. "What is in here? A microphone, perhaps?"

"Don't be ridiculous, it's just an old silver cross."

He handed them to Wilhelm. "See that these are taken far from here."

"What about the disk, sir?"

"I don't think she would be able to tamper with a functioning disk. Dispose of those quickly and come back. I have need of your talents. Oh, and have Etxebarria join us. I think he will enjoy watching you work." He locked eyes on Kat and said, "Now, who would be out there tracking you?"

"You are completely delusional. Do you think I command a vast army of ninjas or something?" she said. "Look ..., it is just a cross. It was my mother's."

"It really doesn't matter what you say now, does it? Wilhelm, as soon as you return, it will be time for her to join her friends in the cell."

"You said you were going to release us after I did the job! I killed him for you. You just saw the goddamn video, so let us go!"

"You should have known that I was never going to let you go. You may have deluded yourself into thinking that I would overlook your rather substantial role in assassinating Petrus. That was a very entertaining video as well, by the way. I assure, you I had no intention of letting you go."

"So, you are just going to kill us, is that it?"

"Oh no, I'm not going to kill you. No, no, of course not. Please have a seat while Wilhelm deals with those treacherous items." Wilhelm forcefully sat her on the couch while Jäger collected his gun and sat in the armchair.

"There is nothing in them, this is ridiculous," she said.

They sat in silence until the giant returned, then Jäger said, "You know the more I think about it the more I like the sound of the disembowelment idea, Wilhelm."

"What?!" She tried to get up, but once again Wilhelm had crept in just in time to restrain her.

"Yes, I think we will do that. The man doesn't interest me, so just shoot him. Then we can get to the entertaining part of the evening. Wilhelm will gut your sweet Meadow like a fish. I prefer watching women die. When you have seen how painful that is, I think it will heighten your appreciation as you anticipate your own untidy end.

He has a knack for keeping people alive for a long time."

"You can't be serious! You're actually going to let that troll cut ..." Wilhelm smacked her on the back of the head.

"Oh, but I am. You know, I find it interesting that you returned. If I were in your place, friends or not, I would have left my people to rot and vanished when I had the chance. It seems obvious to me that someone in your profession would have expected this sort of end as inevitable. I will see you shortly. But then again ..., you will probably be too distracted to notice. Wilhelm, escort the lovely lady to the cell."

A small car left the back of the fortress and headed down the mountain. The driver had the jewel case and the cross on the seat beside him and his instructions were to take them as far away as possible.

The transition from the grand cathedral like spaces of the glass spires to the cellars below was like traveling through a time machine. Down the wide steps to the first sub-level, they passed through an ancient kitchen with a huge stone fireplace and brick ovens that had been cold for centuries. There were storage chambers and a cavernous room with a wide, shallow well that could have been the laundry. Beautifully cut stone columns and arches with detailed carvings formed the bearing walls that held up what used to be the Abbey di San Christos.

Wilhelm pushed Kat onward to another set of stairs much narrower than the first. He turned on a light switch and they descended into a cold place, and at the bottom was another large chamber with a cell built into the wall on the right. Kat saw Conner at the bars staring at her silently, Meadow was crouched in the corner hiding her head.

Like a giant funnel the floor sloped gently to the center, terminating at a hinged iron grate. Beneath it was a box-like hole a meter square with a drain in the center. "At one time," Wilhelm said, "it was used as a torture chamber. Heretics were locked in it and left to rot. When it rained, the water would flow down there, the prisoner's body would plug the drain and he would drown. Unfortunately, the water no longer enters the basement. I could have put the man in that. On a day like today, he would be sure to drown." He stopped to let her look inside the chamber. "By comparison, your deaths will take longer and be more painful. I will try to keep you alive for as long as I can."

Kat couldn't bring herself to comment, she just looked at him with a mixture of horror and disgust. Wilhelm laughed. "Soon, I will gut you and butcher you like a pig." Pointing to Conner he said, "I will start by putting a bullet in his head."

She looked at Conner and Meadow and saw the terror in their eyes.

"I am so sorry," she said.

"Silence!" Wilhelm said, delivering a back hand to her head. She staggered and fell hard. Before she could orient herself again, he grabbed her by the arm and hauled her to her feet, as if she weighed nothing, then pushed her toward the cell. She connected with the bars painfully and hung on for support. Holding her by the neck, he removed the key from his coat pocket and held it at the mouth of the lock. "You, stand back from the bars," he ordered. Conner immediately backed into the corner beside Meadow. They were covered in bruises and dried blood. Wilhelm inserted the key and turned it then pushed the door open. With more force than necessary he tossed Kat in. Once again, she landed painfully.

"Fucking troll," she said, with the taste of blood in her mouth. He smirked and slammed the door closed, locked it, and then padded away to the stairs.

Conner helped her to her feet. "Thanks," she said. He put his finger to his lips and pointed to the light fixture above them. It was just a bare bulb in a steel cage as far as she could tell, but he was certain there was a bug hidden in it. Kat nodded and said, "I don't think what we say to each other will matter now, Conner." She looked at Meadow who was still trembling in the corner with her hands covering her mouth and her arms held tight against her chest.

"That ape raped her right in front of me," Conner said. "He told her that he was going to do it again just before he gutted her. She's been like that ever since."

"Jesus, Meadow, I am so sorry. I'll ..."

"You'll what? Stop him?!" she shrieked. "I saw what he did to you Kat. There is nothing you can do to stop him. That man is going to rape me again and then he's ..., he's ..."

"Meadow." Kat went to her to hold and comfort her, but Meadow screamed, "No! Stay away from me!"

Conner drew back. "Meadow, for Christ's sake, this wasn't her fault."

"Wasn't it?" she challenged, through her tears. "WASN'T IT?"

"I'm sorry, Meadow," Kat repeated.

"NO!" Meadow shrieked again. "You don't get to apologize!" She turned to face the wall. Conner had nothing else to say, he just sat on the floor.

To distract herself Kat began to look around. There was nothing in the cell but them, no bed, no blankets, no sign of food and no waste. There was a small hole in the floor which, she assumed, they had been using to relieve themselves.

She began to look more closely. The cell's three walls were brick while the rest of the dungeon was stone. Beside Conner and Meadow there was an arch shaped alcove in the wall with a stone sill and a crude painting depicting Mary and the baby Jesus. The top of the alcove was covered in soot, probably from burning candles and incense. It was obviously an altar, so the room wasn't originally intended as a cell. Perhaps it wasn't meant as a dungeon after all, but a prayer room, large enough to accommodate all the monks of the abbey. But why would they build something like this underground?

She was about to examine it more closely but when Wilhelm reached the top of the stairs, he switched off the lights plunging them into total darkness. "Holy shit, is this what it's been like the whole time?"

"Yeah, no food, no water, no light," said Conner. "Be careful, the hole in the middle."

Kat leaned her back against the wall near the alcove and slowly slid down until she was firmly planted on the floor. At least, she thought, it will all be over soon. The DVD will guide the bomb in and that'll be it. She didn't tell the others in case the people up above were listening. All they could do now was wait. Please let it come soon, she said to herself. She put her hand on her tummy and felt a small bump. "Christ, I have been such a fool, my sweet little baby. I'm so sorry."

Historical Reference

What no one realized, was that one thing was missing from the brochure's brief history of the abbey. The lowest level of the abbey was where they kept their preserves and wine.

The room had an alcove under the stairs which was faced with red brick over the stone. The wall with the arch was built to divide the alcove into two chambers with a carefully balanced stone door opening onto the smaller chamber.

With a great deal of foresight, the abbot commissioned an escape tunnel to be dug from that small chamber, down to the forest at the back of the mountain. It was an amazing feat of engineering that had taken many skilled craftsmen several years to construct. The tiny chapel was placed in the alcove with the altar to hide the door and, when bad times came, neither the French nor Jäger knew that it was there.

On the Mountainside

All Capt. Holt knew was that Kat's tracker had been motionless for a while. There was no way of knowing that she was sitting in the pyramid with Jäger. As their conversation stretched on Holt became increasingly anxious. Col. Davis was concerned as well because she had already given orders for the Predator to launch.

"Fox 1, what is happening down there, can you see any activity outside the fortress?"

"No Sea Gull, the status up there is unchanged."

"She is still with the target?"

"As far as we know, Ma'am."

"How is your team doing in the tunnel?"

"We had a progress report from them ten minutes ago, and they were near the top."

"They are running out of time, Fox 1."

"Ma'am, I'll call them right now and get a SIT-REP then call you back."

"Do that. The package is on its way, repeat, the package is on its way. If Jäger sets foot outside I want to know about it. If he heads to the chopper before the Reaper gets there, then you have to take him out. Do you understand Fox 1? See that he doesn't get off that mountain."

"Yes Ma'am."

"Keep me posted."

"Yes Ma'am, Fox 1 out." He turned to his radio man and said, "How the fuck does she expect us to do that and get off the mountain alive?"

Holt contemplated the implications of her order for a moment and then called Lt. Ray. "Gordy, what's your status?"

"We've reached a corridor, Cap. It curves around to the left and I think this is the top now."

"Well hurry the fuck up!"

"Copy that."

Precious minutes ticked by and the DVD's signal was still in the center of the glass pyramid. Capt. Holt was about to contact Col. Davis when Kat's signal began to move. "Hey, there she goes now. Well son-of-a-bitch, she's done it. "OK, Timble, Ho and Penn get to the bus and intercept the vehicle." The three men got up ran down the mountainside. Holt clicked on the radio, "Sea Gull, we see activity and it appears that our asset is on the move."

"I see that too, where is she going?"

"There is only one road down from there. I've sent some men to intercept. There is no visual on her outside, but she is moving away from the buildings." He checked his watch and saw that they only had eight minutes before the strike. "She is moving fast now, Ma'am, and heading off the mountain."

"You don't know how relieved I am to hear that Captain. Any sign of the target?"

"No. All I know is the that the RRT is in the center of the largest part of the building and hasn't moved since it was delivered. I assume it is still in his computer and he is with the computer."

"As soon as you have secured the agent, let me know."

"Yes Ma'am."

The men reached the bus quickly and the car was already heading down the lane.

The commandos sped up the road, skidding through the turn at the farmhouse then the raced off to Strada Statale 79. They beat the car broadcasting Kat's signal to the intersection of the abbey lane and Via Panoramica and blocked the road.

Two commandos jumped out with their hands waving, signaling the car to stop. It didn't. It was heading right for them. "Holy shit! Fire into the engine to stop it," said Ho.

As the bullets slammed into the area between the headlights, the car skidded to a stop into the retaining wall. Their lights fell on the lone figure as he reached out of the window with a gun and was immediately shot.

They ran to the car and found the jewel case and the cross on the floor of the passenger side. Timble radioed back to inform Holt, "The asset was not in the car, Sir. The driver was a decoy, he had her cross and the CD case."

"Copy," he said, and looked back at the glass edifice. "Fuck!" Holt radioed Col. Davis. "Ma'am, that was a decoy. She is still inside."

Col. Davis said, "Copy that. We must assume that our asset has been eliminated. The package is on the way. It is 01: 08, ETA is 01:18. Is there anyone moving outside the building?"

"No Ma'am."

"Then get your people off the mountain now Captain. There's nothing more you can do."

"Copy that, Ma'am."

THE CELL

Sitting in a cell beneath thirty feet of solid rock felt like being sealed in a tomb. She thought that it was a good thing that Jäger had taken the cross from her. The only hope she had now was that the bomb would kill them quickly before the monster started gutting them one by one.

Kat heard a scraping sound coming from the wall. Carefully she stood up and feeling her way she moved toward it. The others heard it too, and the three of them stood there staring into the black hoping for a miracle while at the same time knowing full well that miracles don't happen.

Kat shouted, "Hello! ... Hello, is there someone there?"

Down the Mountain

Holt signaled his team to withdraw "You heard the lady, let's clear off this rock." He was about to radio his people to get them out of the tunnel when the radio squawked. "Cap, we're at the top. That corridor that curved to the left brought us to a huge stone set into the rock face. I think it's a door."

"Can you get it open?"

"We're going to try."

"Do it then and hurry. We've got less ten minutes before the mountain blows!"

"Shit! Copy that."

"There's no fucking time. They're not going to make it. OK, move, move, move."

As he ran down the slope, Holt called up to the Recon Plane. "My team has found a door at the top of the tunnel. They are almost in. We need a little extra time to locate the asset. Can you have the drone circle until they are out?"

"That's a negative, Captain. The agent is dead. Now if your people don't get out of there in ten minutes, they are not going to survive either. Get them out now!"

"But Ma'am ..."

"You heard me Captain, nine minutes twenty seconds. Now get out of there! And Captain, I'll need you to go in after the explosion and report on casualties."

At The Top

01:05:15

Kat pressed her forehead against the crack in the rock and shouted, "Hello, we're in here!"

"Hello! Listen the stone in front of you is a door. Can you push on it?"

She tried." I can't, there's a stone shelf in the way."

"Well, see it you can move that out of the way."

The radio squawked, "Gordy, time's up. Come down now!"

"Hang on, Cap. We've found her."

Kat pulled the shelf away from its housing and dropped it on the floor. That action was the key that released the latch and the door moved. "It moved!"

"Good!" the lieutenant shouted, "OK push!" As the gap began to widen, they squeezed their fingers into the crack and pulled. The secret door was remarkably easy to move for a stone that large.

The captain shouted into his radio, "Shit, we don't have time for games! Get out now!"

Three faces appeared in the beams of their helmet lights. "Cap, you're never going to believe what's on the other side of this wall. We have three hostages in a cell, two women and a man. They look OK and we're heading down now."

"Jesus! You've got less than nine minutes! Move it!"

"Shit! OK people, let's move! Follow the sergeant and watch your step, the stairs are steep and there is a fuck load of them. Run! Keep going!"

The lights came on in the cellar as Meadow ran through. "Christ," Kat said, "they're coming. Conner, go!"

Wilhelm stepped off the stairs in time to see Kat disappearing. He warned Jäger that something had gone wrong. Jäger immediately turned and, pushing Etxebarria out of the way, ran up the stairs. Shouting into his radio Jäger ordered the helicopter to be ready to take off the moment he got to it. The bomber was right behind him.

Meadow was unsteady, so Conner wrapped his arm around her and was practically carrying her as he ran. Kat was the last out and Wilhelm was at the cell door fumbling with the key in the lock. In a few seconds, he would be right behind her.

They were just turning the corner down the slope and she could hear the troll thundering down the tunnel after them. Ray turned off his light, stopped to let Kat get by. He waved her on then took a knee.

He didn't have to wait long. Wilhelm was moving fast with a light attached to his gun. The light swung from side to side as he came around the bend.

The troll's huge form filled the tunnel and Ray sprayed the corridor with his submachine gun. Wilhelm took some hits but stepped back behind the bend and fired back. Ray moved to a new position and Wilhelm advanced.

When Ray fired again there was nowhere for the troll to hide and, this time, he took the full burst. He fell face down and didn't move again.

Switching on his light, the lieutenant turned and raced after the others. They heard more men running after them, and soon bullets were bouncing off the tunnel walls kicking up dust and splintered brick and stone. The turns and steep angle of descent were what saved them.

Following Les Allen's light, Kat could see that Meadow was holding Conner back, so she took her saying, "I'm in better shape than you. I'll take her from here. You just move as fast as you can and be careful."

Lt. Ray shouted, "Keep going, they're right behind us."

It was taking far less time to descend than it had to climb the stairs. They reached the open circular stairs through the cavern. At the bottom, Ray held back to pick off the pursuers as they came out onto the stairs. He took out two who fell and disappeared into the blackness, but there were more waiting behind, and the next man started firing blindly with an automatic weapon. Ray bugged out to find another defensive position further down.

Allen was thinking about how long it took to get up and was afraid that there was no way they'd make it to the bottom in the time they had left.

Kat was getting tired and really beginning to feel the effects of a concussion. She slipped and Meadow fell. "Oh Jesus, Meadow, are you alright?" She scooped her up and carried on. "Sergeant, how far down does this thing go?" she shouted.

Sgt. Allen let Conner go past him and, as Kat came near, he said, "Not too far, ma'am, keep going." He took Meadow up in his arms, "I've got her, now go."

"But how far is it?" Meadow asked.

The sergeant said, "Just keep moving," he shouted, "they're right behind us."

Kat ran taking the steps three and four at a time, risking a twisted ankle or worse, and the distance between her and the sergeant widened.

Lt. Ray fired, and two men toppled over as they came into view on a landing. The rest held back for a second then came at him firing.

The ricochets were coming awfully close, so Ray made a judgment call. He lobbed a hand grenade up at them and jumped down to the next landing. A man scrambled forward to get to it, but he was too late.

The explosion was deafening, far beyond anything a grenade could have produced. The roof in the upper section of the tunnel came down burying the pursuers. Smoke, dust and debris rushed down and chased Ray to the bottom.

At 01:18 the GBU-12 Paveway crashed through the glass right onto the Mac laptop.

Out on the surface, the horrific explosion sent out a shock wave that bent the trees as if they were made of string. The sky lit up with orange and red flames and billowing black smoke. Debris began to cascade around the mountain. There were secondary explosions and large shards of golden glass came flying through the air like daggers, embedding themselves in trees and setting off several of the remaining Claymores around the mountain.

Inside the tunnel, it seemed like the whole top of the mountain was coming down on them.

Capt. Holt and his men had found the mouth of the tunnel and taken shelter as the ensuing fire storm raged over them.

It threatened to envelope the town as well, but in the moments before the explosion, the rain had become very heavy and the flames were kept down. What was left up top was nothing but a smoldering, steaming crater laced with twisted steel.

The dust and smoke blasted down the tunnel almost suffocating Kat and the others. Luckily, the tunnel collapsed before the fire could reach them. Even so, they were caked in dust and trying to breathe using their shirts as filters. When Lt. Ray caught up to them on the smooth sloping floor at the bottom he was shouting, "Keep going, we're nearly there!"

They ran right into the arms of the SF team captain and they all spilled out into the rain. The dust instantly turned to mud and it was nearly impossible to tell who was who.

"Fernando?" Capt. Holt shouted.

Doubled over and coughing, Kat raised her hand. "Here."

"Did the target get the package?"

"Yes," she said, gasping for air, but then she stopped and stood up straight. "Wait a second." In the relative silence, she heard something. "What's that noise?" It was the helicopter in the distance. "Oh, God no!"

Holt didn't like the sound of that and asked, "What?"

"Don't you hear that?"

"No, what?" He was surprised that she could hear anything after the explosion.

"The helicopter!" Kat held up her hand and pointed at the flashing red light disappearing into the black. "The helicopter. Oh Jezzus, he got away. I've fucking failed."

"Holy-fuck," Holt said. "Sea Gull, come in."

"Go ahead, Fox 1."

"Sea Gull, did you see an object fly away from that on your radar?"

"No, why?"

"We think the target got away. Can you get a fix on it?"

"We can't see anything on radar. Captain Holt, are you sure it was him?"

"We may never know, Ma'am. Holt out."

CHAPTER 35

MONTE SAN GIOVANNI

Hikers found the helicopter in the mountains north of Monte San Giovanni. The only body was that of the pilot, presumably the only occupant. It was determined that the weather had brought it down. Kat was shown pictures and she identified it as the Bell 525 Relentless owned by Jäger. She also identified the pilot as the man who flew her up to the mountain from Rome.

The cause was difficult to pin down, but there was some gold impregnated glass from the fortress embedded in the tail section. That suggested that it had been damaged by the explosion as it took off. It looked like he could have been the only one to escape the inferno, only to die moments later.

After the command system was destroyed, the attacks on Americans stopped.

If Jäger and his bomber friend had escaped - and according to the experts, it would have been impossible - then they must have fallen off the face of the earth without a trace. The general assumption was that they had been inside the Golden Fortress when it went up. The authorities confiscated every asset belonging to Jäger they could find. If he had survived, they were going to make certain that he would have nothing to live on.

Part 4

CHAPTER 36

A Family of Two

Mulmur, Ontario, Canada, Monday, April 18, 2005

The little mystery was solved on Tuesday, December 14, 2004, at Mt. Sinai Hospital in Toronto. The baby was a girl and Kat named her Sara. She had been sure from the moment she knew she was pregnant that it was a girl. At eight pounds seven ounces, she was perfect, and Kat was deliriously happy. She was probably going to be just like her mother, except that she had blue eyes.

Spring had come and it was a beautiful, warm, summery kind of day. Kat knew that there was always the chance of another snowfall in her Camelot but that was OK, life had become consistently quite wonderful. The baby was asleep in her arms after a small midmorning snack and Kat was hoping she would wake up soon and work on the other side. It was getting painful and she was tempted to wake Sara up just to relieve the pressure.

As if in answer to her wish, Sara opened her lovely blue eyes and smiled at Kat. "Oh, there you are. Who is Mummy's beautiful little girl?" The baby rewarded her with an absolutely beautiful smile. "Are you hungry again?" Sara didn't seem interested. "No, no, funny girl you are hungry, believe me," she said, and Sara obediently latched on and closed her eyes again. "Hey there, little one," she said, tickling Sara's chin with her finger, "don't you go to sleep again, you have a job to do." Sara began to suck and make little noises. "That's right."

Her beautiful blue eyes were the only feature she got from Paul Devlyn. Lucky little Sara. Kat stroked the baby's soft black hair with her finger.

She was so overwhelmed by how wonderful Sara was she began to cry soft happy tears. The baby was the answer to the emptiness she'd felt.

Sitting in a comfortable chair, Kat was looking out a large picture window with a view down to the Pine River Valley. Only a few tiny sections of the winding river could be seen through the forest canopy. The old forest stretched along the valley, and on the far side, where the land was cleared in the mid-1800s, were lush green fields. She was in Mulmur again, back where Deacon Loats's beautiful house once stood. It was gone now, pulled down after what had happened there. But she had made a quiet promise to herself that her child would grow up here, in Mulmur.

Out on the distant hill across the river valley, there was a small lake where she and Deacon swam and made love. They rode to it on horseback, picnicked on the soft grass of its tiny island and made love again. She thought about that every time she looked out the window.

She and Sara were living in an attractive house she found not far from Deacon's farm. He was in the city now, a hundred kilometers from her. It may as well have been a million, because he had no idea that she had returned. During the short time with him in Mulmur, she had fallen in love again, with him and this quiet country. The memory of that was enough for now. Out of all the places she had been around the world, this was the closest to perfection she had found.

It was a big house, bigger than she needed, but the location was what sold it. Kat and Sara shared it with her nanny Rosario, who was a nurse back in the Philippines. She started off with Kat as a temp, while she waited for a better job, then decided that being with Kat and the baby was all she really needed to be happy.

"Kat, can I get something for you?" she asked, as she came into the living room.

Kat looked up at her and smiled. "No, we're fine thanks." Her voice was light and happy as she gently rubbed Sara's tummy. No, she needed nothing, her world was as close to perfection as it was ever going to get, she thought.

"OK, I'll go into Shelburne now. I have a big list of things to buy. Is there anything special that I can get for you?"

"Oh, you know, there is one thing that might be nice," she said.

"Maybe you could pick up some chocolate, you know the kind I like."

Rosario grinned. "I know. I won't be long." Kat nodded and looked back out the window. "OK, bye."

"Bye."

She took Kat's Range Rover and headed off down the lane. A triple beep from the remote alarm on the end of the drive told Kat that the car had left the property. Now it was just the two of them. The sun was brilliant; the sky was a color chart of blue from the palest hue on the horizon through to the deep rich blue at the top of her window. It was dotted with what she liked to call fluffy, white lambs for Sara's benefit. She touched her tiny hand and her perfect little fingers curled around the end of her finger and hung on.

The phone rang.

The double ring meant that it was long distance. She looked at the Ident-A-Call screen and didn't recognize the number, so she tried to ignore it. But it would not be ignored. It continued to ring until she finally picked it up. "Yes?" At first there was silence, so she said, "Hello... Who is this?"

Then the familiar voice said, "Anita darling, where is your accent?"

Hearing that voice sent a shiver up her spine and made the hair on the back of her neck stand on end.

"You don't know what a pleasure it is to hear your voice again."

"You've got the wrong number, there's no Anita here," she said, and was about to hang up, but what he said next brought her to full alert.

"It is April 18th, our anniversary. Do you remember?"

Her voice betrayed the panic that took hold of her, "Jäger, what have you done?"

"I have sent a present for you and Sara. It is on its way to you now. I am sure it will be a big surprise when it arrives."

Kat had already dropped the phone, jumped from the chair, and ran, crashing through the screen door without bothering to open it. She raced across the deck and jumped down to the lawn five steps below and kept on going.

Jäger was still talking, but she was too far away to hear him. "... I just wanted to repay an old debt. Goodbye Anita."

She ran to the other side of the yard and got through the cedar hedge just as the house disintegrated. She was knocked to the ground by the shock-wave and Sara spilled out of her arms and rolled in the long grass. She scooped the baby up and continued to run for the bush.

Sara was screaming and wouldn't stop. Kat was terrified that something had happened to her when she fell. She gave the baby a quick inspection and she looked alright. Until that moment, Kat had ignored her own condition. She was barefoot and bleeding, her shirt was still open, and her bra was still pulled down. She crouched down holding Sara on her knee so she could pull herself together, all the while trying to think where she could go to hide.

Was the bomber still there?

Did he expect her to run?

Did he have a rifle with a scope?

No, he expected her to die inside the house.

But maybe he had been watching.

Did he see her escape? She looked back and even though she saw nothing but the fire, she ran.

Without concern for the thorns on the raspberry canes that clawed at her pant legs, or the stones that bruised and scraped her feet, she ran. She didn't stop until she was deep in the bush, far from the burning house.

Half-way into the valley she stopped and dropped to a knee again, panting, her heart pounding against her chest as if it were going to burst out any second.

"Oh Sara, it's OK now sweetheart." The baby was calmer now and looked bewildered, but apparently unharmed. "We'll be alright, Sara, I promise." She moved down the steep slope to a rolling cornfield where last year's stalks had been cut short and yellowed. They were hard and sharp and made running difficult. Moving down the muddy rows with Sara clinging to her shirt, she stopped once to look behind her. All she could see was the smoke above the trees with orange flames licking at the sky.

The fire could be seen from as far away as Honeywood. Volunteer firefighters from all over the area raced to the fire in their pickup trucks or to the fire hall for their equipment. Now she could hear the sirens coming across the valley, but no one was following her.

Kat turned away again and moved as quickly as she could to the farmhouse below hers.

A man in his seventies rushed to open the kitchen door as she banged on the glass. His eyes were wide with concern. "My-god-woman, was that your house that blew up?" She'd seen him before, in town and around, but they had never been introduced.

Kat nodded. "Please can I come in and use your phone?"

"Jesus! Well of course ..., Jesus. Here, come in, come in." Her feet were leaving a track of mud and blood across his floor as she walked to the kitchen table. The man took the baby and helped Kat to a chair.

"Have you called the police?" she asked.

"I called the fire department after I heard the bang, they are on their way, but they won't get there in time to save the house. I'm sorry. They never do, out here. They say they save the foundations. God, how are you?"

"I'm fine. I'm just worried about Sara. I dropped her when I fell. Is she OK?"

He touched Sara's cheek with his finger and the baby smiled at him. "Yes, she looks fine."

Kat reached out for her daughter. "I need to hold her."

"Oh sure, of course, here you are." The exchange was awkward, and she was anxious. "You got her now?"

"Yes, thank you."

"OK, I'll get something to clean you up. I think I have some bandages in the washroom."

For the first time, she looked down at the trail of red and mud she left behind her. "Oh, I'm sorry. I've tracked mud all over your floor."

"Never mind about that." He brought back a wet cloth, a hand towel and a box of small bandages and began washing her feet. "I don't think these little Band-Aids are going to do you any good."

"It's OK, thank you. Can I use your phone? My nanny was out doing the shopping and if she gets home to that ..."

"Of course, I'll get it for you." He went over to the counter and picked up his wireless phone and handed it to her.

"Thanks." Kat made the call and Rosario practically screamed in response.

"Kat, oh thank God, I thought you were inside." Through the tears she managed to ask, "Is Sara alright?"

"She's fine, she's alright, we're both alright."

"Oh my God, what happened? Where are you?"

"I'm at the white farmhouse with the corn field down in the valley."

"I know the one."

"Can you come and get us?"

"I am coming, Kat, I'll be there soon." She got back in the car and raced north on the dump road.

"So, she is OK then?" the man said.

"Rosario is OK. She's fine. She's coming for us now. I should make one more call. Do you mind? It's long distance."

"Sure, go ahead, I got a plan with Bell."

She dialed her special number and the voice on the other end said, "Maryland heating and air conditioning."

"My furnace isn't working. I'd like to speak to the manager please." The old man looked at her like she had just lost her mind.

"Serial number please."

"MI 55-31-86."

"That number is listed as inactive."

"It's an emergency, I must talk with G-2."

"Hold."

There was a long pause and then the general's familiar voice came on the line. "What's this all about Katrina?"

"Jäger is alive. He just spoke to me by phone. And Etxebarria is alive too. He was here. He just blew up my house."

"Hold on." There was a pause and then the general came back on. "I have you located in Ontario, Canada. A township called Mulmur, is that correct?"

"Yes."

"You are in a farmhouse off River Road that belongs to ..., Fred Goodale. Is that correct?"

She looked at the old man who could hear the conversation but couldn't figure out what the hell was going on. "Are you Fred Goodale?" Fred nodded and smoothed back his thinning white hair. The look of concern on his face deepened. "Yes, that is correct. He is my neighbor to the north. My house is burning."

"I can see that; I'm looking at the satellite feed right now. How do you know it was Jäger?"

"I will never forget his voice. It was him, I'm sure of it. The moment he said it was our anniversary, I ran."

"Any indication of where he called from?"

"No, just that it was long distance. Area code 786."

"That's Miami. I'll get the Miami LLEOs (local law enforcement officers) to put out a BOLO."

"Etxebarria is probably still nearby though."

"Do you have a safehouse?" Wolf asked.

"Yes."

"Go to it now and call me when you are secure."

"The operator said my serial number is deactivated. How do I get in touch with you?"

"I'll fix that. Go to the safehouse as soon as you can." Kat touched the off button and handed the phone back to the man.

"What the hell was that all about? How did he know where you were?"

"He saw your name and address on his computer."

"And it sounded like he's been tracking you."

"It did, didn't it," she said, and it had never occurred to her that they would be doing that.

"Say, are you some kind of spy?"

"Mr. Goodale, you've been very kind and I am grateful, but I ..."

"Hang on a second there, Missy. You are a spy, aren't you?!"

"No. no, I was a Federal Law Enforcement Officer with US Army Counterintelligence. I'm retired now."

"Yeah counterintelligence, that's government speak for American spy. Isn't that just typical. You people are bringing your terrorist shit up here again ... wait!" he said, as the penny dropped. "Your name wouldn't by any chance be Fernando?"

She became concerned and headed for the door, instinctively turning Sara away from the man. "Yes."

"Katrina Fernando?"

"Yes," she said cautiously. "Have ..., have we met before?"

"I thought that name was familiar. You were part of all those killings over at the Loats' place a couple of years back. The papers said you were dead! Now, doesn't that beat all? So now you're back and you brought your goddamn guns and bombs with ya."

"I'm not involved with that anymore ..." Kat began.

"Oh yeah? You should have told that to the son-of-a-bitch who blew up your house!"

"I think he already knows that. Look, Mr. Goodale, I'm sorry to bring this to your door, but I had nowhere else to go. Rosario will be here any minute now and I'll be gone. The police will be coming too I suppose, but ..."

"Yeah, I heard that G-2 man on the phone, nothin' wrong with my hearing. Never mind with that bull crap, because I want you out of my house, now!" Goodale was angry at first, now he was scared and angry, thinking that he'd just let something poisonous into his house and he didn't know what to do about it. "Get out! Get out and wait down by the road."

After she left, he collapsed in the chair she just vacated and thought about how he had reacted. He was wrong and he knew it. "That was a damned stupid thing to do," he said. He got up and went to the door, but it was too late. She was gone.

Chapter 37

Following the Explosion

Toronto

General Wolfson immediately put out an alert to be on the lookout for Etxebarria that went right across North America. The photo taken from the security camera in Munich was the only image of him they had, and it was sent out to all agencies. The order was to follow, not apprehend. Wolfson was sure that he would lead them right to Jäger's door.

Carl Blanché, an agent with CSIS (Canadian Security Intelligence Service), was transiting through Pearson International Airport on his way back to Ottawa. On his inbound flight to Toronto, he received a call telling him to check in with the RCMP to pick up a photo of a wanted man.

It was Blanché who spotted Etxebarria first. He had long hair and a beard, but Blanché was certain that it was him. He phoned in the sighting as he followed the wanted man to an Air Canada flight heading for Miami. He showed his ID at the gate, explained that he was on government security business and boarded the plane. He walked right by Etxebarria who was sitting in business class. He found an empty seat at the back of the plane.

Etxebarria changed planes in Miami and continued to Port of Spain, Trinidad, where they had an eight-hour layover. Blanché did his best to stay out of sight until they both boarded an Air Jamaica flight to Georgetown, Guyana.

They landed at Ogle Airstrip on the eastern side of Georgetown. Blanché followed him at a discreet distance and watched as Etxebarria bought a ticket for a flight to Bartica Airport on a small commercial plane. The agent phoned in his report to CSIS, then went to buy a ticket to Bartica. He was surprised when he got out onto the field that there were only two passengers boarding the plane.

King St. Safehouse

Tuesday April 19

Kat called Wolfson again when she got to her safehouse and the general gave her the short form of the report they received from Blanché. "So, what are you planning to do about this General?"

"I took this all the way to the President. The FBI, the CIA, AHS and Joint Chiefs have been informed and are considering their options. I have to tell you that, honestly, Katrina, there isn't much we can do. Since the Rote Faust problem seems to have been resolved, and Europe is getting back to normal, any further action must be taken through local authorities and diplomatic channels. Our ambassador to Guyana will bring it to their attention. If they can find him then we will extradite him. Legally, there's nothing more we can do, I'm sorry."

"Has Blanché reported since he arrived in Bartica?"

"Not that I am aware of, but it's not like the Canadians are giving us daily reports. Listen, Katrina, bottom line here is no one wants to see another Golden Fortress. We're not sending in the troops, we're not dropping bombs, we're done."

"So, what am I supposed to do?"

"You are a civilian now, Katrina. Officially, I am telling you to leave this to the professionals. My advice to you is that your responsibility is to look after your daughter," he said cryptically. "You should know how to do that better than anyone. Oh, and check your email. Be advised that your access to CI and its services will be terminated in seven days, repeat, seven days," he said, and hung up.

Kat checked her email and found something from Shep W. Not much of a mystery that it was from Lt. Gen. Shepherd Wolfson, Deputy

Chief of Staff, Intelligence G-2, so what was he playing at?

There was a short message and an attachment which she downloaded and printed. The image was from a security camera at Pearson and it made her blood run cold. The photo was of a man with a hat, his thinning long hair was tied back like a rat tail and he had a bushy mustache and beard. The Message read:

Jesús Maria Etxebarria, Bartica, Guyana.

CHAPTER 38

TORONTO

11:00 pm

From the sidewalk on King St., it looked like nothing more than a dirty brown, steel door, perhaps leading to a storage room beside the used furniture shop. Up the steep and narrow staircase was a large, two-story apartment, with a modern service elevator at the back. Kat bought the building when she arrived in Toronto and had the space above the shop renovated, complete with an advanced security system and a secure garage off the lane behind.

She was sitting with her feet curled under her on a comfy loveseat in front of the TV. The evening news was on and, as usual, they were covering the wars in Afghanistan and Iraq and the latest Hezbollah rocket attack on Israel, but Kat wasn't paying attention. She had the email and photo of Etxebarria Wolfson sent on the coffee table and was pondering what to do about it. Wolfson had resorted to that stupid old cliché they use in the movies; it's up to you to get the bad guy, but officially we don't know what you're doing and we can't help you if you get into trouble.

"Well, isn't that just peachy?!" she said.

"Pardon, Kat, you said something?"

"Sorry, just talking to myself." The baby was having one of those rare moments when she was sleeping peacefully in her crib. Rosario was knitting in a chair nearby. Kat was about to get up and go to bed and would have missed the story if it weren't for the tease before the commercial break. The news reader said...

And coming up, a Canadian diplomat has gone missing in Guyana. Details after this.

Kat immediately sat back down. Rosario was startled and dropped a stitch, so she put her knitting down. "Is something wrong?"

"No ..., ah, there was just something on the news. The story is coming on after the commercial and I want to hear, that's all," Kat said.

"OK, I'm going to bed now, good night."

"Good night, Rosario."

34-year-old Carl Blanché, a diplomat serving in Ottawa, was reported missing in Guyana today. He arrived in the former British colony two days ago, on a low-level trade mission to Georgetown. Police say that he was last seen boarding a flight to Bartica. No one in Bartica remembers seeing the diplomat get off the plane. Guyanese Police said they have investigated and are saying that Mr. Blanché probably missed his flight and will turn up soon. The RCMP is looking into it.

In other news...

"Aw damn!" she said, "If he got on that plane with Etxebarria then he probably got out before it landed."

Kat went into her study, closed the door, and sat at her desk. She was trying to come up with a way of making this go away that didn't involve her leaving Sara. The problem was, according to Wolfson, there just didn't seem to be one. If something happened to her, then Sara would be left with no one. The only other person in the world who cared about her, besides Ramsey Hershoff, had just gone to bed.

For a while she had been able to forget about everything, as if her life began with Sara. But it did not, and she couldn't help wondering if this was retribution for all the lives she had taken. There had been so many. She had been too self-absorbed to see that bringing Sara into her world was wrong. The only person responsible for this mess was herself.

She drafted a letter appointing Rosario Cherethites Guevarra as Sara's legal guardian. In her absence, if something happened to Sara, then, on the advice of a physician, Rosario could authorize whatever medical treatments may be necessary to preserve her life and physical wellbeing.

There was another letter giving Rosario access to a separate bank account Kat had set up, called Sara's College Fund. It was for the express purpose of seeing to the continued care, nurturing and education of Sara Fernando until she turned eighteen. Account number to be supplied in a separate document.

She had already drawn up a will with a lawyer in Toronto that left everything to Sara and appointed Ramsey as trustee to see to it that the money was handled wisely until she was eighteen. She just hoped that he lived that long.

There was more to do before she left. Her pediatrician had told her that she could rent herself out as a wet nurse, so she had been storing milk in the freezer since they moved down to the city. She went to her room to pack. She kept a complete wardrobe in the apartment for emergencies. She packed casual things that would work in the tropics. A pair of comfortable hiking boots, jeans, a couple of t-shirts, a long sleeve cotton shirt, underwear and a spare bra. She also put in two packages of breast pads and a breast pump. How long would she be away anyway? No, she didn't want to think about that.

She went online and looked up Guyana, Georgetown, and the town Agent Blanché was heading for. There were three ways of getting to Bartica; the first way was by air to Bartica Airport from Georgetown. Taking that flight had probably cost Blanché his life.

The second choice was taking a bus or a series of buses and a lot of stops, which would take about six hours. In her condition, her boobs would probably explode before she got there. There was no way to avoid a bus ride, but it was shorter to travel to Parika, a small 'resort' town on the shore of the Essequibo River. From there she could take a river taxi up to Bartica.

The travel guide said it would take a speed boat about an hour and fifteen minutes to travel the 35¾ miles. That would be her route. She phoned the airport to find the next flight to New York and booked it and the passage from there to Georgetown.

Sara was awake and hungry. Kat lifted her out of the crib to feed her one last time then she went to bed for a couple of hours. She woke up an hour before she had to leave for the airport which gave her time to tell Rosario what was happening. "I'll only be gone for a couple of days, there is milk in the fridge and freezer. Rosario, listen to me. There is a chance ..., that I may not be able to come back."

"What?! Oh, no Kat, then you can't go!"

"I'm sorry. If I had a choice, I would never leave her, you know that. But I don't have a choice. As long as those men are alive, Sara, you and me, we are all in danger. These are for you. They are the documents you'll need while I'm gone."

She gave the nanny the pages she'd printed out, copies had already been emailed to her lawyer. Rosario promised that she would stay with Sara forever if she had to. There was nothing more she could do so she left, locking the door behind her.

New York

10:20 am

When Kat first went to New York it was on her way to St. Petersburg, Devlyn told her to get an apartment and a safety deposit box. She since let the apartment go, but kept the box containing passports and other ID, money and a gun. After retiring, she thought she would never need them, but she thought it was prudent to keep them just in case.

She hadn't been near the bank in years, but it had what she needed to continue her journey, money, a passport and a gun. Kat selected a passport she had never used that identified her as Barbra Carr from Carson City, Nevada. There was also a CI badge and ID card for Special Agent Barbra Carr. A back story still existed in the data base in Maryland.

She sealed her real passport in a secret waterproof pouch inside the backpack and tossed in the gun, a SIG P226, the silencer and two extra clips. She counted out $9,900 US, put the box away and then up on the banking floor she bought a hundred thousand GYD for $480.00. Back on the street, she went to a deli on Madison for breakfast where she used the restroom to dump some breast milk and change the pads, then took a cab to Kennedy.

At JFK, she went to the international desk of Air Jamaica, introduced herself to the ticket agent as Special Agent Barbra Carr, showed her badge, ID and passport and told him that she was carrying a gun in her backpack. He keyed that info into his terminal and gave her a boarding pass.

Her reservation was for a first-class seat to Georgetown.

"Agent Carr, your flight leaves at 5:20 pm, in Terminal 4. The airline requires that you check in with the flight crew when you board and tell them about the gun. They will keep your bag locked up at the front of the plane."

"I can do that. Thanks very much."

"You are entirely welcome and have a safe flight."

GEORGETOWN, GUYANA

The overnight flight took fourteen hours and fifteen minutes, with an eight-hour stopover in Trinidad and Tobago's capitol, Port of Spain. During the flight, it seemed that all she had to do was think of Sara and she'd begin to lactate so she spent some time in the lavatory pumping milk and flushing it away.

It had been raining over the north coast of the lower continent and the plane descended through thick cloud cover. She had an immediate flashback to arriving in Rome a year ago in bad weather with the two doomed goons.

Her first sight of South America was of a vast steaming forest as far as the eye could see. It was at 8:15 am when the plane touched down in Georgetown.

She was bone tired, very sore and starving. Opening the door only made everything worse. The full ambiance of the tropical city and all the Guyanese smells, tastes and sounds flooded in on her. The day was deplorably hot and humid, the air was as thick as soup and had a taste she couldn't describe.

Without pausing, Kat found the desk for the airline that flew to Bartica and showed the agent her ID, badge and Etxebarria's photo. "Have you ever seen this man?" she asked.

"I may have. Why do you ask, has he done something wrong?" he said, in crisp English.

"I just want to ask him a few questions."

"It is Mr. Emile Fayette. He is a mining engineer at the Lumstrum Mine in Bartica. He comes through about once a week. You are not the first person to ask about him."

"Oh, who was the other one?"

"A Canadian diplomat came down here asking about him first and then a Canadian policeman. The diplomat disappeared and our police have been looking for him. The man just vanished. It happens sometimes down here."

"What about the policeman?"

"I don't know. He was here yesterday."

"OK, thank you. Oh, just one more thing, do you know where to get the bus to Partika?"

The sun was hidden behind dense, smoky gray clouds as she boarded the crowded No. 32-bus bound for Partika. People were carrying all kinds of things; chickens in cages, dogs on leashes and a goat restrained by a rope and a large man's leg over its back. An elderly woman plunked herself down beside Kat and dragged a large fabric bag up onto her lap. She offered Kat a toothless smile and then promptly fell asleep. Kat slapped at a mosquito on her arm, regretting she had no time to get bug spray, or to be inoculated against tropical diseases for that matter. She slapped another on the back of her neck as the bus jerked into motion.

The official language of the Co-operative Republic of Guyana is English, but most Guyanese use an English-based creole, with African or East Indian syntax. Kat found it difficult at first, but people were chattering away all around her, listening carefully she began to understand them ..., a little, but without the local terms of reference she missed a lot.

The bus traveled through Georgetown, passing colorful little houses tucked away behind iron gates and gray block walls. There were gardens with stands of palms, their fronds hanging low over bushes thick with fuchsia blossoms. The pastel-colored houses were separated from the Partika Road by narrow, water filled canals, covered with lily pads and bright pink flowers. Some of it was very pretty but it reeked of rotting fish, fruit and urine.

Rusty cars and small smelly buses rushed by, horrifyingly oblivious to the cyclists, pedestrians, donkey-carts and oncoming traffic. The bus turned south at the mouth of the Demerara River and rumbled through small villages that seemed to seamlessly merge, one into the other.

It was a poor country with dirt roads running along the Atlantic coast and along the banks of the river. Beyond the thin line of civilization to the south, clear-cut plantations and irrigation canals stretched back to the distant rain forest.

She hadn't expected to see many tourists, but she was not the only foreigner on the bus. The young couple were gawking and snapping pictures of everything. There was a moment of great excitement when the highway crossed the river on the Demerara Harbor Bridge. It was floating on dozens of huge pontoons anchored to the river bottom. The crossing was an odd experience as the bus bobbed along.

A little more than half-way across, a section of the bridge rose acutely over a narrow boat channel where a few fishing boats passed beneath them. On the other side, it dropped down once more onto the pontoons and the bus bobbed along again like a noisy, smelly, fun park ride.

It was not a pretty river. That stretch of the Demerara was more than a mile-wide and the strong current was red with mud from the eroding rainforest. But there was beauty, she saw luxuriant trees along the bank on the other side.

Elegant white birds nested on their thick branches that reached down to the water.

Kat looked forward to seeing the rainforest, but the only sign of it was that deceptively thin band of trees along the riverbank. Everything else in sight had been cleared off and under cultivation. It wasn't difficult to see why so much of the soil was draining out into the Atlantic.

The bus followed the coast the whole way and she was shocked to see that the ocean was just as muddy as the Demerara. Eventually it became evident that the silt was from the Essequibo River as well. The scale of that river was completely unexpected; the delta was twelve miles across and the dozens of islands in it were stripped of their trees and under cultivation.

Finally, the bus trundled into the town and stopped in front of the Parika Police Station near the river. A block west the street ended at the ferry dock. Kat thanked the woman for the use of the blanket, it had been a life saver. She was one of the last to get off and crossed the street to a little market shop where she bought a blanket of her own.

Leaving Parika, Guyana

She was starving and found a restaurant up the street and had fresh fried fish and a local beer for lunch. Feeling hot and sticky, but a little more human, she walked down to the dock looking for a water taxi. She couldn't see anybody who looked like an official, so she asked a man sitting on the dock mending a fishnet. "Could you tell me where I get a water taxi?"

"They're all gone now, missus."

"Oh," she said, looking at the river. The tourists must have taken them all while she was eating. "So, when will they be coming back? Do you know?"

"Can't say."

"What about hiring a boat, does anybody around here do that?"

"Where ya goin'?"

"Bartica," she said.

"That's me home, I can take ya there in me boat, but it'll cost ya."

"OK, how much?"

He thought about it for a few seconds then said, "Two thousand dollars."

"Two thousand, eh?" He was a serious man, a little too thin with a deeply lined face and sad eyes. He had a little white hair showing beneath his worn and faded cap and his tattered red t-shirt and beige pants looked clean. His gray canvas shoes were tied on with string and had so many holes they barely stayed on his feet. Two thousand dollars was a lot of money for this man. He seemed harmless enough, but would she trust her life with him out on that river? She hesitated, wondering if it would be better to wait for one of the river taxis to return?

What choice did she have? "What do ya say, missus?"

After overhearing horror stories on the bus about murderous bandits, she was having some serious trust issues. In plain view of him she removed the gun from her backpack and stuck it in her belt.

He certainly noticed but the gun didn't seem to bother him. Coming to the decision that it was a risk she had to take, she slung her backpack over her shoulder again and said, "Alright, you have a deal. Where is your boat?"

"That's it down there," he said, pointing.

There were so many, and they all looked pretty much alike, so she had no idea which was his. "I'll pay you the money when we get there. Is that alright with you?"

He nodded. "Whatever ya say."

"Lead the way."

He gathered up his net and showed her to his boat. It was a narrow boat with a shallow draft and a long punt-like bow that reached out over the river. It was in desperate need of paint, among other things, about eighteen feet long and filled with rope and a pile of nets at the front. He tossed the one he was mending on top and crouched down to take hold of the gunwale to steady it.

There was a brown and white Evinrude 10 hp outboard bolted onto the stern that had to be at least fifty years old. It sported a broom-pole lashed to the throttle to extend its reach. At the far end of the pole was a banged up red gas tank with a thin cushion on it. He said, "This is me boat, missus. Sit ya-self down on that pile." There were no seats and there was oily water sloshing around inside so she agreed that the pile of nets was the best place for her.

"OK then," she said, after taking a deep breath. She stepped carefully into the tippy craft and cautiously made her way to her perch while hanging on to the gunwales for balance. She turned around and sat down facing her driver and asked, "Can we leave right away?"

"Yup." He parked himself on the gas tank and asked, "Will ya be huntin' with that thing?"

She touched the butt of the gun and said, "You never know. You hear me?"

"Yeah, I hears ya, missus, I hears loud and clear," he said.

"OK then, let's go." He leaned back, pulled out the choke, wrapped a cord around the flywheel on top then tugged on it. Grey blue smoke with a heavy oily gas smell sputtered from the engine and drifted up to her before the breeze cleared it away.

He knocked the gear lever into forward and, steering with the pole, he slowly steered away out of the cluster of similar boats into the open water.

The engine noise was less irritating than she had expected, and the ride was surprisingly smooth. "So, what is your name?"

"Clarence."

She smiled and said, "Mine is Barbra."

Soon they were cruising up the river at about ten miles an hour. The wind seemed to cool her somewhat and the swirl of the current was mesmerizing. She began to relax and enjoy the view. It was amazing how small she felt in that vast expanse of water.

Small houses dotted the east shoreline all the way up the river and, behind the houses, the forest seemed so dense that she couldn't imagine what lay beyond. Occasionally, wonderful exotic birds, disturbed by the drone of the engine, rose up from the islands and flew overhead. She saw river otters fishing by the shore. A pod of river dolphin kept pace with them for a while, playing in the wake. Then something more interesting must have crossed their path, because suddenly they were gone.

Once again it was just Kat and Clarence on the quiet river. Her skipper never said a word during the whole trip, he hardly paid any attention to her. All he did was watch the river with a keen eye. She wondered what he was looking for. What dangers lurked beneath the surface? She could imagine how easy it would be to dump the CSIS officer out of the plane into that and he would never be found. Perhaps, it was best not to think about it.

Nearly three hours later the town came into view low on the horizon. It spread out on a point of land where two rivers met. He kept to the Essequibo on the east side of the point. Eventually he steered over to a dock where several other fishing boats were tied. "This is Bartica." The boat slipped in beside the dock and he put out his hand to stop the boat and held on. She climbed out onto the dock and walked back to hand him his money.

"Thanks, missus. Up there is Front Street and the road what goes by the shore is First Street. If ya go north by the shore, there will be the de Relax Inn Hotel. My cousin, he work there. Reginald is his name. Tell him Clarence say hallo. He'll fix ya up good 'nuff."

"I'll do that, thanks Clarence." She gave him his two thousand dollars, stood up and turned towards the town. Some children had spotted them coming in and ran down to greet her, chattering away happily as they surrounded her. Before she reached the end of the dock, she handed ten dollars GYD to the girl who seemed to be the leader and they all cheered and ran way bouncing up and down all talking at once. Clarence smiled for the first time, waved goodbye to her, pushed away from the dock and was soon out of sight.

Kat found the Relax Inn, a tired two-story building with a balcony over the veranda. A few spots of color indicated that it had once been painted pale green, but that was a long time ago. The veranda steps creaked, and the thin floor sagged beneath her as she walked to the door.

She had a feeling that entering this place was a bad idea. Hell, the whole trip was a bad idea from the get-go.

Even so, she pushed on the screen door and stepped into what could have been a storage room for worn out wicker furniture. The concrete block walls had been finished with a thin parge coat and painted coral pink. There were a few crude paintings of the river screwed onto the wall. The few bits of furniture were arranged at the end of the room on the right with a skinny man snoozing in one of the chairs. The front desk was to her left. Other than the sleeper she was alone, she walked over to the counter and looked around. There was no sign of a clerk, but next to the stack of postcards and maps was an open guest book, and beside that, a tap bell. She put her pack down and gave the bell a tap. The snoozing man opened his eyes and slowly got up then walked over to her rubbing his face. "I was just waitin' to see if ya changed ya mind," he said. "We don't get many tourists in here, missus. What can I do ya for?"

"Do you have a room?"

"As it happens, I do." No surprise there, she thought.

"Are you Reginald?"

"Yeah, that's me." He smiled showing lots of white teeth. "So how do ya come to know me name?"

"Your cousin Clarence brought me up from Parika in his boat."

"Oh, well now, Clarence, he's not a mon who takes to strangers. So that makes-ya practically one of the family. I tell ya what, I give ya the best room in the house for no extra cost. It's on the second' floor with a fan and a window what look out to the river. Now how do that sound t'ya?"

"That sounds fine. How much is it?"

"Five hundred dollars American."

She barked out an incredulous laugh and said, "How about this, I'll give you a two thousand GYD, does that sound fair?"

His brow creased as he rubbed his chin in thought, then he smiled again. "OK, not a problem."

"I thought so."

"Sign the book then I be showin' ya to ya room ...," he read her name upside down, "Missus Barbra Carr."

"Reginald, before you show me to my room could you tell me where I could get some food?"

"I can fry up some fish for ya after I show ya the room. How does that sound?"

"It sounds fine, thanks."

"You comin' here to see the sights?" he asked, as they headed up the stairs.

"No, I'm looking for a..., a job."

"Is that so? When they reached the top of the stairs he said, "A lot of people come down to Bartica to get rich. Most people leave here as poor as when they come, other's leave in a box. But there ain't much happenin' round here now. If I was ya, missus, I'd take a water taxi back to Parika and get on the plane to go back to where I come from. It be plain to see ya got a baby what needs ya."

"Now how would you know that?"

"Cause ya be drippin' milk from ya big titties, missus."

"Oh shit!" She took off her pack and held it against her chest.

"Not a problem, missus. I've seen it before, I got babies of me own at home."

"Glad to hear it."

"You'll find the WC at the end of the hall. I'll go down an' fix ya dinner now while ya clean yourself up," he said, and left.

She washed and changed then went down to discover that Reginald had set up a table on the back veranda overlooking the river. He sat with her and they chatted over a couple of cold beers. He talked about the glory days when small groups of gold seekers they called "pork knockers" used to come up on big boats to Bartica. "They come down here to buy their rations and supplies. Then after they get the gold and diamonds the pork-knockers come back to Bartica to sell what they work so hard for. It was dangerous work and some never come back to Bartica, but ya can bet their gold and diamonds made it here without them." He laughed sadly and sipped his beer.

"Ya say ya come down here for a job."

"That's right, I'm a mining engineer. A man in New York offered me a job at the Lumstrum mine. Do you know it?"

His expression turned serious. "I know that name, missus. The big company what done take over all the mines."

"You don't seem to think very much of it."

"That be true enough."

"Oh ..., well, I'm only here to have a look at it. If it looks OK, I'll come back with my daughter. If not, I'll look someplace else."

"Ya best look careful. Who was the mon who offered you the job?"

"Emile Fayette."

"Oh, the Frenchman," he said quietly. "I know that man. He like to drink at the Platinum Bar."

"Where is that?"

He rubbed his chin as he looked her over. "Down at the end of the street. But ya know, now that I'm thinkin' about it, I don't think that a fine woman like yourself would be wantin' to be workin' for a mon like that."

"That's interesting, why is that?"

"Because he works for Mr. Lumstrum and he's a cruel and hard mon. Like I say before, some people go down there and they don't come back, if ya follow my meanin'."

"Don't worry, I'll be careful," Kat said, with a hint of a smile.

"Hear me now, missus, ya gotta be careful in Bartica, not all the peoples be as friendly-like as me." He got up to take away the dishes.

"I'll keep that in mind." she said, surprised at how he abruptly cut off the conversation. "Thanks, the fish was delicious." He shook his head as if to say, he'd done all he could.

Kat went back up to her room and locked the door. She put her gun and her knife under her pillow. After turning on the overhead fan she lay down on the bed for the night, this time she lay down fully dressed.

BARTICA, GUYANA

When she woke up, she thought she could give breakfast a pass. She washed, pumped and changed into some clean clothes, putting a light long sleeve shirt on over her jersey to hide the gun she placed in the small of her back. She left the silencer in the backpack and folded the knife and put that away in her right pant pocket.

Stepping out onto the street with her blanket over her shoulder she looked at the strange and isolated little town with a more rested eye. She became even more aware that what she was doing was potentially suicidal. A disturbingly familiar feeling for her.

It was 6:20 am, the humidity was oppressive, and she was becoming uncomfortable. The mosquitoes and other biting insects were out filling the air with their buzzing and the sky was looking even darker than the day before. There was a heavy smell of tropical rot and the air carried the taste of rain. It would be coming soon.

She stopped where a man with dark chocolate skin sat by a pile of coconuts with a machete across his lap. He had big hands and she saw that the left one was missing a couple of fingers. His eyes were bloodshot, but his broad smile showed every one of his perfect, white teeth.

She handed him some money which he stuffed in his shirt and, without standing, selected a coconut, then with an expert slash he hacked the top off. He took a paper straw from a box beside him placed it into the coconut and handed it to her. "Thank you."

"Alright missus, ma pleasure."

She sipped the milk as she strolled up the street. The town was waking up and moving slowly in the coolest part of the day. People wandered out of their houses with baskets and seemed to be heading north. She had nothing better to do so she followed them.

They led her up to First Avenue and through the Bartica Mall, the shopping center of the town. There she found more people talking and laughing around stalls selling fruits and vegetables. People were friendly and she got lots of smiles as she bought a bag of local plums. She stopped at a few more booths just to see what they had. She picked up a loaf of bread and casually walked out onto Cool Square.

It was aptly named because there was indeed a refreshing breeze coming in from the Atlantic via the Essequibo River. There was no hurry, it was too early to surprise Etxebarria. She sat on a bench and watched the river flow by while she ate the warm bread and fruit, occasionally wiping the plum juice off her chin with her sleeve.

At 8:00 she wandered back down to the town mall where the crowd was swelling. It seemed like the whole town was up and shopping as she weaved her way through the people to get to the shops. It occurred to her that it might be a good idea to hide her face somehow, so she bought a big hat and sunglasses in one shop and a scarf in another. Looking at the result in a mirror, she thought she could easily pass as a tourist while she looked for the Frenchman. At least she hoped she could. She stuffed her purse in a colorful straw bag and continued to wander.

A visit to the drug store for bug spray and some after bite medicine gave her an opportunity to cool down a bit. After she checked out the postcards, she asked the pharmacist, "Where would I find the Platinum Bar?"

"Go north on First Avenue, it's near the ferry dock. Not far."

"Thanks," she said, heading outside for some more wandering, some more looking in shop windows. Eventually, she crossed paths with two couples in their fifties doing pretty much the same thing.

They were Brits, the men were talking about fishing while ignoring, as much as possible, the women who were preoccupied with shopping for souvenirs. Kat had an idea that she might be less conspicuous if she was with a group. It would play better if she were invited to join the couples, rather than force herself on them, so she decided to do a little fishing herself.

She stopped to adjust her backpack in the path of the men where they couldn't help but notice her.

There was little chance that they wouldn't as she gave them a very effective profile view while she lifted her arm up to adjust her shoulder strap. It was too easy, they both smiled broadly and the bigger one said, "Hello-allo-allo, all alone, are we?"

"As a matter of fact, I am. Hello."

"Well, aren't you a spot of sunshine on a cloudy day. What do you say, Ned?"

"I'm practically speechless, Ralph, to be honest."

"Doing a bit of hiking I suspect? My name is Ralph and this lump 'ere is me mate, Ned," said the tall man. "That there is Jennifer, my better half, and the other lovely lady is Ned's ball and chain, Winnie."

"Oh Ralph, must you?" Jennifer complained. The wives' radar had already picked up on Kat long before she decided to reel the men in and had hoped their men would have the good sense not to pick things up off the street.

"Must I what?" said Ralph, and Kat could see the disappointment in the women's eyes as their men fell for her trap.

"I'm Barbra," Kat said, ignoring Jennifer's hostility. "Isn't the mall interesting?"

"If you say so my dear, but I'm sure Ned will agree when I tell you I am bored to bloody tears, I am. It's the wives who dragged us over 'ere."

The wives, Jennifer in particular, were hiding their anger behind plastic smiles for the benefit of the men while throwing virtual daggers at Kat.

Winnie started up a conversation about the shops, "I saw a lovely little print dress in the shop just ..."

But Ralph wasn't going to be sidelined by the women. Kat was his find, so he said, "Well let's have enough of that, shall we. I see it's close to 11:00 and I think it is high time for beer."

"Goodness, Ralph, it's always sodding beer time for you, isn't it?" Jennifer said.

"Never you mind that my darling. My feet are fucking killing me, and I've got to sit down."

"Ralph, for God's sake, language."

"Tell me Barbra," he said, ignoring her admonishment, "are you up for a pint?"

"Sure, where do you want to go?"

"The Platinum Bar is close, and I hear it's nice," Ned said. Kat couldn't believe they were doing her work for her.

"You'll join us, yes?" Ralph continued.

"I'm sure this young lady has better things to do with her time than sit with you two ogling miscreants," Jennifer said. The men rolled their eyes.

Much to Jennifer's disappointment, Kat laughed and said, "Yes, I'd love to, thanks." Arm in arm the three of them headed off to the bar looking like Dorothy between the scarecrow and the tin man. Jennifer and Winnie tagged along miserably.

"Have you seen the waterfall, Barbra?" Winnie asked. We're going up there this afternoon." Jennifer punched her in the arm. "Ouch."

"But Winnie darling, I'm sure Barbra must have already been there."

"No, I haven't. I had no idea there was a waterfall," she said

"Then perhaps you'd like to come with us," said Ralph, and Jennifer turned on Winnie with a withering glare, then stretched her mouth into an approximation of a smile for the others and said, "We'd be glad to have you along, of course, but I have already booked the tour for four and there are no seats left. I am sorry, my dear."

"That's alright, I have some business to take care of this afternoon anyway."

Jennifer sucked in her cheeks and rolled her eyes. "We can't keep you from your business, now can we?" she said." And what business would that be, precisely?" Kat ignored the question.

Up the road they saw a building set back from the street with a large patio in front. Colored lights and small flags dangled from a network of wires overhead and the building was festooned with more flags. The sign over the door said Platinum Bar. The men were immensely enjoying brushing up against her and regaling her with their adventures on the river.

Jennifer meanwhile began plotting with Winnie to get rid of her as quickly as possible.

There were two European men in the bar when they walked in, one bald and the other with long thinning hair tied at the back and a full beard. Kat hadn't expected to run into them like this. She tensed and immediately shrank down behind Ralph. Much to Kat's relief, the failed emperor and his minion ignored the loud party of five and didn't seem to notice her at all.

The tourists chose the table on the far side of the room where a lizard had been resting on a plastic menu. It vanished in a flash as the laughing men closed on him. Kat sat between Ned and Ralph, hiding in the big man's shadow.

True to form, Ralph drew all eyes toward him as he enthusiastically ordered. "Beers for everyone."

"The ladies will have Dark and Stormies, please and thank you very much, heavy on the rum," said Jennifer, in a competitively loud voice

Kat tried to shrink into her chair hoping that she was still below Jäger's radar.

The wives sipped their aptly named drinks, having apparently been ostracized by their husbands. The men on the other hand, were in their element talking incessantly about lizards, monkeys, parrots and piranha. Kat accepted a beer but didn't touch it.

When Ralph and Ned were ready for a second round it started to rain. "Goodness, we're well out of that, I'm happy to say," confessed Ned.

All eyes turned to the door as it opened, and the Chief of Police walked in and shook the water off his cap. He was certainly not a local and from his appearance she pegged him as an expat German. Kat kept her head down.

After scanning the room, he went directly over to Jäger and Etxebarria, greeted them in German, confirming her suspicion, dropped his cap on the table and sat down.

Isn't that peachy? she thought.

The three men continued in German and it was loud enough that she could hear them over the rambling stories Ralph was telling. This new wrinkle was a big complication for her, although she should have expected that he would own the local authorities. Jäger had always bought his loyalty wherever he went.

In this policeman's case, he might have been imported for the job.

Ralph's volume rose as he started in on his second beer and Kat was trying desperately to block out his babble. It was hit and miss, but at one point, she clearly heard the policeman say, Barbra Carr and the Relax Inn in the same sentence. Jäger asked if he had a photo of her and the cop responded by lifting the flap of his tunic pocket and producing a Polaroid.

Oh, now that's perfect! Who knew they still had fucking Polaroids?

The picture must have been taken before she bought the hat and scarf, or they would have been on her the instant she walked in. The cop apologized for the poor quality saying the light wasn't good but asked if either of them wanted her.

Wanted her? she asked herself. Does this mean that he doesn't know who I am. Was he just out there procuring women for the monster?

Jäger passed the picture to the Frenchman who tossed it on the table. Both men nodded. They certainly knew who she was, and her heart began to pound. She had a sudden urge to pull out her gun and shoot them, but outwardly she remained calm. None of them looked in her direction. Perhaps they didn't know that she was under that hat and scarf.

Oh right, dream on, stupid, she thought.

The conversation ended when the Chief said, "Ich werde mich persönlich darum kümmern." He picked up the picture and put it back in his pocket. They shook hands and the cop stood up, replaced his cap and walked out into the downpour.

Jäger and Etxebarria talked for a moment longer then Jäger quickly gestured towards the door and they pushed away from the table and left.

Kat waited a moment then excused herself and went to the window to watch what they did next. There was an old Land Rover parked at the curb. They had probably driven down from the interior.

Jäger got behind the wheel on the right side and Etxebarria climbed in beside him. It kicked up quite a roar when it started up pumping out copious quantities of smelly black diesel exhaust and then took off along First Ave. heading west around the point.

The police car remained on the far side of the street and the officer was clearly looking at the bar. Did he see her? How could he not? Kat returned to the table thinking about Sara. Jennifer stared at her chest and smirked. Kat looked down. "Oh shit, now that's just totally perfect."

Using a stage whisper Jennifer said, "Why, my dear, you seem to be lactating." The men's attention was suddenly drawn to her breasts, her jersey was soaked through. The long sleeve shirt had been left unbuttoned but now she pulled it together to cover the stains. "How dreadfully embarrassing this must be for you." Then without a hint of restraint she continued, "Future clients of yours, were they?"

"Excuse me?"

"But my dear. I got the impression that those men wanted your services. Is that policeman your pimp?"

"What?"

"Well Barbra darling..., he said he would take care of you personally. Obviously, you are a whore, yes?"

Kat turned and looked out the window again and saw that the policeman was still staring in her direction. If there was a back door it was probably covered. She wasn't going to get out of this without a fight and she had no illusions about how that would turn out. She wondered if it would be possible to defend herself without getting the tourists killed. She realized that the only way that they would survive, was if she gave herself up.

Ralph stood up and said, "Jennifer! What on earth would possess you say such a thing?"

"Oh, do shut up, Ralph."

She was sure that she would be killed the moment she walked through the door. Maybe it was time. Maybe Sara would be better off without her.

She turned back to them as Ralph said, "Have you completely lost your senses? I am so sorry, Barbra. Something is wrong, isn't it? You are in trouble, aren't you?"

"Ralph, you always were a fool for a little T&A and trust me ..."

The rain seemed to intensify, to add weight to the unfolding drama. It was coming down in torrents as if someone just tipped over a lake.

"Ralph," Kat said, cutting off her tirade, "Thank you for that and I'm sorry I dragged you into this. I'm a Special Agent with US Army Counterintelligence."

"You are such a liar," shouted Jennifer and Kat just lost it.

She picked up her backpack and slipped the straps over her shoulders. "This mess, Jennifer," she said, pointing to her chest, "this is because I left my four-month-old baby at home to come down here and arrest those bastards you just referred to as my clients. That cop just gave me up to them. I don't know if they want to fuck me, but I do know that they want to kill me, just like they killed the father of my baby. The moment I walk out that door, I am as good as dead."

She had no idea why she was saying all this to them, maybe it was because it was her last chance to say how she was really feeling. She picked up the new bag with her purse inside. "There's just one last thing I've got to say to you, Jennifer. You are an ignorant cow, and I feel sorry for Ralph, because he's stuck with you. Enjoy the rest of your day."

They watched from the table in stunned silence as she pushed open the door and stepped out into the rain. She was instantly soaked to the skin as two heavily armed policemen appeared in rain gear, pointing their assault rifles at her head. Two more joined them, took her by the arms and dragged her across the street. The car door was opened, and they forced her inside behind the driver. The car pulled away from the curb, slipped around doing a U turn, then vanished into the downpour.

Ralph ran to the window and the others followed and watched in horror as she was driven away, knowing Kat was being taken to slaughter. Trembling with anger Ralph turned to his wife and in a voice barely controlled declared, "She was right, you know. You are a fucking cow, and as of this moment, you and I are done, Jennifer. You can find your own way home."

And with that he walked out into the rain. Ned followed him. Winnie hesitated for a moment and without saying a word went after Ned, leaving Jennifer alone.

Into the Jungle

There was another man in the car that Kat hadn't seen from the bar window. From across the street, it looked like the car's suspension system was broken, but now she knew why the vehicle sagged so low. The man obscured on the dark side of the car was as black as night and huge. Kat thought he looked like a giant slug. He was so overweight that his body had little definition from the head down. She wondered what possible function a man like that could serve. Perhaps he was the South American version of Wilhelm, the German troll who nearly killed her.

With ponderous effort, the slug twisted around as far as he could and reached over the seat back. The car shook as his arm dropped down on her side of the chair-back, then he squeezed it between that gargantuan appendage and his monstrous body like the jaws of life. Stretching his other arm across his chest, he rested his hand on the steep slope of what passed for a shoulder. The gun he pointed at her looked like a toy in his grotesque hand.

"Boss mon say he wants to see ya," he growled, in a mucous colored bass baritone. "He say it don't matter if ya be livin' or dead. If ya be packin' a gun, best give to me, elst I kill ya right now."

Obediently, she moved forward and using two fingers she took the gun from the small of her back and handed it to him. "Just drop it on the seat," he said, so she let it go.

Satisfied that he'd done his due diligence, he let go of the seat and the car trembled as he settled down facing front. The German said nothing.

That's it? she asked herself in disbelief. They're not going to search me?'

The German was headed in the same direction the Land Rover had gone. At the end of First Ave., he turned south and eventually came to a fork in the road. This was her Yogi Berra moment she thought. When you come to a fork in the road, take it.

The heavy downpour made it nearly impossible to see the road they took. The driver gripped the wheel with both hands, trying to maintain control of the dangerously unbalanced car, while he dodged craters in the pavement.

Despite his efforts, it aquaplaned through the torrents and puddles and slammed into countless potholes.

The big man's attention was also focused on the road ahead. They were both frightened by the weather. Kat took advantage of their distraction and went for the weapon in her pant pocket. Being soaking wet made it difficult, but she managed to slowly pull her KA-BAR out, without them noticing. She opened the blade and held it against her hip. It was a short, wide blade and razor sharp.

She looked at the base of the huge man's skull, locating the spot where she would plunge it. She wondered if she'd have time to kill the German too, before he killed her.

All she could do now was wait for the moment to strike.

Progress was slow. They followed the twisting road past isolated houses, squeezed between the road and the jungle. Eventually there was nothing but forest. Huge trees, pummeled by the rain, drooped over the roadway, occasionally blocking the deluge for brief moments, but the downpour was relentless. Kat was stiff and cold, her breasts were engorged, leaking through her shirts and aching unbearably. All she could think about was Sara.

Wham!

"What the fuck was that?" the German said, visibly shaken.

"I think we just hit a big snake on the road."

"Mein Gott, I hate this place," he grumbled.

It felt like they went over a speed bump and it jolted her back into the here-and-now.

The big man was trembling and gripping the dashboard. "Can ya slow down mon?!"

The German slowed. "It's not far now," he said. "Just try to keep it together, will you?"

"I hates snakes."

A couple of minutes later the German made a left turn onto what was once a dirt road but was quickly turning into a river of mud.

"It look like the river's floddin' the road. Ya can't drive down there, mon," the slug said, but the German kept on going.

The further he went, the more the wheels spun and the deeper the car sank into the mud, until it stopped altogether and sank down to the rocker panels. They weren't going anywhere now, and the men began to argue. Though they didn't know it, she was getting some valuable information from them. The German wanted to walk, he said it wasn't far, a quarter of a mile or so at most.

The big guy didn't like that idea at all. There was no way he was getting out of the car until the rain stopped and the mud dried. "It ain't gonna rain forever, mon. What-cha-gonna-do, go out there and drown in the mud? Don't be stupid, mon!"

"What are you arguing about?" Kat asked.

The hysterical slug shrieked like a little girl."The snakes! The snakes will be out in the flood! I ain't goin' out in that, now way, now how."

The German threw up his hands. "Scheisse! The house is just around the corner," he said, as he pounded them down on the steering wheel then sat back in disgust.

"I can't walk in that mud. I just drown myself." The big man sagged into the seat. They stared out into the river of mud through opposite windows as the rain pounded down harder than before.

She had to shout to be heard. "Can we walk through this mud?"

"Ja, but this fat piece of garbage is afraid to get his feet wet," the German yelled back, without taking his eyes away from his window.

"It's the snakes. I hates the snakes," shouted the slug, without moving his head.

The time was now, and she had to act quickly. She slid over behind the big man then, striking like the snakes he was so afraid of, she stabbed him in the neck at the base of his skull, severing his spinal column. He was so big he didn't tip over. His blubber shuddered a bit, but his death was instantaneous and, in the pounding rain, silent. The German had no idea what had just happened. She slid over again and, taking him totally by surprise, she stretched around with her left hand and grabbed his forehead. He grabbed her wrist, but there was nothing he could do. She rammed the knife into his neck. His hands fell away, and it was over. When she released him, he slumped forward on the car horn.

The noise was drowned out by the rain, but she pulled him back and leaned him against the door.

Aching and cold, she sat back shivering. Suddenly she was aware that the car was still sinking. She he had to get out before the door was blocked. She bent over the seat to retrieve her gun then practically fell out of the car into the knee-deep mud. It was a struggle to get to the road's edge with the straw bag over one shoulder and her pack over the other. It seemed to take forever, and she was getting panicky as she reached the side. Fortunately, the ground was firmer on the south shoulder of the road.

When at last she crawled out, she stayed on her hands and knees and let the rain pound down on her back. It was painful, but at least it was washing the mud and blood from her body.

Kat had lost a boot and sock to the sucking mud and wondered if she would be better off losing the other one as well.

She lifted her jersey, opened her bra and squeezed her painful breasts until all the milk was expressed. When the pressure was relieved, she covered up again and stood up. The question of the remaining boot was ignored for the moment, she had to get moving. Walking east, she hoped that the house was as close as the German said it was. A quarter of a mile he said. How far had she gone?

Something moved in front of her.

She stopped in mid stride.

The big guy had been right about the snakes. A Guyanese Parrot Snake slithered by her from the flooded road. She didn't know the species, but she knew a viper when she saw one. It was a couple of meters away and passed without paying her the slightest attention before it disappeared into the bush.

If there was one, there would be others, she thought, and they would be heading for the higher ground to the south. Cautiously she forced herself to push on, but after just a few steps she froze once more.

Something very large moved across the surface of the road. She slowly reached back for her gun. If it was a snake it was a big one. Maybe it was a caiman. She chambered a round. It was hard to tell what, but it was heading her way.

With the rain pelting down so hard it had no real definition. Then it rose out of the mud just a meter from her feet.

At the same time the tip of its tail lifted out of the water. It was perhaps four meters long, more or less. The skin was chocolate brown, making it almost indistinguishable from the mud. She thought at first it was an anaconda. But then she saw the viper's head, it was a Bushmaster, one of the few snakes they talked about years ago, when she did her tour in Honduras. They said it was very aggressive. There was one quote in particular that she remembered; it is the silent bringer of death. Oh, terrific. She closed her eyes and waited.

This time, the bringer of death just slithered on by. She thought, maybe the predator avoided me as a professional courtesy, and almost laughed.

She walked faster now and around the bend she saw lights through the rain. It was a house, but was it his house? And, why in God's name, did it have to be on the other side of the fucking road? She forced herself back into the mud and struggled to keep upright.

She was more aware of the sensations she was getting on the sole of her foot, the sharp twigs, stones and roots that grated and scraped across her skin with each step. What would happen if one of those sharp sensations was from the tiny fangs of a coral snake? Would she even know if she was bitten? Feeling she might never make it to the other side she began to panic. It seemed that everything was going wrong, then the left boot started to let go.

"Oh!" There was no way to save it. "Wonderful," she whispered, as another snake slithered by. It was so close that it nearly touched her. She just closed her eyes and held her breath. Maybe it didn't know she was there. She was so cold that the snake's heat sensors didn't pick her up.

The house was in a three-acre clearing, covered with coarse tropical grass. It squished like a spongy carpet beneath her feet. Closer to the house, the ground was paved with flag stone and defined by a knee-high stone wall claiming an area of civilized subjugation from the wild and unfettered forest. As she gained a foothold on the stones the relief was extraordinary.

She could see lights on at the front of the house, but all the windows had been closed off behind steel hurricane shutters. That was a good sign, she hoped. Whoever was inside couldn't see her coming. Unless of course, there were security cameras.

To her surprise there were none visible. That didn't mean that there weren't any. It just meant that she couldn't see them. She avoided the front of the house. Keeping low and looking for more reptiles, she moved around to the side. The front was just a two-story façade with a garage on the left. The driveway sloped down to the back and she followed it. As she reached the rear of the garage, she saw that the rest of the house was just a large bungalow, elevated on dozens of concrete columns, maybe ten feet above the ground. There was a large rectangular concrete structure at the back with the pipes, pump and heater for the swimming pool. Beside it, near a large generator, was the Land Rover they left the bar in.

This was indeed Jäger's house. There was another Land Rover, suggesting that there were other people inside.

On the back wall of the garage was an unlocked door. She went through it, closing it behind her. The noise of the rain was instantly reduced. She touched a light switch on the left, illuminating a space with two golf carts plugged into the wall. There were two more doors, neither of which was locked. One was to an elevator, the other opened onto a small landing with a set of tiled stairs on the left.

Leaving the doors unlocked was a careless mistake.

Before she ventured up, she checked to see if there was another way in. Outside there was set of open stairs leading up to a screened in patio at the back of the house.

Retreating into the shelter of the garage, she put her bag down and removed her backpack, took out the silencer and threaded it onto the barrel of her SIG. She put the two magazines in her pockets, checked the round in the chamber, then opened the door.

Carefully she stepped onto the landing and closed the door quietly behind her. Pointing her gun up into the gloom she waited to see if someone had heard her.

After a minute, she padded up the steps as quickly as she could. Her bare feet made no noise at all, but she was leaving a trail of muddy water behind. They might not be able to hear her but, if someone walked in, they would certainly see the water and know she was in the house.

At the top was a small laundry room and light was coming through a doorless opening on the right. It led to the kitchen and as she moved to the opening, she heard distant voices and peeked in. The kitchen was empty. Looking over the counter she could see a dining area and just to the right of that she could see a bit of the much larger room where the men were talking.

She moved across the kitchen until they were in full view.

It was Jäger speaking in English. "They won't make it down the road in this," he said.

"We should have taken her out at the bar," Etxebarria replied irritably.

"Then we would have to kill all the others. We couldn't keep that quiet."

She listened for other voices, but there were only two. Jäger was sitting in a throne-like chair with his back to her. Etxebarria was showing his profile from a chair facing the front door. He had a cigarette in his hand and was looking down into his wine glass. She stood still for what seemed like an eternity, just listening and watching.

They were talking about her, as if there was no doubt that she was coming. Jäger was going on about the torture he would inflict. "I wish Wilhelm was here to do it for me, he was so good with the knife."

It was so revolting that she had to put an end to it. "Ah, excuse me, assholes," she said. "Yeah. Hello, you sick-fucks ..., hey, over here."

Jäger turned slowly as he stood up to face her. Etxebarria dropped his wine glass as he shot up and they just stared at her in disbelief. Their expressions were priceless. "Hi, I was just in the neighborhood and, well, I thought I'd stop by and kill you two bad boys." Her hands were at her sides and she looked harmless. Etxebarria reached for his gun. Almost casually, she lifted hers and shot him in the head. In the tiled house, the metallic pop was louder than she had expected. She walked closer to Jäger. "Oops. I killed your little friend."

"How did you...?"

"Don't you remember asking that nice policeman and his pet slug to bring me here?" He just stared at her un-blinking. "So, funny thing. We almost got to the house, but their car got stuck. Wasn't that awful? They didn't want to get out because of the snakes, so I just killed them and left them in the car."

Jäger backed away, carefully stepping around the Frenchman. "Who else is in the house?"

"No one," he said.

"Aw, and you said you never lied. There are two cars downstairs so there must be someone else. You don't look after this place by yourself, do you?" she said sweetly. "Where are the maids, the housekeeper? Surely you have a cook and perhaps a bodyguard or two. Perhaps a new Wilhelm?"

"No, it is just the two of us."

"You should sit down; this must be a terrible shock for you." He returned to his elaborately tooled antique armchair. His hands were clutching the arm rests as he leaned forward, turning his huge head like a gun turret to keep his eyes on her. Kat thought he was preparing to bolt.

"Oh, come now, relax. There must be a few bodyguards somewhere to keep you safe. So, where are they hiding?"

"It's a little late to be wondering about them now, don't you think?" he said, finally gaining some courage. He patted the arms rests and then folded his hands in his lap. "So, what shall we talk about in your final moments of life?"

As if on cue, the rain stopped and there was almost complete silence in the house. Kat could see the wheels at work in that irregular globe on his shoulders. He was trying to distract her, but she wasn't going to let that happen.

She heard a very subtle scuff of rubber on tile.

Instinctively she located the noise, turned and fired. The man dropped his gun as he fell, and it clattered away down the steps to the front door. A second man immediately reached out from the corner and fired. His shot went wide, but hers was right on the mark and the bullet ripped through his head. He collapsed on his companion. She turned in time to see Jäger bending down, reaching for the Frenchman's gun.

"Stop!"

He did and dropped to his knees with his arms extended, reaching for the gun. A third man appeared in the doorway at the far end of the room but before he knew what to do, Kat put two in his chest.

She walked around Jäger's chair and stood in front of him. He looked like a dog pointing at the gun.

"Is that it? Just the three of them?" He didn't answer. "I'll take that as a yes. Local guys, eh? Did you just hire the first bandits you met? Yeah? Well too bad you didn't find better ones, because they didn't do a very good job, did they?" She kept scanning around her, but her attention was never far from Jäger.

"How did you find me?"

"Funny thing about that. I'm not actually an assassin. No, before I retired, I was an Army Lieutenant Colonel, a Special Agent with Counterintelligence. I've got a shiny badge and everything. I'd show it to you but it's in my backpack.

"Anyway, we were trained to track down assholes like you and your little limp friend there. He left quite a trail you know." Jäger looked back at the body with utter contempt. "It really wasn't his fault. If you had been half as smart as you think you are, you would have left me alone. But no-o-o-o, you couldn't do that, could you?

"After I killed Petrus I quit, I'd retired, I was completely out of it. Then you sent your men after me in Ukrainian. I was just trying to find some peace. But you woke me up and you forced me to come after you. This ..., this is all your fault. You should have learned a lesson from the failure in Ukraine. But you didn't, did you?

"Here's an interesting bit of trivia. Did you know that after you vanished, it was quite possible that no one would ever go looking for you?" His brow wrinkled. "I know right, but it's true, they'd given up. Oh, and I had retired again and set up a new life for myself. I bought a nice home, had my baby, Sara, oh and she's beautiful by the way ... and I tried to forget all about you. But you're a fucking megalomaniac, aren't you? Everything is about you. So, you sent that piece of garbage after me and my child. Big mistake. This ...," she waved her gun at him, "this is the direct result of that mistake. You've had your three strikes."

He looked puzzled.

Oh, I'm sorry, you're German, so you may not understand that reference. It's a baseball idiom that Americans use, Arnulf. Three strikes. That's all you get, three strikes and you're out."

He reached for the gun, again she fired, and the bullet smashed the tile beside his hand. "A-a-a, another one of your bad ideas."

"You won't do it, will you? You Americans play by the rules, so you've come to arrest me. True?"

"You are completely delusional. Who the fuck do you think dropped that bomb on you?" She was in agony now, every part of her hurt. She was wet, cold, tired, frightened and in no mood to put up with any more bullshit. "Before I kill you, I have a confession to make. Vladimir Mogilevski is very much alive."

"Liar! I saw the video."

"What you saw was pure theater, special effects. He's my friend! In what universe did you think would I ever do anything to hurt him? You may have thought you'd be Emperor of Europe when you started all of this, but you failed. Now you are just a corpse in waiting. Oh ..., by the way ..., the wait is over."

She squeezed the trigger three times, and the bullets pierced the crown of his head like the finger holes in a bowling ball. He went face first onto the tile, on his knees. His arms slid out in front of him as if he were bowing down before her, begging forgiveness.

At least, that's the way it looked to her.

Retracing her steps, Kat returned to her things under the house and left the garage. Once again, she was standing out in the muggy jungle air and a steaming mist hung over her like a shroud.

Even though Jäger would spend eternity bowing down to her, it all seemed so anti-climactic. She couldn't believe that it was over and, more significantly, that she had survived.

"Perhaps," she said aloud, "you're being a little premature about that. You're still in the fucking jungle, thousands of kilometers from Sara.

"How the hell am I going to get out of here without drowning in mud, or dying from a snake bite?"

As she was pulling the pack straps over her shoulders she looked out to the side and could see something that had been hidden from her during the rain. She could see the tail rotor of a helicopter sitting behind some tall shrubs.

She ran to it.

"Holy crap, it's an old Huey. Now how lucky is that?"

She opened the door. It was in good shape inside. The cabin was filled with crates of weapons.

"Now what the hell was that bastard planning to do with these?" She couldn't check the fuel until it was switched on, but she looked for dings in the paint, missing screws and broken connections. "Wow ..., I think this will work. The only thing it's missing is the key."

She returned to the house, ran up the kitchen stairs, prepared to search every room, but that proved unnecessary. There, at the top of the stairs in the laundry room, were three sets of keys hanging on the wall. Two sets with Land Rover fobs hung on the first hook and, on the second, a key tag that read: UH-1 Iroquois.

She took the key and held it to her chest then closed her eyes to think. Imagining a list of positives and negatives, she started with the negative side; she was wet, cold, dirty, hungry, and thirsty and she had a headache. She was far away from civilization, down an impassable road surrounded by poisonous things that bite.

On the positive side, all the villains she knew about were dead. She now had what she presumed was a functioning helicopter. She had the house to herself and she had some time, time to rest. There was probably food in the house, all the water she needed to wash and drink, and even a bed.

Standing by the washing machine, she hung her waterproof pouch containing her real passport around her neck, stripped down, emptied her backpack, and put everything into the washer including the pack. She added detergent, turned it on and let it do its thing. While it worked, she found some pills for the pain then, ignoring the bodies in the living room, went in search of the master suite.

The bathroom was huge with a big marble shower and the water was hot. She was going to wash her hair but naturally Jäger didn't have any shampoo. Screw it, she used soap. Wrapped in a large towel she returned to the laundry and put the things in the dryer.

After finding something to eat and washed it down with a bottle of water as she headed to the master suite. Then the thought of sleeping in his bed stopped her cold. There was an unused guest room at the other end of the house where she slept for an hour.

At 6:35 pm she woke up rested, warm, and anxious to get out of there. She dressed in jeans and a t-shirt. As she dressed, she began to create a ritual in her mind to signify the end of the nightmare.

She wrapped her gun, the ammunition, the silencer and Barbra Carr's CI badge in a pillowcase. Then she ran the passport and ID through the shredder in the office then tossed a match into the pail. When she was satisfied that she had left nothing behind she ran out to the Huey. Before she took off, she undid the straps that held the cargo down and pushed the crates to the open door. Lifting off she headed down river for Georgetown.

She flew out over the Atlantic, opened the cockpit door, dumped the pillowcase into the ocean and watched it splash and disappear. Then she flew in a tight circle in a steep bank and the crates slid out. The chopper shot up as the load departed. "And there," she said, "endeth the lesson."

Kat turned east toward the city and called the airport for landing instructions.

They directed her to the helipad by the Air Services Ltd. Hanger. She set it down gently, switched it off and got out while the blades were still turning.

The people inside must have been warned against getting too close to the people from that bird, because no one approached her.

To her amazement, it was as if she had timed everything perfectly. The flight home departed at 8:42 pm.

Chapter 39

Heading Home

The key was still in the Huey's ignition when the authorities arrived an hour and a half after Kat's plane took off, and by that time she was sitting in the lounge in Port of Spain's Piarco International Airport reading a detective mystery. The rest of her trip was uneventful, and she landed in New York at 10:45 am. Even so, she felt odd, as if there was still some danger lurking out there. She put her book away without bothering to finish it and began to walk up and down the terminal until it was time to board the connecting flight to Toronto.

She should have been feeling safe by now, but she didn't, and wondered if she ever would. After boarding the Air Canada flight to Pearson, she tried the book again and re-read the same line five times before she put it away. She called Rosario. "Rosario, hi."

"Kat, are you alright? Oh, my heavens, I have been so worried about you."

"I'm ..., I'm fine, how is my baby?"

"Sara is fine, but she has missed you very much. She is sleeping now. When are you coming home?"

"I'm on my way now, I should be home around 4:30 this afternoon. Is everything alright?"

"Yes, don't worry about a thing, just get home safe. I am so happy that you are OK. We will be waiting for you." As the Air Canada Airbus began its descent into Toronto, Kat filled out her immigration declaration saying that she had been in Trinidad for four days.

Arriving in Toronto

3:30 pm

The customs and immigration officer took one look at her declaration card and he saw a problem. Kat was tired but she read the signs and kept her cool. "You are an American citizen living in Canada?"

"Yes."

"How long were you in Canada before you went on this trip?"

"Does that matter?"

"No, that's fine. And how long were you away?"

"Four days," she answered easily.

"And what was the purpose of your trip?"

Kat's face told the story of pain, suffering and death, there was no need to fake it. But that wasn't the story she was going to share with him. "I was visiting a sick friend. I was with her in the hospital to hold her hand during her final hours."

"And you bought nothing while you were there?"

"Well, I got this book at the airport in Port of Spain."

"Was it any good?"

"I don't know, I couldn't finish it."

He circled the question box concerning health risks and said, "Ma'am you checked off 'no' for communicable diseases. Are you saying that the illness your friend had was not contagious?"

"Yes, that's right. It was pancreatic cancer. She only found out that she had it a few days ago, and she knew she only had a couple of days left when she called me. I flew down right away, but we didn't have enough time. It took her so quickly."

"I guess that was a mercy of sorts."

She nodded and put her hand on his desk to steady herself. "I left yesterday morning right after her funeral."

"There is never enough time," he said. "My sympathies and welcome home, Ms. Fernando."

"Thank you."

He stamped the card, gave her a pass slip, and said, "Next."

Standing outside the terminal Kat was finally feeling the stress drain away. It was over and she would be home soon with Sara.

The line-up at the cab stand was getting shorter and she was lost in her thoughts about her home coming when a limousine came to an abrupt stop. Her head jerked up and her eyes widened as she reached for the gun she didn't have.

The car backed up quickly to the curb right in front of her as the rear window slid down.

She froze.

There was nowhere to run, nowhere to hide.

She closed her eyes.

"I can't believe it!" said a familiar voice and opening her eyes again she saw the face she had thought about so many times beaming out at her. "Is that really you, Kat?"

"Deacon?" she said, trying to hang on to her composure, but failing miserably. "Oh Jezzus, you scared me..., I ..., uh ..., Hi," she said. As much as she had longed for this moment, she never expected to see him again.

"Listen, you can't take a cab; I'll drive you wherever you need to go."

"Uh ... I uh ..."

Her seemingly reluctant response worried him. "Please Kat, anywhere you want to go. I need to talk to you." He opened the door. "Please." Moving over he said. "Come on."

"Hey lady," the dispatcher said, "get in, don't get in, I don't care. But that limo's gotta move out of here."

She stepped off the curb and slid in, then sitting on the edge of the seat she put her purse and backpack on the floor. The Dispatcher closed the door behind her and waved Deacon's driver to pull out.

"You were traveling light, I see."

"Deacon," she said, and paused. Her heart was pounding, and her hands were trembling a little bit. She worked up a tentative smile. "I ..."

"Kat, I can't believe it, you're alive, I mean ... after they ..."

Looking towards the driver, she touched his lips to caution him not to say any more. Filling the void, she said, "I know ..., most of the time I do too, but here I am." She couldn't think of anything to follow that. She had just been thinking of him, that she loved him.

"What's the matter?"

"Jesus, I ... I don't know what to say to you, Deacon. I never thought I would see you again. I mean, I let everybody think I was ..." she looked at the driver and revised her declaration a bit, "Well, you know and ..."

"And yet, here you are," he said. Deacon looked so happy and expectant and she didn't know what to do. He waited for her to say something else. When he realized that she wasn't going to, he said, "And it looks like I'm rescuing you this time."

"So it would appear. Deacon, I am so sorry about the way I left you."

"It had nothing to do with you, I understand that. Listen Kat, it was a terrible time for all of us. But that is all in the past, isn't it?"

"You are such a sweet guy, Deacon. I just ..."

"Aren't you just a little happy to see me?"

"Oh, I am. I ..., I just can't believe it yet."

"The only thing I care about now is that you're here. Apart from looking tired you look wonderful, you always have."

She needed to shift the subject away from her. "Were you just coming from someplace exciting?"

"Mexico City. I was there for a year." That surprised her and he laughed. "No, I'm just kidding. It was only three days, it just seemed like a year. We're opening a new factory down there."

"Of course. God, you must be so busy. I read about you in the paper. You were nominated for the Nobel Prize no less, I mean wow. I gather the Phoenix Project has become huge."

He just looked at her. "Jesus, you look so ..., I don't know, so ..., sad. Are you OK Kat?"

"It was a difficult trip, and I haven't had time to decompress yet."

"Were you on the job?"

She rubbed her palms on her jeans while she figured out what she was going to tell him. "You know I can't talk about it."

"Yeah OK, I get that."

"Let's just say that it's been a tough week and a really long flight, so ..."

"We'll call it a business trip then."

"OK, that works." She looked at him and thought there was no point in lying to him now. "Deacon ... I ..."

"Wait, before you say anything; are you staying in the city a while, or are you just passing through. What I mean is, what hotel am I taking you to?"

"As it happens, I am living here now." He looked stunned. "I know eh ..., surprise," she sang, and finished with a weak little laugh. "I'm hoping they'll let me make it permanent."

"You ..., you're really living here now?" She nodded with a shy smile and he said, "Wow, I never saw that coming. I mean that is fabulous!"

"I'm glad you think so."

"Absolutely, so where am I taking you?"

"We have an apartment on King Street, just east of Jarvis. It's above a used furniture store." He gave her an 'are you serious' look, so she qualified it by saying, "I know, it doesn't sound like the greatest location, but it's actually better than you'd think."

"Right. Did you get that Jim?"

"Yes sir, King St. just east of Jarvis."

"Thanks." Deacon put up the divider so they could have some privacy. "OK, first tell me what you were going to say before I cut you off."

"I was going to say that I was just finishing up my very last assignment. I had to go down to South America. Look, I just wanted to tell you that ..., that..., that part of my life is over, I am officially retired now."

"God Kat, you don't know how relieved I am to hear that. It's beyond wonderful to see you again." His excitement faded as something she said dawned on him. "OK, whoa, let's back up for a second. A moment ago, you said 'we'." The disappointment in his voice was unmistakable. "Does that mean you're living with someone now?"

"I'm living with two people actually. My daughter Sara, and her nanny Rosario."

"So, the father is somewhere near by?"

"No, there is no father," she said.

"OK, so we don't believe in immaculate conception, which means what ..., artificial insemination ..., alien abduction?"

"Her father died before Sara was born."

"Oh damn, I'm sorry. I was being stupid and insensitive."

"I'm sorry too, he was my partner. It was a..., a one-time thing in a moment of intense stress. One of those times when you do something without totally thinking it through. I wanted a family. I didn't want him as a husband, but I will always be thankful for his gift; Sara is totally wonderful."

"I'll bet she is, so how long have you been here?"

"Since May, I came back from Europe and decided this was where I wanted to be. I wanted her to be born a Canadian."

"We're honored. How old is she?"

"She was born on December 14, which makes her four months and five days."

"Wow," he said.

"You look good, Deacon."

"Thanks, I've been very lucky." He fidgeted with his watch. "So, you didn't love him."

"Deacon, I've only loved two men in my life, Harm was the first," she said, putting her hand on his, "and then there was you."

He took hold of her hand and just looked at her for the longest time. "Would it be alright if I came over some time? I'd really like to meet Sara ..., and I would truly love to get to know you again." She was about to say something, and he thought it might be no. "Oh, not right now. I meant when you're rested."

"Would you really like to meet her?"

"I would, absolutely. How about this? Why don't I let you have a couple of days to come down from your trip? When things get back to normal ..."

"I have no idea what normal is, Deacon."

"Right, well now that you are here permanently, that too shall be a thing of the past. Anyway, I was thinking that maybe I could take the two of you, I mean the three of you, out to a park, or something?"

"I think we'd all love that."

"Terrific. Can you tell me something?" She smiled and nodded. "Why did you come back to Toronto?"

"Yeah …, I thought you might ask me that. I made a promise to myself that if I ever had a child, I would want her to grow up in Mulmur."

"But you're here in Toronto."

"When I arrived in Canada, I went straight up there and bought a house very close to your place."

"Wait a second, if you have a house in Mulmur? Why am I taking you to King Street?"

"King St. is my safehouse." He looked totally bewildered. "OK, we ran into a bit of a problem in Mulmur and had to relocate here. I may tell you about it sometime. Until then let's just get me home to my baby."

They rode the rest of the way in silence and when Jim pulled up in front of her apartment Deacon said, "I tell you what. I'll come by the day after tomorrow. If the weather is good, we can take the baby for a walk and we'll talk some more."

"Deacon I …"

"The day after tomorrow at ten."

"Are you sure?" Kat said.

"I'm positive."

"OK then, we'll see you the day after tomorrow, at ten. Thank you, Deacon. I can't begin to tell you how wonderful it is to see you again." She kissed him on the cheek and stepped out of the car.

Her door opened and there was Rosario with Sara in her arms. They'd been watching for Kat from the window. Kat ran to her and swept Sara up to her cheek. "Hello little one, hi there." The baby grinned. "Did you miss your mummy? You did? Well, mummy missed you. Yes, she did."

Epilogue

Deacon waited for Kat to look back and smile and when she didn't, he sat back feeling deflated and sad. "Do you want me to take you home now, Dr. Loats?"

"Let's just sit here for a moment, Jim."

"Sure, no problem."

Deacon looked up above the darkened furniture shop, wondering what kind of a home she had created behind that tired and dreary looking façade. "Alright Jim you can … no, wait."

There she was at the window with the baby in her arms. She was pointing down at him and waving Sara's little hand. The baby wasn't sure what was happening, but Kat looked so lovely, smiling down at him. She touched the glass as it she could feel his hand and he felt compelled to mirror her gesture. She waved to him and disappeared from view. "That was worth waiting for," he said aloud.

"Shall I take you home now?"

"Yes, alright."

Kat had only stepped back from the window so that Deacon couldn't see her. The moment the car moved she returned to watch and, as it drove out of sight, she thought about her future.

Could she ever become the normal human being she had always longed to be? Would loving him, being with him, put him in danger? It was so easy to revert to that person she so desperately wanted to leave behind. At the first provocation, the claws were out, and people died. Could she ignore that side of her?

Long ago, Death had become her companion, the men she killed were at best bad men, and at their worst evil personified. It had become so easy to take a life without pity or remorse.

Killing them had become almost … satisfying, like an accomplishment or a good deed well done. There was little thought given to the cost of it to her personally. Thinking of the godforsaken place in Guyana, she wondered...

When did I become so callous?

How have I become so brutal?

Not too many years before, Vlad had likened her to a tiger, a top tiered predator. At the time, she had secretly taken that as a compliment, but it didn't feel complimentary now. It was said that a tiger can't change its stripes, so was Kat naïve in thinking that she could change hers?

Deacon had been a calming influence. When they were at his house in Mulmur she began to think about raising a family there. She desperately wanted that life. Now, after being with him during that short drive, she desperately wanted him to be a part of it. But to do it she would have to exorcise the tiger. That frightened her. Was it even possible? Could his kindness help her become human again? She couldn't shake the feeling that if she let Deacon back into her life, she could be responsible for his death. She decided to take a chance and thought that by moving forward very slowly, she could pull back if she sensed she was putting him in danger.

Sara stirred in her arms. Stroking her cheek with her finger Kat soothed her with a tune, softly hummed. Sara cooed and Kat kissed her on the forehead. "I love you so much. I love you bigger than the CN Tower."

Sara smiled.

****

<h1 style="text-align:center">THE END</h1>

About the Author

For many years, Hugh Russel was a popular radio personality, hosting a daily show on Toronto's number one FM station. Now, the writer, sculptor, illustrator, musician and architectural designer lives with his wife and partner, Cheryl in the home and studio complex he designed and built. Their home sits on rolling hills in the Niagara Escarpment  Region north of Toronto, surrounded by extraordinarily beautiful hills and valleys, forests, pristine rivers, wildlife galore, and truly wonderful friends. He and Cheryl have two terrific kids and four amazing grandkids. For this artist and writer, he believes that it's hard to imagine anything better.